LAND OF HORRORS

CHELSII KLEIN

Cover design: Genesis Graphics
Editing: Julie Kramer
Formatting: AJ Wolf Graphics

CONTENTS

Acknowledgements

Thank you to my amazing husband, family and children for all the time you allowed me to sit at my computer and get my stories out to the world!! It's a true blessing to have your support and love for my writing!
To my past, current, and future readers- I can not simply thank you enough for believing in me! The love you have for my books and crazy characters is what gives me the fuel to keep going! On the days I want to throw in the towel, you are here to cheer me on and that means the world to me!
Without you all, Author Chelsii Klein wouldn't be out in the world.

Content Warning

My books contain triggering aspects that could negatively affect readers. If you can not handle these warnings, then I ask you to please not read King of Horrors and Land of Horrors. Triggers are as followed: Rape (Non-Con), Coerced Sex Scene (Dub-Con), Animal Death, Torture. While some of these scenes can be skipped, these warning aspects are part of the characters emotional and physical growth, and it can affect the storyline or major plot later in the series.

King of Horrors

My name is Neek.

In order to survive, I feed from a mortal's greatest fears *or* their greatest pleasure…but the task is getting harder as the years pass, and more and more humans stay away from my reach. The jinn of the Fae race are far and few between but next to royalty, we are the strongest of the Fae. And with that, can come with the strongest fall. I was captured and bound to this land, to be its leader. Leader, or no leader. Either way, this land was a fate worse than death. A trap, for even myself. The only way I can make it out now is if my soulmate survives the land. But first, I have to get her here.

A CandyLand board game Horror/PNR retelling.

PROLOGUE

To say I'm old is an understatement.

I was there when a human called Jesus was hung on the cross.

I was there for discoveries, countless wars, and the invention of an app called *TikTok*.

And I was there when Earth was overrun by demons, angels, and the paranormal.

The humans called it the Apocalypse. We Fae called it the end of Earth.

I was there when the few survivors of the human race were offered sanctuary in our realm, and I was there for the subsequent uprising against the Fae King and Queen for their mistreatment of humans. Hell, I was one of the ones leading the masses. Last but not least, I was one of the ones captured and punished for my role in the rebellion.

Gold enchanted cuffs were slapped on my bleeding wrists and I was magically chained to a land within the Fae Realm—an enchanted land the King had created for his Queen so that she would always remember her favorite Earth game: *Candy Land*. They ended up naming it Sweet

Land, but we all knew what it was. The land wasn't a board game, though; it was a real-life death trap. And as a punishment, I was made its King.

I'd have rather been bound in a fucking bottle and left alone like the genie from that Disney movie, *Aladdin*. But this isn't a movie, and I'm no Genie.

I'm a jinn.

So yeah, I'm old. Old enough to have watched the humans try to cross Sweet Land, hearts brimming with hope for a better life, only to never make it out alive. Old enough to know that no humans ever will. And way past old enough to know that even if they did, I would still be stuck here.

It started like this...

Vampires, demons, ghouls, ghosts, and all manner of nightmares wreaked havoc on Earth during the Apocalypse. Most Fae—half-angel, half-demon ourselves—returned to our own realm. We liked to stay neutral in most cases pertaining to Earth. *Hidden*. Most of the supernatural world didn't even know we existed until the day the Fae King ripped open a giant portal to Earth. It was said that it was so quiet when the King stepped through you could hear a pin drop. He had good timing, though; the last of the humans had holed up in a camp, but were quickly being surrounded by deadly supernaturals.

The King offered them sanctuary and held back the supernaturals with his armies. And like the desperate, very mortal beings they were, the humans accepted his terms to live in one of the most dangerous realms in all existence—one worse than Hell itself.

It didn't take much convincing. Fae are all about wordplay. The humans didn't even think to ask questions. *How long will we be safe?* For instance.

They could have inquired about this or a million other things, but their leader was desperate, and soon they were crossing. Many perished on the way, but most made it—at least thirty thousand of them. But what they crossed into wasn't what they were expecting.

They'd crossed into the part of the Fae Realm called the Bad Lands. A barren, cracked, dry, and hot atmosphere surrounded them. Not a plant or animal in sight.

On that day, the Fae King and Queen supplied the humans with a tent, city, water, seeds, and minimal animals for breeding. These survivors had brought a lot of their own supplies with them, so they weren't totally helpless, but it would take them a while to get on their feet—about fifty years, to be exact. The humans eventually found supplies and built houses, forged weapons, and achieved a semi-bearable living environment. But at night, the supernatural residents roamed the land and tore through the humans without mercy.

A lot of us nobles didn't agree with this death sentence. If the humans were here, let them be here; let us coexist in peace and get them out of the Bad Lands. Unfortunately, the King and Queen didn't agree, and that was the start of the rebellion I led. We lost, and because of it, the humans were treated even worse. The day I was captured, three hundred years after the humans first crossed into our lands and one hundred years after our uprising began, our punishment went into effect.

They drove a magically lit board into the brittle earth of the Bad Lands. It was so big everyone could see it for miles around.

Start Here

Welcome to the Bad Lands. Here you are required to procreate. You are given enough to survive, but never to thrive. At night you are subjected to the elements and my subjects as food and fair game. You only have until sundown to be outside. If you are unhappy with your current land and wish to move to another, you may seek an audience with your regal rulers, King Ace and Queen Thelia. To achieve an audience with the king and queen for this purpose, you must first cross Sweet Land. Individuals or multiple humans (a maximum of four to a group) may step on the lit square below this sign, which will read your heart's desires. If all you desire is to live in a different land, you will be transported into Sweet Land – a world inspired by Queen Thelia's love of Earth's delicious sweets and her favorite game, both of which are no longer around.

Rules

Once you enter Sweet Land, your goal is to make it to the Sweet Castle. The path is how you progress through the land.

There are eight territories you must make it through. Each territory has a leader. If you defeat the territory's leader by challenging them at the start of their territory, their subjects will allow you safe passage to the next. Sweet Land is home to my adoring subjects, the supernaturals, so be vigilant as you pass through. If you cannot survive this land, you won't survive any others. Only the strong, fast, and clever will survive and prove themselves worthy of our attention. This land will test you, haunt you, and tempt you.

Good luck.

After the sign was placed, there was chaos.

There was a mad rush of humans trying to get out of the Bad Lands. They didn't just want a better life; they needed one. But I wasn't just bound to the land as its leader—I was bound by the rules of the land as well. And those rules stated I was *never* to let a human make it through the game. So what they wanted or needed would never come to pass.

See, the land wasn't just a punishment for the humans, but for me as well. Whereas most of those involved in the rebellion were sentenced to death, those of us who fought the hardest for the humans were thrown into this land. Instead of securing a better life for the humans, we were now in charge of making them suffer, scaring them, killing them, and ultimately making sure they never saw a better life.

It's not their fault they never make it out. It's mine.

The groups that helped lead the rebellion were thrown into the land with me. They were a group of supernatural leaders who resided in the Fae Realm called the Equals. Not many jinn were left. In fact, I was the only one. With me were a werewolf, ghoul, vampire, ghost, siren, and witch representative, along with their clans. We all wanted human rights in the Fae Realm, but the King and Queen wouldn't allow it. Now we'd been thrown into this land as human tormentors.

It wasn't our fault we turned into the very monsters humans saw us as. Because as the years passed and more and more humans stopped trying to cross, our food supply took a hit. But the land wouldn't allow us to perish; the King and Queen ensured that by keeping a group of servants in the Sweet Castle, Fae spies who magically kept us alive and in a dormant state until humans entered the realm. Then when humans *did* enter, they found themselves pitted against lots of starving supernaturals. Those odds never work out.

I've been hibernating for seven hundred years, and as every horrible day passes, I starve even more. Unable to die, yet unable to live.

I'm old enough to know that I will never change my fate… unless I find my true mate.

CHAPTER ONE

I'm trapped. Bound to this land with no hopes of escaping.

But then she came along…

Her nightmares were what called to my jinn like a beacon on the darkest night; she had trapped me with her enchanting power ever since our first encounter.

The first time I answered her mind's call, I was starving, with no way to nourish myself. So when the colorful soul of an innocent mind flashed before me like the aurora borealis, I came running. I no longer cared for my morals, or how *any* innocent life I took added more time to how long these golden manacles would stay around my wrists.

I found myself standing in a heavily wooded forest, during a full moon in the realm called Earth. I only knew where this dream took place because of the distinct plant and animal life that were alien to the Fae. Crazed to find the source of the call, I reached out the best I could, letting my weakened powers transform me into my smoke form.

I followed the bright red trail until I was soaking

in color, absorbing the power of fear—the most potent of all emotions, and therefore the most filling. Too ravenous to do anything but feed, I watched as a female human cowered behind a tree, surrounded by a group of werewolves. A howl ripped through the air, signaling their prey was trapped and ready for the alpha.

"Rowan… It's me… Please," she begged. Her fear was so powerful that even after my starvation, I was filled within seconds, yet still the fear floated around me, only partially absorbed. I moved through the air to get a better look at this nightmare, more out of boredom than anything else. It'd been so long since I'd found a mortal to feed from, so long since I'd done anything other than sit on my throne and slowly meld into the fabric.

So I stayed… and watched.

And that was when her eyes had found my form.

They were such a bright green that even through the darkened night, they shone through me like a thousand emeralds. From that moment on, I knew I was fucked. I knew that someone had finally brought me back to the land of the living, after all my years in the land of the dead.

Her stare had been so brief that anger shot through me at how it had been stolen away. She watched a naked form stepping through the wolf's circle—that of the alpha. She needed to look at me, not him. But it was a nightmare, and I hadn't really been here. And if I had been being honest myself, she hadn't really seen me, even if I had wanted her to.

"I love you, Rowan! Even if you can't control it. It's me." She closed her beautiful eyes as he knelt, grabbing harshly at her chin, forcing her to look at him. Tears left a trail down her face through the dirt and bruises that marred her skin. It was obvious she'd been through hell.

Her whimper changed my form to human as rage boiled my blood. The sight of his hands on her delicate skin had me ready to kill. I stood silent, out of sight and pissed I was feeling like this. There had only been one other being to make me feel like that, and she'd been long dead.

The jinn had a lot of powers. Dream control was one of them. I could have changed the dream. I could have eased her pain. But if I did, I risked her seeing me. If I interfered, I would have exposed myself, and I knew this was just in her mind. Whatever was happening wasn't really happening. Was that worth showing myself to a mortal?

A scream tore through the air, and the alpha werewolf sunk his fangs deep into the space between her neck and shoulder—the place where they usually went to turn a human.

I twisted into my smoke form, shooting through the colors of fear and right into the fray. As I let my powers disperse, the wolves and their alpha caught on fire, then collapsed into a pile of black ash.

She blinked, looking around while pushing her sweaty,

dark red hair from her face. I floated past her to absorb the blood from her skin and heal her wounds. It was a dream, and I was the captain. Anything in her mind was possible, yet I had been in control the moment I entered.

"What are you?" she asked.

If I showed myself, my muscles would be taut with frustration and my dick would be straining against my pants. Why was she so… enchanting? Her beauty stole my breath away.

"Who are you?" she tried again, with a quiver in her voice.

Her accent only deepened my infatuation. It sounded Staveic. She piqued my curiosity in a way nothing else had in a long time. As old as I was, it was hard for me to get enthralled by anything or anyone. Yet there I was, ready to transform and show myself.

"Who do you want me to be, little one?" I whispered; my power allowed her to feel my breath against her neck. I watched in delight as goosebumps covered her skin and her nipples peaked through her tight fabric shirt.

A chill of pleasure ran through me at the sight and I growled, unable to help it. "You like my voice; it pleases you. Yet you cannot truly see me."

I watched as she pushed her hands through the loose dirt gripping it. The color of bright azure shot into the air, and I sucked in a breath as a different kind of power fed me.

Pleasure.

It didn't ram into me like her fear previously had. It twisted around and through me, feeding me what she felt, and it pleased me… immensely.

"How can one creature…" I stopped to find the words, enjoying how her head was now tilted back against the tree and her eyes were glazed over. "…one beautiful creature be so enamored, so fascinated by just a voice of a form she knows not?"

A flicker of magic that had never awakened in me harshly and suddenly sparked to life, harsher than I had thought it could and all I could do was stare in shock. I watched as a green shimmered line formed between us. I gasped at the same time she did. I realized too late what was happening as she broke from her trance, her pleasure dissolving. Jinn have a lot of power, but the outward show of magic could only be awakened in them by their soulmate—or as some called them, their true masters.

"It can't be," I whispered in the language of the jinn.

She stood slowly on shaky legs, looking around in a daze, and I realized she was becoming aware of her dream. And for the first time, I realized she was wearing what the human hunters from the Bad Lands wore. I know, because only they were trained in weapons and wore black. For something that should have angered me, it only furthered my lust.

She wore a tight black camisole that showed her toned

stomach, and tight black pants with a belt of weapons around her hips, for killing supernaturals. Boots I could bet held more defensive items and a black leather jacket laid on the ground next to her. She was a hunter, and obviously strong if she had somehow matched my soul.

I studied her as she studied me back. I watched as the confusion continued to hammer her brain and her fingers flinched, no doubt wanting to reach for a weapon, but not knowing which weapon. It was clear she'd never encountered a jinn before.

"What's happening?"

"A call." I needed her. Not in a dream; I needed her in reality. It was clear she was the only one to save me now.

"To where?" she asked. The dream land started to fade away and I knew she was waking up, but holding a dream was something I couldn't waste power on if I was to visit her again.

I moved closer, inhaling her unique scent. It reminded me of frost over a spring flower: startlingly refreshing with a hint of sweetness.

"To me," I whispered against her neck, wanting to pleasure her with my voice again.

It worked, and I watched as her plump lips parted on an intake of air. A flush covered her skin, and if the world around us wasn't dissipating at such a fast rate, I would have tasted her flesh just to see how my touch would have enhanced her experience.

"Find me, my emerald."

Her eyelids fluttered. "Where?" Her voice was barely audible now.

"In Sweet Land."

Her shocked gasp was the last thing I heard.

The dream faded, and it wasn't five seconds later I had the first female I laid eyes upon, one of the servants, pushed up against the wall with my dick buried balls deep in her, trying to fuck *my emerald* out of my system. The servant's moans of pleasure turned to whimpers of pain, but I kept trying, needing release. Even as I imagined it wasn't dull brown eyes staring back at me in fear, but enchanting green ones filled with lust, it still wasn't going to happen. I had yet to find pleasure since I'd been here. The females here didn't satisfy me. And now that I knew what I wanted, I was screwed until I got it. *Until I got her.*

Who was she, to be able to match my soul and awaken my magic? I dropped the now-limp servant to the ground, realizing I may have been a little too rough, but fuck it. Fuck everyone here. They were all spies from the kingdom.

I walked away, realizing how the state of the castle had remained pristine even during my starved slumber. I scoffed, wiping the sweat from my forehead. Of course it had. The Fae King and Queen made sure it was looked after as their spies milled about, ensuring I did my job as the gamemaster, King of Sweet Land, or whatever they wanted to call me. Just a title and job to watch over their twisted little game with the mortals. Make sure the supernaturals stayed in line and the mortals never made it out alive. I wondered if they enjoyed watching me and the rest of the supernaturals of this land starve because mortals feared entering it.

I'd called her here to this sick land, and I didn't even know why. She was the one who could free me, but there could be no exception to the game. I was bound to this land and the rules of it by the cuffs on my wrists. If she entered, she would have to play. But she couldn't save me if she was dead.

An enraged scream tore from my lips and I transformed, flying up and out of the castle, coasting over the land. I flew past Savannah's sick and twisted Frosting Land, where she and the other vampires reigned. I remembered when she was the sanest one of us all, but this land had transformed her, just like it did us all. Most, if not all, of the creatures would be in a slumber until a mortal walked the land again so they wouldn't starve. I wasn't supposed to be awake, but I was.

I was awakened because I'd found my soulmate.

If she could free me, then I had to find a way to break the rules of the game. But that's the problem with freeing a jinn—once you taste their magic, you want more. Her blood sang to me like the sirens call to their prey. Jinn are a type of Fae, but they don't have the power of seduction. *No*. That pull, that pleasure she got just from hearing the tones of my voice, was from our connection. Add that to the first time she gets an inkling of my power. I didn't know her. Would she absorb it and become her true self, which was my mate, and set me free? Or would she get power hungry and end up locking me away to siphon my powers?

I transformed into my Fae form and stood at the border to Sweet Land, where I knew she'd arrive. I couldn't keep still, even if I wanted to. I clenched my hands to keep them from shaking and tried to slow down my heart rate. She'd just had that dream, so I had time. Time to prepare the players, time to prepare the game, and most importantly, time to prepare myself.

CHAPTER TWO

The Fae realm—well, most of it—was enchanted to keep supernaturals of all types fed with food like animals and plants. This way there was no killing and we could co-exist. There were exceptions to this, however—namely the Bad Lands and Sweet Land. They mimicked Earth when it came to how a supernatural must survive, which meant they must prey on humans.

"How is it fair to all the supernaturals of Sweet Land that the first territory is guaranteed to get humans, while the rest of us starve if they don't survive that long?"

That was the question thrown at me during a meeting—a meeting called when fewer and fewer humans attempted to cross. Wolves, witches, and ghosts didn't soley need humans to survive, but vampires, sirens, and ghouls did.

I did.

Well in a way, a very small way, the ghost faction needed interaction with the human race to keep from Fading. Possession and causing fear gave them a power boost. Witches and wolves needed humans to eat, since the land didn't supply a sufficient amount of animals. Wolves needed meat. Witches needed blood and ate human organs. Those two factions were always at war. Ghouls ate anything from a human—the whole thing, sometimes in one swallow—and they had quite the reputation for craving babies. So I guess we all needed the humans, once we were thrown into these types of environments.

All of us trapped in this land were once the most peaceful of the Fae supernaturals. We didn't want the humans harmed, let alone to *eat* them just because our other side was now in control. At first we kept our wits and ate from humans with restraint and remorse. We didn't have a choice. Then, the more starved we became, the more monstrous we got, and we lost control.

To make it so that everyone got a chance to eat, I spelled the land to rotate territories every time there was a new batch of humans who tried to cross.

Some humans made it past the first couple territories, but never more than that. So still the rotation didn't guarantee sustenance every time. But back in the day when humans tried to cross all the time, it worked.

My emerald would be entering, and the first territory set to receive humans now belonged to Adrian and his two wives. Ghouls. They looked like human corpses, if the corpses had been seven feet tall, hairless, and possessing pitch-black eyes and fingers that transformed into knives. They were terrifying. Although back when we lived outside of this land, Adrian, Fushia, and Jasmine were the most caring of us all. In the Fae realm, they had looked like every other Fae, suffused with supernatural beauty and charm. Adrian had beautiful mocha skin, stylish hair, and a blinding smile. Fushia had looked like a human toy called a Barbie Doll, with bright fuchsia hair that somehow worked. Jasmine could have been her twin, except she had brown hair instead. They were always the hosts of our monthly dinner parties. Adrian would make everyone play some type of game that we all tried to get out of, and Fushia and Jasmine would always get drunk and fight about who Adrian loved more. It was normal, entertaining, and dare I say, human. Now they were anything but, and it still pained me to talk face-to-face with them.

It was clear my soulmate had never encountered a jinn in her time as a hunter in the Bad Lands. And that made sense, since I was the last jinn left in existence. We could only reproduce with our soulmate, and finding one was extremely difficult. But had she ever encountered a ghoul? Would she know how to survive them? Would she kill my former friends?

Considering the monsters we'd become… would I care?

The rules of the land prohibited any of us supernaturals from killing each other. So even if it came down to it,

I could only do so much. Ghouls in their natural form, which is what they were in now, were blind. They relied on sound. They also had the ability to blend into their environment. No human had ever made it past them. But even if the ghouls themselves weren't a challenging enough event…

Their territory was made out of giant candy canes.

They were a type of sweet the humans used to eat on Earth. They tasted and smelled of the mint plant if it was dipped in sugar. They were as large as trees in size, white and red striped, and shaped like a cane. The end of the cane was pointed in order to stab down at the humans as they tried to make it through the ghoul's territory, but only if they didn't challenge Adrian, who, after going completely insane from bloodthirst, had started to call himself Mr. Mint.

And if by some stroke of luck the humans were able to pass through a candy cane field that tried to impale them, *and* survived the ravenous ghouls, the only sustenance for a human were the candy cane chips littering their path. It was left over from when the canes hit the path and broke off. And I was old enough to know that humans needed a lot more than sweets to survive.

It was a lot. This land was a lot. And every territory was just as terrifying as the one just described, only the farther you got, the worse it got.

Right as I was about to enter the candy cane fields to

find Adrian, red colors shot into the sky, so bright I had to shield my eyes. It was my emerald's fear. Was it because she was my soulmate that I could connect to her emotions even from so far away? I hadn't been able to see anyone else's fear like this before.

I transform into my smoke form and go into the dream realm, where I find her in an abandoned warehouse, running from a clan of vampires. Why was she always dreaming about us hunting her? Her nightmares were in settings on Earth that no longer existed, and Earth had been destroyed a thousand years ago. How would she know what it used to look like?

Right before I went to feed from her fear, I stopped short, feeling a sudden guilt. She was my soulmate. Was it right to survive off something produced from her being terrified? A lurch of hunger hit me and I couldn't hold back any longer. So I took just a small amount, keeping in mind that the more I took from her, the more she would lose her emotions altogether. That was how jinn feeding worked. We fed on human pain or pleasure until there was nothing left but a shell. I couldn't do that to her. I wouldn't.

A scream tore me from my feeding trance. I looked to see a female vampire with a black pixie cut smack my girl across the face, sending her flying into a group of barrels. I almost transformed into my Fae form, like I did in her last nightmare, but held my shape so that I wouldn't fall to the ground. It was fear. My own fear. I was realizing my emotions for her messed with my transitioning. Seeing her in pain, in fear, hurt me, scared me. I knew we were soulmates, but how could I feel so deeply for someone whose name I didn't even know?

"Alana, help!" She screams as the vampire bites her leg and pulls blood from her. Her whimpers and cries feel like they could crack my chest open and I fly back and forth, trying to keep calm. I need to feed, but I should stop this nightmare. I know it's not real, but I can't keep watching her get hurt.

A small-framed female with long, curly black hair runs into the fray, and she's like no hunter I've seen before. She's a tiny badass. That's when I realize this female, who must be Alana, is in the hunter's uniform, but my emerald is in regular Bad Lands clothes—dull, brown, ill-fitting clothes that are torn in places. Alana comes in, staking vamps left and right like she was born for it. It's like watching a dance, and where one might think she wouldn't fare very well as a tiny female surrounded by huge, strong vampires, she twirls, stabs, and kicks out, taking them all down in a matter of minutes.

"Thank you," my emerald says in a shaky voice.

That's when it hits me. These aren't just nightmares—they're memories. But how?

I fly down to where they converse, and while Alana doesn't see me, my soulmate does and falters in what she's about to say next. I then dissolve the vamps and Alana. I need it just to be us. I have a lot to relay to her and not a lot of time. Dream states only last minutes in real life.

"You again?" she says to me, and if I was in my Fae form, my heart would be pounding. But I couldn't reveal myself to her yet.

"Do you remember our last dream?" I inquire, floating closer to her, and I see that my voice has the same effect on her as last time. It was perfect, because hers did the same to me.

"I do," she says in a breathy tone. It drives me mad.

I want to transform now. I want to feel her skin! *Fuck!* It kills me being so close, yet so far away. But I have to get her to the land—the dangerous land that could potentially kill her—but she *has* to be mine. I would do anything, even if I have to turn her. I would do it. Make her suffer the same fate as me, just to be selfish. Just to seduce her in person. Please her. Love her. Make her mine. I continue to hold back my fantasies as I tease her with my power and voice.

"What is your name?" I need to know. Even though I would always know her as my emerald, I couldn't not know her beautiful name.

Her head tilts in a way that tells me she's intrigued, but doesn't answer. "What are you?" she asks instead.

"Someone important to you." If she knew what I was, would it make a difference? She has to know that

I'm a supernatural. She has to be feeling the same pull soulmates feel toward one another.

She sits up, straightening her clothes, and brings her knees to her chest. "I remember you from the last nightmare, but I don't know what you are. Why would you save me in my dreams and then ask me to go to Sweet Land?" She pauses, and a look of what seems like realization crosses her face. "You are just part of my dream, aren't you?" Standing, she tries to walk closer to my form, but I float back so I won't smell her unique scent. It would tempt me too much. She continues to advance before she grabs at her head. "It's guilt, isn't it? It's my guilt for preparing to lead us into Sweet Land. But why now?"

She starts to pace. She believes that I'm a figment of her imagination. Manifested guilt, because apparently she'd been planning to come to my land all along. But I'm more than that. So much more. And I will show her soon. I'll show her in a way she's never been shown before. There is no way I'm holding back the moment I get my hands on her. It will be more than me being starved for emotions, because the only thing I'm starving for now is her flesh. To taste it. To trail kisses up it.

Her shirt lifts, and I'm able to see a strip of her toned stomach as she grabs her head again.

"Tell me your name," I command in a rough voice. I can't help it; I don't know how much longer I can hold back. I can't continue to meet her like this.

She stops pacing, her eyelids hooded when she looks at me before biting her lip. I smile behind my form. I love that I'm driving her mad with just my voice. It's confirmed when the color of her lust snakes through the air. *Fuck yes.* It comes seductively toward me, and I try to hold it back as I watch her continue to try and figure me out.

"Tell me what you are and I will come to Sweet Land."

I laugh deeply. No one has tried to counter or argue with me in such a long time. "You were coming to Sweet Land anyway, it seems, so negotiations won't work."

Crossing her arms, she cocks her hip. Her attitude is going to be greatly punished. *I can't wait.*

"Well, I won't come then."

"Emerald. Do you like that name? *My emerald…*" I push my power to carry my voice all around her. Her muscles stiffen before relaxing, and I can see her heart is racing by just how fast her chest rises and falls. A darker blue shoots through the previous colors and latches onto me so fast I can't stop it.

My form flickers, and I know she sees it because she gasps. But I can't do anything, because it's like the best foreplay ever. The pleasure she is throwing into the air is building inside me, and I'm shaking. She's shaking. And fuck! If her emotions feel like this, how would touching her skin feel?

"Fellen," she answers on a breathy sigh.

And just when I thought she couldn't be more

enchanting, a name is attached to her beautiful face, and I'm a goner.

I float closer as she lifts her hand to touch my form. "Come to Sweet Land, make it through alive, and I will let you touch me," I promise her. "The *real* me."

She drops her hand and sighs. "Why do you keep saving me from my past? Why am I so drawn to you? Why are you doing this to me? You make me feel..." She swallows hard and bites her lip again before finishing her sentence. "...things I've never felt before."

The dream starts to fade, this time at a faster rate than the last, which tells me someone is waking her.

"Are you alone?" I ask, unable to help the jealousy that laces my words.

She catches it and tries to touch me again, but I fly back. "Does it matter? You are nothing but a ghost." She seems angry now, maybe from the tone of my voice or the frustration, but I can't let her leave like that.

"It matters because you're drawn to me. You belong to me. And this ghost..." I let her feel a hint of my lips on her cheekbone, and she moans and closes her eyes. "...is going to devour every inch of you as soon as you step into my land. So hurry..." I pull back, pleased with the lust in the air. "Because I'm starving, and only your taste will satisfy me."

CHAPTER THREE

Four more nightmares have passed, yet she still isn't here in my land. I'm a King, but I've found the one person I can't command.

I taunt her. Tease and seduce her. Promise her the world. Still, the closest I've gotten to an answer of when she will be here is *soon*.

But I can't wait. Knowing she is out there and can change this fate for not only me, but all the supernaturals in the land, is one of the only things that has me going insane.

Our meetings start out informative now. We talk more, but then it always ends in us panting and wanting more of each other.

I've learned from our short visits that she isn't the only one coming into the land, and that she had been planning this for some time. I also learned that she is a Bad Lands hunter just like the others coming along, and they are all experts in their fields. Fellen's ancestors hailed from a place called Russia, which explains her accent. I've learned that she is an expert werewolf hunter and has a dog named Chip that is her best friend. When I had tried to ask why in her first nightmare she was running from werewolves, she evaded the question and our dream ended. I steered away from that for now, but would find out more when we weren't meeting in dreams that kept fading.

I also found out about the other hunters coming with her, and was somewhat relieved as they were also all experts in different fields of supernatural hunting. Alana, the small female in her second dream, had once saved Fellen from a clan of vampires. It still didn't explain the warehouse, and when I asked, all she said was that the Bad Lands had evolved since I'd seen them last. A lot can happen in seven hundred years, but had they evolved that much? I wasn't sure. The whole situation felt off, but I left it and continued to find out information. Alana was a vampire hunter and lover to both the other hunters coming into Sweet Land.

Their names were Deven and Mollock. Mollock was a witch and ghost hunter, whereas Deven was an expert on all supernaturals, but especially sirens. So,it sounded like they had their bases covered, but I wasn't sure it would be enough. Every dream that passes, Fellen asks me what I am. She grows impatient in wanting to find out. What's worse: That I'm supernatural and that she's a hunter, or that I'm the King of the dangerous land she has to survive, and also the last leader she must defeat? When she finds out the second part, I'm not sure how she will take it. And since she had never even heard of a ghoul, I highly doubted she'd heard of a jinn.

And while she'd told me those things, I tried to prepare her as best I could, but it was getting harder and harder for me to hold dreams the less I fed. Now when I entered her nightmares, I didn't take anything, and it was showing.

"My friends, the hunters who I will enter with, keep asking me how I know what I know."

I float in the air but stay back. If I make her pleasure come out, I will have no choice but to feed.

"And what do you tell them?" I ask as she starts to walk down the shoreline. In this nightmare, a group of sirens almost lured her into the water, but I dissolved them and showed myself right away.

"I tell them I have dreams," she says slowly, like she's trying to find the right words. A soft breeze lifts her wind-torn hair up and her mesmerizing scent surrounds me. It almost knocks me out of the dream, it's so pleasurable. That and the tempting white dress she wears that ends right below her tight ass.

"You wouldn't have to tell them anything if you'd just enter the land, my emerald."

She stops and runs her hands up and down her arms as goosebumps take over her skin. I change the air to warm, and she shivers with a smile and bites her lip. *That fucking lip*. I can't wait to bite it myself.

"Tell me what happens after the ghouls," she implores me. "We leave at the week's end."

I sigh. She is right. She needs to be prepared, but telling her is only half the issue. She will have to survive the land, and only she can do that. I know I shouldn't be so impatient, but every second I spend away from her, I can see our soulmate tether growing dimmer and dimmer. I don't know what it means, but I can't have it go out. She had to get here fast.

"Next is Aspen and his pack, the werewolves."

"*The Dazed Forest*," she replies with a nod, and I'm impressed.

"Yes. How do you know about it?"

She smirks. "I've done my homework."

"There are eight territories. The ghouls and Candy Cane Fields; the werewolves and the Dazed Forest; the witches and the Maze House; the ghosts and the Climbing Woods; the sirens and the Lake; the Swamp; the vampires and the Frosting Land; and the jinn and the Sweet Castle is the last territory."

At some point during telling her the order, her smirk drops to a frown. "We have no choice but to cross the land. We have *all* the Bad Lands humans counting on us." She turns her back on me and looks to the water, but not before I see tears in her eyes. "Why can't you tell me your name or what you are? You tell me stuff and I tell you stuff, but we don't talk about what's important. Those questions you just evade, and it makes no sense!"

She turns around and stomps toward me, and I back up as I float on the wind. "You feel the same way I do! I know you do! You have to feel it, and it's driving me insane. We feel so strongly for each other, yet every meeting while these feelings grow, you keep me at arm's length and continue to beckon me into some land that could kill me! Is it because you're part of that land? Are you one of the monsters that will kill me there?"

She's shouting, and tears are freely falling down her face. I can't take it.

I lower and transition to my Fae form.

Her mouth drops and she sucks in a shocked breath, but doesn't say anything. And all I can do is stare back. I did the one thing I wasn't ready to do yet—I showed myself. She grips the ends of her dress with shaking hands and takes a timid step forward.

"You..." she begins, and I can now see my reflection in her round, awestruck eyes. My skin is tanned, more so than her sun-kissed flesh, like what she would consider Arabic heritage. Where her eyes are emerald, mine are dark chocolate to match my hair. I don't wear shirts, courtesy of my demonic blood, because I cannot keep cool. But I do wear a pair of faded jeans that lay low on my hips, which she is now devouring with her eyes. I never thought anything about my Fae form, but knew a lot of women were swayed by it.

"Fellen," I finally say. Then before I can stop myself, I add, "*My emerald.*"

Her pleasure is immediate and she is flushed. The azure swirling around her brings out her dark red hair and bright green eyes. It floors me, and I can't hold back. I make my way to her, and when she steps back with a look of fear, I know she is a liar, because I can see her lust. It is now surrounding and filling me.

"I won't stop myself."

She stops in her retreat when I'm a foot away, and my heart pounds out of my chest as our soulmate bond flares and wraps around us. She can't see it, but I know she has to feel it, and I can tell that exact moment, because she gasps and then I'm grabbing her.

My world explodes.

Her lips crash against mine, and I swallow her moan while I drive my tongue into her mouth. She tastes like her unique scent of frosted sweetness. I grab her hair and use it to pull her down and onto the sand before my hand is snaking up her flimsy dress. She gropes along my ribs and back. To have her hands on me almost makes me combust.

"Wait," she moans, but I ignore her and rip her skimpy lace underwear clean off. I didn't even check the color, because the color I want is her pretty pink flesh between her thighs. "Wait. Wait." She tries to scoot away and I growl as I hold her in place, looking into her eyes.

She licks her lips and I reach down and unbutton my jeans. I'm not waiting. "I want your name first, please," she says before biting her lip. She gasps, watching as I take my throbbing cock out.

I slowly push up her dress. A look of defiance crosses her face, and I know she is going to fight me. She tries to shut her legs, and I growl and force them back open.

"I'm giving us what we need," I tell her, gently kissing up her legs as I breathe in her heat. It's fucking intoxicating.

"I need your name."

"And I need to be buried in you." I'm past her kneecap now, and as I tease her clit, she wiggles and keeps trying with breathy pleas that just turn me on more.

"And if I say I don't want it?" she asks.

I make sure to lock eyes with her while my face is parallel to her soaked cunt. "Then I would call you a fucking liar." I growl before licking straight up her center. The taste of her is more than I could imagine and I almost combust right then and there.

Fellen throws her head back and cries out, gripping my hands as I hold her thighs apart and continue to taste her. As I swirl my tongue in her, she continues to say she doesn't want this, but her moans of pleasure and bright blue aura tell me otherwise, and I'm throbbing. She's soaked.

Fuck this.

I use my powers to dissolve her dress, not giving her a chance to figure out what happened. I grab her face and pull her into my deep kiss.

"Tell me," she whispers, pulling away. I smirk.

"You want to know, Emerald?" I grab her breasts, and she arches her back as her lips part in pleasure.

"Yes."

I move my hand into her hair and grip it hard, making her cry out, and the tip of my cock starts to dribble. I ignore her panicked look and kiss her once before settling myself between her legs.

"No," she says, her lust sobering a bit. Before I know what's happening, she has her legs wrapped around my hips and flips me over. I smile, and it must not be a friendly smile, because a faint trickle of fear intertwines with the blue. Fellen crawls back across the sand and away from me. I can't read her expression.

"Don't you know what no means?" she asks.

Getting up on my knees, I make sure she has a good look at my girth as I stroke my shaft. And she watches, hunger in her eyes. She's such a tease. "I can see you craving me. Craving this." I look down and stroke faster, and make a show of groaning and closing my eyes while throwing back my head. I give her a taste of her own medicine and bite my lip. She gasps.

I keep it up a few seconds longer before I stand and

stalk closer to her. She slams her legs closed. "I don't know what you are. I don't know *who* you are. I'm not just giving you a part of myself."

"Come now, Fellen—we've been meeting like this for weeks, months." I smirk as she shivers and throws an arm over her perky breasts. I push my foot between her legs, the sand building up between my toes. "You think one simple little word is going to stop me from taking what's mine?"

I push my knee between hers and spread her thighs enough to fit my body through, but she still refuses to loosen up and let them fall.

She tries to scoot back again, fear now more evident through her blue colors. *Good.* Hunting my women has always added to my pleasure. Leaning down, I throw her back on the sand again. If she's being honest with herself, she'd know she's allowing this. She isn't really fighting, and I'm not even sure why she's throwing out words like "no."

"You don't want this?" I grab my cock again and she swallows hard. The blue deepens.

"No," she whispers.

I let go, making sure my fingers are coated in my seed before leaning over her and rubbing it across her bottom lip, which is now trembling. "You don't want to taste this?"

But she gives in and her tongue shoots out, licking it

up before her eyes shut on an intake of air and her head rolls back. "No." Yet she keeps trying. My beautiful little liar. This is also the time that her legs relax enough for me to hold them down again.

She's mine now. There's no turning back.

"You don't want to feel this?" I tease my cock between her slick folds, rubbing it back and forth. She's wiggling now and the red is gone. Blue exploding in the air.

"No," she pleads with a shaky voice. "Tell me and I'll give consent. Tell me your name."

"I'm taking this with or without your tiny, disposable *consent*, Fellen."

"No."

"That's not my name." I groan and push in my tip. It takes all my self-restraint to keep from ramming it in her like I want. She wiggles, and she says no, but her colors, perky nipples, and soft moans tell me she wants it.

"Please." She shivers, and I lean over her enough to bite that fucking lip and taste blood, making her cry out.

"You want to know?" I tease.

"Yes."

"Yes to me?" I push in deeper and she whimpers.

"No. I mean… yes!"

I'm smiling. She's desiring me so much she's lost her mind.

"It's... *Neek,*" I finally say, unable to hold on anymore.

And she screams it as I drive into her.

CHAPTER FOUR

I've fucked a lot. Made love, some. Messed around. Jacked off plenty. But this shit is on a whole other level. Her screaming my name will forever be the best fucking sound in the whole realm. Once I'm buried deep in her, I pull out and slam in again. She is nothing I've ever felt before and I'm losing control, but she takes it hard and fast. Even with the sand burning my knees and no doubt her back, we are lost in lust, just taking every inch of each other. She's clawing, biting, and sucking on everything her mouth can reach from her pinned position. And I'm slapping, gripping, and driving into her with a force I didn't think was possible.

At one point we'd both come to release, me with a roar and her screaming, "Oh God!" I told her there was no such thing, and then she was slapping me and flipping me over before crawling down my body and fitting my whole cock in her mouth. The whole fucking thing. To say I'm impressed is an understatement, because no woman has yet to achieve that accomplishment, but then she's swirling her tongue around my tip and I'm exploding in

Just like that, she pulls a release from me when it's taken me so long to find it with any other being. And she's madness. A rough little thing. I choke her from behind and pound into her ass. That's on our fourth round. I could do this forever, but this is just a dream, and when it gets too hard for me to hold, we have no choice but to pull away from each other with our hearts beating out of our chests and slick sweat dripping down our bodies.

It won't be enough. It never will. I want to be buried in her for the rest of eternity. She awakened in me a desire I'd thought long gone.

The dream starts to tear away and I hold Fellen tight, placing gentle kisses up her neck. "You'd better hurry. Now that I've had you in your dreams, I want you for real."

She turns toward me, running her finger down the side of my face. "So this wasn't real?"

I swallow, unsure of how much is too much to reveal. "Think of it as a really fucking hot wet dream. But Fellen…"

She's starting to fade, and I'm growing angrier by the second. Fucking dreams.

"Hurry," is all I can manage before she's gone.

I thought I'd have more time with her, but dreams never finish the way you want.

Now I'm pacing in front of Savannah's Winter Castle, or *Frost's,* as she likes to call herself. She is the vampires' clan leader and one of my exes. We'd been together for close to a decade, and I believe it had been more from convenience and boredom than anything. Just like all of us stuck here, she was one of my closest friends. She'd also been born a vampire and had lived in the Fae Realm all her life. So when we were thrown here, it was the first time she'd resorted to blood. At first, herself and the clan would fight the werewolves and witches for what few animals remained, and they would drink from them. She'd tried so hard not to turn into her true monster. And she was strong. The second-strongest next to me, and the last to give in to human blood.

When the rotation finally determined the vampires would receive the humans first, she didn't hold her clan to the same values and let them feed. We were starving by that point. She had asked me to hold her down in chains with a stake poised at her heart, but we both knew I would never kill her, even if the game would allow it. It was pointless. It was like the whole land could smell the moment a human's blood hit the air, and she went crazy. Bloodlust transformed her beautiful face to something unrecognizable. Her skin wrinkled and her fangs seemed longer, sharper. Her eyes turned bright red, and maybe I didn't have the chains down tight enough, because even with me pleading for her to stay calm, she had broken through them like melted butter and was gone. That was the end of it—the end of her "humanity," I guess you'd say.

After that when the time came for her to get sober, it just never came. It was like she was locked in a constant state of raging bloodlust, and eventually we all had to band together and lock her away. If I listened close enough, I could still hear screaming, and I didn't understand. The magic of the land was supposed to keep us in slumber when there were no humans. Yet she never stopped. I just hoped that meant she couldn't be summoned. The land and its rules didn't allow for exceptions. If Fellen and her crew made it to Savannah's territory and they called upon her for a challenge, she would appear—no if, ands, or buts.

There are a lot of uncertainties in this existence, but one thing *is* for certain: If it took all of us banding together to lock Frost deep in an underground tomb, Fellen would not be able to defeat her in a challenge.

Thinking back to Savannah's bright smile, my chest hurt. It wasn't because I loved her or missed her romantically. She'd been one of my best friends. One of my confidantes. Someone I could get advice from, and now she was gone just like the rest of them. Turned into an uncontrollable monster, and I didn't know how to fix her. Getting Fellen here was the goal, getting her out alive would be a miracle, but what would it take to change all of our fates? Would we ever be able to go back to how it was?

So I guess that's why I keep hopping from territory to territory, thinking about how many of my friends I'd lost. How much I want to tell them I'd finally found my soulmate, and how much I wish they wouldn't try to kill her. But those are the rules of the land, and there wasn't anything I could do.

I had no doubt the monarchy's spies had run straight to them to reveal I had awoken, and with no humans reported in the land, they would be wondering why. This poses a real threat to me, the land, and especially Fellen if they were to find out who and what she was to me. My mind flashes back to her eyes lighting up the first time we climaxed together. They sparkled and reminded me of our tether. I didn't know a lot about soulmates, because the jinn race had died out so long ago; many considered us the stuff of rumors. I'd heard tales of there being a tether linking you to your soulmate, or what some considered your true master. And now I knew that much was true, but the others I wasn't sure about.

A soulmate was considered your true master because of the ways of the jinn. We were half-angels and half-demons. And like those beings that are now extinct after the Earth battle, they could be trapped, claimed and forced to do someone's bidding. Unlike a demon circle or angel trap, jinn could be possessed by two things: knowing their full name or physical cuffs. Utter a jinn's full name, and they are forced to grant you three services. It was why a jinn's name was a sacred thing. Not even my friends knew it. I went by Neek, but that was all I would give. Physically cuff a jinn with pure gold, and you can magically bind them to anything. Like myself, bound to this land and rules. The King and Queen then became my masters and until they released me, I had to stay bound for all eternity. Jinn can live forever but can still die. Just like all the rest of the Fae realm. So it was a miserable and perfect punishment for them to place me here and let me suffer.

But Fellen was my soulmate. My true master. That above all else was the only thing that could free me *if* I could get her in front of the King and Queen. A true master can only claim a jinn if they announce their claim to the current masters. I had to get her out alive, deliver her to them and then above all else, reveal my true name. I was putting a lot on the line for myself and everyone here. I would make sure she went through with it like a good girl. Even if I had to trick her, fuck her, ruin her, I would win this game... no matter the cost.

Shaking myself from my thoughts and haunted memories, I step into Savannah's frozen castle and the slamming of the door behind me echoes throughout the empty grand entryway. The vampires are magically made to slumber, but we don't attack each other and I can wake any of the supernaturals at any time. So yeah, they might be pissed I'm waking them, but I have to try to talk some sense into them. All the territories were dangerous enough without the humans having to fight the residents. But would that be possible?

As I walk into the den where their coffins are placed, the smell of dust and sugar swirl through the air. It's nauseating and makes me hate this place even more. They lived in a land that mimicked ice and snow, but tasted like frosting and icing. Seven coffins, all black, lay before me and are held up by pedestals. They are in order of hierarchy. So I know that the first one is Savannah's second in command, Dagger.

I unlock the latches to his coffin and flip open the lid, a creak filling the room. I press a finger to the magical tattoo on his right shoulder and hold it there, reciting the words that will awaken him. I may be bound by the rules of the land, but the other supernaturals are bound and controlled here by an unbreakable magic symbol placed on them by the King and Queen. This was also how the Fae servants put them to sleep. I'd learned long ago how to reverse certain magic. This magic was child's play compared to the magic that held us captive here.

Daggers' eyelids slammed open. His blood-red eyes immediately met mine and he snarled, "I don't smell food."

I scoff as I step back and give him room to climb out of his coffin. "And you won't. I need to talk to you."

Dagger was rough-looking. Huge muscles. Scars. Long hair and bad attitude, but once you had his loyalty, you had it for life. He was a turned vamp that had a MC club on Earth during the end times. He had fought alongside humans to fight off the other supernaturals. That life must have stuck with him, because he still dressed like a biker. Monster or not, he was still him. And I needed his loyalty now more than ever. If I was going to convince the leaders of the territories to let her pass unscathed, it was going to take a miracle and Dagger by my side.

After catching him up on Fellen and the recent dilemma, he sat quiet for a long time, stoking a fire neither of us needed, but had made out of pure boredom. "If she's your soulmate and we can get her to Ace's Castle, we have a chance." He cracked his knuckles, a nervous habit and one I recognized. "But it's going to take all of us."

"The servants. I say we use them." I'd been thinking about it for a while. Vamps needed blood, and it was a crime punishable by death to kill a Fae, but who was here to enforce that rule? Why had we left them alive for so long? At first it could have been fear, but then what? Did we just forget?

"And what happens when Ace and Thalia's spies stop reporting and the King and Queen come to investigate?"

"Then even better. We won't have to get them through the land, just get them in front of Fellen."

Dagger squinted. "You already sealed the bond?" He was inquiring about the soulmate bond. Your tether is sealed forever once you consummate your bond, and while we did have sex in her dream, it didn't count.

"I will," I assured him, and he chuckled.

"Your love life doesn't exactly have the best track record," he said, and I rolled my eyes but he held up a hand and continued. "Either way, how you planning on dipping your dick in her when she is running around trying to survive?"

I stand from the stool I was sitting on by the fire. "That's why instead of trying to kill her, we try to save her. Protect her through the land."

He stands now too and shakes his head. "I don't know, man. We can try. They might be more likely to help if they know there is a guarantee of us getting out, but you need to play this right. I'm barely able to keep up this conversation, I'm so weak. The moment they step into this land, it will take every ounce of strength in us to hold back, and what if we slip?"

"And what if we don't try?" I ask in a raised voice. "Are you just going to give in and eat your way out of here?"

"And what happens when she gets to your territory and the land forces you to fight her? Have you forgotten the only challenge in yours is to get past you? You don't think the land isn't going to possess you to fight?"

I clench my fists. "That's why we need all of us. Even better if the royal pricks come here. Then they won't have to challenge me."

Dagger sighs and runs a hand through his shoulder-length blond hair. He knows there will be no other chance but this one, and we have to try. It's all we can do. "Fine." He pushes the poker harder into the fire before tossing it into the corner of the room. "But we are eating the Fae."

"You'd be doing me a fucking favor, man."

At this he laughs, and we take off for my castle. I'd get him a snack, and then we needed to make our way to the territories fast. We couldn't mess this up.

CHAPTER FIVE

"So you're cheating?" is all she asks after I explain that me and Dagger have been working to convince the leaders of the other territories to follow our plan. We've only made it to the first three and the leaders and members are evenly split down the board. Half agreed to help and the other half wouldn't agree. Ghouls, no. Werewolves were split 50/50, and the witches were a no.

I look over at Fellen. Something is off with her. She won't look me in the eye and it's driving me mad. I step forward, but she puts up a hand. "Don't."

"What the hell is your deal, Fellen?" I growl. "The last time I saw you we couldn't get enough of each other, and now you're acting like we're strangers. What the fuck?"

She reaches up and plays with her hair that she has braided off to one side. She is in her hunting uniform as well. I watch as she opens her mouth, but doesn't speak, and that's when I notice her glance at my wrist cuffs.

"I know what you are."

I sigh. "You would have found out eventually." I take

a step toward her, wanting her close, but she backs up until she's a foot away from a tree. I barely hold in the urge to yell. "But that doesn't change what we are to each other."

She crosses her arms and attitude flares in her eyes. It makes my heart race from the unknown. "And what are we, *jinn*?" Before I can recover, she continues. "After our last dream I couldn't stop thinking about you, and I needed to know what you were, so I borrowed some books from Deven. I'm so glad I never told him why I needed them." She scoffs and I hold my breath. "I thought the cuffs were just a fashion thing, but then I learned what you are. That would have been fine. I wasn't sure where you came from, though. Were you in the Bad Lands and a threat to my family? Then I remembered you constantly trying to get me to Sweet Land and all your knowledge of it. You said you are trying to convince the leaders to keep back from us, meaning you are in the land, and after everything you've said, the only territory left for a jinn would be… *the King*."

I knew she would eventually find out, but this wasn't the right time or place. Her prejudice toward supernaturals as a human would have to be slowly approached. But the subject of me being a Sweet Land resident, let alone a king, was going to be tough. Now I watch her mentally leaving me before we've got a chance to be together. I'm shaking and my chest hurts. Either I have a good poker face or she can't see my hurt. Either way, it's obvious she doesn't care, because she keeps on.

"So tell me, King of Sweet Land… Did you spy on my nightmares and think I would be easy to take down and destroy in your land? Or was it when you found out I was a hunter and strong enough to hold my own that you found a different tactic? Did you think if you just slept with me one time I would fall madly in love with you and risk it all?"

She walks toward me in anger, but I grab her by the throat and push her back against the tree before she can blink. I had to stop this.

"This is just a dream, *Neek*. You can't actually hurt me here," she wheezes, and I squeeze a bit harder.

"I am more than some title to you, Fellen." I look down at her cleavage pushing out of her shirt. Her breath is coming fast and I didn't even see the fear until it was trying to shoot through me, but I reject it and focus on her raging eyes instead of her body. "Yes, I might happen to be the *King* of Sweet Land *and* your last challenge, but I'm more than that. I can't just enter anyone's dreams, and if you read up on me like you said, you would know that."

I release the pressure a bit on her neck, even though I know she's breathing fine and a faint pleasure floats through the air surrounding us. I press myself against her while she tries to turn her head to look away. I let her, but not before I readjust my hand on her neck and slam her head back against the tree. She clenches her jaw, but her nipples poking through her shirt let me know just how much she *thinks* she hates me right now.

"You belong to me," I remind her, "and I will never let you go."

She laughs, but it's humorless and harsh.

"This is fucking crazy, Fellen!" I hiss. "Does it fucking matter what I am? I know you feel this pull between us!"

"I thought I did, but apparently you were just using your Fae magic to seduce me," she spits. I shake my head in astonishment. She has it so fucking wrong.

I know she still feels our pull, and I grind against her just to prove it. She may look pissed, but one deep inhale along with the blue colors slithering through the air tells me she's soaked.

"Just because you can turn me on doesn't mean this is anything other than lust. You betrayed my trust. *Tricked me.*"

"And how do you think I did that? *Huh,* Fellen?" I squeeze tighter on her throat until I see a spike of fear. "Did I betray it by telling you knowledge no human has been graced with before entering my land? Or was it when I told you I'm trying to get you through the land *alive* because you are my soulmate? Believe what you fucking want, but I didn't trick you, and I would never betray what's mine."

She bucks underneath me, and I can tell her anger has

reached a breaking point. Tears now flooded her eyes. "Get off me! You're a monster!"

"I'm *your* monster," I say, letting go of her throat. I keep her pinned with my body, blocking her in with my arms. "One you'll never escape."

She looks at me with tears falling down her face, but doesn't try to buck me off or speak. I take it as progress, but I'm not sure. I lean forward and lick down the shell of her ear, grinding into her again. But she's like a corpse, with no reaction to me. I won't let her do this.

"You're not mad at me for what I am, but who you *think* I am."

After another beat of silence, I keep trying. "You can't tell me I'm faking this just to kill you. I'm fucking *helping you*. And I know you feel our soulmate bond," I whisper, and she freezes.

"It's impossible from what I read. Humans and jinn cannot mate. So I know you're lying."

"What you read is wrong. You *are* my soulmate. I can see our tether of magic."

Something changes in her stare, and it almost looks like she believes me, but I can't be sure. "Just tell me what the hell I have to do to get you off me." She's back to mad in the blink of an eye.

"Give me a chance, Fellen," I say in a low voice. I lean close to her lips, but don't kiss them. I see the debate in her eyes. She looks from my lips to my eyes. She wants me.

She and I both know she does, and she's right—it might be just lust right now, but that will change in time. Our bond will strengthen and our love will be like no other, but she has to give it a chance. She has to give *me* a chance.

She scoffs and rolls her eyes, which results in more tears falling down her cheeks. I move over and kiss them away as she sniffles. "I don't know how to do that. I don't know how to trust you when I've been training all my life to *kill* you."

Her eyes plead for me to understand and for some reason, I do. "You just have to have faith, Fellen."

"Why are you trying so hard to get me out alive, other than the soulmate thing? If I make it out, then what? You will leave your castle and come with me? Or expect me to live with you in that horrible place? Is there even an us?"

She's shooting questions at me rapid-fire and panic has taken ahold of her. It's evident in the air. "Shh. Listen. Just listen, *my emerald*. First, there will always be an us. Even if I have to pin you to a tree to get you back every time, I will." I lean forward and kiss her gently. I almost cry out in excitement when she kisses me back. "Second, if you can make it through, we might be able to change the fate of Sweet Land. You may be the key to everything. Our freedom, human freedom—all of it."

Sucking in a breath, she stares at me with wide eyes. "How?"

"By winning." I step away from her and give her some

space now that I know she's not a flight risk.

She is in a debate with herself, and the dream starts to fade, but I keep her asleep. "If I really am going to give you a chance and trust you… then you're going to need to tell me more. How am I supposed to win, and how will that fix things?"

That was the one card in my hand I couldn't play until I was absolutely sure she was on board. If I told her the power of the soulmates and she turned it against me, I would put not only myself, but my friends in the land in danger. I'm asking her to trust me, but I can't trust her. Not fully. And not yet. It has to be at the right time.

So I smile, and it produces a skeptical look on her face. I know I have her, though. "I will tell you the moment you step into Sweet Land, and only if you do so in two days."

She opens her mouth to argue, but I transition to my smoke form and fly away as I fade the dream.

The ghosts can appear as anything they want. Humans. Objects. Animals. The only real way you can tell they're ghosts is by the slight bluish tint around their forms.

Dagger and I approach Zeek, and before I can wake him, Dagger is sneaking back behind one of the huge lollipop trees. I mean, they are called the Climbing Woods, but are really huge-ass candy suckers. All I can do is roll my eyes. Dagger and Zeek were best friends at one point and notorious for pranking each other. With our sad fucking lives, there hasn't been much fun. So I let him have this one, even if he looks stupid as hell trying to hide behind a lollipop.

"You're really going to try and scare a ghost?" I say, crouching to examine what looks like a sleeping gray cat. I know it's Zeek, because that's the form he likes to take when he sleeps.

"Shh!" Dagger says. I shake my head and chuckle. Just like fucking children.

Zeek wakes slowly and looks around before yawning. Before he can change into his Fae form, Dagger jumps out with a loud vampire hiss and Zeek lets out a screech before shooting three feet into the air. In the blink of an eye he transforms into a human movie villain called *Michael Myers* and swings a huge bloody knife at Dagger, who barely dodges it from laughing so hard.

Zeek turns toward me and tries to swing, but I put a stop to the madness. "Don't even think about it!"

He falters with his knife still in the air before he transforms into his normal Fae form. "Much better," I say, and Dagger comes over, giving Zeek a hug with a series of slaps to the back—man shit.

"Oh, come on, Dad, we've been asleep for hundreds of years. You can't be so serious all the time," Dagger says. One minute he's a tough biker, the next he's back to being the youngest supernatural in our messed-up group.

"Fuck off, I'm not your dad. And I'm not serious all the time, but this *is* serious shit."

Zeek stills at that, dropping the smile and putting on a blank face. "What's happened?"

His voice catches me off-guard for a moment. I forgot how much I missed my friend. The Fae form he likes to take on is a six-foot-seven male with a red afro. It's weird as fuck, but it's him.

We gather around in a section of his territory that won't try to kill us, and once Adrian and some of his pack members arrive, we recap events, catching him up to speed. Zeek agrees to help right away. I had no doubt he would. But we still have the others to convince and come up with a plan for those who disagree.

It's a long night, to say the least. Before it's over, we have the help of the siren leader but not his clan, and three more vampires that are a part of Savannah's harem. Adrian and the ghouls are split on their decision now. We all know Savannah is off the list, being a big obstacle if she's to get free. We've done all we can at this point, and we are on the last night before the humans step into the land. So I decide to wake everyone. Whether they are on board with helping us or not, I throw a little party.

This one just happens to be a Fae-eating party.

I watch from my throne as a Fae with half her face bludgeoned in comes running through the throne room, screaming bloody murder. Taking a pull of her fear, I watch two werewolves tear her apart.

"See, that's what happens when you're an evil asshole who works for an evil kingdom," I shout before taking a drink from my goblet, enjoying the rich taste of raspberry wine the witches brought to the party—in exchange for blood, of course. Zeek spits out his drink with laughter. How the fuck did we become okay with being sadistic? Oh, right. We were trapped here and starved as a punishment for being nice.

I'm drunk. That's okay.

My soulmate was preparing to cross this land, survive a fight with me, and then free us all by asking pretty please. Fuck my life, this was a train wreck. I drink some more and shout to a male Fae servant, who I'm pretty sure shit his pants at one point because of the reek coming off him, to fetch me more wine. I can get my own wine, but I'm using up his fear until he's a shell, then I'll throw him to vampires. They get the next one. It's fun. Adrian even brings his two wives, and once they eat enough Fae, they are back to looking normal and non-hideous. In fact, everyone was looking normal.

"A toast!" I call out and stand to address the room. Everyone stills in their killing, and I continue only after Dagger snaps the neck of a really annoying screamer. "Whether we are all on board with this next round of humans or not…" I look around the room and make eye contact with every leader I can. "...my soulmate will make it through, and we will soon be out of this shit hole!"

I raise my glass high as the room explodes in cheers, and then it's back to the killing festivities and I down the rest of my wine.

"Nice speech, Kingy," Zeek says, helping a witch named Leah onto his lap.

I glance over and flip him off before I try to find Ashley, Leah's coven leader. I spot her trying to seduce Aspen, and the pissed-off look on his mate's face tells me there's about to be a fight. She's most likely drunk as Hell to be on him like that, because up until they went into a slumber Ashley's coven and Aspen's pack fought tooth and nail.

"How much you wanna bet she sucks his cock and Rune tears her head off before the end of the night?" Dagger says, walking over while pushing a siren off him.

"I'll take that bet and raise you two dead witches if I can frame them," Zeek says, and Leah rolls her eyes and twitches off somewhere, making us all laugh our asses off. They do it to themselves.

Ashley used to be a friend with our group. She joined the Equals and even loved baking shit for game nights. But then the rebellion took place, and her husband was beheaded and his body burnt at the stake while they forced her to watch. Getting thrown in here with us after that was just the icing on the cake, so to speak, and she turned into a wicked witch. Casting harmful spells, turning normal witches into hags who grew old and decrepit before they eventually died. We couldn't die, so she could do all the evil she wanted and never turn into the hag she is.

For the first hundred years, she made all of our lives miserable, hiding hex bags meant to harm us and casting spells to annoy us, but eventually she stopped her shit and just retreated into witch territory and ignored us all. Until now, apparently. I almost feel like it's an act. We ask them to help letting the humans pass, they decline. Next thing we know they are bringing us shit for this party. Something wasn't right.

"I agree," Zeek says, and I realize I must have spoken out loud. I was drunker than I thought.

Before I can even respond, azure shoots across the sky over my glass-roofed throne room. What the fuck?

There was only one person who pleased Fellen, and that was me.

Someone was going to die.

CHAPTER SIX

I'm fucking shocked. Completely aroused and totally into this shit.

She's dreaming about me.

More specifically, about our time on the beach.

I watch from a distance as the dream version of me hovers over her, kissing down her neck. From this angle, she is breathtaking. I watch as her luscious breasts rise and fall beneath me as she moans and grabs my ass. Fuck, this was crazy. Should I make her aware she's dreaming and go please her myself? Or should I just enjoy the show? She cries out my name as I slam into her. My throbbing cock is out of my pants and in my hand before I know what I'm doing.

I'm far enough away, standing in the tree line, so she wouldn't be able to see me even if she was aware. Doesn't make me feel any less like a creep, but fuck it. Using my powers, I focus in closer. So close I can watch a bead of sweat trail down her neck as our sweaty, sand-covered bodies fuck hard and relentless on the sand. Squeezing hard, my breath stalls as I stroke myself faster, concentrating on her ass, lips, breasts, and hands that are starkly beautiful in contrast to my dark skin. My other hand gives me balance as I hold onto a nearby tree.

She cries out again, and I do too as I come in my hand. I pump myself a few more times, then transform into my smoke form right as the dream version of me is about to go for round two. Fuck this. I fly over to her and make my other self disappear, and suddenly she's aware.

"Neek?" she asks in a sultry voice. I'm hard again and ready, but all I want is her pleasure.

"Lay back," I command her.

She does as I ask, but confusion fills her eyes. "Transform. I want to feel you."

I slowly brush over her, letting my power represent soft kisses all at once on her skin.

"Oh fuck, Neek. Oh my gods," she moans, throwing her head back. Her right hand flies to her soaking cunt, but I force it away.

"Please," she whimpers. It's hard not to give in, but this will be better.

"Emerald, *scream for me.*"

Then I shoot my form up into her body.

And scream she does.

After she succumbs to exhaustion and starts to pass out in her dream, I tear myself away and plant a kiss on her forehead.

"Next time I see you will be in real life. Prepare yourself, Emerald. I'm coming for you."

It's funny how you have a picture of someone in your mind, and then when you see them in real life, they aren't what you thought they'd be like. Or maybe they were, and that's the shock. My dream visits showed the real Fellen, but they must have been a dulled version of her because she's here now in the flesh, and every feature that drove me mad before is highlighted and shoved in my face.

I'm on fire with lust and barely able to stay hidden, but I do. I watch and observe as her and her team step into my land. Alana looks how she did in Fellen's dream, so she isn't a shock. The males I'm surprised to see, though. The tallest one has the darkest skin I've seen in a while and looks like a warrior. He stands directly behind Alana in what I can tell is a protective stance as he looks around. From the salt pouch on his waist, I take it he's Mollock, the ghost and witch hunter.

That leaves the other male, who she called Deven, and he already lands on my shit list. He stands beside Fellen, a little too close, a little too protective. His hand is just inches away from hers, and I itch to break it. But I needed them alive. I needed them as fodder. I had to ensure she survived; the rest would be good protection until then.

I'm most surprised by the white and black-spotted

dog at Fellen's other side. It looks like it's seen better days, but is obviously a smart choice in bringing along because it growls out, hair raised and chin pointed toward where I am hiding twenty feet away. And I know for a fact that I'm the closest supernatural. It would also come in handy in protecting my asset.

It is daytime where they are, but perpetual night where I am and where the entrance of the path into the land is. It knows. The land knows that humans are here. And so do the supernaturals.

I watch as Fellen takes the first step and leads her team, starting down the path. The air around me thickens, and not just the fog; it's a feeling. The one that quiets everything around you, raises the hair on your arms, and gives you the feeling that someone is right behind you. The land is preparing. Wetness under my hand has me lifting it off one of the giant candy canes to see where the red in its stripes are now dripping blood.

A haunting howl rips through the air. Aspen has changed, no doubt against his will. And just like the land, the supernaturals are preparing as well. The air drops further in temperature the closer they get, and I transform into my smoke form and hide. This was it. They would either try and make it through Adrian's land and he would try and keep the other ghouls back to honor our alliance, or one of them would challenge the leader and we would all be fucked. I told her not to. And hopefully she heeded that warning. I could get her through as safely as I could, but she had to stick to the plan.

The moment they are all surrounded in the night air, I can feel the land as well as myself and the others around hold their breath. "*Still,*" I whisper on the wind to them. They needed to let them pass, hungry or not.

"I know you're out there, King of Sweet Land!" Fellen yells, clenching her hands tighter around a weapon I've never seen before. It holds blades on both ends of a long staff. "But we only trust our kind, and because of that..."

She pauses again, taking a step forward, and I hold my breath. In anger. In fear. I needed her. They needed her. I wanted to fly to her and shake the shit out of her. What the fuck is she doing?

"I alone challenge the leader of the first territory!"

I have nothing to say before ghouls I hadn't seen slide down from their hidden positions on the canes and rush toward her. My heart is slamming out of my chest, but when I go to intervene, the land knows and I hit an invisible wall.

No. No. No! Fuck!

Adrian walks out, and I can tell he is fighting the change. He looks at me with pleading eyes as his wives pull on his arms to hold him back, but a rush of wind blows the humans' scents right into his face and his pupils dilate. I know then that my friend is back to being lost to the land.

Ghouls surround Fellen, and I watch as her teammates fight the same invisible wall I am trapped behind. They pound on it, shouting. I can tell they knew nothing of Fellen's plan either by the shock and fear in their eyes. Adrian whistles, and as quick as the ghouls descended, they disappear back into the candy cane fields.

"They call me Mr. Mint," Adrian laughs, fully transformed into the terrifying creature that haunts even *my* dreams. Fellen is looking for him. I only see him because I am the King of the land. She doesn't look scared, though. She looks pissed, and I just hope it's enough to get her through this alive. We need her to make it out alive, but now she has to kill one of my best friends in order to make it through the land, and it's all too real. This wasn't what we planned, but I harden myself for the inevitable. She is here in the land, just like I wanted.

The land is waiting for me, and I grit my teeth, but know there is no point in stalling, no matter how pissed off I am. Taking a deep breath, I release the word that will start this game.

"Begin."

Instead of looking at Adrian, who is now in clear view of her, crouched upon the closest cane, she looks to me. I'm shocked. She talks to him, but looks at me when she says it.

"Bring it on, you piece of shit!"

My Happy End- To her getting here.

Land of Horrors

My Name is Fellen

My destiny is to save the human race, but there's more to this destiny then I might be willing to accept.

The day before we are set to leave on this journey a seer foretells my future, I think she aims to surprise me. However, the King of Horrors has been gracing my nightmares for sometime now, so I'm well prepared. Maybe not for him, but I am ready to defeat this land and all it throws at me.

I just have to get myself and my team out alive. Can I ignore the physical and sexual pull to the one being I'm set to kill to complete this mission? Or will this "destiny" stand in the way of saving the human race?

A CandyLand board game Horror/PNR retelling.

THE BAD LANDS
FELLEN

"Hold on, Chip! Hold on, baby girl!" I plead repeatedly, while pushing open the door heading back into our healer's medical room. I readjust my grip on her when she starts to slip, the blood coating her body and her squirming makes it hard to hold her.

Are you sure it isn't a supernatural bite?" The healer asks again.

"Yes!" I snap at her, unable to help it. I'm frantically shaking as I get to the table and lay her down carefully. Chip continues to whine in pain and I don't realize I'm crying until the tears obstruct my vision. I lean forward and hold her head to mine as I pet and comfort her. "I told you it was some other dog, but not a werewolf! It's that pack of strays that keep getting too close to the village!" My voice starts to rise with the hysterics of the situation, but I take a few shaky breaths to get it under control.

The healer, Jules, rushes past me and gets to work

gathering materials on the counter to tend to the bite on Chip's back leg. I lost my family and the only thing I have left is Chip. The white and black spotted pit bull puppy, my father gave me on my eighth birthday. She and I have been inseparable since and I thought I'd trained her better than this! After all, she was a dog to a hunter. When I say run, she should listen, but I know she was just protecting me from the pack of strays that veered too close. Unfortunately, she paid the price for protecting me before I could shoot the bastards away. Now I'm terrified and second guessing all the things I should have done differently.

Jules comes over and pours a clear liquid on Chip's injury, resulting in a louder whine from her. I hug her tight to try and keep her still but look away. I'm not exactly blood shy, but for some reason, seeing her injured is breaking down all the walls I built around my heart to stay strong. I'd built them for a reason. I wouldn't let myself feel sorry for being alone and I knew one day I would lose her. I guess I just didn't think it was a possibility it would be this soon.

The sound of the door swinging open behind me has me shifting my head to see Alana and Mollock rushing in. Alana is wearing a pair of torn skinny jeans, a white tank top, black leather jacket and boots. She always wears those boots, she refers to them as her vamp stomping boots. It's her normal attire when she isn't in hunter clothes. Which are all black and have places for us to hold our weapons. Mollock is also in normal clothes. Jeans and a long, gray fitted t-shirt that he has rolled up to his elbows. Where Alana's style is more punk rock, which is what the old humans would call *her style*. Mollock's is very casual. Except his hairstyle, which he wears shaved close on the sides of his scalp but the middle long and in braids that he styles down his back. Most male hunters have their hair shaved closed to the head, but Alana won't let him shave his.

"Oh my God, *no*!" Alana gasps, rushing over. I sit up and make room for her to comfort Chip as Mollock heads over and wraps me in his arms. I turn my head to see Alana crying and kissing Chip. She moves her long black hair out of the way to lay her head on Chip's.

"She'll be alright, Fellen. That dog is stronger than all of us put together." I take a deep breath, holding back a round of tears and step out of his embrace. Damn him. I was trying to keep it together.

"I know." I whisper. I didn't. Neither did they. But they've been my family ever since taking me in after my parents died . Chip was just as much theirs as she was mine, and I know Mollock is just trying to comfort us all.

"The muscle here." Jules is talking to me, pointing to something on Chip's leg, but I can't look. The previous look of her leg confirmed it was pretty much flayed. I look up to Alana and she nods and heads over and talks to

Jules. I tune out what they're saying, only catching bits and pieces. It's all too much. Either she was going to make it or she wasn't. We've evolved since first migrating to the Fae Realm, but not enough for something like medicine. Apparently when humans had their own realm we were advanced. We had luxury, health and happiness. Now we just struggled to survive day in and day out in a Realm meant to kill the weak.

We hardly had water. We hardly had plants. We hardly had animals.

So *no*, we didn't have medicine. Apparently our ancestors who migrated, overused the last of that kind of stuff and didn't think to make more. Or from what we'd been taught, couldn't make more from lack of equipment. In a way, it was okay, because we evolved to survive our environment. Too bad that didn't account for things like injuries. We might be faster and stronger, but we weren't invincible. And the same was true for Chip. It killed me to see her hurt. And it would kill me, if she couldn't survive this.

"FELLEN!"

I look up to see Deven waving his hands in front of my face. When did he get here?

"Did you hear me? The Chief is coming, give me your gun!" He urges, frantically looking behind him at the door. I cuss and stand from my knelt down position, digging it out from the back of my pants before handing it to him.

"What the hell were you thinking *Fell,* you know we need to be on good standing before we head into the Land." He referred to our mission to Sweet Land, and I didn't give two shits about that. We were the only ones qualified to even *try* to save everyone. As far as I was concerned they should be kissing our asses, or at the very least throwing us a funeral as a goodbye party.

"Hey back off, okay! This is Chip we're talking about!" Alana says, standing up for me. Deven just shakes his head and darts out, no doubt to hide the weapon before the Chief can think to take it. Yeah, we don't have modern medicine, *err,* old way medicine, but we still had a lot of weapons and they were for emergencies only. I'm sorry, but I believe saving my dog's life *is* an emergency and if he had a problem with that he could go play in the Land.

"I have it wrapped and a splint on it, but Fellen… that's all I can do." Jules looks down and I know she wants to do more, but she's already done more than she should. We all know the rules, the healers were for human use only. Especially when it came to the medical supplies.

I pull my wobbling lips into a thin line and bite hard while looking at the ceiling, trying to stop the fresh emotion blooming again. When I look down, already the white fabric she'd wrapped around Chip's injury was soaking through with blood. "Thank you," I say as I swallow hard.

"Come on, we need to get out of here. I got her."

Mollock says, stepping forward and gently scooping up Chip, who's lying still now and only quietly whining with every breath she takes. Chip loves Mollock like she loves us all, so she doesn't put up a fuss when he scoops her up.

"Thanks, Jules." I say, reaching back, taking the elderly healer's hand. I don't want to get her in trouble. She's about the only one of us left with a heart. Which is hard to have in a place like this. She squeezes my hand back and gives a quick nod before turning around to clean up her medical room. I hope to everything in this hell hole she doesn't get in trouble for this.

It takes no time to get to the home we all share and get Chip settled on her bed in our living area. Alana, Mollock, and Deven all lived here prior to finding and taking me and Chip in. But they did so with no questions asked. And also gave me a purpose, a calling…the life of a supernatural hunter. We all had a job here in the village. Village X, the ones closest to Sweet Land and the ones trained to be hunters to protect all the villages in the land from nightfall. Nightfall was when the Fae were permitted to purge on us humans. This purge consisted of any and every type of supernatural in the Fae realm, which as we know are up to the hundreds in different species. And that's just what we know from the small land we are living within the Fae realm.

It sucked ten thousand assholes, at first anyways, but now I'm used to it. It was a shit life and a short one for a hunter, but it was what we were dealt.

I even trained my ass off and rose within the ranks. All of us had, and we were known experts in our areas of study and hunt. Mine was werewolves. Alana, vampires. Mollock, witches and ghosts. And Deven, Sirens and well…pretty much all the other ones. But that's what we wanted. We wanted to grow strong, because the only way out of this cesspool was to get an audience with the Fae King and Queen. And to do that we had to cross a land a hell of a lot more dangerous than this one. Our front door opening didn't pull my attention from petting Chip, who now was asleep. When I hear it not shutting, I looked up.

Ah, Hell.

Standing, I sum up the will to use my manners. Normally, manners didn't come so easily for me. "Chief Oak," I greet, while stepping in front of Chip. Not that it matters much; he'd obviously heard about what happened or Deven wouldn't be burying our guns somewhere in the dirt right now.

"Fellen." I ball my hands into tight fists to keep from correcting him. It was *Sergeant Fellen* to him and everyone in this land, but he saved a special place in his beady little heart just to piss me off. "I heard the gunshot, as well as the rest of…well, *everyone*."

I raise my chin. "And?"

He sighs before stepping all the way into our living space, shutting the door. I didn't remember inviting him inside, but whatever. Glancing behind me, I notice both Mollock and Alana weren't around. *Chicken shits*. Probably rushed out the back when they saw him coming.

I look back to see the Chief approaching me or really, Chip, from where his eyes are trained. I suppress a grunt of irritation and step aside while holding my breath. The guy always had the worst body odor. It was like he didn't know how to bathe. He was also huge. I'm not talking about being overweight. I'm talking, he barely fits through a doorway. A person's weight didn't bother me. But it was his lack of shirt that showed his ton of rolls and a weird green and purple necklace, which he said was an ancient plastic lei, that disturbed me. He also wore a weird skirt that did absolutely nothing to hide his bits. That. The smell. *Just all off it* and take in that the guy thought he was some superior God, it was beyond irritating on the best day.

"All this *waste* of supplies over an animal that doesn't further our people in the slightest."

He looks at me condescendingly like I'm not going to reply but he should know better by now. I'm not going to take his shit. He needs me. That and I'm so pissed, I'm sure my face is the color of a tomato. "Did you forget that *this* animal helps with every protection and hunting detail *and* does a fine ass job of it. The supplies are mine, none were used from the village supply."

I start to say more but he holds up his hand in front

of my face. I glare at him, daring him to touch me. "Shh. Shh." He drops it and looks over to our makeshift seating area and points to it. "May I?" And then he's walking, almost knocking me over with his huge, smelly ass all without waiting for my reply. I count to ten in my head. Over. *And Over.* I watch as he sits on a wooden chair and it creaks under his weight. I pray to any being out there that the chair breaks and the wood shards shoot right up his overconfident ass.

"*Please,* join me Fellen. There are some things we need to discuss. The coming days will move quickly and I need to make sure we are prepared when you all leave."

I almost snort but I don't. The door opens and Deven walks confidently in, not a bit scared that the Chief sits in his house. And he shouldn't be. The only people that should be scared of this idiot are the ones that give him the power to act like this.

"Chief Oak," Deven greets in a strong voice, shaking his hand before the Chief tells him to take a seat. I'm sure Deven thinks he's here as some sort of protector for me, but he's really still a little obsessive since our failed relationship last summer. He's with Alana and Mollock romantically now, but he still likes to play protector, which irks me. Deven is extremely handsome, tall and muscular. His ancestors are from a place on the gone human realm Earth, called Japan. His dark eyes always hold a smoldering danger and he's probably the best kisser in this village, but our romance was like all the other ones for me. Short lived. And when it ended he begged for me to take him back. But I made it my life goal to only have flings. Because feelings hurt and shit. It was the reason for my walls. He eventually moved on and Alana took him as her second lover.

"I will deal with your little defiant act once I finish the important issues. Me and the other Chiefs in the villages have prepared a dialog for the Fae Court when you, *or one of you,* makes it through Sweet Land." He says, pulling out a rolled-up scroll from somewhere behind him. I lift my eyebrows and stare at the thing. There's no way in all the lands I was touching something that he probably pulled out from his ass crack. My hesitation has Deven reaching forward and taking it. He unrolls it and starts to read to himself. All I can think about is how presumptuous of the Chief to think we wouldn't all make it through. I sit up and start to say as much to knock that stupid look off his face, but Deven speaks before I can.

"I don't understand."

I look over and Deven is frowning, his jaw is clenched tight. An angry Deven is a yummy one, but yummy or not, I need to concentrate. Plus, *that land wasn't meant to cross*. As our people would say when talking about a failed relationship. The Chief sits up straighter and chuckles. "It's pretty self-explanatory."

Deven thrusts the scroll into my hands and I unroll it

while ignoring the dampness. *Yuck,* but it probably said something bad if Deven was acting like this, so I take it and try my best to ignore the nasty paper. I read it once. Blink and look up at the Chief's smug face and then read the most stupid parts a second time before I fly up from my seat. "If you think for one minute that we are risking our lives for you and every human in the Bad Lands only for the Chiefs to be granted immunity and not the rest of us, you've lost your damn minds!" I shout as Deven stands and grabs my arm. Right as I'm about to say more the Chief's guards rush in and I hear Chip growl and then whimper. She's no doubt trying to get up.

"Easy, Fell." Deven whispers. I shake his arm off and laugh humorlessly while looking at the piece of shit that wrote this. The message he wanted us to pass on to the Fae King and Queen, asked for safe passage to the new land, for the Bad Lands Chiefs. *Only* the Chiefs. Nothing about the people. Hell, nothing about the four of us who were going through the land to get this audience.

"How do you know we will even pass this on? You can't make us."

I watch as he struggles to stand up, eventually getting the help from his personal guards. "Why Fellen, we were tricked by the Fae before and that can't happen again. You need your elders to go to this new land and make sure it's safe for our people."

I scoff and shake my head. "And then what? You're

going to come back and get us all." I ask, incredulously.

"Fellen, lower your voice." Deven says, leaning into my hair. It irritates me more.

"No! This is bullshit and you know it! He knows it!" I say, flinging a hand toward the Chief. His guards raise their guns at me, but I'm too mad to care. And I know he won't shoot me.

"You are going on this journey because I'm allowing it, little girl."

"*No*, I'm going on this journey because I'm one of the best hunters you have. You need me and you know it."

I know I have him by the balls when his cheeks start to redden and a slight shake starts in his balled-up fists. "You will do as you're assigned!" He shouts and steps toward me. "Or you will stay here and be locked up on the whipping post. Your choice."

"And how do you know that once we make it through we just won't skip this shit hole and leave you all here to rot?" I growl out, which gets me shocked faces from the guards and a sigh from Deven. I would never do that. Unlike this asshole, I actually care for the people, but he doesn't know that.

"It looks like you need to know I'm not bluffing. Maybe a little taste of your would-be punishment will set you right." Deven tries to speak, but the Chief yells for the guards to take me and then they are attempting to grab me. I don't make it easy. They need me and by their hesitation, they know it. My outburst and little act of defiance isn't one of an immature girl not wanting to follow the rules, but of a woman who has the self-sacrifice and strength to enter a dangerous land to save her race. And with every day that passes with this piece of shit in charge of our village, more and more people suffer and lay down, taking his shit. I've had it. He's nothing but a self-serving dick and I plan to tell the Fae King and Queen as much when I barter for all our freedoms. All but his.

I slam my fist into one of his female guards' stomach, snatching her gun while performing a spin kick and knocking the rifle out of the second guard's hands that also attempts to rush me. The other two guards stay by his cowardice ass and when he realizes I'm not going to be taken that easily he bustles out an angry command, spit flying everywhere for his guards to take me. I laugh as Deven steps in front of me right as Alana and Mollock rush in the house.

"STOP!" Mollock shouts and the room grows quiet. Behind them more of the Chief's guards rush in. "Whatever is going on, stop now."

Chief Oak steps forward. "What's going on is you just lost one of the hunters you needed on your mission. Instead, she will be sentenced to death. By stoning."

I stand still as the reality of what he says takes hold. It went from punishment to death. I sigh as my high starts to go down. I'm not scared for two reasons. One, they need me and I'm the best they've got. Two, a death can only take place if the whole village is there to witness and agree to a trial. If circling back to the first logic, it's safe to say his little power trip won't happen. Before he can say anymore, I smirk. "I request a trial then." I'll appease him. He already knows it's pointless and we all know it. It's the reason he's now stomping out of our house.

"Tie her up on the post and ring the bell. We need to show our people what happens to those who defy my orders." I hold my hands out for his guards to take me as I hold in a laugh. I hear the guys sigh and I do hear a laugh from Alana. This was going to be fun.

"I want steak tonight after my stoning." I yell back as the guards drag me out of the house. This does get the guys to laugh and Alana to laugh harder.

"I gotcha, babe!" Alana shouts back right as the village bell rings.

I'm laid down on the burning ground and my wrists and ankles are tied up to posts in front of *the sign*. A pile of red dyed rocks is stacked up not too far from where I lay and the crowd of the villagers has started to grow in size. I hear their whispers and from the ones I can see, their expressions show shock and anger. It makes me laugh. The nasty old, shithead Chief better have a compelling story to convince them. I've saved most of the people in this village from a supernatural trying to eat them at one point or another. So, it would take a lot for them to turn on me. That, and most of their children love my dog. That's worth a thousand points alone.

"My people! Gather around and quiet down! You all have been called to cast your votes in for death by stoning. The offender, Fellen."

"SERGEANT FELLEN!" I interrupt, which gets me kicked in the side by the female I punched in the stomach earlier. I hold in the grunt of pain trying to slip out. I probably deserved that, I'll let her have it.

The Chief glares at me but continues. I look over his shoulder to see only Alana decided to show. The guys are probably back making dinner. This was the second to last night we had left in the Bad Lands before we left for our mission. So, yeah. Not only did we want a good meal, but we had the next two nights off and needed some sleep. Food was scarce, but as the day for our departure grows closer, surrounding villages have left us piles of gifts and well wishes. Alana's mom sent some steaks, which is extremely rare since most of our beef is made into jerky to preserve.

"*Sergeant* Fellen. The crime is disobeying a direct order from the Chief. Now, let me explain the situation and then we will cast our votes." The sun decides to take that moment to poke through the clouds and I now have to squint to see his fat ass try and sway their votes. Sigh. I wish he would just hurry up so I could be with Chip.

"Our history is important and it's one that we should know and try to learn from. So to make my point I will remind us all of the great passing and the sign, we all stand in front of." I can tell a lot of people are already done with his shit by the groans of annoyance in the crowd and I have to bite back a laugh. I don't need bruised ribs going into the land. "One thousand years ago our ancestors lived in peace and prosperity on our own realm called Earth. But it was said that we'd angered our once God of that realm and he decided to destroy our kind. Hence, the Apocalypse of Earth. A terrifying time when the God ripped open Heaven and Hell and unleashed all of the supernatural beings to finish us."

The Chief's voice bellows out over the people as he raises his arms for the show. I roll my eyes. "BUT! Before we were completely eradicated a new type of supernatural entered Earth and held back our enemies. This supernatural was the Fae King. And we rejoiced. He offered us sanctuary in his Realm, the Fae Realm…and we rejoiced again. We were safe! Along the journey through the portal some of us drove vehicles called cars, trucks and semis. That are no longer around. But they were filled with things from the realm to help us survive. Not once did the King object to us bringing stuff, but helped hold back all the creatures set out to kill us while we made it through." He paused for effect, looking around at the crowd. Who still looked bored as shit. We'd all heard this how many times? We all knew our history, so this was super annoying to everyone here.

"It is said that around thirty thousand humans made it through the portal from Earth to the Fae Realm, but the moment the last human crossed, the portal was closed and a great sign fell from the sky and landed magically into the dirt ahead of the massive crowd. *This sign...*" The chief said, pointing to it, before then reading from it.

"***Start Here-***

Welcome to The Bad Lands. Here you are required to procreate. You are given enough to survive but never enough to thrive. At night you are subjected to the environment and my subjects, as food and fair game. So you only have until sunup to sundown to be outside. If you are unhappy with your current land and wish to move to another, you may seek an audience with your regal rulers, King Ace and Queen Thelia. To achieve an audience with the King and Queen, to enter a different land, you must first cross Sweet Land. Individual or multiple humans (max 4) may step on the lit square below this sign which will read your heart's desires. If all you desire is to live in a different land, you will be transported into Sweet Land. Inspired by Queen Thelia's love of the delicious sweets of Earth and her favorite game, called CandyLand.

Rules to Sweet Land-

Once you enter Sweet Land, your goal is to make it to the

Sweet Castle. The path is how you progress through the land. There are eight different territories that you must make it through. Each territory has a Leader. If you defeat the territory's Leader, by challenging them at the start of their territory, the Leader's subjects will allow you safe passage to the next territory. Sweet Land is home to my adoring subjects, the supernaturals, so be vigilant as you pass through the land, little humans. If you cannot survive this land, you won't survive any others. Only the strong, fast and smart will survive and ultimately be honorable enough for our attention. This land will test you, haunt you and tempt you. Good luck."

More groans from the crowd can be heard but I'm resting my eyes from the sun and trying not to fall asleep. "WE WERE TRICKED!" He shouts out and I jump. I can hear Alana laugh at this and I pucker my lips to keep quiet. "We should have known that the Fae weren't just like every other supernatural but worse! We should have checked to make sure we wouldn't be trapped in a barren land that did nothing but deplete our race! Since that time we have lost more people than gained, due to us trying to make it across Sweet Land. At first the ones who stayed behind thought that the people leaving were making it through, but then Mother Adelle, our wise Seer, revealed the truth." He thrust his hand out again and I, along with the crowd gasp. Mother Adelle is standing among the crowd taking in the show. She never left her home! Ever. It was either a good thing she was here, or a really bad one. Seeing her now was making me squirm and the nerves that I should have had now came to life, live and rampant. "Humans were not making it through because they weren't strong enough. We were getting slaughtered by the thousands. If we weren't getting killed trying to hurry and build up our villages and homes, we were dying trying to escape. Or dying because of the lack of food, water or medicine! Until we are what you see now."

"Well, my precious people, we are going to be smarter about it this time. We have come up with a negotiation of sorts to pass to the Fae King and Queen. We will not be tricked a second time!" He yells out to the crowd and I see that some of them are getting swayed. "But your *great Sergeant Fellen* has refused to not only pass on the message but has threatened to not save anyone but herself!" Gasps of surprise and cussing rings throughout the crowd.

"BULLSHIT!" I yell out, but it's lost to the sound of the crowd that's growing angrier by the second. "ARE YOU ALL GOING TO KEEP LISTENING TO THIS OLD SHIT AND HIS LIES?"

The Chief steps closer to me and I avert my eyes in order to not look up his skirt. Gross. Okay, maybe do kill me. "BECAUSE WE CANNOT LISTEN TO THIS CORRUPT HUNTER'S LIES, SHE DOES NOT GET ANY LAST WORDS!" The chief yells out pointing down to me. I roll my eyes. Yeah, the crowd seems to be angry by his words, but that doesn't mean they believe him.

One of our elders in the village steps forward. There are six elders under one chief. This one is an old man with white hair and famous for his skepticism. "NO. We will hear her talk. That is the ways!"

A harmony of *yeahs* sounds through the crowd.

"And why isn't Mollock, Alana and Deven here? If she really was in the wrong and about to die, they'd be here defending her!" A woman calls out.

"Now just wait." The Chief tries to talk but someone else yells out. "Yeah! I just saw Deven and Mollock cooking by a fire, not a bit concerned and look!" A pause, I can't see the man who's talking. "There's Alana!"

This puts the crowd in a frenzy calling her name and asking her to speak and no one is listening to the Chief anymore. I smile and look over to see Alana also smiling as she steps forward with the scroll in her hand. *Gotcha, mother fucker.*

"To the great Fae King Ace and Queen Thelia- We have sent these messengers-"

"DON'T READ THAT!" Chief Oak yells and starts for Alana but the crowd steps forward blocking him and then the guards are pointing guns at the crowd, but Alana keeps reading.

"In our stead to secure passage to a new land. One better. One where we will thrive and prosper. Be rich with bellies full." I snicker at this part, the stupid part, and get another kick in the ribs. It was worth it though. "In a non-dangerous land, for the six chiefs of the Bad Lands villages." She could go on. There's a shit ton more stupid stuff in there, but at the last sentence the crowd is now in an uproar and turning on the Chief. They demand my freedom and demand his blood and it's chaos.

I fucking love it.

While I'm watching the now angry mob advance on the Chief and his useless, corrupt guards, Mother Adelle makes her way over to me with her cane and I stiffen. Nothing good comes from the Seer and she was the only one in this place someone should be scared of. I can't help but recall all the people that went to her wanting to know something about their future, only for her to paint how exactly they will die like a brilliant canvas. Just to be cruel. And all those times her visions did come true. It's terrifying. "Fellen, how you will soon blossom for your true mate." Holy fuck. No. Do not give me a prophecy. She must see the terror on my face, because she leans her head lower and cackles. The sound shoots through me like a knife and I'm suddenly shaking in fear. "*Yes*! Yes, I see your dreams. I see the one that saves you. You must save *him*."

"Neek," I say in a whisper as my heart rate picks up. I know who she's referring to. The crowd has pushed Chief Oak away from this spot and I now only see Alana, the Seer and me are here under the sign as the sun sets.

"It's real. It's your blood. It will doom you, if turned.

Free you, if found. Or kill you…if hidden. Your answer lies with frost." Her eyes flash white and then she's turning and hobbling away.

"*Oookay*. What in the seven villages was that?" Alana asks me, and gets to work freeing the rope from my wrists.

"There are only six villages." I say, and she rolls her eyes.

"Dear baby vampires. Old lady Adelle visits and gives you a prophecy and all you're concerned about is my math?" She unties the last rope and I shake them free as I stand.

"No. I got what she said."

Alana pushes her long hair over one shoulder and raises an eyebrow. "Oh, you got that you are supposed to have a true mate, like some animal. And that you're supposed to have something weird with your blood and all this right before going into Sweet Land. Oh my god..."

We reach the front of our house and watch Mollock cooking steaks over a fire. Yum. Both him and the steaks. "What?" I ask as I stop ogling her husband. He is the tallest, darkest and dare I say the most handsome hunter in all the villages. Together Alana and Mollock have the most adorable twin babies that her mother takes care of in the gathering village, Village V. The safest village that the others surround. It's made up of mostly women and children. We all plan to go there tomorrow on our last day to kiss those sweet babies goodbye.

"What if your true mate or whatever," She pauses to wave her hands around. "Is some supernatural in the land?" She asks, as we stop in front of Mollock, who looks at us like we're crazy.

"What in all the lands are you two going about with mating supernaturals?" I'm not sure how to answer that as my heartbeat is suddenly going so fast it hurts my chest. My mind flies back to the last dream where Neek, my mystery love, saved me and then made love to me on the beach.

I stay quiet and let Alana recap what happened with the Chief as I go to check Chip.

Putting the Seer out of my mind was going to be hard. There was only one man that had ever saved me and it was someone from my dreams and not someone I even knew was a man but as a supernatural. He only comes to my nightmares to save me but has never come to me in real life. He'd been visiting me for months now and I hadn't dived into wanting to know what he was, because, *ignorance*. I'd asked him over and over, but he refused to tell me what he was. He knew I was a hunter, just like I knew he was some type of supernatural. The time for keeping my head in the sand needed to be over. We were leaving in two days' time and I needed the truth. Going into Deven's library, I ask him for a book about supernaturals who no longer exist. He gives me a funny look but hands me the book. After moving Chip to my room to keep an eye on her, I think about everything I know about Neek.

Thinking of his human qualities is easy. He's breathtaking. He has a mocha complexion. Dark brown eyes and hair and a sharp jawline, but that won't help me find his supernatural side. So I think of all the non-human things about him instead. I know that he has a dark blue, smoke form. I know that he can enter, manipulate and exit dreams. I know that I can feel his touch and I'm sexually swayed by him when he's in his smoke form. From the first time I was aware of him in my dreams, he's been begging me to enter Sweet Land. Our dream meetings got longer and it turned to spending the first half exchanging information about myself, to the second half him seducing me. And as I flip through the pages of a book I've already read a thousand times, the only thing that seems off to me is a picture of a half smoke, half Fae form next to a bottle. The man in the picture wears the same gold cuff looking things Neek wears, and suddenly I'm an idiot.

A man has been entering my dreams, begging and seducing me to come into Sweet Land. He's even told me knowledge of the land and leaders. So that could only mean one thing. If he was the same thing as the supernatural in this picture was, that would make him a jinn. And there was only one territory in the land that we didn't know the supernaturals of. The King's.

I'd been tricked.

Was Neek a jinn? Was he the King of Sweet Land?

The rest of the night goes by in a blur. I can't focus and Chip isn't doing too great. I can't leave her here, but bringing her with me to Sweet Land will only seal her death. I guess all the stress finally hits me because the second I close my eyes, I'm haunted with another nightmare and just like every time before, he saves me.

NEEK

King of Horrors Chapter Insert

I saved her from a group of werewolves, like I had the first dream with her. Now we stand in the dream realm off in the woods.

"So you're cheating?" It's all she asks, after I explain that me and Dagger have been working to convince the leaders of the territories to stand down for her. We've only made it to the first three leaders and those members are evenly split down the board. We still had five territories to go. Half agreed to help and the other half wouldn't agree. Ghouls, no. Werewolves were split 50/50 and witches, no.

I look over at Fellen. Something is off with her. She won't look me in the eye and it's driving me mad. I step forward but she puts up a hand. "Don't."

"What the Hell is your deal, Fellen?" I growl, unable to

help it. "The last time I saw you, we couldn't get enough of each other and now you're acting like we're strangers. What the fuck?"

She reaches up and plays with her hair that she has braided off to one side. She is in her hunting uniform as well. I watch as she opens her mouth but doesn't speak and that's when I notice her glance at my wrist cuffs.

"I know what you are."

I sigh, because what else can I do in this situation? "You would have found out eventually." I take a step toward her, wanting her close and she backs up until she's only a foot away from a tree. I barely hold in the urge to yell. "But that doesn't change what we are to each other."

She crosses her arms and attitude flares in her eyes. It makes my heart race from the unknown. "And what are we, *jinn*?" Before I can recover, she continues. "After our last dream I couldn't stop thinking about you and I needed to know what you were so I borrowed some books from Deven. I'm so glad I never told him why I needed them." She scoffs and I hold my breath. "I thought the cuffs were just a fashion thing, but then I learned what you are. *That* would have been fine. I wasn't sure where'd you come from though. Were you in the Bad Lands and a threat to my family? Then I remembered you constantly trying to get me to Sweet Land and all your knowledge of it. You said you are trying to convince the leaders to keep back from us, meaning you are in the land, and after everything you've said. The only territory left for a jinn would be…*the King*."

I knew she would eventually find out, but this wasn't the right time or place. Her prejudice of supernaturals as a human would have to be slowly approached. But the subject of me being a Sweet Land resident, let alone a King was going to be tough. Now I watch her mentally leaving me before we've got a chance to be together and I'm shaking and my chest hurts. I have a good poker face or she can't see my hurt. Either way it's obvious she doesn't care because she keeps on.

"So, tell me *King* of Sweet Land…Did you spy on my nightmares and think that I would be easy to take down and destroy in your land? Or was it when you found out I was a hunter and strong enough to hold my own that you found a different tactic? Did you think if you just slept with me one time that I would fall madly in love with you and risk it all?"

She's walking toward me in anger and I grab her by the throat and push her back against the tree before she can blink an eye. I had to stop this. "This is just a dream *Neek*, you can't actually hurt me here." She wheezes and I squeeze a bit harder.

"I am more than some title to you, Fellen." I look down at her cleavage pushing out of her shirt. Her breath is coming in and out fast and I didn't even see the fear until it was trying to shoot through me, but I reject it and focus back on her raging eyes and away from her body. "Yes, I might happen to be the *King* of Sweet Land *and* your last challenge, but I'm more than that. I can't just enter anyone's dreams and if you read up on me like you thought you had, you would know that."

I release the pressure a bit on her neck even though I know she's breathing fine and a faint pleasure floats through the air surrounding us. I press myself against her and she tries to turn her head to look away, I let her but not before I readjust my hand on her neck and slam her head back against the tree. I watch her clench her jaw in anger but the feel of her nipples poking through her shirt shows me just how much she *thinks* she hates me right now. "You belong to me and I will never let you go."

She laughs, but it's humorless and harsh. "This is fucking crazy, Fellen! Does it fucking matter what I am? I know you feel this pull between us!"

"I thought I had too, but apparently you were just using your Fae magic to seduce me," she hisses. I shake my head in astonishment. She has it so fucking wrong.

I know she still feels our pull and I grind against her just to prove it. She may look pissed, but one deep inhale along with the blue colors slithering through the air, tells me she's soaked for me.

"Just because you can turn me on doesn't mean this is anything other than lust. You betrayed my trust. *Tricked me.*"

"And how do you think I did that? *Huh*, Fellen?" I squeeze tighter on her throat until I see a spike of fear, but contain the monster within me from feeding off it. "Did I betray it by telling you knowledge no human has been graced with before entering my land? Or was it when I told you, I'm trying to get you through the land *alive* because you are my soulmate. Believe what you fucking want, but I didn't trick you and I would never betray what's mine."

She bucks underneath me and I can tell her anger has reached a breaking point. Tears now flood her eyes. "Get off me! you're a monster!" She threatens, but it's weak. We both know it.

"I'm your monster." I say, letting go of her throat but I keep her pinned with my body and block her in with my arms. "One that you'll never escape."

She looks at me with tears falling down her face but doesn't try to buck me off or speak. I take it as progress, but I'm not sure. I lean forward and lick down the shell of her ear and grind into her again. But she's empty. I won't let her do this. "You're not mad at me for what I am, but who you think I am."

After another beat of silence I keep trying. "You can't tell me I'm faking this just to kill you. I'm fucking *helping you*. And I know you feel our soulmate bond." I whisper and she freezes at the last part.

"It's impossible from what I read. Humans and jinn cannot mate. So I know you're lying."

"What you read is wrong. You *are* my soulmate. I can see our tether of magic."

Something changes in her stare and it almost looks like she believes me but I can't be sure. "Just tell me what the Hell I have to do to get you off me." She's back to mad in the blink of an eye.

"Give me a chance, Fellen." I say in a low voice. I lean forward close to her lips but don't kiss them. I see the debate in her eyes. She looks from my lips then back to my eyes. She wants me. Her and I both know she does and she's right. It might be lust right now, but that will change in time. Our bond will strengthen and our love will be like no others, but she has to give it a chance. She had to give *me* a chance.

She scoffs and rolls her eyes, which results in tears falling down her cheeks. I move over and kiss them away as she sniffles. "I don't know how to do that." Her voice breaks and I'm patient as I give her a chance to speak. "I don't know how to trust you, when I've been training to *kill* you all my life."

Her eyes plead for me to understand and for some reason, I do. "You just have to have faith, Fellen."

"Why are you trying so hard to get me out alive other than the soulmate thing? If I make it out, then what? You will leave your castle and come with me? Or expect me to live with you in that horrible place? Is there even an us?"

She's shooting questions at me now with rapid fire and

panic has taken hold of her. It's evident in the air. "Shh. Listen. Just listen, *my emerald*. First, there will always be an us. Even if I have to pin you to a tree to get you back every time. I will." I lean forward and kiss her gently. I about cry out in excitement when she kisses me back. "Second. If you can make it through, we might be able to change the fate of Sweet Land. You may be the key to everything. Our freedom, human freedom, all of it."

Sucking in a breath, she stares at me with wide eyes. "How?"

"By winning." I step away from her and give her some space now that I know she's not a flight risk.

She is in a debate with herself and the dream starts to fade, but I keep her asleep. "If I really am going to give you a chance and trust you…then you're going to need to tell me more. How am I supposed to win and how will that fix things?"

And that was the thing. The one card in my hand I couldn't play until I was absolutely sure she was on board. If I told her the power of the soulmates and she turned it against me, I would put not only myself but my friends in the land in danger. I'm asking her to trust me but I can't trust her. Not fully. And not yet. It has to be at the right time.

So I smile and it produces a skeptical look across her face. I know I have her though. "I will tell you the moment you step into Sweet Land and only if you do so in two days."

She opens her mouth to argue but I transition to my smoke form and fly away, as I fade the dream.

CHAPTER TWO
THE DAY PRIOR

"FELLEN!"

I barely registered my name getting yelled out before something cold and wet, something like water, is splashed over my face. "What the hell?" I sputter, as I open my eyes and look at the mess of my wet shirt and blanket. "On my bed?! Really?" I glare at Deven, holding an empty metal cup and a look of fear on his face.

"You were in here screaming bloody murder, Fell! Alana just went to get a healer! We couldn't fucking wake you!"

I recap the groggy dream I just had with Neek. He must have held me in the dream longer or put me in a deeper dream state for them to have trouble waking me. If that was even something he could do? And why was I screaming? Either way, I couldn't let them know about Neek. Not yet. He wasn't something *I* was even ready to digest yet. So I wasn't sure how to explain not waking up.

"Must be stress," I immediately look down to see Chip

watching me from her spot on the floor with concerned eyes. "It's okay, girl." I get up and love on her. I notice she has clean bandages, which tells me someone has been in to take care of her while I was asleep. "How long was I out?"

Deven scoffs, before running his hand through his hair. "Long enough to miss dinner. It's still night. Probably why they are having trouble getting a healer here."

"Shit," I cuss, making my way to the living room. I don't make it there before Deven juts out his hand, blocking my path. "What supernaturals were flagged tonight?" I ignore that he's leaning in *waaay* too close to me. There were certain supernaturals you just didn't risk getting a civilian out around. Werewolves and vampires especially and with us not working tonight, there was no telling how the hunters and guards would fare. We were leaving at least two groups of six hunters and about three guards trained well enough behind, but it still made me nervous. That meant there were thirty other guards that we felt weren't trained well and three other groups of six that didn't meet our standards. I know I needed to trust them, since we were leaving them behind to protect everyone while we went to the Land, but it was hard. No matter how many extra hours we all put in to make sure everyone was well trained. All it took was one little distraction from a guard or an extreme run, what we called multiple factions of supernaturals hitting us at once, for the walls to the homes of interior villages to be breached. From there things could get out of hand fast.

It could happen to any of us, at any time. I wasn't saying that our small group of four was the save all. We made mistakes, but we were the best trained and most capable. I just hoped we could make it through Sweet Land fast. Every day gone is another that we aren't here to protect the villages.

"Let me pass," I growl, giving my best scowl.

"I was concerned about you, Fell." With his other hand, not blocking me from getting through the doorway, he goes to run it down my face before I smack it away and step back.

"I will beat the ever-living shit out of you, I'm not in the mood for your bullshit. Move. *Now.*"

Deven just gives me a heated look and I try the one last card I have before having to injure one of my teammates going into the Land with me. "Or how about I tell Alana and Mollock that their new lover isn't being pleased enough not to stray."

"You wouldn't." He frowns before trying to give a smolder; it just irritates me more. How many times do I have to tell him that I'm not interested? "Come on, Fell. You know you miss me. When I heard you scream my heart dropped, you know I care about you. You know I still want you, and I know you still want me. I see the way you look at me."

"And you told them that you never got over me?" I lift an eyebrow. I knew he hadn't. Poor asshole went and ran to the first person that would take him in after we broke up. That just happened to be Alana and Mollock after they all had too many drinks one night, well, technically one day. We work nights. And I walked in with Chip to see way more naked bodies than I ever wanted to see in my life, as they hooked up in our living area. She was going down on Mollock as Deven was taking her from behind. I swear I thought my eyebrows would get lost in my hair. Alana tried to invite me to join and that was a BIG no for me. Ex-boyfriend, best friend and her husband. Hard pass. That was a shit load of drama in one house just waiting to happen. When she came to tell me what happened, part of they're agreement to hook up was that Deven promised he was over me. Yeah, he was obviously *not*, but I didn't tell her that. I just knew that I was never getting back with him, so it wasn't a problem. But him pulling this 'I need you Fellen' shit was getting pretty old.

"It doesn't matter."

I scoff. "Aren't they coming back with a healer for me? Why are you even trying anything right now?"

He opens his mouth to answer but I'm saved by the slam of the door and soon after hear Alana cussing. "Holy shit it's like a war zone out there. Werewolves. They got through the entrance." I duck under his arm and bolt into the living room to see Alana helping Jules to sit down, who's limping. Shit, not good. On two accounts. Our entrance, the one that leads to the living quarters, is usually heavily guarded so that supernaturals can't get any closer to us than needed. Two, our healer is obviously injured.

"Why would you risk her?"

Alana gives me an incredulous look. "Well, we didn't fucking know what was wrong! You were screaming bloody murder in your sleep and we couldn't wake you!"

I saw her point, but losing a healer in a village was a big deal, and our village got the best healers since we got the most injuries. Which made them more valuable and a loss of one, a bad deal. "What happened?"

Jules looks up from where she sits on our couch, holding her leg and wincing in pain as she rocks back and forth. Not good. I could see the sweat forming across her forehead. I hope that doesn't mean what I think it does. Alana looks up and swallows hard. "She got bit." Deven cusses from where he just entered. And then moves closer to me. I fight the urge to move away from him.

The door opens as a round of gunshots go off and Mollock rushes in before slamming and barring the door. He's breathing heavily and has his uniform ripped across his shoulder from a scratch. Thank god you can't turn from those. Alana rushes to him. "You okay?"

Mollock nods and kisses her on the forehead. "It's bad tonight. Something has them acting up more than usual.

There are at least three separate packs out there. It's a run. They came in disguise. Their Fae form and fooled the entrance guards. There is a shit load of hunters dead and a lot more still out there. We're all needed." He's talking in short bursts from being winded. It's weird to see him out of breath when he's in great shape, but if he says it's bad. It must be bad.

"Right." I say as I start to rush back to my room to get my supplies. I stop as I remember Jules and turn around. "Jules-" A bite from a werewolf meant she would turn. Which meant she wouldn't be allowed to live. We all love Jules. She is the grandmother of the village and someone who has comforted us all through different points in our lives. Healed us. Loved us. Broke the rules for us. It wasn't fair, and it wasn't fair that she got bit and had to die because of me. Because of my stupid dreams with Neek. It was all my fault and I couldn't tell anyone.

She looks up with tears in her eyes. "I know. I just ask you to make it quick. I'll need a pen and paper to write down instructions for my study. She's only been training for a month." I nod and swallow down my rising emotions. Hunters needed to be numb to their feelings to get the job done. I had a job to do. I would mourn for my friend later when we gave our respects. This life wasn't fair, but if I wanted to save anyone else from the same fate tonight, I needed to go.

The howl of a wolf right outside our door has me

rushing back into my room to get ready. We'd never had a supernatural this close to our hut before. This was bad. Werewolves were known for their incredible strength and it would only take one running full blast at our door and they would be in. It was insane that they got this close and right before going into the land. Something didn't seem right. I pack up supplies as quickly as I can and rush through the house. Werewolves in the Fae Realm weren't known for being able to talk English. So how were they able to trick the guards? The guards are well trained not to approach anything or let anything approach them, human or otherwise, once night falls. If it's not one of our hunters on schedule for that night and the signal of an incoming hunter isn't sounded, they don't engage. Unless the wolves learned the rotation schedule, learned english or our sound, they shouldn't have gotten in. They shouldn't have been able to trick any guard. Thoughts of our slimy chief run through my head but I don't have time to worry about the whys, I needed to help fix this before it got anymore out of hand.

"Ready?" I ask as I walk through the living area. Deven is holding two machetes. Alana is holding a sword. Mollock is loading bullets into a gun. And I have multiple knives loaded on my belt, a machete, and my signature weapon. A staff with two special blades on each end that works perfect for this type of threat. There is a reason why I'm an expert in werewolves. I had a past life that I've slowly started to remember since my eighteenth birthday through dreams. In my past life I lived on Earth during the end times, my boyfriend had succumbed to the fate of a werewolf bite and turned. I dedicated my life to hunting him before he finally turned me. I won't let that happen in this life. I'm glad I was able to remember my past life through dreams. Enough for me to have the knowledge to hunt them. And although none of my friends believe these dreams are real, I know in my soul they are. How else would I have had the knowledge of werewolf hunting I have now?

"Let's do this."

I sent Mollock and Alana to spend the day with their babies, since this was our last one. We were all supposed to be visiting them, but I didn't feel right leaving all this carnage for the village to pick up alone. Elders, guards, hunters and even healers were out today tending to the massacre that happened last night. All because a guard let in a werewolf. It just didn't make sense. As I move the bodies I go over it time and time again. Werewolves here didn't know English. At least not the ones we'd ever encountered. I play devil's advocate and wonder if they have known English this whole time and just haven't played that card yet. Maybe they were acting dumb. But out of all the times I was about to blow some wolves' head off and they transformed to beg and appeal to my human nature they *always,* always spoke in the language of the Fae.

"I see the wheels turning in there." Deven says, grabbing the feet of a fellow hunter we lost last night while I grab the upper part of her body, under her arms. We swing her onto the burn pile. "And you're quiet. It's a dangerous combination."

I sigh in frustration as we go for a healer who was beheaded. She was young. Way too young. "I've gone over this attack so many times in my head. They don't speak English. How were the guards tricked?"

After both her head and body are on the pile we walk over to the prepped buckets of water and start to scrub our hands clean, or somewhat clean. "I already know what you're going to say, but is there really any point?"

"What? What am I going to say?" Maybe it's the hot sun or dead bodies of our friends. Maybe both, but I'm in a foul mood and I can't seem to step out of it. Of course he knows I'm thinking it's the chief's fault. I honestly can't think of anyone else in this entire village that is as slimy or corrupt as him. Well, Madame Adelle was sketchy, but that wasn't her fault. It's said that she's close to almost two hundred years old. When she was a little girl, before the villages had evolved to where they are now, a group of witches attacked Village M where she grew up. During the battle, an explosion of magic flew out and she was exposed to it. And that was what gave her the power to see prophecies or glimpses into people's futures, as well as slow her aging. But I couldn't see her doing something like this. After all, she was one of the most vulnerable people here with how old and frail she was.

Deven gives me a deadpan look, which is actually a refreshing change from his usual flirtatious one. "How would the chief have anything to do with this?"

"Because maybe he was pissed that I didn't get killed at his stoning attempt and he let them in to kill me?"

Okay, that's an overreach, but still. I felt deep down there was foul play and his name somewhere on it.

"Yeah, you're probably right. He killed a quarter of his own village just to get to you. *Wow*. You're something special, Fellen." I must have hit a nerve because he stalks off, shaking his head without another word. Fine by me. We were both tired from working the night before and now all day, on top of dealing with a major tragedy.

"Welp, I guess I'll just go home alone then," I mutter under my breath.

"But you won't be entirely alone, will you?" The creepy sound of Madame Adelle's voice directly behind me has me almost jumping out of my skin.

"HOLY GHOST PUPPIES WHERE'D YOU COME FROM!" I spin around as I try to keep my heart from exploding out of my chest.

She stands there with a faraway look on her face, like she can see right through me. I make a show of how excited I am by groaning in frustration. "Really? Why?" I whine. I really couldn't handle any more prophecies right now.

This makes her cackle. I hadn't thought she could get any creepier…I was wrong. "So young. So old."

Yup, I was not spending my last free day listening to crazy. "Yeah, and as fun as this is…" I trail off and hope she gets the message as I turn away and head to take a bath. It might be the one chance I get alone time and a good soak before heading into the land.

"You are right."

This grabs my attention.

I turn back around with eyebrows raised. "About?"

Her wooden cane wobbles and almost slips into a crack in the barren ground, I don't think twice as I reach out and catch her frail elbow before she can fall. "About your wits, child. They will be what *really* saves us."

She takes her elbow back defiantly and walks away from me as I watch in shock.

Okay, that was weird. She never leaves her home and now I've seen her twice. Just out and about. She refused to tell us our future going into the land and now she's talkative, but only if it's in riddles. She said so young, so old. Could she be referring to my past life? How would she know? I thought she could only tell the future or prophecies?

I get home and start to work on a fire to warm my bath water, while I debate for the millionth time about bringing Chip. She would be better off staying with Alana's children back in Village M. It would also help having her there to protect the village, but the one time I had tried to leave her there when I first started as a hunter, it hadn't worked. She wouldn't stay and they couldn't contain her. So she went with me and learned to become a hunter as well. If I were going to try it again, I would need to leave soon, but then there was always the possibility we couldn't make her stay and she could hurt herself more trying to follow me.

I make my way over to her with a treat and smile when her ears perk up. "You know that if you go, it will hurt your leg more." I stroke her soft fur and kiss her head as she eats her dried meat treats. "It will be dangerous."

Her head tilts like she actually knows what I'm saying. Who knows? Maybe she does. "It would be better for you to stay." She whines at that word because she knows what it means and she hates staying. Like during the attack last night I had to all but scream and force her to stay in the hut. I hated treating her like that but with her leg it would be too dangerous. Just like going with me to Sweet Land. "But- " I conclude in my head. "I may never come back. If I made it through the land, I would want you by my side."

I go back to getting my bath ready and Chip lays her head back down to sleep. Each of our rooms holds a small bathing spot, so once my tub is full, I shut myself inside my room and flip the wood switch to lock the door. Thankfully, we don't have one like the other huts where they are a community bath and located in the middle of the living area. A sigh escapes me as I enter the warm water and take a second to relax my head back and close my eyes, but I don't get too comfortable so I don't fall asleep. I didn't want any unnecessary visits from Neek. I needed to be on my game the next time I saw him.

He wanted me to come into the land and for our team to just survive the territories without challenging the leaders. His words, not mine. I pick up a washcloth and get to scrubbing the dirt, blood and stench of burning flesh from my skin. The team, being Alana, Mollock, Deven and myself, previously planned to not challenge the leaders. For some time now that's always been the plan, because we didn't know if the leaders could be challenged by all of us or just one, and those stakes were too high. But if you defeat the leader, then the territory has to let you pass, so fight one and get a free pass or try to run through and survive all the problems at once. Since Neek's visits and him telling me we can't challenge the leaders, now I'm conflicted, too. Because what if this was a trick?

Thankfully for Deven drawing the proverbial short straw, he's been visiting Madame Adelle for months now and getting precious intel of the land and taking notes that we'll need to survive. She's never been to Sweet Land, but she's foretold hundreds if not thousands of deaths, and that's valuable. And since she refuses to tell Deven his future or show him, she instead shows us all the others she's predicted in the land. No matter how morbid they are.

We knew, even if Neek hadn't revealed to me, that the Candy Cane fields were the first place we would come to and where we would enter, and it also had ghouls.. We also pieced together that the start territory rotates. After sitting and putting all this information together with a lot of late night hours, plus brain power, we also figured out what creatures went where. So Neek helped, in his own way. He helped to reveal that the last territory was a jinn, and that it was him. Again, not that I could tell my team that. I quickly make work of my tangled hair and clean it the best I can and when I finally step out of the cold water, it's a nasty rust color.

I look to my bed, where the book that led me to the information of Neek sits like it's a bomb waiting to explode.

My heart speeds up as flashbacks of some of our more heated dreams flash through my mind. He tricked me. I feel like there's more to all this that he isn't telling me and I highly doubt the moment we enter the land he will tell me like he promised he would. A part of me wants him to be fake, just a dream, while a very real part of me *knows* he's real. Of course Madam Adelle's creepy ass prophecy doesn't help matters.

I hear the others arrive as I dress and go over what she said in my head. I didn't need to write it down, because her words have haunted me on a deeper level than I thought they would. And ever since she'd said them, they have been flashing in and out of my mind on repeat. *Fellen, how you will soon blossom for your true mate.* I silently scold myself when I feel my cheeks heat. Neek thinks I'm his soulmate and I can't deny I feel a pull toward him. Not just attraction. I'm used to hooking up with hot men and getting the lust out of my system, but with Neek it felt… molecular. More permanent. His voice alone pulls more of a sexual pleasure than any man has given me before. Did that mean we were soulmates, as he put it? Or true mates as Madame Adelle had? I wasn't sure.

It's real. It's your blood. I can't think of what that can mean. I'm human and my blood has never been significant, but I honestly believed I had a past life. Could she mean that? *It will doom you, if turned.* I was turned into a werewolf in my last life. I grab at my head as I think. She is talking about the future, not my past. *It will doom you, if turned.* I repeat it over and over, trying to question what it meant.

If I was physically turned?

If my blood, meaning myself or an ancestor is turned?

"Urgh!" I stand and toss the book on the floor.

"Knock, knock," I hear Alana say out loud, as well as physically knock. I let out a breath of frustration and plan to leave this mood in the room as I unlock the door. If I had to guess, half the people that had gone to the Seer died because they were caught up on her damn riddles instead of concentrating on surviving. Plus this is my last night; I shouldn't stress. That was coming soon enough.

"How was your visit?" I ask as she comes in and sits on my bed. Her hair is down and curled from the braids she had in last night. She looks beautiful in a simple red sundress and sandals. We didn't have much as far as fashion. Not like the humans on Earth had from what we can tell in books, pictures and magazines left over, but we do have some clothes they brought and our crafters can make some beautiful things every once in a while. There's a touch of sadness, and there usually is, after her and Mollock go and see their babies. They hate leaving them and I know that if she had a choice, they would move to that village to be with them in a heartbeat. Unfortunately, once you are registered and trained for a certain job in a village, that's what you are stuck with. And Village X, our village, did not allow for children. We were welcome to go wherever we wanted off duty, meaning we could visit and stay with our children in Village M, but we could not let children here. It was too dangerous.

She sighs. "They are getting so big." I sit next to her

and give her a side hug and rest my head on her shoulder in comfort. "They are walking now."

This surprises me, but I don't let it show because I love them and miss them too. I know at times it really takes a toll on her. I squeeze her in support. I'm not really sure what to say, so I just let us sit there in silence for a bit. "I think I'm going to take Chip with us."

She flinches back and I lift my head off her and move away as she gives me a shocked look. "Fell…"

I interrupt. "I know, but you know if we leave her she's just going to try and follow and I'm worried about her hurting herself more." My chest clinches.

"And you don't think she isn't going to hurt herself going into Sweet land?" She asks incredulously, and I don't blame her.

I stand and go to lean against my dresser. "I know. I just–I don't know."

Her eyes shine with understanding. "Okay."

"Okay?"

"Yup." She stands and grabs my elbow. "If that's what you want, there is no point in fighting. We have this one last dinner together in safety before going in the land and we have no idea how long any of us will last in there. So we might as well enjoy it while we can."

We head out of the room and Mollock and Deven are pouring a clear liquid into four glasses. I stop and shake my head as Alana laughs and attempts to pull me toward the table. "Oooh, no! Nope! I am not drinking." I pause. "You all are *not* drinking before we go into Sweet Land!" I point to each one of them as my voice rises.

Chip's eyebrows raise from where she lays on her bed, but otherwise she doesn't seem to care about my freak out. I hear her blow out a doggy breath of tiredness and Deven laughs. "See, Chip thinks you're overreacting like the rest of us do."

Mollock hands his wife her cup and then they are all holding theirs, looking at me. "Come now, Fell, we need to honor the dead and have one last drink together in joy with the hunters' prayer. Tomorrow is not guaranteed for any of us."

He always has a way with words and the room sobers with the realization of what we were about to be waking up to do. Nerves fill the air and I shake out my hands. "You're right." I head over and grab my glass and look at my team. "This is our night as a team." I pause as I look into each of their eyes. "As friends." I lift my cup in the air and they meet theirs with mine. I swallow hard. I hate emotions. "We all make it, or none at all."

"None at all!" They repeat and we all laugh. Before any of us take a drink, Deven recites the hunter's prayer and we acknowledge the names of our fallen village members, taking special time for Jules. We would miss her the most. After we all came back from the attack in the early morning hours, we said our goodbyes and gave Jules a quick and respectful death just as her transformation into a werewolf started to take place.

Because of the chance of disease and people coming back from the dead…*Yeah, zombies were a real thing here-* we couldn't bury her like we wanted to, but we did build her an honorable pyre and buried some of her personal belongings that she loved under a cross with her name on it. Her necklace, personal journal, and wedding ring of her husband, who passed away about ten years ago. Jules didn't have any family to place her cross next to, so we placed hers behind our home, as family members would have done to acknowledge and honor their dead.

One drink turns into two and we decide to go over the details one last time before breaking apart for the night and packing up. "Territory one," I quiz.

Deven sits straighter. "Candy Cane Fields. Ghouls. They can blend in with the canes. From the vision, we are guessing at least ten ghouls total, if not more. The plan is to stay together and move fast. We veer off the path to the right and head to the farthest field on that side, where the canes are thinned so we can concentrate on the ghouls. Once the ghouls are killed, we will collect what food we find and rest until we get to the next territory. We can only collect the cane chips *after* the ghouls are gone. If any are still alive and we try to consume the candy cane chips, they are poisonous and we will die."

"We assume," Alana says from where she sits on

Mollocks lap.

Deven nods. "There has been one death Madame Adelle could find in the Candy Cane Fields that wasn't from the ghouls and it was from consuming the cane chips. That guy almost made it clear through the territory without getting killed by the ghouls but as he ran and hid, in hunger he tried to eat the chips and died. Blood poured from every orifice of his body."

I shudder. "And did Adelle show him that or just a riddle?"

"He refused to see after she told him his future. The canes will kill you in hurried hunger, was the prophecy."

I laugh. I don't mean to. "Oh my shit, are you serious?"

He sighs. "Unfortunately. And if he would have just let her show him the vision, that guy might still be alive, or at least made it longer."

"But that takes up the question of the canes being edible at all. Are we sure we will be able to eat them even after we defeat the ghouls?" Mollock asks.

"I told Adelle the full plan like I was supposed to two days ago and like I said, she had nothing to say."

"But nothing could just mean there is no death. That we make it through the land. So if we stick to the plan, then we don't die," I add.

Alana sighs. "Yeah, I guess but what about the prophecy she told you?"

This gets Deven's attention. With everything going

on, we forgot to tell him. Oops. We fill him in and then continue on about what ifs. Two days ago we were in agreement of the plans and now we were back to being unsure. I chalk it up to nerves and after we go over the rest of the territories and finish packing, I crawl into bed, completely exhausted. I don't mean to, but my mind flies back to the dream of Neek and I on the beach and the time he ravaged my body and gave me the greatest pleasure of my life.

NEEK

King of Horrors Chapter Insert

I'm fucking shocked. Completely aroused and totally into this shit.

She's dreaming about me.

More specifically, about our time on the beach.

I watch from a distance as the dream version of me hovers over her, kissing down her neck. From this angle, she is breathtaking. I watch as her luscious breasts rise and fall beneath me as she moans and grabs my ass. Fuck, this was crazy. Should I make her aware she's dreaming and go please her myself? Or should I just enjoy the show? She cries out my name as I slam into her, and I have my throbbing cock out of my pants and in my hand before I know what I'm doing.

I'm far enough away, standing in the tree line so she wouldn't be able to see me even if she was aware. Doesn't make me feel any less like a creeper, but fuck it. Using my powers, I focus in closer. So close I can watch a bead of sweat trail down her neck as our sweaty, sand-covered bodies fuck hard and relentless on the sand. Squeezing hard, my breath stalls as I stroke myself faster, concentrating on her ass, lips, breasts, and hands that are starkly beautiful in contrast to my dark skin. My other hand gives me balance as I hold onto a nearby tree.

She cries out again, and I do too as I come in my hand. I pump myself a few more times, then transform into my smoke form right as the dream version of me is about to go for round two. Fuck this. I fly over to her and make my other self disappear, and suddenly she's aware.

"Neek?" she asks in a sultry voice. I'm hard again and ready, but all I want is her pleasure.

"Lay back," I command her.

She does as I ask, but confusion fills her eyes. "Transform. I want to feel you."

I slowly brush over her, letting my power represent soft kisses all at once on her skin.

"Oh fuck, Neek. Oh my gods," she moans, throwing her head back. Her right hand flies to her soaking cunt, but I force it away.

"Please," she whimpers. It's hard not to give in, but this will be better.

"Emerald, *scream for me.*"

Then I shoot my form up into her body.

And scream she does.

After she succumbs to exhaustion and starts to pass out in her dream, I tear myself away and plant a kiss on her forehead.

"Next time I see you will be in real life. Prepare yourself, Emerald. I'm coming for you."

CHAPTER THREE
SWEET LAND

All six villages have arrived to see us off. This is a one time allowance by our *great* Chiefs. Eyeroll. It's nerve wracking stepping outside for so many reasons it isn't funny. We are nervous, and it's not because all the members of the villages are lined up from our hut to the sign; it's a mixture of things. All our lives we've been told of our history and why we have suffered. All our lives we've been told the dangers of Sweet Land and how no one has made it through. And all our lives we have known the significance of someone making it through the land and getting an audience with the King and Queen. It would change this horrible fate for everyone. It's a lot of pressure, and one that we are prepared to take, even if I can see all our hands slightly shaking and know that my team's hearts are probably beating hard, just like mine is.

We all stop in front of our now closed door. The mood isn't one of celebration like you'd think it would be. It's quiet, nervous, and sad. Almost like we are marching to our deaths, and we probably are. For a thousand years humans have tried to cross Sweet Land and none have made it, so that is probably the reason for the sad atmosphere and faces we are getting. We are packed heavily light, as I put it. Alana and Mollock laughed when I told them that. We won't be able to run if we are carrying lots of gear, but we do have a full backpack of supplies strapped tight to each of our backs. Dried meats, nuts, fruit and vegetables. Bottles of water that we will most likely need to cherish like a forbidden treasure. One set of clean clothes, a small rolled cot and medical supplies. Hopefully it will be enough.

I look down to Chip and another round of nerves hits me. She is limping, but at least she's walking and I know deep in my heart that I'm a shit owner for letting her come. I tried first thing this morning to let her go with Alana's mom. I handed her a leash and her supplies, but Chip was too strong and flew out of her hands, just like I figured she would. In reality we could lock her up in my room, but once she got out, she would look for us and not stop until she found us. We all just came to an agreement that this is what she wanted. She had hunted with us the better part of eight years now and this is the only time she'd been injured. She was an asset and a part of our team. I just hoped nothing happened to her.

"Better not keep them waiting," I mumble and look at my team. Mollock nods, Alana gives a small smile that doesn't reach her eyes, and Deven shows me nothing other than a clenched jaw. Seeming to think the same thing, we all look back at our home one last time and then we are walking toward the sign. People utter their thank yous and good lucks under their breath as we pass and it does nothing to calm me. We stop in front of the sign and are met with the six chiefs of the villages. They each give us a hand shake and a well wish, all but our own Chief, who just sneers in anger. Probably because of the little ploy he tried to pull yesterday, the village has decided to vote in a new chief. Good. He's finally getting what's been coming to him for a long time now. Sucks we won't be here to see what's probably going to be the biggest meltdown in history when he officially loses his title. It also gives me hope that the village might be okay now that he won't be leading them.

"Step on the lit square below this sign, which will read your heart's desires. If all you desire is to live in a different land, you will be transported into Sweet Land." I read the part of the sign aloud that tells us what to do. The lit square below the sign has to be swept once a day to keep the dirt and sand from covering it. I honestly don't know why we clean it, but it's just something that for as long as I can remember was the responsibility of the chief of Village X. It shines a bright white color as dirt swirls over the top of it from the wind blowing today. It's big enough for all of us to stand side by side in a line and we get in position.

"No matter what happens, we stay together." Deven states, and my heart flies up into my throat. I want to tell them about my dreams of Neek and how I'm worried that if we go along with our original plan and what coincidently Neek also wants us to do, that there is a chance we will be tricked and killed. I start to open my mouth and it gets stuck. It's too late and that isn't fair to my team. But I have a plan that formed after waking in the way early hours after the dream with Neek. If he wanted us to do something, him, as the King of Sweet Land...he couldn't be trusted and because of that, we would need to do the opposite, which meant challenging the leaders.

Since this wasn't our plan and since I can't throw that in their faces at the last second, I would alone challenge the Candy Cane Fields leader. I knew I could do it, I had no doubt. That would also allow us safe passage through the first territory. I just hated lying to my team and making plans behind their backs, but for their safety, I would do it. Even if they'll be mad at me afterwards for it. At least they'll be alive.

"On the count of three," I say, and everyone nods.

"One." I pause and watch as Alana takes both Mollock and Deven's hand and squeezes. Nerves splay over all of us, but she looks the most nervous. I have no doubt it's because she has the most to lose if we die and don't make it through.

If we can't change this fate. No one else could.

"Two." Deven follows and I face forward, the anticipation of the unknown making my skin itch and my clothes feel too tight.

"Three." We all say it together and step onto the square, Chip following at my side.

I hold my breath and by pure determination only I manage to keep my eyes open, even though I want to slam them shut from fear of the unknown.

At first nothing happens. I panic and think about my will to save the human race. How I want us all to be released into a plentiful land full of food and water. Another second happens and still nothing. I start to really panic and I can tell by the others' expressions they are too. No one has tried to cross in so long. What if it wasn't an option anymore? What if we were all truly forgotten and the Queen and King didn't care to hear our pleas? I grab Mollock's other hand and squeeze as I slam my eyes shut and think as hard as I can about what I want. What I truly want and what I know that my heart wants. I want us to be able to live a safe life. To not worry about the sun setting. To be able to thrive, enjoy our lives and not struggle anymore. To not be scared and chased by predators every day of our lives.

That's when I felt a heat grow from the ground.

I open my eyes and look to see the lit square below us lighting up like a thousand suns. The heat grows as the light does and I worry about having a heart attack from how hard my heart is slamming against my chest. Keeping a hold of Mollock's hand that is now squeezing mine incredibly tight, I squat down and pet Chip with a shaky hand to keep her calm. A brighter flash of light happens and I can't see anything now; the light being too bright forces my eyes closed. I hear Alana whimper and I start to say it's okay, when suddenly the light vanishes.

I tentatively open my eyes and when I blink, I see we're in a whole new land.

We made it.

We are officially in Sweet Land.

My heart is still beating hard with no signs of slowing as I take in the land. All of us are now in hunter mode as we get into a prepared stance and immediately check our surroundings. Where we stand it's day, just as it was in the land we left, but in front of us where a stone path trails forward and into the Candy Cane Fields, it's darkness. Night. I swallow hard and shove down my fears. I am no longer Fellen, but a Bad Lands hunter, and I needed to be on my toes. I step forward, not asking if any of us are ready, mainly because the longer we stand here the longer our nerves will swelter. We are at risk of being surrounded.

As soon as I lead the team over the invisible line between night and day a chill, along with a haunting feeling falls over me, causing a shiver to flow through my body and down my spine. It feels like a warning, and I know it's one telling my instincts not to go any further, but it's too late now. The cool air smells of mint and sugar, and something I can't place until I take a large inhale of breath. *Blood. Decay*. It doesn't immediately come to you like the sweet smell, which I assume comes from the giant candy canes that are larger than any tree or building I've laid eyes on before, but it's there. Lying underneath. Chip starts to growl at my side and I catch where she's focused on and know he's there. I know, not because I can see him, but because of the feeling of an invisible tether I get. It's uncomfortable and seems to want me to go closer to him.

He's no longer the man in my dreams, but the King of Sweet Land and now my enemy. I can feel we've wasted enough time standing here as my team takes in the land and I know they are expecting to start our plan, so it's now or never. I want to say sorry, but sorry isn't going to cut it. The time for sympathy is over. I needed to assure my team's safety, no matter how upset it makes them.

I grip my caned weapon tighter as I step forward and

project my voice to where I know he is. Neek. "I know you're out there, King of Sweet Land!"

"What the hell are you doing, Fellen?" I hear Deven hiss at my back. I step forward more to where I know he won't be able to reach me. I swear I can feel the shock in the air almost, as if the land is surprised by my addressing it's king. Or maybe it's *his* shock. I wondered what he would do with my actions. I was his soulmate, as he claimed, the soulmate he's trying to make sure stays alive through the land. Will he save me? Will he confess the promises he told me he would in my dreams? Or will his true self be revealed now that he's got me in his clutches?

"But we only trust our kind, and because of that..." I continue, my nerves giving way to brave foolishness. I wasn't going to wait and find out and see what Neek would do. I couldn't. I can see things, ghouls, move about, hopping from cane to cane and approaching closer to us the longer we wait without moving. Alana whispers the same question Deven did. I hated this...this betrayal to them, but the show must go on.

"I alone challenge the leader of the first territory!"

I hear the gasps of my teammates and the howl of Chip behind me seconds before I hear a knocking sound. I glance back to see what I can only describe as magic. They are right behind me, but they can't move forward because of an invisible barrier that is now between me and them, and they are banging, kicking, flying into it, frantically trying to break through it. To help me? To throttle me? Who knows? It's too late now. The barrier must be soundproof as well, because I can see that they are yelling at me, but can't hear what they are shouting. Probably a good thing.

A mixture of howling and screeching sounds in front of me and brings my attention forward. Goosebumps coat my skin. This was it. *Ghouls*. From what I could tell, there were at least ten or more that now jumped, or slid down from their hidden positions in the fields, rushing me all at once. Some leap from cane to cane. Some run with arms arched high, screeching with jaws that are stretched wider than I thought possible. Others run toward me with deformed backs on all fours, growling and snarling. They were getting closer. I crouch and prepare to arch my weapon in a wide sweep to take out a line of them at once. This wasn't the plan. I challenged the leader, not the lot of them, but I also wouldn't just stand here and let myself be taken over. So, fight it was.

"Begin." The words of the king float as a whisper on the wind through the land and over all the noise of the approaching death racing toward me.

I can see him now. Clear as day.

Not the king that just whispered the start of my fate, but the leader of this territory and the first territory leader of Sweet Land I've ever laid eyes upon. It's hard to make out his exact features because even though he is within range of my sight, high above me crouching down on the arch of the closest cane, the darkness makes my sight blurry at best.

Luckily or unluckily, the leader slides down the cane and the other ghouls retreat just as fast as they started to approach me. And they were seconds away from reaching the slice of my blades.

I don't have a lot of experience with ghouls. None, actually. But I take him in. His gray wrinkled skin reminds me of a hairless cat. His bald head, fangs, pitch black eyes and knifed fingers are super creepy. I know that a good beheading would be the best course of action as any. After all, I know not a single supernatural that can survive without their head, but then again, I've been surprised before.

"They call me Mr. Mint," he snarls. The smell of blood and decay are now amped up the closer he walks toward me and I realize that while the land is where the sweet smell comes from, its residents must be where the other smells originate. I'm shocked to hear a supernatural talk in English. There isn't one in the Bad Lands that talks anything other than Fae. I didn't give two shits what they called this guy. *Dead,* is what he would be called when I finished.

I look over on instinct to where I know the annoying tether is telling me the King is still hiding. *Coward.*

"Bring it on, you piece of shit." I mean that more to the supernatural hiding to my far left than I do to the one approaching me.

Mr. Mint, *man that is a creepy ass name,* looks to his right, almost like he knows I'm talking to his king more than himself before looking back at me. He stops. "You know he advocated for you."

The words freeze up my muscles. Was Neek being honest? If so, why wasn't he trying to stop this now?

"Too late now I suppose, as the land controls us all. Once you challenge a leader, we fight to the death." He drops his bottom jaw and moves it around as his long black tongue shoots out in a slither. Like a snake. I grip my weapon tighter, reading the body language. He was about to strike and I couldn't get distracted by his words. He's right. It's too late now.

"Are you just going to stand there and talk all day?" I ask.

This gets him to move...but not in the direction I want him to. I expected a creepy screech and possibly a lunge attack. Neither happened. I stand there a full ten second in shock and watch as he shoots straight up in the air before totally disappearing.

"Shit!" I look around but can't see anything. Logistically if he wants the fighting advantage, he'll draw me into the fields and I know that's exactly what he's doing when I hear a creepy laugh from further back into the land.

Wasting no time, I run as fast as the heavy weapon in my hands will allow and follow the laugh. My boots crunch the cane chips under my feet. Some are so large they are like boulders that I have to run or dodge around, while some are the size of tiny pebbles. I almost forget about the canes and their stabbing ability until the one immediately ahead of me slams it's arched top down to the ground, stabbing the path with a strikingly fast ability. I scream in shock and almost slam into the cane, barely able to slide into a stop at the last second.

Another laugh, this one less creepy and holding a lot of amusement, sounds and then I'm running again, this time dodging the canes that are super fast at trying to kill me.

Is this a trap? Possibly. But I'm a hunter. I won't stand around and wait to be preyed upon. The other humans that have tried to make it through this land were not hunters but farmers, gatherers, or desperate parents that left their children behind to try and get an audience with the King and Queen for a better life. They didn't have fighting knowledge, or half the time, survival knowledge. It didn't matter if he thought this was the advantage. Whereas before the supernaturals in this death trap were the hunters, we are, and now they are the prey.

The laughing stops and I can feel that I'm close. I don't need my instincts or the hairs rising on the back of my neck to know that he is somewhere up high behind me.

I train my eyes up and press my back against a cane as I slowly move around the base. The pointed end is going crazy and stabbing twice as fast as the others. As if it's alive and can't stand that I'm touching it or that it's end can't reach me. Chips fly up, striking my body, and I have to cover my face at the flying candy. I try to catch my breath while steeling myself for the attack soon to come. And other than the candy canes slamming down, which is extremely loud, the air beyond this chaos is quiet and there are no ghouls laughing. He's about to make his move, I can feel it. I take a slow breath out and continue to check my surroundings.

I don't have to wait long.

"SURPRISE!" He roars, as he appears to my immediate right and slices out with his knife-like fingers. I crouch just in time but can't move too far from his attack because now at my back is the cane's pointed end, which will gladly finish the job if I retreat any further.

"Fuck!" I cuss out when swipe after swipe he has the advantage and almost slices my throat. I'm fast though and spin kick his legs out from underneath him, half surprised it actually knocks him down. To hesitate is to miss your shot. I drive the edge of my blade, hard and fast aimed at his neck, but at the last second he rolls out and under the cane's pointed arch. Which stops and doesn't strike him. Freaking great, they don't hurt him, but they'll definitely hurt me.

I grab one of my throwing knives and manage to throw it out from the cane's stabbing field, striking true to the back right shoulder blade of the leader's back. I'm gifted with a horrible scream that jolts the cane to stop it's striking. I run. I don't think and I throw another as he jumps to disappear again, or tries to. This time the knife strikes his back left calf. Another screech and black putrid blood pours from where my knives lay embedded in his skin as he falls to the ground. Grabbing my staffed weapon, I dodge a cane at the last second, approaching him and he doesn't give chase. I had him. He knew it too by the look on his face.

"If this is the only way to really save the rest of you, so be it."

What?

I halt, doing the one thing you're not supposed to because now the leader of the Ghoul territory is transitioning into his Fae form and holding his arms out wide. Blue smoke appears off in the distance, the King watching the show. I don't get what's happening. This has to be a trick. He wants me to get closer, but then why is the King watching? My tether to him is shooting sadness at me. Just like the land did to my friends, the ghouls are now screaming and running at an invisible force field, trying to stop what's about to happen. All but two, who are in their Fae form, females holding hands while crying.

Holy fuck, he's sacrificing himself.

"The land is forcing me back. It's now or never, Fellen, but make it count. For the record, I would have let you pass if you hadn't challenged me."

My ragged breath stalls for a second. I hear what he says and it makes a buzzing in my ears start up. Neek had been telling the fucking truth. I shake my head, ignoring the pounding guilt projecting from the King, who still watches in his smoke form, too cowardly to stop this or show himself. "I can't say I'm sorry." And with that I arch out and behead the leader of the ghouls. Screeches sound from the ghouls that are blocked from attacking me. They're pained ones, sad ones, ones that cry for their fallen leader. I don't look at them and only after I bend down with a lighter to light his body on fire does Neek actually grace me with his presence.

"Don't," he says. It's a command and it's coming from the King of Sweet Land. Not Neek, as there is no other emotion in his voice but cold hatred. "Return to your friends. You may pass through territory one safely."

I start to pull back my hand from finishing the job but delay. "What if he comes back?"

His jaw works and I watch as he swallows hard and looks away. "He won't." I don't get any other explanation, because he turns into his smoke form and suddenly the body of the leader and himself are gone, along with the ghouls. The canes have stopped stabbing the ground also. Holy shit, I did it. I actually survived and got us through by challenging the leader. I hadn't thought it would have been this easy, but maybe with him saying he was going to let me pass, that was why only after two knives were thrown at him he gave up?

Right as I bend down to retrieve my black blood covered knives and wipe them clean, I hear the bellowed call of my friends yelling my name.

Shit.

I hadn't thought about what would need to be said to them about my actions, but it was clear I fucked up and would have to come clean. For them, and myself.

CHAPTER FOUR
MR. MINT

NEEK

I watch from the front row as Adrian, Fuschia and Jasmine hold hands as another co-leader to their clan lights the funeral pyre aflame that holds their precious daughter on it.

It's hard not to go up and hold them right this second as their cries grow louder. It's exactly what I will do when given the chance. Jasmine never wanted children, but Fuschia wanted them so bad. Her and Adrian have been trying for the better part of two years before she found out she was with child, but the magic of this land is thick and makes it hard for supernaturals to have a successful birth. Their daughter died sometime during child birth and fuck if it wasn't the most devastating thing. I wished I could use magic, change this and save her, their baby girl-Lyca. But I couldn't. No one could.

All I can do is stand here holding Savannah's hands tight and willing the tears in my eyes not to fall. I never had a desire for children. Not a lot of supernaturals, other than the wolves, do, but that didn't mean I didn't understand it. All of us. Myself, Savannah, Zeek have been together for as long as I can remember and this pregnancy has been the highlight of our supernatural lives. Her death knocked us all hard on our asses. I guess we were so blinded by love we didn't think of the reality or the dangers of death. It's hard to remember it can happen when you are immortal.

When the funeral is over and the gathering at their home has past, I sit outside with Adrian under the two moons, drinking a hard liquor to help numb the pain.

Him clearing his throat breaks my stare from the tree line surrounding their house, to his tear soaked face. "Living for all eternity really puts death in a different perspective."

"How so?" I knew what he meant to an extent, but it was different for everyone here. Some wanted death and hated living for eternity, others relished in it. I wasn't sure where I stood on it just yet.

He chuckles lightly before taking another long drink. "I just mean. We can't expect to live forever. One of these days, one of us, or all of us will die." I can tell the liquor has hit him, but there's no judgment. He needs it. Just like I need to be here to see him through it.

"Man, that's a long way off. There's no war, and no reason for any of us to die." I swallow the lump in my throat and give his shoulder a hard pat. "Death makes us think of it and realize how easily it can happen to us or any of those around us. It's hard not to think of, I get it, but I'm here. I would move all the realms in this universe to protect you guys, so just know your

time isn't coming yet."

"Yeah." He pauses and grabs the bottle, not bothering with the glass this time, taking a big swig. "Yeah, I guess. Just wish I would have been able to be a father for just a little while, you know. I was so ready for her. To hold her. Teach her. Love her. I wonder what she would have grown up to be like, or look like." He wipes his face with the sleeve of his shirt and sniffs before another drink goes down. "Fucking sucks and it just makes me think."

He pauses for so long, staring down at something on the ground, I almost think he's too drunk to finish what he was saying before he finally looks back up to me in a concentrated stare. "Just make sure, promise me-"

"Anything." I interrupt.

He reaches out and holds my shoulder in a tight grip. "That if anything happens to me, just know that I loved the shit out of you man. I loved the shit out of all of you, and know that you made every single day worth living having you as my best friend. Promise me you'll take care of my loves and the others."

I swallow down my emotions and take the bottle from his hand, taking a much needed drink. "I promise."

The conversation plays loud in my mind, torturing me with flashbacks of his sad face from long ago. I look over to the other supernaturals that surround the unlit pyre and want them all to yell at me, scream at me, try to beat the shit out of me. Anything but what they are currently doing, which is not a fucking thing but standing there silently crying and staring at Adrian's wrapped body.

I hate everything about this, and there's a pain in my chest that feels like my heart is ripping apart.

Here lies my best fucking friend in the universe. *Dead*. Fucking dead and it's my fault. My fault for trusting her. For thinking that I could, and hoping to save everyone with niceties, false hope and wishes like some asshole. Adrian was skeptical and he had every right to be. I should have listened. I should have tried harder to make Fellen understand how important this was to me, or maybe hide my identity. Why did I have to show her my supernatural side? Then she wouldn't have guessed who I was, or maybe a different approach altogether would have changed this.

As the King of the land, I guess they are waiting for me to light the pyre.

I don't want to.

I don't want to fucking move.

But Jasmine looks at me and I know I don't have a choice. I can't imagine what they are going through. If she's telling me it's time, I guess it's time.

I take a deep inhale, trying to calm the growing pain in my chest, and let it out slowly through my nose as a tear breaks free. I grip the torch tighter and clear my throat. I can't let his death be in vain.

"Adrian..." I start, but my voice isn't right and I clear my throat. *That if anything happens to me, just know that I loved the shit out of you man.* "Fuck." I blow out another breath and try again.

"Immortality makes it hard to think about death. Especially for those of us here that I know have craved it for so long now." I look around at more than the ghouls; all the supernatural residences of Sweet Land are here outside of my castle. A lot look somber. Some, pissed. Some, shocked, but the majority looked devastated. "Adrian thought about death, well before we landed a life sentence here." I look at his wives now and they know what I'm talking about, but I don't delve into that; it's not fair. "In those thoughts he'd confessed to me that if something ever was to happen to him, he wanted everyone to know that he loved us all, because that was the kind of person, leader, husband and best friend he was."

"He carried the clan of the ghouls for thousands of years and grew you from a secluded community to a well loved, involved and important part of the fae society before the uprising. He was loved by so many people other than his immediate clan and because of that, his life being gone will stain our hearts and minds for as long as we live. His death doesn't have to be in vain though. It fucking doesn't!" I can see some in the crowd shaking their heads, thinking this isn't the right time for this, but fuck them. This is exactly the right time for this.

"I fucked up!" Some nod now. "I went about this the wrong way. I won't let my best fucking friend's death be in vain and neither will you!" I raise my voice as the anger starts to bleed into me and my powers start to reach out to feed. "I am no longer asking for your help in getting these humans through the land, I'm telling you. You will let them pass!"

"No!" Aspen steps forward with angered determination in his glare. I clench my jaw and try to hold in the anger I feel at his protest, but stay quiet. "No, I'm not going to just sit here and be promised that they won't challenge me like you had Adrian. You fucking lied. That or you couldn't control that bitch, either way I'm preparing to kill her fast and hard. Even if they don't challenge us and we let them through, do you really think she will get past Savannah, or you for that matter? The land is too fucking strong! It's pointless! End this!"

"If she makes it through, she is the only one that can release Neek and in turn release us!" Argues Zeek, stepping forward from behind Adrian's wives, who still don't break their stare from their slain husband.

Aspen just shakes his head. "Unless you can control them and come up with a plan for the last two territories all of this is fucking pointless." He pauses and shakes his head again, disappointment showing. "I won't hold myself or my wolves back. You won't be burning a single one of my pack. This ends the moment they step into my territory and out of those candy canes." With that he turns and walks back through the crowd, with the wolves following.

He has a point and I can't argue. There is a time when being a leader, King, is hard. This is one of them. I want to throw my weight and order them to do as I say, but I can't. I don't know what else to say, because Savannah and myself will be the problem. I just couldn't let anyone else die. Fellen needed to understand. She just had to. We weren't all monsters, but she and her team were forcing us to be.

I turn away from the bullshit of this and back to my friend. "I'm so fucking sorry, brother." I swallow hard, wanting to say so much more, but I can't. His wives nod and unlike the majority of ones around me, I don't look away as I light his body on fire.

FELLEN

"Spill," Deven says, sitting down across the fire from me.

I look up from petting Chip. We got settled into a good spot with enough vantage points that we *think* it may be safe to sleep in shifts. At least for a little while, but before we settle down I needed to explain and even if I didn't want to, they weren't going to let me be silent. As soon as I heard them calling for me I rushed back to them, and after the hugs I got a good slap to the face from Alana as she bawled like a baby. She was so pissed, and I didn't blame her. So feeling like I bathed in a lake of guilt, I take a deep breath to calm my nerves and sit up straighter squaring my shoulders.

"I've been keeping something from you guys," I start, and when they don't look surprised, I take it as my signal to continue. "I've been having dreams-"

Before I can continue Mollock shakes his head and interrupts, running a hand down his face. "We know all about the dreams and past life shit, Fellen, we need to know what the hell your actions back there were about, and why did it look like you were talking to the King of Sweet Land? Like he could hear you or you could see him?"

Fair point. "Just listen, it's different dreams. I've been having them for months. A man or rather, a supernatural has been entering them."

"*Fuck*!" Deven stands and grabs his head, not giving me a chance to continue. "That's why you wanted that book?"

I nod. "Yeah. That's why, and also why I knew some of the things that the Seer didn't tell us."

"Let me guess, it's the King that has been in the dreams?" Alana guesses, with a raised eyebrow.

I take a deep breath, trying to unclench my stomach. It's in knots and I can't stop shaking. Why didn't I tell them sooner? Leaders don't lie. I feel like the biggest fuck up, but I needed to get this over with. As well as I can remember them, I recap the dreams, leaving out the sex part and brushing slightly over the soulmate part, but they still catch it.

"And you being his soulmate is why he's claiming to want to help us get through?" Mollock questions, as Deven sneers and Alana cusses.

"Yeah, and when I found out what he was in this land, the King, it was the night before we were set to leave. Not a lot of time to come clean to you guys, but I just couldn't trust him. His plan aligned with ours, so I decided to do the opposite. If it was a trap, I would be leading you all straight into it and I couldn't bear to live with myself if I had."

Alana sits up and huffs, "That's just the thing, Fell, it wouldn't have been a trap! We'd plan to take all of them on and *not challenge the leader*. Trap or not, they would have still been coming for us all anyway, right? You doing the opposite only put yourself in danger for no reason and then what? You even said you think the King was telling the truth, from what the leader of the ghouls said and did by sacrificing himself!" She was pissed. I didn't blame her, and fuck if she wasn't making a good point.

"Yeah, I guess." I didn't know where to go from here,

which was strange. I always had my head on when it came to being a hunter. I still did, but I just didn't know where to go when it came to the leader of Sweet Land.

Seeming to read my mind, Deven speaks up. "We need to figure out what to do about this soulmate shit." I scoff at him, wanting to speak up about his jealousy showing, but I bite my tongue.

"Oh shit, Fellen, the fucking prophecy!" Alana gasps as I hang my head. That too. "She was talking about the leader, the fucking King!"

"Hold on now." Mollock puts a hand on her shoulder to calm her and bring her back to his side. "We don't know that for sure." He starts but she doesn't let him finish, moving back and turning toward him before thrusting a hand at me.

"Yes we fucking do! What was it again?" She asks me but doesn't let me talk. "Something about blossoming for your true mate and how he saves you in your dreams. That's your dreams, it's him! So he must be telling the truth!"

I sink further into myself. How bad did I fuck us if he is? Would he still be on our side after I killed a leader of his land?

"What was the rest of it?" Deven asks, looking at me. The gleam in his eyes that is normally there has now vanished, and in its place is a darkness that unsettles me. I know he's jealous and the others will pick up on it too, but now is not the time to deal with pointless infatuations.

"It's real. It's your blood. It will doom you, if turned. Free you, if found. Or kill you…if hidden. Your answer lies with frost." I repeat the prophecy, word for word. I can't unthink the damn thing ever since her creepy ass said it.

"Frost, one of the territories is the vampires. Their leader. That must be her, but we have no intel on that," Deven states.

"You will." A new voice joins the conversation. One I know all too well and my heart drops, as I stand and spin not sure what to do. Defend Neek? Defend my friends? Either way it was too late. The King was here.

I stare at Neek with an open mouth and eyes wide as Chip barks like crazy at my side. I shush her and try putting a hand on her, but she still growls as I hear weapons being unholstered behind me. I raise my other arm, not on Chip, slowly while looking back at my friends. "Easy."

"No, not fucking easy, Fellen, if we kill him now this is all over!" Mollock growls at my back.

Was he right?

"No, it won't work like that," Neek answers, taking a step closer to me and it's weird. I just saw him after killing the Ghoul leader, but I don't think I was actually seeing him. Not like I am now. It's different from the dreams. Before it was like a memory, or like there was always a weird cloud around us, but now it's been lifted. His voice is deeper, sexier, all man. His body and shirtless torso has a deeper color to it and his muscles are more defined. Against my will I feel my heart start to race and my body heat up in a way that embarrases me. I still must be in shock, because it takes me a minute for my eyes to reach his face and once they do I take a step back.

In my dreams there was always a heated stare in his dark eyes.

Now there is nothing but cold hatred.

Even if he takes my breath away, I know that we are enemies and I need to snap out of my lust. I was right, he hated me and killing the leader was a big mistake. "See something you like, *hunter*?" He asks and it's not lost on me that he didn't call me by my name or Emerald.

I suck up the hurt from it. They were just dreams, and it was time to survive. I had a job, and it wasn't to play prophecy and soulmates with a supernatural King to monsters. "Absolutely nothing." I take a step back before getting back to the subject. "You were obviously listening to our conversation. What do you know about Frost?"

"I know that you should have told me about a prophecy that included me! And you needed to listen to it and know I was telling the truth instead of acting like an irrational child!" He yells out while clenching his fists. "Regardless." He looks away and I follow his stare to see two other supernaturals step into sight, coming to stand on either side of him from the darkness and I'm temporarily struck that we had no idea they were here.

I look around, wondering how many more are out there watching us, but I can't see anything or anyone. Had we let our guard down that much?

"She will be extremely strong and near impossible to pass." It's one of the new supernaturals that finishes for Neek. He's huge. Same in height as Neek, but huge in bulkiness and muscles. Nothing but black pants, boots and a vest covers his tattooed body. His sandy blonde hair is pulled back in a low bun. He looks scary and rough, and strangely dresses like Alana. His eyes give away what he is though. Vampire.

The other supernatural has yet to say anything and he is the strangest looking of any human-shaped supernatural I've seen. I wonder slightly if he's a giant, as he towers over Neek and the other one, looking to be nine to ten foot tall. Bright orange, shaggy hair and eyes that match. It's unnerving and I have no idea what he could be, but the light blue glow around him makes me think maybe a ghost, but I'm not sure.

"So she's a leader of the vampires?" Deven asks, stepping irritatingly close to me. It's obvious he's trying to stake his claim on me. I glare at him, a warning look, but he ignores me, so I look back at the potential threat in front of us, only to be met with Neek's intense stare directed at Deven's hand close to my hip. A blue smoke starts to form around his clenched wrists and his eyes slowly turn from a dark brown to a crimson red.

"Step away from her before I punch your heart through your chest and make you swallow it."

My eyes fly back to Deven, only to see a smirk on his face. Fuck.

"Enough!" I step away from Deven, holding out a hand to make sure he doesn't follow. "This isn't the time for measuring dicks." When I see Deven finally quit his shit and Neek's eyes slowly turn back to their right color, I continue. "If you aren't here to help us, you are here to hurt us. So either get on with what we need to know, or you force us to attack."

Neek's lips lift up in an irritatingly sexy smile showing his bright white teeth, "Oh Emerald, how I wish you could." He runs a hand down his face. "It's not the time though for teaching you a lesson or wishing you could make me do anything." I hate how I can feel my body change just from his words. He breathes in deep, making a show out of it. "Hmm, you smell ready for me. If you follow through and do as I say, you might just make it through alive so I can take you as mine."

"Like hell you will." I almost forgot about anyone else being with us until Deven speaks up. Shit. I shake myself out of whatever trance he has me in.

"Stop," I look at both of them, my sight finally landing on Neek. "No more riddles. Tell us who she is and how to beat her."

"On one condition." Neek answers.

I look at my team and then back to him. "What?"

He smiles and it's the evilest thing I've ever seen. "I will tell you all that you need to know, but only you, and only in private."

CHAPTER FIVE
HOW YOU WILL BLOSSOM

NEEK

"You're dangerous."

She raises an eyebrow and tilts her head, trying to be cute. "Deadly, even."

I can't help the blue flames that erupt around us, as my temper explodes. "THIS ISN'T A FUCKING GAME, FELLEN! YOU KILLED MY BEST FRIEND!" I take a deep breath and step back, glad that my outburst finally knocks that condescending look off her face. It may have helped her expression, but did nothing for my own self-willed battle between wanting to strangle her to death or strangle her until she cums. All the heartbreak of Adrian aside, our soulmate bond is going strong ever since she stepped into the land, and I can't help but be close to her even if she pisses me off. "We have feelings, lives, families, friends and we are trapped in here just like you are now! We need to just put all this shit between humans and supernaturals aside and work together."

This animates her once more and her cheeks redden, her chest rising faster with heavy breaths. "I know this isn't a game, I never said it was! But I didn't know if I could trust you! I still don't!" She grips that damn weapon tighter and I want to tear it from her grip and break it in half. It's the same weapon she took *his* life with. Obviously her signature one, because she wasn't going anywhere alone with me without it. I hate it. I hate that she can't trust me, and I hate that I can't trust her.

I scoff, shaking my head and taking a step back from her. "Yeah, and killing an innocent person is the way to do it."

"You mean *monster*, and all of you monsters are far from innocent!" She argues. It pisses me off. She doesn't know the fucking half of it.

We both take a break and a much needed breath. I need her to chill with challenging leaders, get her prepared for the wolves and get her team on board with Savannah's realm, on top of trying to seal our mate bond. A shift in wind and a chill in the air tells me that the land is getting impatient waiting for them to continue on, and they won't have that much time left in this territory before it forces them on to the next one. Adrian's death and the smell of the pyre we just left are thick in my mind and it's hard to move on from it. Impossible to forgive her for, but being older is to be knowledgeable and I take a second to think like her. I can see her point of view. I can also tell from watching her team before we made ourselves known that she does feel some—albeit small—remorse for what was done and what she had to do.

Her attitude is coming more from fear of the unknown and I don't even have to see the stark colors in the air to be able to tell that, as I slowly approach her. She doesn't try to step back, but she also isn't as receiving now as when I had her pushed up against a tree and my hard cock pushed up on her. "Fellen, the only way we both get what we want here is for you to put the prejudice aside."

I watch her beautiful emerald eyes look up into mine. "And there is none of that coming from you against humans?"

And this was it. I knew she wanted to know the truth. I knew and I promised her coming into this that I would come clean. I can't trust her with everything, especially with the key to our bond, but I can explain some. If anything, it had to change her view on some of us and maybe help us. "I told you we were trapped here."

"And?"

I lift a hand before I even know what I'm doing, completely compelled from our bond, and reach out to brush a strand of hair back from her eyes. "Let me show you." I drop my hand, giving her a second to think on it. Slowly she huffs out a sigh and nods. "Okay."

"Okay?"

"Yeah."

I'm shocked with her distrust of supernaturals that she would let me use my powers on her, but don't dwell and grab her hand pulling her body flush against mine. It produces a gasp from her and her cold hand rests on my chest. "How is this showing me?" The breathlessness of her voice isn't lost on me.

I lean my head forward and brush my mouth against her ear. "Like this," I whisper. She melts further into me and I'm getting hard as more azure colors surround us. We are bathing in our lust for one another and I fight the urge to act on it. I reach into my powers and let my smoke surround us before entering her mind. The moment we are, I show her. I show her my life with my friends before all this: game nights, fun times and even the funeral memory between Adrian and me. I then move on to show her the uprising. The Fae King and Queen, my torture. All the supernaturals' deaths who acted in the coup. My friends' deaths. Our prison sentence and the struggle of trying to stay on our Fae side before we were forced to where we are now. The only thing I leave out is how my soulmate with the power of my true name can control me. She won't get that until I know I can trust her.

The moment she is done seeing what I project, she gasps and steps back away from me with shock and sadness in her expression. "You led the uprising to save the humans?" The awe in her voice almost knocks me on my ass. *Fucking. Finally.* "And this is your punishment. Making sure the humans get killed trying to get to a better place."

I nod.

I watch as she continues to piece, or tries to piece, everything together. "But, how do I or I mean, how does my team make a difference in getting you out? If humans do make it through the land, does that mean you guys get free also?"

"No."

She sighs in irritation, switching the weapon from one hand to the other. "Then what?"

"Because you are my soulmate." I want to tell her, but I can't. So she would just have to wait until that moment. "I know you can't trust me. I can't trust you either it seems, but we need to come to some sort of agreement and understanding. *Because you are my soulmate,* it makes you different. It makes you capable of freeing not only the humans, but also me. If you free me, I can free the supernaturals and then Sweet Land will no longer exist, once I destroy it and then destroy the King and Queen. But that's all I can say for now."

I watch as she bites her bottom lip. I reach forward, brushing my thumb along her lip, releasing her bite. "The prophecy confirmed everything I needed to know and after me showing you the past, if you think hard on it, you would realize you're the key to freeing us and your race as well. I just have to get you through the land, alive."

The moment I heard the prophecy I knew that it was real. Not because I knew whatever Seer they referred to, but because it finally made sense why she *was* my soulmate. I just couldn't confirm my suspicions out loud and until I could, I just had to trust my gut, get them through the land alive, and figure out how to get her in front of Savannah without dying.

"Okay." She nods, almost like she's talking more to herself than me. "Okay, we will work together."

She doesn't really have much of a choice, but instead of pushing my luck and telling her that, I give her a smile I know produces that delicious lust in the air. "There's one more thing."

This worries her and almost makes me laugh when she steps back. I know she's not scared. She's trying to stop her lust for me that obviously has her wet and pounding with need right now. *Good*. That was my next task. "This soulmate thing won't work correctly if we don't seal the bond."

She tilts her head and squints at me. "The bond? Sounds made up."

I do laugh at this. "I assure you it's not, and it's part of the reason why you're soaking fucking wet right now." She opens her mouth to continue, and I use my speed to appear in front of her and back her up against a cane. She gasps in pleasure and almost drops her weapon as her eyelids flutter. "It's the reason why I can smell your heat, see it floating in the air, and want to bathe in it." I press my erection against her and this time I get a moan, as her other hand that was hanging lifeless now grips tight on my right bicep, making my erection throb with need. I reach up and trail my knuckles against her exposed cleavage. She came to kill and fight in a suit that makes her look like every guy's wet dream. Where her normal hunter uniform has baggy pants, she is in pretty much nothing but tight black leather. When we get out of this alive, I will burn it so no one else sees what's mine. But for now I'll take advantage of it and push my hand down under her zipper until I reach her hardened nipple and pinch it.

"What...wha-"

She tries on two accounts to talk or question me and fails. I love it. "What's what, Emerald?" I'm about to lose the fucking plot here. Teasing her isn't easy when I've already had a taste and am now *starving*. I grip her throat and angle her face up before sucking hard under her ear, and right in the spot that I know takes her breath away. She moans and I continue my assault while grinding against her, squeezing her breast.

I move up her jaw to her irresistible lips, slowly kissing them. "Remember how I made you scream my name on that beach?" I whisper.

Her closed eyes slowly open and she finally finds her voice. "Yeah." She says, thick with lust.

"That's how you seal it."

FELLEN

I feel so hot right now.

This isn't right. The download of information I just got needs to be taken to the others and we need to be forming a plan. Going over Frost and how to survive and, *and...*

Neek grinds into me again and this time I drop my weapon when he bites my neck, making me gasp and lose all motor functions. "We can't." There are so many reasons why we shouldn't but the main one is, if he makes me scream like he did in that dream we would have a big problem on our hands.

"Fuck your friends." He stops his assault and looks deep in my eyes. "This is bigger than what they think of me...and also-." He brings his lips in, looking away before looking back at me with a pissed off look on his face as he starts to squeeze me tighter. "I want that little fucker to hear you. He needs to know what's mine."

Right as I start to say his name to argue, he kisses me. Full on, and his tongue takes my breath away. I can't fight it. I want more. I want all of it. Just his voice alone ignites my heat, but his fucking touch and skilled tongue blows me away and I'm no match. He could be planning to slit my throat for all I know, and I'm fucking loving his pleasure so much I would watch with eyes wide open as he did it. I'm so fucked.

He turns, taking me with him as he kicks out my legs, not gently, and lowers me to the ground before attempting to rip off my outfit, but I stop him.

"Unless you want me fighting through the land naked, I need that." He growls, but obliges and goes a lot slower, unzipping the front of it down to my belly button and exposing my top half. He stops and takes in the sight of me with lustful eyes. I wiggle in anticipation as he squeezes my breasts; my eyes roll back with pleasure. I want him in me. Now. This isn't like me, but it feels like I'm out of control for him. He's built me up too much just with a simple kiss. I need him. Memories of our dream flash through my mind, I've never had that much pleasure before in my life.

"I want to devour you, worship your body like the fucking goddess you are, but we don't have that much time. Zeek and Dagger can only stall for us for so long." He slowly peels off the rest of my clothes, balling them up.

"Lift that sexy ass, Emerald." I do as he says, and he shoves the clothes under there. Not once breaking eye contact, he leans down and kisses me deeply.

He pushes down his jeans and his cock is long and hard. I ache, I want it so bad. A whimper escapes me before I can stop it. "Fuck me, Neek."

He licks his lips rubbing the tip of his cock against my entrance, making me suck air through my teeth and making him smile. "With pleasure."

NEEK

She's fucking soaked.

I love it.

I love it more that she is shaking, her fingernails digging into my arms. *She wants it bad.* Her body knows who owns it and responds accordingly as I tease her. I wish like hell we had more time, but we don't and I don't want anyone interrupting us, so I only tease her a second more and then I can't stop myself before slamming into her, hard.

She cries out before I can stop the sound and put my hand over her mouth, grunting out my own pleasure. From our time on the beach I remember she likes it rough. So I don't go easy. Fuck, she feels amazing. *So warm. So tight.* I'm lost in it. Pounding into her with no way of stopping until we both reach that high. She's clawing into me and other than her muffled sounds, my haggard breathing, and our skin slapping together, there's nothing but silence. It's hard to listen for anyone coming, but I'll be fucking dead before I let anyone see her vunerable and getting fucked. I lied when I said I wanted him to hear. Her sexy as fuck moans, screams and cries of pleasure are just for my ears and no one else's. Just like her body.

Her eyes alternate between rolling back in her head and being slammed shut, her face in pure ecstasy as I keep her mouth covered. I wish like hell I didn't have to so I could hear my name being screamed from her sexy lips, but it won't be long. Once this is over we will have all the time in the realm to be loud. I hit her in the right spot while sucking one of her nipples in my mouth and I feel her clenching around me and her screaming muffles get louder. It's the best feeling having her cum all over my cock. I'm fucking gone and can't hold back. I follow her shortly after and remove my hand, letting us both catch our breaths.

It's only then that I see the tether seal completely moving around us. The bright, white light circling both of us, before forming a line between me and her. I choose to shut my mind off from seeing it to look down at her beautiful face, only to see her completely freaked out. Without thinking I pull out of her and jump up to face the threat. There isn't one. What the fuck is she…

"What is that light?" She gasps, pointing at the soulmate tether that bonds us.

I'm stunned before a laugh busts out as I grab my jeans, pulling them on. How is she seeing that? Did my powers transfer to her somehow? I wasn't sure how human to jinn soulmate bonds worked, but I didn't think she would have anything supernatural transfer to her. Instead of acting shocked like I am, I roll with it. "Told you there was a bond."

I watch as she tries to touch it before failing and grabbing her clothes getting herself dressed. "You were telling the truth."

"I have been Emerald, you've just been failing to see it."

She scoffs, adjusting her uniform before zipping it up, allowing her cleavage to once again show. Next time I'm cumming all over them. "So, now what?"

I walk over to her, loving that she can't keep her eyes off my abs. I pull her close before grabbing her under her chin, rough just like she likes it, and kiss her deeply. She responds hungrily and I pull away, but not before grabbing a handful of her ass. "Now we find every fucking excuse we can to do that a million more times."

"Neek, I'm serious."

I kiss her, covering her irritated groan. "So am I."

She pulls away and reaches down for her staff. "We are soulmates, fine. You just proved it, but I still don't know what this means. I don't know if I can trust you."

I watch as Dagger approaches from afar. "You don't have a choice."

Chapter Six
Supernatural or Monster

It almost feels like a walk of shame going back to the others and I'm constantly looking down at this weird light thing. I hope like hell they can't see it. Would they be able to tell I just had one of the most amazing orgasms of my life while my head pressed up against a giant candy cane while the enemy King fucked my brains out? After I learned Dagger's name and that he was officially a mother freaking vampire, Neek told me to go ahead and fill in my team on his past and that they would catch up shortly. And I'm still not sure how I feel about the whole thing.

His past explains why he acts like he does, if it's real. I don't know a lot about jinn. Could he have faked all of that and projected it into my head? I couldn't be sure, because in the memories there was a guy he called Adrian that looked just like the leader that I killed. Also, the soulmate bond thing was officially real, since I can see that with my own eyes. The crunching of canes on the ground breaks my inner dilemma. Lifting my weapon, I'm ready for whatever it could be. Chip barrels around a cane, running straight into me and jumping up with her front paws on my stomach, causing me to almost shit myself and let out a very embarrassing screech. *Some hunter I am.* I roll my eyes at my own stupidity before kneeling down to greet her and putting down my weapon. "Holy shit, baby girl, you about got unalived!" It's obvious she's feeling better with how fast she was running. Good. She would need to be in her best health for the rest of this. Especially if I fucked up with how bad I think I did by killing the first leader.

With all the truths Neek has been giving me, if he was trying to convince the leaders to stand down and let us through, it was obvious they weren't going to now. I may have really messed this up for us. I continue to give her love before she gets too excited and starts licking my face. "Nope. None of that." I laugh and stand up slowly realizing the wind has died down and for some reason it's too quiet. Grabbing my weapon, I start to slowly turn, feeling the hair on my arms start to raise and a feeling of being watched fall over me as my heart rate increases. Shit. This wasn't good. I continue to look around the best I can and wonder if it's one of the supernaturals Neek brought with him.

I'm shocked when I see two females approach through the fog. Ghouls. I only know because they were the same ones that were holding hands in that form and crying while all the other ghouls around them tried to break through the barrier. There was no way this was good, but oddly enough, they didn't seem like they planned to attack and Chip wasn't growling, but sitting calmly by my side. My tilted head must have shown my confusion and prompted them to speak first.

The one with bright pink hair sighed. "You'll have a lot to learn if you make it through this land and onto the rest of the Fae Realm." Her English is perfect. Why the hell can the monsters in here talk but *not* the ones that attack in the Bad Lands?

"I'm not sure what that's supposed to mean." I withhold any of my usual attitude, generally curious about that statement.

The other girl next to her laughs. "You were surprised when we walked up that we weren't attacking or a threat. You sensed it. As did your dog."

How did they know that?

"Ghouls are empaths. We can't read your mind, but we can pick up emotions and feelings of thoughts," Brunette hair says before waving her hand in the hair. "Not that it matters. We couldn't attack you anyway. The rules of the land are not just measly written rules that can be broken on a whim.They are binding, body controlling ones." She pauses and takes a deep breath, putting her arms around herself. "You killed our husband, and we know that you *kind of* didn't have a choice."

"I..." For the first time in a long time, my smart ass mouth has nothing to say because the supernaturals I was trained to hunt were savages with no human or humanistic qualities. Yet these ghouls stand here looking and talking, obviously feeling human from the tears I watch trail down their faces. I've never had to learn of the consequences of killing a supernatural before. The ramifications. Was that someone's mother, father, sister, wife, son? Didn't matter because they were animals, deadly creatures and a threat to our species. I really don't know what I was going to say, because I've never said or felt sorry for killing one, yet the guilt has slowly been bleeding into me since I killed their husband.

"Problem?" Neek comes up right beside me and I didn't even hear him approach, nor did Chip growl again.

This above all else shakes me out of my stupor. I was a survivor and I wasn't acting a fucking bit like it. I was next to three supernaturals and haven't even had a bit of sense to protect myself or be cautious. Let alone be on guard. This all could have been a ploy to kill my team. Now I do look around and use my senses. Everything sounds fine, the same eerie quietness as it was when we entered other than a slight wind is still the same. No new smells. Empty candy cane fields with nothing but two bright moons staring down above us.

"You aren't in danger, you're just learning what you should have learned from the very beginning of your species stepping into the Fae Realm...not all supernaturals are dangerous." The pink haired one says.

"I don't know what to trust." I pause and stand up straighter. "No one has made it out of here alive. No human anyway, so don't be shocked if I don't immediately fall for every monster in here being nice."

"*Monster*?" The brunette steps forward with shock in her voice. "You killed our husband and we're the monsters?"

"*Jasmine,*" Neek says to her in warning.

Enough of this. "Oh, so you weren't in your other form barreling toward me like all the other ghouls in here to rip me apart when I first entered?"

A huge pause and I don't back down.

"Yeah, but-"

"And you would have done so without any delay regardless because before I entered, the last thing I heard from Neek when it came to this territory was that you were against us passing and then undecided. I shouldn't have to explain that to a human it's killed or be killed when it comes to the whole Fae Realm, and I didn't just come in here as a human but a hunter. Whichever god you pray to has big laughs to put the one human in charge of saving you that hates supernaturals the most."

I ignore their open mouths and raised eyebrows. Fuck them. I look at Neek. "Let's go." Then without waiting I head back to my team, whistling for Chip to follow.

They had me for a minute there. Thinking I was almost sorry, and shit maybe a small part of me is, but would they have blinked an eye if I had gotten ripped apart? Would my team go to them and try to guilt trip them into saying or feeling sorry? No. Of course not, because that's not how this worked. We were here to help our race first and foremost. This soulmate bond has complicated things more than I could imagine, and I'm playing along because there seems to be a truth to it that could help us all get out alive. But that didn't mean I was here to make friends. Especially if at any moment this could all be a huge trap or ploy.

Deven stands up first from the fire at my approach, right away sensing my mood. "Take it from the pissed off look on your face the negotiations went as well as expected."

"They weren't negotiations." I pause and look around for the giant supernatural we left them with. "Where's the tall one?"

I hear Alana sigh. "Turns out he was a ghost."

I immediately look at Mollock. "Shit. Please tell me you didn't kill him, I've already fucked up enough for all of us."

This gets a laugh from a new voice and I spin to see the tall, apparently ghost, come out of nowhere. Literally, one minute nothing but laughing air, next, poof, tall ass ghost man with orange afro. "I would like to see you lot try to off me, but no. I prefer my cat form better, but that didn't go over well with Rambo over there and he started throwing salt."

Sigh. Big sigh.

Here were these horrid creatures that were to tear us limb from limb. We should be fighting for our lives to get through, yet every one that we've met is more human than us at times. I shake my head, not knowing what to say, right as Neek and the vampire show up. It's not lost on me that Alana puts her hand on a stake hanging from her belt, making him laugh.

"Enough, we need to get on with this meeting or whatever it is so we can get some rest and be ready to move on." I look at Neek, who looks severely pissed. Probably because of what I said to the ghouls, but not a single thing I said wasn't the truth. And just because I liked his cock doesn't mean I was about to be BFF's with every supernatural that came my way. Until we made it through this land and got our race safely out of the Bad Lands, I wasn't going to play nice. "The wolves are the next territory. In the dream you stated that some were on board to let us pass and others weren't, where are we at on passing?"

Neek shakes his head and runs a hand through his hair, frustration seeming to seep out of him. "They were on board until Adrian."

"Adrian?" Deven asks with an attitude.

"The territory leader for the ghouls. And fuck!" I answer before Neek can go break his neck. Which the latter looks more likely from the look he's giving him. Of course Deven is squaring up right back, so I didn't have any doubt they would fight eventually. Right now wasn't the time.

"So what? What does that mean? And how does that even make sense? You think they would be more on board to letting us pass since Fellen did kill the previous leader. They should be scared that one of us will challenge theirs," Mollock protests.

Neek looks over at Dagger, a silent conversation seeming to pass between them before he answers. "None of you will be able to beat Aspen one on one."

"Werewolves are what I've trained all my life to kill. They are pack animals. One on one is a hell of a lot better than fighting a pack. Especially if you all have been trapped in here as long as you say you have been. They will have a very close bond and know down to the wire each one of their pack members fighting strengths, weaknesses and style. Not to mention how they can communicate through their pack. We will be completely fucked if we try to run through the pack lands in hope to survive."

"And let me guess, you will be the one to challenge the leader again?" Neek asks and suddenly everyone is talking, or arguing at once until Neek's voice booms over everyone's, causing the normal wind to break into a howling one that immediately puts out our fire and everyone standing on alert. "You will not challenge him. None of you will."

I will myself to calm down and take a deep breath. "Then what?"

"Talk to them," Dagger says. It's the first time he's spoken. "Just like you did when you all entered the Ghoul territory. Don't give them a chance to rush. Ask to speak to their leader first."

"And say what?" Mollock challenges. "Ask nicely if they'll let us through?"

"Wouldn't fucking hurt, man." Dagger cracks his knuckles. "You know, I was human just like you. Whereas these fuckers were born here in the Fae Realm." He shoots his thumb to Neek and then to the ghost whose name I have yet to learn. "I was twenty seven when the end of Earth happened. I was turned during it and instead of fighting against the humans, I turned the rest of my MC Club and we fought to defend the humans. Right before the Fae King and Queen showed up on Earth to save the last humans, Neek saved me and a group of us and brought us to his realm. I've been fighting alongside him every since and I've always trusted this motherfucker with my life." He looks at Neek and shakes his head, giving a light chuckle. "It wouldn't fucking hurt to take some advice, no matter how much you think you know."

The ghost guy stepped forward. "All of us monsters,

as you and your team like to put it, are trapped in here because we tried to help your race and were thrown in here as a punishment to remind you why you hate us, and it worked. Not that we blame you. But until the day we were thrown in here, a lot of us that were born in the Fae Realm had never acted on our side of what we were born to be. We were simply just like all the other Fae that look, eat, talk, walk like humans. The land, spelled by the King and Queen, are what makes us these creatures. Starves us."

"Turns us against one another," Dagger adds.

"And kills us. Just like you." Neek says. "So regardless of feelings or wanting to suck you dry, we are here fighting that nature to try and see a bigger picture where we can get out of this hell hole and back to the life we once had."

Mollock talks first, me still too stunned to know what to say. I mean, I saw Neek's past but didn't really delve into it and still questioned it. Either these guys have had a lot of time to rehearse this little speech or it's true. "I don't get that though, because the supernaturals that attack us back in the Bad Lands nightly are anything but humanistic. They never, or hardly ever, transform into a human shape and always communicate in Fae."

"The Bad Lands are where Fae are thrown as a punishment. They are stripped of all intelligence or Fae natures other than the language. Which is a dead, old language that only savages use. Which is what they are. In the real Fae Realm, other than certain lands within it, this one and a few others, supernaturals are more human than even humans and because the land is spelled to sustain us we don't act on our natural sides unless we want to. We are immortal and have everything we need to survive."

All we can do is sit and stare at each other. The information is too insane to process. "So there really is a way we can make it out."

I watch as Neek's jaw clenches, along with his hands, before he answers. "A small one, but there are a lot of territories still left to pass and out of all of those, the only ones completely on board with you passing straight through are the ghosts."

Mollock scoffs and I can't help but scoff also. "One down at least." Alana bumps her shoulder into his.

"So wolves, you expect us to ask pretty please. What about the others? What about Frost? And you?" Deven asks.

"We'll have to play it territory to territory. Wolves you stand a better chance of talking with them. Let them know you don't want to kill them. Let them know that you have talked with me and know now that you can help everyone get out of the land and ask for them to give you a chance."

"And if they don't?" I ask.

Neek just shrugs. "Then they don't, Fellen, but either way we are telling you, your team has a better chance at making it through the wolf territory alive by going through together. Aspen is way too powerful for a one-on-one. And before you interrupt or try to argue, let me put this into perspective. The Fae Realm is about the size of five of your previous Earths put together. A world that had over a billion people on it. Aspen is one of the oldest Fae alive and controls all of the wolves in Fae. In the normal realm he isn't just some territory leader. He's known as the Wolf King." That does shock me, I stay quiet. "Before Adrian you had the wolves split fifty-fifty and that still might be the case. There may be a lot still on your team's side to just let you pass to avoid bloodshed and those few might be able to convince Aspen if you and your team can open dialogue and try to win them over."

Dagger and the other guy nods. "And the wolves are like fucking rabbits. There's a shit load of them pregnant right now. I doubt they want trouble. At least those families."

"How are they able to conceive if what you showed me about you all being starving is true?" I ask Neek.

Dagger is the one that answers though. "With these." He turns and points to a tattoo and I don't get it until the ghost guy shows the same exact mark. "We are put into a restless sleep and only awakened when humans step into the land. But at one point, there were humans trying to cross all the time and so, we were awake all the time. When you have nothing to do, fucking eachother is about as close as you'll get to getting rid of the boredom."

"And by then everyone is insatiable with hunger." Neek sighs. "Making their Fae side retreat.."

"And their animalistic side comes out," Mollock finishes, looking exhausted.

"Yes. So you're fighting Fae that don't want to be the monsters you claim but have no choice. Just like the moment you walk into their territory you're not just fighting their hunger, you're fighting the land as you saw with the canes and if you challenge the leader, the land will compel him to fight, kill and win whether he wants to or not."

"But then-" I cut off, having that stupid guilt shit flood back in.

"Adrian?" He asks, and I nod. "I think when he saw me in the distance is when he fought it and gave up." It's not lost on me that the other two now look to the ground. "I told him about you being my soulmate and how you could change the fate for all of us trapped in here. He sacrificed himself to give others that chance because that's the kind of *monster* he was. And also, Fuschia and Jasmine were just trying to be nice. Which is big for them since you did just slaughter their husband. They told me to tell you not to let his death be in vain."

My team just gives me confused stares, but I shake my head. "I'll tell you later."

A gust of wind picks up, carrying a howl that has all of us standing and Neek closing his eyes and tilting his head to the sound. "It's almost time. The land will reactivate and push you to the next one if you're not out soon. Get some rest. We will cover the rest later." They turn to leave and I want to shout for Neek to wait. I have more questions but I stave it when Deven offers for me and him to have the first watch, but not before I hear Mollock mumble that he thinks there's something weird about all of this.

Turning around, I catch the team up on what Neek showed me from his past and we go over what to do. As the guys pack everything up other than the sleeping mats so we can run and go at the last minute if need be, Alana and I go find a place to relieve ourselves. "I know there's more to this than you're telling me," she says with pursed lips, trying not to smile.

"What does that mean?" I ask with a laugh.

"It means." She pushes a finger into the side of my neck.

"OW!"

"That you have a hickey." Fuck.

I cover it with my hand like that will make it disappear. I've never been embarrassed by my sexuality, but for some reason coming clean that I was having sex with not only a supernatural, but enemy number one was making me feel weird to tell me friends. "I have a soulmate bond with him."

That causes her to burst out laughing. "Stop acting so embarrassed by it. I mean, yeah we will probably have to off him to get out of this alive, but I don't blame you girl. Soulmate excuse or not, that guy is fucking *hoooot*."

"Ha. Ha."

We walk on a little more in comfortable silence before she breaks it again. "What do you think about the wolf thing? I mean, with your past life stuff and all? Does he know about that?"

I sigh. "I haven't told him about the past life and about the wolf stuff, I have no idea. Everything so far about this place has been shocking and nothing like I expected it to be. That either means that we were way wrong and this will go easy, or that we are about to have the fight of our lives ahead of us and if Neek and his friends seem to think Aspen is as dangerous as they said he was, we may need to figure out a plan to not challenge."

She nods. "I think that maybe that's for the best. Maybe talking with them really will work. I mean, we were literally just talking to a ghost, vampire and a freaking jinn and didn't have to fight to stay alive." She shakes her head. "A motherfucking vampire, Fel, and his name is Dagger."

I take a shaky breath in, feeling weird about all of it as well.

"This is either going to be really bad or really good but either way, I won't let anything happen to you guys."

CHAPTER SEVEN
The Dazed Woods

None of us were expecting to be awoken by the slamming of candy canes, but that's exactly what happened and it sucked a thousand assholes. It sucked the first time and it sucked worse now because I feared for my teammates and Chip. Running for your life, packing your shit in a bag and constantly looking behind you to make sure everyone was okay was less than ideal, but it's where we were. It felt like I only just shut my eyes before Alana was screaming to wake up and shaking me so hard I'm surprised I don't have a broken neck from that alone. Although, I don't blame her. Apparently they didn't get to see the candy canes' nifty tricks when they were stuck behind that invisible barrier and the first time seeing something like that, well, it's fucking terrifying.

"Pick up the pace!" I scream, looking back once more to where Deven was lagging behind the others but I see why. Chip. Shit.

I slow down, barely dodging out of the way from

a sharp cane right as Alana and Mollock run by. "I got them. You two go, it's right up ahead!" I don't wait for a response and we know the code. Do we leave anyone behind on our team, well, absolutely we do if we know they are a hundred percent gone, but in this case the canes may be terrifying but not something we can't survive, so I run back and pick up Chip as she yelps. It's so much harder to run and dodge out of the way of things that are trying to stab through my body, but I could see the change in the land ahead.

It's not how any of us wanted to be bolting into wolf territory, but we didn't have a choice. With the perpetual night, it was hard to tell how much time had passed and when we needed to get going. Back home we told the time from sun dials, and unless someone could crank a moon dial out of their ass, we would just have to micro sleep and not stay down in one place for too long.

Right as Deven, Chip and I cross into a new territory, the canes stop stabbing and go back to just menacingly pointed, death trees. I set Chip down and move to the front of the team; a hand lands on my shoulder and I look back to see Mollock's stern face. "Stick to the plan this time." He doesn't have to worry. I learned my lesson, but instead of smarting off I nod and get into hunter mode.

It is way too quiet here.

Just like the last territory, there's a path. This one is a hell of a lot easier to see as it's not littered with candy cane chips or chunks. Just a gray stone path leading us into a wooded area. I slow my breathing and concentrate, taking my time to look for any reflective eyes of the wolves that I was sure had to be watching us. Nothing. And if they were in their Fae form, I guess there wouldn't be any reflective lights from their eyes. Maybe that was a good thing and showed that talking would work.

"We wish to talk." Geez, that sounds stupid. There's a reason usually Mollock and Deven do the official delegation for our team. I have too much of a smart mouth and temper, and Alana makes everything into a joke to where the other party usually doesn't take her seriously. But I volunteered, since this is my field of expertise. We all respect when it is time to lead and when it is time to fall in line. This is my time. I just hope I don't fuck it up.

Nothing answers back but silence. "Let's take a closer look. Mollock and Alana, concentrate on our flanks and Deven the rear, just in case this is a surrounding tactic." And in which case we were royally fucked, but I don't say that part out loud.

We move as one unit, just like we did in the Bad Lands when it was time to hunt. I hold up a hand and we all pause as one. Even Chip. Looking around, I still don't see anything and we are almost to the tree line. Were they going to let us pass or was this a trick? A tactic maybe to catch us off our guard? "We talked with Ne- ." I pause to correct myself. "Your King. We don't want this to go the way it did in the first territory." I take another pause, making sure to look carefully around at our surroundings as I continue to talk in a slow, steady, yet stern voice to show no fear. "Come out and talk with us. We just want to pass through with no death to us, or to you."

Nothing again. Not even a damn breeze from the wind. This isn't right. Something is wrong or this is a trick. Their nature wouldn't allow them to be starved and let prey pass by them. They would act against that rational side. They were predators. Hunters. So no, I didn't believe for one second they were going to let us pass, unless they were all dead? Either way it's safe to say I'm confused as fuck, and that isn't good. I need to concentrate. I start to walk again, putting down my hand, and we continue on further into the wooded area that thickens as we travel further down the path, to the point the moons no longer lit our way and I pause again.

"Torches," I say in a low voice, still straining so hard just for a hint of anything that may come out at us, that my damn eyeballs feel like they may pop out. No whines come from Chip though and I know she's able to see and hear better than us, I'm not totally freaked. Having an early warning detection from her will help. Alana is preparing in the middle and Mollock has dropped back, side by side to Deven. Mollock facing out and forward while Deven facing out and to the back, leaving them to cover all our sides. We are so used to hunting together it's like a choreographed dance at this point. We know exactly *how* to move, and *when* to move, covering almost any of the situations that may arrive, which reminds me that I need to be looking up as well. Being in the woods gave our predators another advantage and us a disadvantage with tree limbs, but we have trained for that as well.

I don't even turn my head a single inch to the side when a torch is thrust into my peripheral and I take it. She will make one more for the rear and then we will move on. Other than the weird silence, chilly night air and the lack of audience, the only other thing that seems weird to me is the trees. They aren't normal. They are a lot bigger in size, huge trunks and the bark flips up and out in square chunks. I move my torch a little closer, doing another quick check and then look back at the bark. There are different color things poking out of the bark also and I had no idea what it meant, but the closer I got to it, the sweeter it smells, making my stomach grumble at the scent. It was almost mouth-watering and reminds me of the canes with a sugary scent but also like baked bread which makes no sense. I try to remember back when learning and studying for this but can't. Would this bark try to kill us like the Candy Cane? The thought puts a chill through me and I realize we've been in one spot too long. If these weird trees try to kill us, I wasn't sure how we'd fare being surrounded by them.

"Shit." I did a quick look back at Alana, who is

spinning in a circle.

"What is it?" I hiss, looking around frantically.

"My fucking pack is gone!" Mollock and Deven look around frantically as well. Theirs and mine are safe on our backs, but hers had no doubt been on the ground when she made up the torches.

"Fuck." We weren't alone after all and it seemed one, some or all were fucking with us in their Fae form. How the fuck did they get past Chip. My heart drops as my eyes slam to the ground and then I turn frantically, my heart shooting back up into my chest and my ears immediately buzzing. She's gone.

"CHIP!" I yell, not giving a fuck to be quiet.

"Fuck!" I hear Deven cuss and his knives slice out of his holsters with a sharp sling. "We need to move, Fellen."

I want to scream. I want to run ahead and then back, and sideways and all around. They took Chip. *How? Why?* He was right. Shaking my head, I nod. "Forward." And this time we are a hell of a lot faster. It was a tactic, a trick. Just like I feared and now they had our early warning system, my family, *my best friend*. They are playing a game with us, while at the same time showing us that they can kill us and have no intention of talking, but then why not just attack? Why drag it out?

We break into a clearing, the bright moon light shining down in one spot and it was less than ideal to bust out into it and be fully exposed, but either way we were probably surrounded as the clearing was in the shape of a circle with woods surrounding it. *Fuck*!

I tilt my chin back and talk to my team. If the wolves are here like I fear, with their hearing they'll catch what I'm saying anyway. "I'm going to try again, once we're out there." I don't have to wait for a response or see if they agree or disagree, I just have to let them know the plan. Either we stop and try to open up a dialogue to expose them, or make a break for it to the other side. Wolves love the hunt of the prey, so if we run that would just seal the deal of our asses being puppy chow.

I look all around and once were in the clearing, we all get to a better formation with our backs to each other, facing out. "You've made your point!" I yell out as nerves of fear for Chip enter my voice and I cuss internally trying to hold it back. The sound of a twig snapping grabs my attention, coming from straight in front of me. "If you're set on fighting, fine. We would rather not see blood shed, but you also threw the first stone by taking one of our team members. You can at least humor us and tell us why you don't want a temporary truce!"

I'm breathing heavily, more from being so pissed than anything now. I hate being ignored. I hate them being too chicken shit to show their faces and as I start to say that, a fully dressed male steps out—barefoot—into the clearing. From studying packs all my life, I knew this wasn't the Alpha as he was alone and not flanked by anyone. It isn't a good sign that they sent an Omega. It meant the Alpha did have us surrounded. He wasn't threatened by us and more than anything else, didn't feel like it was worth his time to open dialogue with us. In other words, a huge f-you to us. *Great.*

"I come with a message from our Alpha." The wolf continues forward in his Fae form. He is stacked with tanned muscles, which confuses me since it is always dark here. He wears a tight black shirt, low riding jeans and his blonde hair is long, hanging down around his shoulders. I bite my lips to keep from talking and taste blood when he smirks. "We will give you back what is yours and allow you through if you can show that we can trust you."

I open my mouth as I step forward, but he holds out his hand, signaling to me he isn't finished. "All the territories bore witness to you going back on your word and watched as Adrian's body was on that pyre. His wives, friends and our King crying in silence over their dead brother, husband and friend. So you prove you can be trusted and we will allow you to pass."

"What would we have to do?" I ask, looking around to make sure this isn't a tactic to get us into place for a thousand wolves to lunge and eat our asses. Although if that was the case, we wouldn't be able to do anything about it anyway, but still. Dying fighting is better than dying without ever seeing it coming.

He thrusts his hand out. "Eat the bark on our sacred

fruit bread." I hold back a giggle trying to make its way out, mainly because I'm pissed at the fuckers for taking Chip but also something called fruit bread is way tacky. And it isn't just fruit bread, but *sacred fucking fruit bread.*

I sigh. "That's it? Just eat the bread and then you'll give Chip, our bag back and let us walk through here unscathed on orders of your Alpha?"

I don't miss how evil his smile looks but ignore it. "Fine, I'll eat the bread."

He shakes his head. "You all have to eat it to be trusted."

"And how can we trust you? How do we know that it isn't poison or that it won't kill us the moment we touch it?" I fire back. It felt like a game.

He starts to walk away but he stops right next to a tree and breaks off a piece of the fruit bread before holding it up in plain view for us to see before eating it. *Hmm.* "See. Harmless. Sacred. And a way you can trust us. I'll even give you some pieces from the same loaf." He precedes to break four pieces off from the same bread he ate from, before heading our way.

"Are you sure about this, Fell?" Alana whispers. I look back at her and the unease in her stare is what I feel in my gut. I want to scream fuck no, but...

"What choice do we have?" I ask her.

"So are you ready?" The wolf is now right in front of me and I look back to my team and after a couple of awkward looks around, they all nod.

I hold out my hand and right as the bread touches my hand I quickly bite into it, waiting and willing to be the tester of this just in case it is a trick. The taste is foreign, just like I expect but also very good. In a weird way. It's sweet just like I thought it would be based on the smell, but unlike other bread that was light and fluffy, this was chewy with weird chewy bits in it. Altogether it left an extremely bad taste in my mouth. Instead of taking off my pack to grab some water like my mouth was begging me to, I stare intently at the wolf in front of me, who gives me a blank expression in response.

"See? It's fine." He says with a shrug.

Okaaay, that was the weirdest test I've had to partake in, but whatever. I look back to Alana, Mollock and Deven. "Go ahead. I mean, I haven't dropped dead yet." I state.

Deven lifts an eyebrow. "Probably because it hasn't hit your lower intestine yet." Alana snorts out a laugh and I roll my eyes.

"Whatever, just eat the crap so we can go." A growl breaks my attention from Alana cringing while chewing her bread, to back at the wolf. "I mean the sacred bread," I correct, and he stops growling. I almost laugh but don't, not wanting to screw up this weird alliance because I made fun of fruit bread that grew from a tree.

Once my team is done eating and the wolf irritatingly checks to make sure we swallow like children, he continues on. "Now we can trust you. You may proceed through the territory." He signals to the way out and I spot the gray stone path starting up again at the other side of this weird flowered clearing.

"What about our dog and pack?" I ask, not budging.

He smiles and it looks friendly enough. "They will be waiting for you at the end of the path at the start of the next territory." Then he turns to leave.

"Wait." I step forward. "Why would you put them there? How did you know that we would eat the bread?"

He only turns around halfway giving me a smirk. "One should always expect to trust first and only doubt someone second." Then he continues on, disappearing into the woods.

Alana steps beside me taking a huge drink of water and I take mine out as well. "That doesn't seem like a very wolfy saying."

"It doesn't," Deven concurs as I take my own drink and think on it as well. It didn't. Wolves were protective, but also paranoid as shit by nature. Never immediately trusting, but if he or they really didn't think that way, they would have attacked instead of making us do a trust test first.

I sigh, enjoying the fresh taste of water clearing away that nasty taste. Although some of it still lingered in my mouth, at least it wasn't as bad as it was after first eating. "Maybe they are peaceful wolves." I guess, making

Mollock snort and the others laugh. Yeah, even saying the words didn't feel right. "Whatever, let's just go and get Chip and Alana's bag before they change their mind."

The gurgling of my stomach has us all stalling but I don't feel any pain with it, although I do temporarily start to think the worst, but it passes. "Ugh." We all let out a nervous laugh. "Hopefully that was just because I'm hungry."

"Hopefully. Let's push on," Mollock states and we move again as one, stepping onto the path and once again are secluded in darkness which is fine since we still have our torches.

Just like the last path, it's quiet. This one, however, has a thick fog that reaches our ankles. Still creepy as hell and we are all on our guard, but nothing is jumping out at us as suspicious. It would normally raise my hackles more, but a tiny part of me hopes that maybe the wolves really are serious about the damn tree bread and *did* plan to let us pass. Another more reasonable and pessimistic part of myself expected a pack of wolves to jump out at us any second.

Almost as if I conjured it, a white blur of a wolf runs in front of us across the path before disappearing again and I falter but only for a second before raising my weapon. "Shit," I cuss. Wolves were organized and obedient, not sloppy. If their Alpha had told them to stand down they would have. I doubt that meant fucking with us, but who knew. This also seems to be a new brand of wolf that would offer peace with bread. A howl sounds and I turn my head toward the sound so fast I get a temporary wave of dizziness but can't see anything.

"I think we're being messed with again," I state.

"I think so too. I think they were just fucking with us about the bread," Deven says from the rear.

"Let's go." We start walking again right as another wave of dizziness hits me. I stop. That isn'tt right. I was never randomly dizzy. Another wolf howls and this time I feel more than dizzy but like I rolled down a hill for five hours. "What the?" I grab my head to try and steady myself as I blink away the weird feeling along with my vision now deciding to cross. Shit.

"Ugh. I feel weird." I hear Alana say and look back to see her in the same state.

"The bread," I slur, right as Mollock nods, not looking a bit affected although with his size it probably hasn't hit him yet. "Or the fog." He adds. Damn it, he was right.

"This isn't good. How are you feeling?" Mollock asks Deven, and he reports that he's fine as I now resort to leaning against him alongside Alana to hold myself up. It felt like I took a whole bottle of alcohol and downed it in one go. "We need to get them out of here."

He no sooner gets the words out and two huge wolves, one white and one gray, step out in front of us snarling, with bared fangs. "*Shit,*" I slur and try to stand up straighter to defend myself, but it's no use. I had to lean on my weapon for support. I should be freaking out right now, but all I can do is concentrate on trying to breathe and blink. Looking over to the trees, the weird colors that were in the bread are now shining like a thousand colorful fires. It makes me laugh.

A wolf flies in front of me, its neck slit as it hits the same tree with the tiny color fires and slides down dead. It makes me laugh more and soon I'm wiping tears from my eyes. I feel like I'm floating on a cloud of ecstasy. Everything feels perfect and amazing. I reach forward to touch the dead wolf wondering why it didn't turn into its Fae form.

"SNAP OUT OF IT, GIRLS!" I hear Mollock yell and I try to turn his way to explain I just need to lay down, when water splashes in my face. I gasp and the dizziness starts to pull away. I shake my head and grip my weapon tight, turning just in time to catch an incoming wolf. I slit its throat, not all the way, and it still bares its teeth and lunges, but Deven steps in front me, driving a small knife into the back left shoulder. With one last roar, the brown wolf falls to the ground before transforming into a female with long brown hair.

She isn't dead. I know because she lays on the ground whimpering. Deven stumbles back into me and whatever has hit Alana and me has hit him and we stumble to the ground in front of the whimpering wolf in a fit of giggles.

I grab one of his knives from his waist and hold it to the whimpering girl's throat.

I look around and there are no more wolves, but that didn't mean they weren't going to send more. We were pretty much done for, but instead of killing the female wolf, we would just take her with us. "IF YOU'RE LISTENING WOLF ASSHOLES!" I slur out in a yell the best I can manage and hear Alana and Deven laugh. "WE WON'T KILL HER IF YOU LET US PASS!" I press the knife further into her neck, making a thin line of blood trail down her naked chest.

"Instead we should have a little fun with her first," Deven says, starting to crawl toward her. The girl swipes out, transforming her hand into sharp claws, aiming for his neck. It only makes us laugh more with fits of *ooooo*.

Mollock falls down next to us. "Let's go back to the clearing," he says, and it sounds like a good idea. I nod and then we are getting up and heading back to the clearing with lots of stumbling and giggling. Along the way the trees sway and blink different colors that float up into the air that I try to catch to ride upon. Is that what Neek feels like when he's a blue smoke floating in the air? The idea pushes more giggles out and then I'm being handed a knife and in front of the female wolf not knowing how I got there.

"Her arms first," Alana says, licking some blood off the female's chest before moaning. I'm confused about what she means.

"Huh?" I stumble back and realize a slapping sound. I focus out and see Deven behind the girl grunting, biting her neck. *What the?* The female wolf is crying and cringing and I realize what he's doing and only the fleeting thought of horror passes me, but it's too quick to hold onto and then Alana is slicing the knife across the female's front shoulder and down to her armpit. This wakes the wolf up fully and she starts to howl before Mollock steps in front of her and punches her jaw so hard it almost looks like it's hanging.

I shake my head, confused by this. None of it seems real. We don't torture and rape. I must be asleep. I turn back to the colors and before I can stop myself my eyes are shutting and I'm falling onto the colorful and swirling ground beneath me.

NEEK

"This won't work. As much as I miss her–." A pregnant pause fills the air and we all feel more than a little uncomfortable by it. "We are all her blood mates. Between us and the damn Fae seal, nothing keeps her from raging and losing control," Braken says, running a hand down his face.

I pull in my temper, barely. "It doesn't matter, we have to try." When I get zero looks of confidence, I try a different route. "This may be the only chance we have at breaking whatever crazy ass spell this land has over her, and getting her out of here alive. Back to a normal life. Do you really think the Fae King and Queen are going to let this go on forever or do you think that eventually they'll just get sick of it and end us? Because I believe us dying is how this really ends."

That does seem to pull some sway and Savannah's harem looks around to each other in what looks like a silent conversation. Maybe it is. I didn't think vampires could do that, but I'm learning after seeing Fellen, a human, be able to see the tether bond of us, that maybe I don't know as much as I thought I did. We are all standing around in her territory where their coffins are. Dagger and I woke the rest of them to try and come up with a plan, but so far every plan we've offered up to try and get Savannah to calm down or at least be able to hold her back, hasn't been agreed upon. The closer Fellen and her team get to this territory, the louder and more ferrous her screams and raging growls get. I know because yesterday it was her normal insanity screams, today it sounds like someone is pushing a hot branding iron into her every five seconds.

"Is there any Fae left at your castle we can bring for her?" Dagger asks.

I shake my head. "No, but that would have been a

good idea. Although even when she's blown through a couple of humans, it still hasn't touched her blood lust. It's likely she'll go through a whole castle full of people before she starts to calm down."

We sit in silence for a while before another one of her harem members, Quinton, speaks up. "How do we even know that her chains will break?"

"It's not about that. We know they will. Go down and see for yourself. They are half way out of the wall now," Dagger answers.

"Can you drink her down?" I ask the room. Drinking down is technically what vampires do before they turn someone. They drink until they die with little to no blood left. Then they are revived, before being forced to drink a vampire's blood. Which forces the change. "We can't die so there's no fear of that, but if she doesn't have blood she won't be able to move much."

"We could try, but the blood bond we have with her means she can control us with just a thought," Dagger says.

"Not that she's ever abused it before," Braken states, running a hand through his cropped brown hair.

I stand, running out of patience. "I'm not sure what to do, but you're her blood mates'. If anyone can figure out how to subdue or control her, it's you. I don't care what you have to do, but get it done." I turn to leave but pause at the threshold to give them something to think about.

"This is the last and only chance we have at freedom. I only have one soulmate and she's here now. It's now or never."

Right as I walk out into the sugary snow, swirling around me on the ground, the flash of bright red colors catch my attention and my jinn responds without thought as I turn into my smoke form and head to wolf territory. Dealing with the vampires has put Fellen temporarily out of my head and that isn't good. Aspen was a wild card and I hated not knowing what the hell was happening with her safety while trying to figure out the Savannah situation.

I immediately knew something is off as soon as I flew over the area.

The wolves are all congested to one side surrounding Aspen, holding a pack meeting and the colors flare from across the territory. That didn't seem right. It looks as if he is letting her pass, but then why is she scared? Nightmare? I fly over until I reach right where her emotions of fear slam into me. The taste is so potent, I can only siphon a little before I feel sick. I wasn't prepared for what I saw.

Tory is dead.

Or close to it.

Her arms are torn off of her and she lays bloody face up with her jaw broken almost clean off. Bloody hand prints cover her where her own blood isn't pouring out and around her. She's tied to a tree with vines around her neck that at some point must have cut into it, because blood is thick around the vines too. I gasp at the inhumanity of it and look around to where Fellen and her team are passed clean out and open to attack. What the hell happened?

I don't wait to see any more of the horror and head into her dream, or nightmare from the looks and feel of her fear. Just like her body was screaming to tell someone, it replays everything for me like it knew I was coming. The horror of what I see almost makes me throw up. They were drugged and tricked by the wolves. The drugs fucked them up. *Bad*. But torture and rape, drinking Tory's blood, fuck. And they called us monsters. I watch Fellen in the dream cry and scream for Chip over and over again. I fly over, making her aware of my presence.

She blinks up, confused. "I don't understand," she says through hiccups and fuck, I've never seen anything other than pure fire in her and she looks totally broken right now.

"Fellen." I pause and crouch down to her, putting a hand on her tear soaked cheek. "You have to wake up, you're dreaming and vulnerable."

She frowns before looking around. "This isn't real?"

I clench my jaw. "This, here isn't. But–."

She catches my hesitation and stands, questions beaming in her eyes. "But?"

"You just need to wake up. You were drugged. You're lying in wolf territory and killed multiple of them."

She still doesn't look like she's in a hurry to move and keeps looking like a lost puppy. I grip her shoulders and shake her lightly. "You have to snap out of this or you will die. I can't believe what I saw you guys do but...it's done now."

"What we did?"

Fuck, she is out of it. "It doesn't matter." I pull her forward and plant a kiss right on her lips, sucking in the amazing lust it spikes in the air. "I'm pushing you awake and then you and your team need to run. At this rate–." I pause, not wanting the words to pass my lips, but needing her to understand the severity of what they did. "I don't even know if you'll make it out alive now."

The pack was fair. Most of the time. It went back and forth. Intruders in their land, meant fair game to kill or claim, but at the same time they attacked humans and the wolves believe if you were killed provoking and attacking first that is fair. But torture. Torture they won't forgive. I give her shoulders one last squeeze for good measure and push the dream to end, waking her before exiting it myself and flying to where I saw Aspen and his pack.

This outcome was bad, and could very well fuck up any alliance I have with him in the future, seeing as Tory was his and Rune's daughter. One of them, anyway. And she is dead, not yet but close to it. I cuss myself for not finishing the job just to end the suffering I could smell curled in the air, but at the same time I remember holding her when she was born and that would break my fucking heart. "SHHHITTTTTTTT!" I roar out to the sky as I fly that way, wanting this just to be over with.

I show up and walk through the crowd of the pack that has formed with in-fighting, members separated into two groups that yell and scream in between the ones shouting demands at the Alpha and I have never, in my entire existence, seen Aspen let this kind of chaos form in his pack. There was a reason why he was the king of all the wolves and it had a lot to do with his discipline and strength. It didn't take long to figure out what was going on. Half the pack wanted to slaughter Fellen and her team and the other half wanted to let them pass. All upset and angry to sit idly by while the Alpha's daughter was tortured to death, her last pleas and thoughts blaring in their mind.

I continue forward, catching Aspen's eye and know that he's not only in shock. He is stoic. It's the calm before the storm, and one I've only ever seen on him right before he took over a rival Wolf Kingdom and claimed Rune for his bride. It doesn't matter what the crowd is shouting at each other and him. Rune on the other hand, who had to prove her strength right along with Aspen's to prove she could lead along with her husband, is showing anything but strength and I don't blame her. I don't think any of the pack does either.

"We can get our revenge on all the humans once

we're free!" An Omega, Alex, shouts from the back before someone else, I don't know their name, shouts even lounder. "FUCK THAT, KILL THEM NOW!"

Hysterics start to break out again.

"AND BE TRAPPED HERE?" A woman cries out, holding a newborn to her chest.

Aspen needs to calm this and I'm not sure why he hasn't, but I approach him and Rune, all the same not surprised one bit when I feel the crack of her hand slap across my face. "How dare you show your face to us!" She growls. It doesn't matter that she looks like a twenty five year old from her immortal beauty, I still feel like a child from her tone.

"Did you plan to drug them?"

Aspen shakes his head. "Once the inner thoughts floated through the pack that Tory planned this, it was too late."

I want to ask why he didn't rush forward and kill them all right then, but from the chaos behind me I now know why. The pack was split and inner fighting wasn't allowed, yet here it was, and the pack made decisions together. Tory broke that rule and she paid the price. "And your decision?" I ask him, even though I should be talking to him and his wife as they are both notoriously known through history to only make decisions together. She's in too much of an upset, even now, she quietly sobs next to him.

The crowd quiets for the first time since my arrival when Aspen stands and steps close to me. It's a show of force. An Alpha thing. I don't back down though. I didn't need his fake show to know who was really in charge. "What if my answer was to kill you?" He threatens and his pack responds with tempered growls like he pushed a button.

"Do it!" The crowd yells, agreeing with *"it's his fault"* and *"end him."* I let it go on a couple seconds more but when a young wolf transitions and goes to bite me I snap my fingers and they all fall unconscious. Damn, I wish I could do that for Fellen and her team, but the land only allows me to be King to the residents, and only when it abides by the rules. No harm comes to the King. I smile as Aspen steps back with a sigh and looks at his unconscious wife, before turning to me again.

"Don't forget your place, King of Wolves," I growl, flexing my hands at my side as blue flames circle my arms.

"War." He sits back down on his throne of sticks and leaves and runs a hand slowly down Rune's face before looking back up at me. "We'll let you pass because once we are free, you've now declared war against the whole wolf nation, and one jinn with a pack of humans, against millions of wolves..." He looks up as his eyes transition to his orage wolf ones, with a burning glow. "I like those odds," he growls. I don't wait to hear any more before transitioning into smoke and flying away. Fellen and her team got their pass through this territory, but I may have fucked their future.

At least they were safe, for now.

CHAPTER EIGHT
THE ALPHA

I'm jolted awake and only have a second to roll over on my side before the contents of my stomach spew out on the ground next to me. Dizziness hits hard and I grab my head. "Ugh." I can't remember the last time was this hungover. A howl sails through the air behind me and I'm snapped to reality. Holy fuck! My eyes fully open as I take in my surroundings. A girl is tied to a tree, no arms, blood everywhere and dead. I stand shakily and turn around. Mollack, Deven and Alana are all naked and laying in a heap using a dead wolf as a pillow. *What. In The. Actual. Fuck.*

A shiver races through me as my body and mind try to wake up, more howls sound closer this time, and realize it's freezing. Not just chilly. I can see my breath and I can barely feel my hands. This isn't good. I race over and shake my team awake who are in the same state as me. Completely hung over and that's when the flood of memories about what happened races back to me. I almost puke again, remembering how Deven raped that female wolf while Alana cut her arms from her body and drank her blood. Shit. I lean over and dry heave, *hard*. There's nothing left to throw up, but apparently my body didn't get the memo and is trying anyway to dispel the disgust I feel.

The wolves are closing in and there's not a lot of time. After what we did, and remembering a little about the dream with Neek now that I've woken up a bit, them attacking to get revenge makes sense. "Get up now!" I scream, and ignore that I sound like a dying cow. We need to move! The temperature feels like it's dropping even more since waking up and is getting to a dangerous level that we hadn't predicted. Deven is still retching, but the others are ready. I wait a couple more seconds but when I hear the leaves shuffle in the wooded area to my right, I take off. Kill or be killed. "DEVEN, NOW!" I yell back as I fly down the path.

Right as we enter into the darker part of the path under the canopy of trees I cuss, realizing we didn't ready torches to light our way, but it doesn't matter. The path is hard to see but not invisible, so we push on the best we can and it's not long before I see another clearing coming into view and I hope like hell that it's the end of this territory. From the growls we are hearing and the shining eyes that surround us as we run, I take it they are holding back, but not for long. I look back and see that Deven made it ,but wolves follow close behind. Either we will run right into the other territory or we won't make it. No human can outrun a wolf.

Another couple feet and we will be out of the dark. Almost there. My heart is pounding and my breathing heavy. I'm in great shape, but after getting drugged, I'm not in the best state today. "ALMOST THERE!" Right as my foot crosses into the lit area and I get a glimpse of the next territory, a tall, white haired, young male steps in my way and I skid to a stop biting in the scream from surprise.

"Not quite," he says. I don't have to guess. He's the Alpha. I can tell as he's flanked on either side of him by two giant white wolves. My team catches up and stops as well before coming to stand next to me in a straight line as wolves snap, snarl and growl behind us. There is something so strikingly familiar about him I can't tear my eyes from him. I continue to stare at him, as the nagging feeling continues to taunt me. Right when I think I have it, to where his similarity comes from is gone as fast as it came. I shake my head and forget it, or try to; it seems like he almost recognizes me as well. I would be stupid if I said I wasn't scared but also from the demeanor, I wasn't getting the vibe that we were going to die. Not yet, anyway. My mouth opens to ask for passage through when a thud catches my attention and instead of shutting my mouth I let out a heartbreaking scream from what landed in front of us.

Chip is dead.

I temporarily forget the hunter's code to push all emotions aside in the face of danger. I can't push these ones away as they flow out of me in automatic screams and tears. I try to run to her, but more wolves step in front of me as my team holds me back. I hear the shock from them as well as I fall hard to my knees on the ground. I should have known. I was stupid to think that Chip would be here waiting at the end of the path like they said. Especially after what happened with the wolf we tortured. We killed Chip ourselves. My sweet best friend and heart lies there completely destroyed, and it doesn't take a genius to see they made her hurt, as she's almost torn in half. It looks like they fought her in wolf form. There's barely anything left. I must have lost my mind because I forget that I'm standing before an Alpha, or maybe he did this on purpose to get me on my knees in front of him. Either way, he's got his revenge.

Why didn't I keep her home?

"Enough!" He yells, and motions for me stand. I cast a glare his way, feeling the heated hatred start to build and burn through my veins. Alana comes over and helps me stand and I thank her for it before looking one last time to Chip and then back at the motherfucker who ended her life.

"What do you want?" I ask in a low tone full of venom.

I wish it could kill him. All of them.

I get growls in return and two more white wolves come from behind him and stand to either side of him, widening their line and growling their response of how I talked out of turn. I don't give a flying fuck. Alpha or not, I wasn't a wolf, so those bullshit rules don't apply to me or my team. *"I said...What. Do. You. Want?"* I take my time and enunciate each word with pure hatred.

Instead of pissing him off like I thought it would, he does the last thing I would have expected and throws his head back and laughs loudly. I look over at Deven, who seems just as confused but doesn't show it, just tilts his head to the side with a clenched jaw before facing back to the Alpha. "Has your soulmate told you the consequences of your actions?" His laughter dies just as fast as it started and it almost gives me whiplash, but I'm so pissed that his back and forth attitude doesn't affect me like he was probably hoping it would. It's also not lost on me how he spits out soulmate like it was venom on his tongue. If I had to guess, he wasn't the biggest fan of his King.

When I give no answer he continues. Really, I just want him to get on with it and make his move. Either he was going to attack or let us by. There was no point in us sitting around and talking about what happened to his wolf and my dog. It's done. "You and your team just brought war upon yourselves and the rest of your race as soon as we are free from this land." He pauses, stepping forward. "So count your days, Fellen, because they are surely numbered."

He means to intimidate me by using my name and threatening big things like war, but I've been at war my entire life. Another day. Another supernatural asshole, so he wasn't any more special then the rest. "*If* we make it through."

He crosses his arms again, looking me up and down with disgust in his stare. "If, correct."

Silence falls over us and I take a deep breath from screaming at him to just get the fuck on with it. "Is there a point to why you're blocking our way if you're going to let us pass?"

"It is curious." I raise an eyebrow at him. "How Neek's mate, or soulmate, as the Jinn call it, would be a human." He walks forward, thrusting out his arm to tell his other pack members to stay behind when they go to follow. I grip my weapon tighter and place it at an angle, easier to cut his head off if need be, but he stops a couple feet away, seeming to study me intently. "Unless you're not human. That would explain a lot," he concludes, with questions in his voice.

I laugh, unable to help it. "Trust me. I'm human."

Now it's his turn to raise an eyebrow and I held in a growl. "Let us pass."

"I have been alive a very long time and have never, ever, in all this time seen a human with a jinn." He goes on ignoring me. Alana and Deven who stand on either side of me are getting just as impatient as I am. Deven's jaw is clenched so hard, I'm surprised I don't see his teeth falling from his mouth and Alana keeps shifting her weight from side to side. At this point we had a beloved family pet die, drugged, all of our supplies to try and nurse or replenish ourselves taken. No doubt they were thinking the same thing I was…without all the stuff we need, how long would we really last running on empty?

"Regardless of what you have or haven't seen, I've seen the soulmate tether with my own eyes, and it is true. So, if you're standing in our way doubting if I can actually save you all or not, don't. However, the longer we stand here feeling the side effects of being drugged without our supplies to survive, that's a whole other issue, isn't it?" I hold back from spitting at his feet in pure rage, but I manage, barely.

He steps closer and my team starts to raise their weapons but just like he did with his own pack, I also signal for them to stand down. They had us surrounded. If they wanted to kill us, they would have by now. Although that still may be the case if we piss them off. We have to tread lightly. "You say you've seen the soulmate tether, but yet are still claiming to be human. I'm curious. Now that you're standing in front of me is there anything else you've seen?" He takes a deep inhale of breath, sniffing the air around me like he can just sniff out that I'm something other than a human. I don't answer his question because I don't know what his aim is. I'm starting to wonder again for what feels like the hundredth time since we came to the wolf territory if we're being messed with. "Has Neek let you in on how you actually save us all? Or do you think you're just going to make it through the land and-." He motions his hands out in an explosion. "Poof. We are all free, along with your precious human race back in the Bad Lands and we all live happily ever after?"

I roll over the fact that he was right. Neek hadn't gotten to that mysterious part of how exactly I was going to save them all by surviving the land and being his soulmate, but I don't let him know that. "It's none of your business," I say in a low voice.

"Oh, ho, ho!" He laughs out and gets in my personal space. I stand tall and don't let it affect me. Not like he thinks it will. "Such a brave little thing. You remind me of someone I used to know." He raises his hand like he means to grab my chin, but I move it to the side before he can.

"Grab my chin and you may have your war with us earlier than you planned on."

"Funny how you see an Alpha in front of you, knowing any second I could rip your throat out, but you keep pushing me." He grabs my chin harshly before I can stop him a second time and forces me to look at him, while my staffed weapon now presses up against his neck. He doesn't even flinch, but neither do I. Right when he opens his mouth to say something, or threaten me more, he flinches. He throws his head back and drops his hand suddenly before stepping back in fear. I don't move a muscle, more confused than anything, but don't let him know it. He stares for only a second more before turning his back to us and walking back to where he came, letting out a whistle. "Let's go. Pass along, little *humans,* before I change my mind."

And then we are left standing there.

"What was that all about?" Alana cautiously asks, coming around and looking into my face like she'll see whatever no doubt the Alpha saw.

I shrug. "I'm not sure." And then look at Chip and then see upon further look our packs were there on the ground next to her. I swallow hard and move toward her as a sob I didn't plan works its way up and out of my mouth that I have no time to cover. I stave it quickly though, kneeling down beside her and petting her one last time. Reflective lights of the pack's eyes still shine bright from the treeline and it tells me we really didn't have a lot of time here. We wouldn't be able to bury her, burn her body, nothing. No send off. I hate this fucking code. I lean down and gently kiss the top of her head before leaning forward and undoing her bloody collar. "I love you so much, and I'm so sorry." I take another second to gather myself and head for the packs, or what was left of them, as I hear the others saying their goodbye to Chip as well.

I knew there was a chance it could end like this for her, especially her coming here right after being injured, but I really didn't think it would be in this way. Not so brutally done and after being taken. I can't help but wonder if she would still be alive if we hadn't killed that female wolf, but questioning the past won't change the future. "Let's go. Mollock, you lead us."

We get in somewhat of a shaky formation and continue on the path, crossing the invisible threshold out of wolf territory and into the witch's.

The freezing air suddenly changes to a damp, warm and stale atmosphere. It reminded me of right after it rained on a humid day with no wind. Fog is thick around our feet, but the open atmosphere ahead of us allows the two moons' lights to shine down and illuminate our next challenge. Which is a house. Mansion even. It's huge with brown brick work and fancy windows. It looks haunted, or maybe just feels that way from the atmosphere around us and the fact there is no light shining from any windows. The path leads straight to the door and on either side of the witch's house is a concrete wall that is too tall to climb and shows no way around. It leaves us with only one choice. Apparently we were going to the damn house. Great. And super not ideal. Tight spaces, witch magic and spots for them to hide themselves or any of their damn hex bags is super bad.

Mollock is thinking the same thing as he addresses us. "I have my tattoo for protection, but you guys don't." He turns his backpack around to his front and digs in it for a bit before pulling out his own homemade hex bags for protection. No, he doesn't practice magic, but he is the best witch hunter around and sometimes you have to fight fire with fire. On a hunt in the Bad Lands, we had captured a group of witches and put in months of questioning, but this was the result. Protection bags that would prevent magic getting casted on us. "Tie these around your waists, on your belts, and make sure they're secure."

We get to work on the task as he continues on. "Grab some water and eat real quick while I get a plan together." He looks back at the house and then back to us. "I don't see them coming out of that house to jack with us, so that gives us a little time to get our shit together. They have us in a bad spot, most likely leading us straight into a trap. I know with the wolves it was different, but I think I should challenge the leader."

Alana bites her bottom lip hard and I can tell she's holding back her protests. He looks over and smirks at her. "It will be fine, baby, I got this. You know I do." He leans over and gives her a kiss on the cheek.

"I agree on the challenge," Deven says, at the same time I agree with it, also. Mollock was a badass witch killer and I had no doubts he could get us in and out the fastest and the safest but..

"On the off chance that doesn't work?" I ask.

"Why wouldn't it?" he counters.

I shake my head and sigh. "Devil's advocate. We always have a backup plan."

He sighs now too and, on looking closer, I see the exhaustion in his gaze. It sucked that we were still recovering from the damn drugged bread. I finish some of my jerky and grab a quick drink, waiting for his direction and see the others finishing some as well. A tiny piece of dried meat and water is way less than we need to get our energy back, but we are in enemy territory. While the witches may not be coming out, I don't think any of us like standing here out in the open to possibly test that theory.

"Then we do like we always have when we hit a house. Keep together. Do not get separated under any circumstances, shout if you do. We move fast and we hit hard. We don't want to be trapped in a room with any spells or hex bags." He looks down and lifts Alana's salt bag off her hip. "While these may work against some magic, there is no way we can tell if it will work for *all* magic, so it's best not to test that theory. If we can't challenge the leader, there is no shame in us running through and slicing those bitches up on the way. Got it?"

We all nod. "Got it."

"Let's go kill some hags."

CHAPTER NINE
THE MANSION

Mollock opens the door hard enough that it bangs back against the interior wall, making me flinch as I continue to look around at our surroundings. I hate, absolutely hate hunting witches for this very reason. They're never the ones to rush out and kill humans openly in the Bad Lands. Nope, they're the ones that would do sneak attacks to our villages with magic and hex bags and then we would have to hunt them out in their creepy little houses, much like this one but way smaller.

It's the same every time.

Magic that created confusing rooms, hallways and tricks at every turn to try and confuse you and get you trapped into one of their casting circles. And every freaking time we hunted them, something bad happened. None of us came out unscathed, making this a lot more nerve wracking being as this is the biggest witch house I'd ever seen.

"Coven leader, I challenge you to pass this territory." Mollock wastes no time and challenges the leader before we even make it through the door. That's fine by me, but also I think he planned it that way in case we couldn't enter upon getting challenged. Kind of like how they were stuck behind a wall. Dead silence answers him and I keep watch of our backs, panning around to see the team looking around in confusion also.

Nothing is happening.

Mollock cusses before grabbing a gun from his holster. "Fuck. Okay, time for plan B. Run through and don't get separated. You know the plan." And then he is moving and we are following in a straight line as Mollock, then Alana and soon Deven in front of me disappear into the pitch blackness of the inside. Right as I get through the door, it slams shut behind me, making me jump once more and then a wicked female laugh that coats my bones in ice shrills out around us. I reach forward, barely making out Deven's outline and right when I start to suggest some light, candles flame to life around us that sit on high top tables off to the sides of the entryway we are in.

"Welcome, humans." We continue to make our way slowly, heading to the left and down the only available turn of the hall, which brings us into a living room of sorts. Everything is fancier than I've ever seen before in my life. Well, other than old magazines and books. It has high class furniture, an unlit fireplace and a black crystal chandelier. We continue to file into the room as I watch our backs, and stop in a line to face the source of the voice. A tall, blonde haired female witch stands ahead of us on the top stair of a huge open staircase. She is dressed in a black, sparkly evening gown and even from where I stand, she has the brightest green eyes I've ever seen. I swear they almost glow. I can also tell from here that her fingernails are pitch black from how long they are.

"Go ahead and speak anything you'd like. This spell–." She brings up her hands in the air and looks around at the supposed spell she refers to. "Keeps us and the land from hearing any of your supposed challenges. *See*, we may not be as physically strong as you bone-headed hunters, but we make up for what we lack, in intelligence."

I can't hold in the scoffed laugh as it blows past my lips and while the evil bitch hisses like a snake, Alana starts laughing also. "Yeah, *okay lady*. So then why did you get mad just now." I look over to see Deven's pissed stare then back to Alana's smiling expression. "She can totally hear us," I surmise, getting another hiss.

I want to tell her to get on with it, but that's Mollock's job as the leader to get us through this territory, so I shove down the smart ass comments when she continues her little speech meant to intimidate us. "You won't be able to make it through this house and our magic." Now more of her Coven steps out from the shadows, standing behind her and again they all are dressed in weird ass evening dresses. It's tacky and I don't know if they were going for a weird power play using their blinding beauty, insert huge sarcasm here, but it only made it harder for me to hold back my laughs. "We've created an impenetrable fortress that not even your soulmate King can break through."

"And you would rather be stuck in here for the rest of your miserable immortal lives, than back to whatever hole you crawled out of and back to freedom?" Mollock asks, crossing his arms and widening his stance.

"Freedom?" She laughs now. "You really think Fellen and your team are going to make it past Frost or even the King himself? I mean, it took every single one of us supernaturals here to band together and lock her away. The closer you get to her lair, the more and more she goes insane with blood lust. If it took all, *and I mean all of our strengths to contain her*, what makes you think that humans with no supernatural strength will be able to make it through her territory or even challenge her?"

All good points, and now we know she's a vampire, so there's that. "So then why can't you use your little magic spell and contain this Frost and the King in the same manner you've done here so we *can* make it through without problems?" Mollock for the win, and another good point.

One that the apparent geniuses didn't think of, because she lifts her chin while subtly glancing at a short, cropped brown haired female off to her left who wears a red satin dress. "We don't have to answer what we do or don't do to a mere mortal. What we can do, however, is offer some..." She pauses and taps her black fingernail of her index finger on her bottom lip in thought. "Courtesy," she finishes, putting on a blinding smile. "You can choose to accept your surrender and we won't put you through the countless tortures that make up our home, we will even make your deaths quick. Or–."

Before she can continue Mollock interrupts. "We chose the second. We don't surrender to any supernaturals. Especially ones that use magic to cover their warts and bald patches."

Ooo. We were probably dead meat now, but it's still more funny than anything and I bite my lip to keep in the giggle trying to escape.

"You little ungrateful cretins!" She shrieks, and the glow in her eyes gets brighter. I raise my staff now, preparing for whatever they plan to send our way. Hopefully they just try to rush us and all break their necks falling down the stairs in a heap and take each other out. Sigh. One can hope. Instead they step back into the shadows from where they appeared. "Good luck surviving us now!" Her warning comes before a phantom wind blows towards us and all the lit candles go out.

"Shit." Deven cusses and I hear one of us digging in our bags. Hopefully it's Alana, since she makes and lights torches made from strips of material faster than anyone I know.

"Yup," I agree as we stand there in the awkward darkness. I wish I could at least look around to see where they may come from, but witches usually don't get hands on when it comes to their fights. They're cowards like that. They were probably off creating traps and the sneaky shit they liked to do. Which only served to piss us off more and encouraged that we made their deaths more brutal in the end. Oh well. Their funerals.

The sound of a snap and then a flicker of light illuminated our faces and Alana moved to make the next one, handing Mollock supplies to make his own while I tried my best with the touch I was handed to check our surroundings, but nothing other than pitch blackness surrounded us. It was definitely supernatural. Probably one of their damn spells. A tingling sensation brushed across my right hip where my protection bag is and I thrust my hand down over it, feeling emptiness. "SHIT!" I twirl with the torch and even walk a few steps away. "They took my damn bag!" I turn around as the others discover the same.

"Shit, a couple torches will have to do. Let's go." Mollock said, putting his non-lit one and the supplies back in his pack and heading off for the stairs. Upon observation when the area was lit, there was no way out or around going up them.

"What do we do about the bags?" Alana whispers, as

we make our way up the stairs.

"We have a couple more tricks up our sleeves," Mollock states, not bothering to turn around as he uses his torch side to side trying to see better as he breaches the top of the staircase. "YOU HEAR THAT! YOU AREN'T SCARY BLOWING OUT A COUPLE OF CANDLES!" He shouts now, turning around and thrusting out his arms. I get that he's not scared but damn, he was also not helping us. That wasn't like him; he's usually the most level headed and last to get upset out of all of us.

I pull Alana's arm and she falls back as we continue to follow Mollock from the balcony into another hall. "Is he acting all right?" I ask, and she shakes her head.

"Do you think they did anything to him? To us?" She asks back and I'm not sure. I feel fine but that doesn't mean anything.

"I don't know. Let's just try to push through without provoking them anymore."

"Can't you like…call on Neek or something? Get his help?"

I huff out a laugh, "Not likely. Plus I think he said something at one point or another about not being able to intervene. Which would make sense with everything we've gone through so far." I pause, checking behind us and still nothing. When were they going to make their move? "Plus, if he could, I'm sure he would have by now from all the claims of him and his buddies saying I can save them if we get through."

"Unless it's a trick," she adds.

"That's why you don't need to be going off alone with him, Fellen, let alone believing this soulmate crap," Deven adds with a lot of attitude from up ahead and I roll my eyes.

"It could be a long con?" Alana obviously thinks something isn't right also, but I saw that light; I felt it and I still feel it. It pulls at me and when I concentrate hard enough; it's almost like it's linked to my very being and urges me to go wherever he is, but I don't tell them that.

"And what about the human remarks from the Alpha back there?" Alana continues.

I shove down the feeling of dread that starts to creep up when thinking about how he acted or what he said. I don't trust any of them.

"SHHH!" Mollock says from up ahead, signaling for us to stop. We've been walking down an empty hallway for a while now and nothing. No doors. Windows. Decorations. But from the glow of his torch, I can see the big empty area we are about to enter. "I don't hear anything, but this could be a trap. Remember, stay together."

He walked forward and we all followed, getting back into hunter mode. Something was off. I could feel it by the hairs on my arms rising and even though I keep an eye out behind us, where nothing is, it still *feels* like someone is watching us from behind. "What the?" The uncertainty in Mollocks voice accelerates my heart, and not in a good way.

"What?" I ask as we all reach him to see what he's seeing and a gasp flies from my lips. Holy shit.

"They are teasing you. Don't let them bait you," I say quickly, as Alana covers her open mouth from the shock.

A sketch of their baby twins sits on an empty table in the middle of the room, with a note that reads *"Drink the potion if you want to save your human offspring."* Four different sized, shaped, and colored glass bottles sit beside the note, all holding a liquid. Rule one of dealing with witches: don't drink or eat anything. But also, what they are insinuating is going to crash into Mollock and Alana's inner intelligence that is no doubt shouting it's a trick.

"It's a trick," Deven tells them as well but they aren't listening and as Alana goes to grab a bottle I rush forward and grab her wrist to stop her.

"Let me go, you know they could have gotten them. What if one of the Bad Lands witches captured them and brought them here or... has them still in the Bad Lands and is communicating with these witches here or–."

I interrupt her, grabbing her wrist tighter to try and encourage her to let go of the tall, green colored glass container she is holding. "Alana, stop. There is no way that they have them or can get to them. They are in the most protected village back home. Don't let your emotions rule you." Indecision shines bright in her stare as she looks back to Mollock.

He reaches forward and grabs her shoulder. "We don't know whether they do or not, but they're right. There isn't a rational way they could *actually* have them here and the chances of them tricking us is far more likely."

"It's a trick, it has to be," Deven said, holding up the paper and taking a closer look, before running his hand over the paper. "No ink, or markings."

"That doesn't mean anything, they have magic," Mollock counters, holding out his hand for Deven to hand him the paper. "But if we ignore this and they somehow do have access to our daughters, then what?"

"Maybe one of us just needs to try and drink it first and see what happens?" I reach forward and grab a slender purple bottle and shrug. "If they really do need me, I mean the other supernaturals, not these bitches, then they won't really try to kill us, right?" I thought about what I just said, taking in the crazy looks I was getting. "Eh, yeah now that I've said that out loud I realize how stupid that sounded. They will try to kill us regardless."

"Ugh, yeah," Alana agrees.

"Bottoms up." Right as I go to lift the bottle to my mouth, the sound of a baby crying sails through the air and my eyes widen.

"NO!" Deven shouts, but Alana and Mollock were already draining a bottle each. "Shit! Might as well do it also, I'm guessing this is going to be like the wolf challenge where we will all have to participate," he adds and grabs the last glass vial.

"Wait! We need to see how they'll react!" I say, grabbing his arm before he can drink one also. A heated look crosses his face and he goes to put his hand on my cheek, which I move away from.

"Are you concerned about me?" Taking a step, he must have forgotten his place with Alana and Mollock temporarily, but I back away from him.

"Quit your creepy shit, Deven, this is serious!" I turn to see Alana swaying side to side where she stands. "Shit!" I steady her. "Yeah, not good."

"You two will drink your potions as well." A whispered voice trails through the air from an invisible source, making goosebumps break out all over me. It was low, female and super freaking creepy.

"And if we don't?" I ask right as Mollock crashes to the floor and passes out. Alana goes down immediately after and between Deven and I we manage to catch her in time and lower her to the ground safely.

"Then they and the babies die." The whispered voice slithers back to us, sounding like it was coming from every direction.

"WE DIE IF WE DRINK IT!" Deven shouts, losing his patience as he stares down at our teammates while breathing like a bull.

"Maybe you do." The voice answers. "*And then again,*

maybe you don't."

"They like to eat from people still alive," I surmise to Deven trying to think rationally. "They are cannibals and notorious for doing it while the victim is awake to watch."

He nods. "They are, and you're right. So the worst case is that they are just trying to knock us out to get us tied up somewhere."

I scoff, feeling the irritation of it all. "So, surrender? Just like they wanted originally. They got their damn way."

Deven steps forward and when I go to back away this time he captures my wrist and tugs me roughly against him as he wraps his arms around me holding me there.

"GET THE FUCK OFF, DEVEN! This isn't the time!" I bite out in anger and disgust, as I squirm trying to get out of his grip. It only makes him hold me tighter and I feel the stubble from his chin graze against my temple and I snap it away. "I swear I will fucking headbut you and slice your damn throat with my staff if you don't get off of me."

"I just want to hold you, Fellen. Don't you miss us? Miss me holding you? Being inside of you?" I feel him getting hard against me and I swallow down the acid rising in my throat.

"Fuck you!" I bring my knee up hard and do just what I threaten, bringing my head back and headbutting him at the same time. He goes down hard coughing and wheezing as he bends down and holds himself.

Out of all the fucking times for him to pull this shit. He's been getting more sleazy, more persistent, but our two best friends—his lovers—are laying on the ground passed out from a witch's potion and he is trying to come on to me. It's unbelievable. "I'm not drinking this shit and leaving my body anywhere near you unconscious, so drink up." I grab a bottle and thrust it into his hand as he glares up at me with pure hate.

"If we didn't have something to do, you would be regretting that little stunt. Don't worry." He fully stands now. "I'll punish you later for it." He's serious, or he believes he is, because if he thought I was going to continue to deal with these attempts, he was way wrong. Even if I had to enlighten Mollock and Alana how much of a creep he is. I will. Before I can respond or roll my eyes back so hard in my head they get lost there, he finally tips the bottle up and swallows the contents.

Finally.

He sits down, preparing to drop like the others. I count to thirty in my head, the whole time holding his malicious stare until he passes out. I give it another minute for good measure and walk over kicking the ass in the ribs hard enough I know it might have left some damage. Still didn't help me feel better about his nasty attempt, but it did let me know he wasn't faking being passed out. I go between Mollock and Alana and lay down on my side facing Deven after drinking my own, odorless, tasteless potion. I hated that I had to watch him, not trust him, and maybe I was overreacting, but I hated being handled like that. Well, other than when Neek did it. Whatever.

I hear another shrill laugh of a witch right before I pass out also.

NEEK

"SNAP OUT OF IT!" I roar in Savannah's face, unable to hold back my anger anymore. There are fifteen of us. Fifteen immortals in this damn dungeon trying to get her to snap out of her rage. She has lost it. It wasn't just blood lust anymore, but like there was nothing in her brain for her to compute words, or even process thoughts.

A hand lands on my shoulder, that I immediately roll back and shrug off without seeing who it is, as I stare into her deranged face. A face that was once so beautiful I almost lost my mind being in love with her. At one time she was my everything and I can't even fathom how we got here now with me wanting to kill her out of rage. We couldn't kill each other, but I could control them and I have tried every trick I have. Even the snap trick that knocked out the werewolves. Nothing. Works. I'm getting drained. I've even tried my jinn power, not just the power of the King. The only thing I can compute is that the Fae spies that were previously here put her in this state.

We are all starved and yes, the land could trigger us to lose our minds and shred into a human within a second of them entering, but we still know it's wrong. But it wasn't like that for her. The day her chains broke after she begged for me to tie her down and she got a taste of human blood, that was it. She was like this from that moment on. I realize I was zoning out, staring at her when a hand snaps in front of my face.

"Snap out of it man. It's fine. You've been at this for almost a full day. We're going to drain her," Dagger says and I finally break my stare from Savannah, who continues to scream, in between snarls, growls and any other inhuman sound she can make as she tries to break free to attack us or maybe just break free.

"Well then do it. Now. It's obvious there are no thoughts in her head so I doubt she is going to stop you via mind control," I demand and Quinton steps forward.

"I'll do it," he says, but looks like he would rather do anything but.

I didn't have time for it. "Man up and at least try, we're running out of time." I was being a dick, but I really didn't care. We didn't come this far, come this close to freedom just for Savannah to turn into her equally terrifying counterpart, Frost, and rip Fellen's throat out.

He doesn't dignify me with a response, but some of

her other blood mates growl in response to my flippant behavior. Fuck them. I love them as brothers, but I've tried it their way for hours now. I've used up and spent every inch of my powers and energy trying to get through to her to avoid this and now it was inevitable.

Savannah, who's in the middle of a growling scream, actually quiets as Quinton gets closer and I wonder if we were doing it wrong this whole time by not having her mates try and break through to her sooner. But Dagger has been down here and tried multiple times. I didn't know much about mates, or harems. Maybe one was better than the other. Who fucking knows.

We all watch with bated breath as she tilts her head, her white, sweat soaked hair sticking to the side of her face as she stares at him in confusion. "Baby, it's me… Quinton." I wanted to interrupt no shit, but maybe she did need to be reintroduced to her harem. Hundreds of years locked into a mad, screaming and crazed state with only four concrete walls could probably mess with your memory. He gulps and moves a little closer and another growl starts back up from her, but it was low. "I miss you, baby," he says and the growl stops. She tilts her head the other way and sighs before stepping back from him.

This is the most differentiation any of us have seen from her. I have half a mind to interrupt and tell him maybe we can give her blood instead of taking it to help her, but I also feel like any sudden movements or noises will set her off. I'm guessing the others in the room feel the same, because no one is moving a muscle other than her and Quinton. "Don't be afraid. Let me hold you, baby." He talks to her gently and while she hasn't started back up with the noises, she does still look confused and unsure. It looked like they had this under control and I needed to go check on Fellen and her team's progress, but I also didn't want to move and mess up the progress. So against my irritation, I stand with the others and wait.

She opens her mouth and the room collectively braces for a scream or other loud noise she usually lets out, but instead she starts to talk. "Quu..iinn?"

Holy shit. There was hope and fuck if it wasn't flaring in my chest so hard right now. Was this it? Did she actually snap out of it?

"Yeah baby, it's me." He takes another step and now he's so close that if he chose to use his speed he could just run at her and bite before she could react. "I'm here. We're all here," he says and she slowly lifts her head and squints, seeming to look and see the people in the room since the first second we entered. Or hell, for even the first time in a hundred years. She casts her eyes slowly around the room before stopping at me and they widen. I'm not sure if it was shocking to her that I was here, but she looks crazed and then a low growl from deep in her throat starts again. *Shit*.

"Baby, look at me." Quinton hurries and steps a little

closer. "Ignore them, look at me!" I know a second too late that he fucked up and so do the others in the room. Dagger screams for him to drain her, at the same time I yell at him to get away from her, but it doesn't matter; we're both too late and with him in reaching distance of her, she grabs hard at his hand, using her supernatural strength and speed and pulls him into her before biting hard into his neck. It isn't a normal bite and she roughly shakes her head from side to side and holy fuck.

"STOP IT!" I command and the ground shakes as the land hears my command, but it doesn't affect Savannah. We weren't able to kill each other but…

Right then the others in the harem snap out of their shock and rush her, biting into either side of her neck, one on her arm and another on a leg. She gives one final growl and shake of the head and Quinton's head rolls to the ground. Fuck. He's dead.

The room is quiet as the rest of her harem drains her and other then her trying to grab them and snap, and growl. They have her now. I turn to the others in the room. A couple wolves and Zeek are not even sure where to begin.

"This is bad," Zeek starts for me.

I nod. "Really fucking bad, and this doesn't leave this dungeon." They nod and I'm still in shock when I feel a sharp tug on my soulmate bond. "I have to go. Don't let her kill anyone else. In fact."

I turn and swallow hard, not giving myself a second to consider my words. "If she's not under control by the time they reach molasses swamp…kill her."

I fly fast and hard and see the colors of fear shooting straight up from witch territory and already know this wasn't good as they've fortified their mansion to not let anyone in. So that meant I was going the dream way and hoped she was asleep. If she wasn't, I would find another way in. I enter her dream to see her running through a hall of mirrors. It was a trick dream. A trap that the witches had them under and one I knew well. They would be preparing their bodies to eat them and meanwhile have them locked into a series of tests inside a dream that unless they unlocked, they wouldn't wake up without the witches releasing them. I wasn't allowed to physically help the humans through, according to the rules of the land, but that didn't mean dreams.

"Fellen," I say and she quickly turns, thrusting a weapon out as beaded sweat sits on her forehead and she breathes hard. I don't blame her. Hall of mirrors was crap that tricksters used to confuse their prey before killing and eating them. They were like jinn, but a lesser power and form and they didn't eat off pleasure, just fear. So they made sure their victims were soaking in it before they went in for the kill. The witches liked to take terrifying things from the worst supernaturals and copy them. They got off watching the torture and fear building up to a death, but didn't like to particate.

I walk over as the fear starts to melt away from her and grab her face. "You're okay," I reassure but she shakes her head from my grip, making me frown.

"I've had enough people touching me without permission today and I don't need another. Just tell me how to get out of here. I don't even remember how I got here and I can't find my team."

I tremble as I close my fist and take a deep breath trying to control my voice. "What do you mean, *touching without permission?*"

Her eyes widen for a second, and her mouth opens and then closes, a look telling me she hadn't meant to say that. Too bad she had a fast mouth and a quick temper and that let her say things before she meant to. "Tell me," I growl, and this time I don't hold back the angry Neek. I slowly but firmly grab her shoulders as I push her against a mirror at her back. "I'll kill them."

This seems to snap her out of whatever she was thinking and intertwined colors of red and blue slowly trail up from her. So she's scared that I'm mad and turned on that I'm protective. I use it to my advantage and step into her, smirking when she sucks in a breath and her eyes droop. I love how fast she responds to me. When her hands slowly move up my arms, trailing on either side of my neck, I clench my teeth shut to keep focused.

"It's insane how much the world around me fades as

soon as I see you," she whispers and my heart slams in my chest. I lean forward, not able to hold back anymore, and slowly run my lips along her soft jawline, her pheromones making me mad with lust.

"You smell like you need me, Emerald," I whisper and she moans, although I can tell she tries to be quiet about it, I still hear it. I love making her go from mad and sassy to melting in a puddle.

"You ready to tell me what I want to know so I can get you out of here." I use my hardness as an advantage and grind into her. She sucks in a breath and squeezes my biceps hard.

"How do I get out of here?" She asks, ignoring the first part of my question as I slowly kiss her neck. "Mmm. Neek, we don't have time." She is loving this and I can't help pull in her arousal. I'm drained.

"I can persuade you to talk." I move my lips to hers and kiss her; I'm a goner. I can't stop and neither can she. I breathe in deep, an aching throb starting in my pants and it's not helping she's rubbing against me.

She pulls back and then is shoving me away. "No. Neek, I'm serious." She says in confidence as her shaky hand wipes our kiss away and I sigh. She's right. Fuck, I was ready for all of this to be over and be done with this back and forth.

"I'm serious too, Fellen," I counter. "You're stuck in a dreamscape right now. So is the rest of your team most likely."

"We took the potion on purpose. They said they had Mollock and Alana's twin daughters. I forgot, but it's coming back to me," she says, and looks around. "How do I get out?"

I start to walk, not needing to look back behind me to see her follow because of all the mirrors around me. "Hold on to me. If you get separated you could be tricked by the mirrors into thinking you're following me." I say and when I don't feel her hand, I look back at her and she raises an eyebrow.

"I'm not a child, Neek."

"And I don't have to be helping you, but I'm trying to save your race and mine. Just do it." I thrust my hand back and ignore the tingle when her warm hand lands on mine. I also ignore her rolling her eyes.

"Just think of this like a maze, and try to not let the mirrors confuse you. It's easier if you have something to mark the floor with." I pause and when she doesn't say anything I take that as a no. "Dreamscapes are places you are locked in and will not be able to wake up from unless you complete a puzzle, trick or challenge." I turn a corner, concentrating on the ground. "There's usually multiple things you have to get through so it won't surprise me if this isn't your only task."

"Why are you helping me all of the sudden? I thought you said you couldn't help us get through."

I shake my head and look up at her skeptical expression in a mirror before going back to concentrating. "I usually can't, and I guess technically I'm not helping you escape the land right now, just a dream." I pause trying to find the right words. "Regardless, something is happening. The land is changing since you and your team stepped foot here."

"How's that?"

"It just…" I decide I don't want to tell her that information just yet, not sure if it mattered or not but something was stopping me. "Just, things are changing."

"*Ookkaaay*? So, when are you going to tell me exactly how I save you all with our soulmate thing?" Damn, she is firing off all the hard shit.

I growl in frustration, unable to help it. "I will tell you when the time comes." I finally see the end of the mirrors and I hurry, pulling her out fast and right when I start to tell her something, within a blink of an eye I'm no longer in Sweetland.

I'm standing in front of King Ace and Queen Thalia inside of the Fae Royal Castle. "What the fuck," I say, more to myself than to them. Was this a dream? Did the witches pull me into their shit also? I look down and pat at my stomach before turning around in a circle and looking at their throne room. It's familiar to me as I once was a royal and then familiar to me as a prisoner where they liked to watch me get tortured.

"What's going on?" I ask, before I lose my mind. Why was I here suddenly? Were they planning on freeing us? Killing me?

"We decided to change up the rules of Sweetland, seeing how this batch of humans have had great success."

I swallow hard and squeeze my hands. My flame doesn't come forward and I'm guessing my powers are dampened here. "Why?"

"Why did you kill your servants?" The Queen counters. "Not very Kingly of you, King of Sweetland."

I don't take the bait. "We can kill each other now. I gathered that. What else?"

This makes the Queen laugh as she takes a drink of wine. "Someone seems rather antsy to get back to their prison." She looks to her husband in confusion and then back to me. "Maybe you need a different land to live in?"

"No!" I say it too fast and then want to punch myself in the face. "I mean, I am suffering. Just ready to suffer more," I say, through clenched teeth.

"Don't be a smart-ass, Neek. You started the rebellion, live with it." The King finally speaks up.

I ignore the jab and decide to keep quiet. I needed to get back to Fellen. I needed her to get an audience with them.

"The whole game is getting old, so I want to up the stakes." The Queen goes back to talking and she glimmers a projection of her powers on the wall and I see Fellen and her team tied up with gags on the floor in the witch's mansion, all of them asleep and trapped in their dreamscape still.

"What are you going to do?" I ask, since clearly she was waiting for me to respond.

She gives an evil smile, one that makes me want to tear her lips from her face. "I decided that for every territory they make it through from here on out, one of the past territories gets desecrated."

"No," I say as my heart drops and I try to think. "That means.."

"That's right." She laughs now. "Bye-bye to your ghoulish friends."

My head feels like there's static inside of it and it's suddenly hard to breathe, it's too hot and I can't form the words.

"*Oh now* Neek, you didn't really think this was going to end any other way, did you?"

I stay silent.

"Kill the girl and her team…or kill your friends. The choice is yours."

CHAPTER TEN
THE COVENS PROMISE

NEEK

After they got a couple more jabs about the fate of my friends or the humans, they snapped me back to Sweetland and right on my throne in my castle. I wasn't even sure where to begin, but I knew sitting on my ass wasn't going to achieve anything. I also knew that apparently they had been watching us like mortal television and there was nothing that I could get past them except…

I stand with a growl when a Fae servant appears out of nowhere, heading my way. "I thought we ate you all." This gets her to stop and she looks around nervously, for who I have no fucking idea, because it's not like her beloved rulers were going to save her.

"I was told to keep up the castle for when you go back into slumber."

That answer tells me that without a doubt they believe I'm siding with my friends. They gave me two options, but I chose neither. I don't grace her with an answer and let her walk on to wherever the hell she came from. At least we had some more sustenance.

Before I can think too hard on it, I do the one thing I can think of that will make sure not to be overseen or heard, I fly straight to the wolf compound and fly right up to Aspen asleep with his wife and dive straight into the dream. It was going to take a while to hit everyone at once, but we didn't have a lot of time. The others I had no doubt would listen to me and understand what needed to be done. The one that would need time and convincing was him and the witches, but I already decided I wasn't even going to try to save them. They were too far gone into their monstrous sides to be saved.

Aspen isn't really dreaming. Not vividly like Fellen does. Instead it was like standing in a huge open space with nothing but blackness and flashes of scenes around me. Using my powers, I concentrate and solidify a dream, until I am able to make him out. Most of the dream scenes flashes around me are of him in his wolf form. This would allow us to talk just like I did with Fellen, and also allow him to remember it when he awoke.

"We need to talk," I say, walking up to him with no time to waste.

He stands staring at a creek bed with little to no water, trickling through and the sun shining down on us through thick trees that cast their shadows overhead. "This used to be her favorite spot to play when she was a pup."

He's talking about his daughter.

I falter in what I'm about to say and snap myself out of it. "This is a dream and the only way we can talk in privacy."

Now he finally looks away from the creek and looks back at me and unlike the previous time I saw him with nothing but malicious stares, now there was sadness. "Seems I can't even go into my own head to mourn in peace. *Why*?" He narrows his eyes on me. "Why are you here? Haven't you caused enough shit to happen in my life?"

"I didn't make your daughter break an order, just like I didn't tell those humans to act the way they did," I say, knowing that the words didn't matter. The act had been done. War declared, and Aspen wasn't anything if not loyal to his own word. So much so, sometimes it was sickening. "Listen." I shake my head and get my thoughts together. "I was pulled to Fae for an audience in front of Ace and Thelia." This does get his attention and he tilts his head and frowns.

"What for? Why now?" He asks.

I sigh, thinking of a way to explain this right the first time to get him on my side. "They've been watching us and I think they are getting nervous about the human potential to make it through."

"So?"

"I think they know her potential of saving us, or they

know something is special about her. I need you to listen and I need you to be on my side, because things are about to get bad." I pause and look out to the trickling water. "Regardless of what we have going on with us now, we need to put that aside. They've changed the game."

He wants to argue. I can see it in his pissed off expression and his clenched fists, but he doesn't speak right away. A gap of silence stretches out between us and he finally breaks it. "How has the game changed?"

I turn back to him and cross my arms. "For every territory they survive, one gets destroyed."

"No!" He gasps and steps back like I hit him. I don't blame him, I had the same sucker punch to the gut reaction not ten minutes ago.

"I need everyone to go to my castle. Every territory, beside the witches."

"Why?" He runs a hand through his hair in frustration.

"They have the humans now. Do you really think they will let them pass if it's them or one of us?" I explain, thinking about how they are still tied up in their clutches.

"This doesn't make sense. They could still make it through and all that would serve to do is have us all squished in the last territories. We may be uncomfortable, but it's not like we can kill each other, so what's the point?" He guesses it the moment he gets done talking and looks at me with wide eyes. I just sigh and nod.

"No one can know."

He scoffs. “They will figure it out pretty fucking fast if we are all stuck in the same place for too long. Fights are bound to happen and it will take one wrong move, someone gets killed and then it’s a bloodbath.”

“So we don’t let it get to that!” I rush on and say, feeling a tingle in my veins from nerves and anger at the shitty situation we are about to be in. “All we have to do is let her and her team make it through. Hell, even just her is enough. Throw her in front of those bastards, she releases me, I kill them and free you all!”

“You act like it will be that simple!” He says with a raised tone. I know it’s nerves because I feel the panic rising. “Why even tell me? Have you told anyone else yet?”

I shake my head. “I need your help on this. They see that we stand united and we have a better chance of explaining the plan.”

“Wait.” He stops and looks around and I zone into my powers, but there isn’t anyone else in this dream. “You said they can see us.”

“They fucking watch us like mortal television from their throne room as they sip their wine.” I spit off to the side in disgust.

“So how the fuck do you think they are going to react if everyone just moves into your castle? How do you know they won’t just blow us all up?”

Good point, but I think I got it covered. “I have a plan.

One I hope will draw them to us instead. I just need you to trust me on this."

I hold out my hand for him to shake and watch the indecision in his eyes. "This doesn't change anything when we get out of here though. My pack will want revenge." I nod, as he grabs my hand in a firm handshake. I could tell him, how about us saving them instead of their threats of war but stave it. One thing at a time.

"I need to hit all the leaders in this same way. Convince them, especially the ones that still have yet to receive Fellen and her team." It's not lost on me the dark look that crosses his face when I talk about them. It tells me that we are going to have to be careful on how to proceed when it comes to the end of this plan.

"The Sirens are not going to help. Death threat or not. Almost all of them are lost." He scoffs.

"They aren't. Stave agreed to let them pass," I say, thinking about the leader of the Sirens and how much different he's changed for the better since being here. The opposite of his squad of Sirens that don't let their humanity side through at all anymore.

"Speaking of Fellen."

"I thought we were talking about the Sirens," I growl, unable to help it and he turns his back to me and starts walking along with the stream, not bothering to answer me. I guess I'm expected to walk and I ignore the heat rising in me from him saying her name. I catch up to him and walk beside him as he continues.

"She flashed blue fire in her eyes at me when I threatened her."

I school my features to not react to that like I knew all along she was showing signs of something other than a human. There were very few supernaturals that held that trait and it didn't add up. She was human. I could feed from her. She was mortal. I didn't understand. The soulmate tether being visible, that could be explained off by us just bonding together. But the eyes? That trait is as unique as it is dangerous, and I couldn't let anyone know. Not even Fellen. "So you believe me now?"

"About the soulmate thing? Yeah, I never doubted it. I can smell both of your blood and it smells the same." The same? I don't have time to react or talk about that. "I only doubted her and your ability to free us once she made it through, and if she made it through. We still haven't gotten to the subject of Savannah or how you plan on killing Thelia or Ace when you couldn't the first time."

I stay quiet, not having an answer for that and he finally stops and faces me. "Being a King means that you're faced with impossible questions and are wise enough to answer them correctly, even when others believe you to be wrong. You lead by showing and proving your right."

"I'm not a King."

He scoffs out a laugh. "Could have fooled me with how you swayed thousands of Fae from all different factions to fight for the humans. Hell, you convinced me. An actual King. And you sure as Hell must have fooled this land and Thelia and Ace for them all to put you in this position."

"As a punishment for leading you all!" I roar out, my temper releasing from the stress of it all. "And look how it's turning out!"

Aspen stays calm and shakes his head. "You need answers for Frost and how you plan on finishing this the right way. You may have a plan to try and save us and to try and get the Fae sovereigns to perish, but try isn't good enough. Not for a King, and like it or not, it's the position you're graced with." He lets out a low growl in his throat. "Which you so rudely reminded my pack and I of when you put them to sleep with a snap of your fingers last time."

I go to turn around, having nothing left to say but telling him to start heading for my territory. Right as I wave my hand to end the dream, he shouts to get Frost together or he will. What he doesn't know is that her harem might have already killed her, if they didn't get her under control. The thought of her dying shoots a bolt of pain through my chest.

The King and Queen of the Fae were right, to an extent. It was between the humans and my friends. I just hope that I could save the majority before it all came crashing down.

FELLEN

After Neek vanished into thin air. *Literally*. I decided to trudge on. With the knowledge that this was a test type coma where once I passed I could awake, I knew I needed to hurry and get through. The longer our bodies were left vulnerable, the longer they had to come up with more defenses or plans to keep us from breaking loose of whatever trap they most likely had us in. It was weird having the knowledge that you were dreaming and then also not being able to wake up. I'd rather just think that I was awake, or I guess it would be like any other dream where I only remember bits and pieces after waking up. This was just mental warfare.

Now I'm stuck in a room with three bottles of potion in front of me and a dead plant. There looked like an outline of a door that would allow me through to wherever else, but no amount of pulling, scratching, kicking, hitting or cussing would open it. So, stupid challenge it is. I wonder if this was the last one. After the mirrors, I had to scale a fifty foot wall to continue on. The climb up sucked ass, the climb down sucked worse. I didn't understand what all these challenges were about, but whatever.

The three bottles in front of me read different things. The red one on the left, *Life*. The blue one in the middle, *Drink Me*. The green one on the right side, *Death*. I'm guessing the challenge was to bring the plant back to life and my hand automatically shoots to the red bottle, but I stop before I touch it, giving it a closer look. The bottle was red. It reminded me more of death than life. I scratch my head. Shouldn't life be green? I continue to look at the bottles and then the plant until I shake my head from the craziness. Neek said these challenges are meant to stall the captive in the dream to give the witches more time to capture them fully. If that was right, they wanted it to look like a riddle so someone stood here trying to contemplate which bottle to pick, but really…the plant was already dead. I couldn't kill it anymore right?

Deciding not to play into the game, I pick up the bottle without another thought and pour the matching contents into the soil. I watch intently and nothing happens. Crap. Okay. I grab the one that says drink me next and pour it in, as I hold my breath. *Come on. Come on.*

Nothing.

I freaking hate witches.

"CAN'T YOU ASSHOLES JUST WAKE ME UP ALREADY!?" I shout in rage as my echo shouts back at me. I'm breathing heavily from the frustration. Without sparing another second I grab ahold of the last bottle, *Death*. A zap of electricity races through my hand and up my arm. "SHIT!" I drop the bottle automatically and it crashes to the floor, glass exploding and the liquid death spilling out all of the concrete floor.

Great. Now what?

I turn in a circle, wondering what to do and right as I take a step to go back to the way I entered, a splash of cold water hits my face and I gasp out and close my eyes as I raise my weapon. Only the weapon vanishes and when I open my eyes, I'm in a whole other place. I'm hoping back to reality and I'm guessing I'm correct, because when I turn my head from my tied down position on the floor, Alana greets me.

"I hate witches," she says and normally I would have laughed, but I was too annoyed with the whole situation to even crack a smile.

I turned my head to the other side and saw Mollock, sitting next to me. Which meant Deven was at my back. We were all tied sitting down, in a pentagram casting circle, our backs to each other, legs tied together in front of us and hands tied behind our backs. I wiggled, testing the restraints and when they had no give, I sighed. "Tell me about it. They had me doing some type of test with a dead plant."

"I had that same one," Alana comments as I look around in the dim lighting. We are in a small room littered with magical items, shrunken heads and what looks like a potion making station. Candles are the only source of light that are carelessly littered throughout the space. The sound of water, almost like a running water, but smaller, is sounding from behind us somewhere and no matter how bad I strain my neck, I still can't tell what it is. Great. That's going to drive me nuts until we get out of here.

"Same," the guys say. So apparently we were all idiots at the plant test one.

"Whatever, I'm just glad to be done with it so we can bust out of here."

An amused laugh sounds, as the witch that talked to us earlier steps into the room. "You aren't going anywhere." I think we all collectively sigh, wanting this to get over with. My stomach growls in agreement and I shift my weight as she walks closer to try and hide the fact Alana is working to untie Mollock's wrists.

"Do you guys go to a witch training seminar every month to work on what to do and say when you capture a human?" I pause for affect and enjoy her face twisting into a pissy expression. "Because you all say and do the same thing. I mean total A for getting everything right."

She looks like she's about to lose it but at the last second takes a deep breath and raises her chin. "It's funny how you quip off to me, yet you're the one tied up and seconds away from my sharp blade running through your jugular. Which is quite delicious, I might add."

Eh. Gross.

"So you really want to go ahead and kill the last hope

you have of escaping?" Mollock asks. It's well rehearsed. We all play our part to distract and keep them thinking they have us. I stay my usual smart ass self. Alana will do the begging. Which Mollock likes way too much, and makes me gag to think of their bedroom play. Mollock tries to reason, and lastly Deven hits them with statistical facts which...come to think of it, I have no idea what use that is. Thinking of him made me want to throw my head back and bang it back into his out of pure rage from him being a sleaze. I suck in an annoyed breath and concentrate back to the task at hand. I can feel Mollock's rope loosening by how much he's wiggling his hands.

"You can keep trying all you want. We are happy here. We don't want to leave." She responds and picks up what I'm sure is some type of small organ in between her long fingernails and pops it in her mouth. It makes a squishing sound as she bites into it and I hold in a gag. Speaking of gags. That's kind of weird. I frown as I think. Usually we are always gagged when the witches have us.

This better not be another freaking dreamscape and I never got out.

"Hold up. Is this real?" I ask, interrupting everything. I look over to Alana and she gives me a look that asks if I'm okay.

The witch scoffs, "Very real, I assure you. Now. Who would like to go first?" She asks, holding up a sharp blade and still my confusion trumped over any fear. I tapped the ground and waited. No response.

"Yup. This isn't real," I announced and right when I thought maybe I was losing it, the air shimmering and changed around me, with my team, room and witch all disappearing.

"ABOUT FREAKING TIME, FELLEN!" Alana screams as she throws a stake and it lands in the stomach of a witch before she could throw the green ball of magic positioned in her hand to attack. The witch falls down with a horrible scream, right as Mollock yells at me to get my ass up.

Yup. This was real.

I jump in the fray with no questions asked and dodge magic thrown our way while Mollock tells us to distract them as he lunges forward like the witch killing beast he is and goes to town. Sweat pours down him and off his muscles that glisten in the dim light. We were right back in the room below the stairs where we first entered the mansion. Magic sailing through the air, whistling past both mine and Alana's heads as I laugh. "Stop drooling over your hubby and get to work."

She laughs, also. "You first."

"Good *Poooiiinnnn–*." White hot pain raced against my scalp as a hand pulled hard at my hair. With my heart in my throat I realize playtime is over. Not thinking twice, I whip up and around with my weapon as best as I can without being able to see the witch dragging me back by my hair, and run the blade hard and fast over what it made contact with. The pressure releases and I spin around, driving it back out and this time hitting home, slicing through her neck. I didn't step back in enough time and the hot, putrid spray of blood fanned across my face, but I didn't slow. I turn and run before diving on the ground, sliding and slicing through the back calves of the witch Deven's fighting. He finishes her off as I look around.

There aren't many witches left but the leader is gone. Officially not killed or we wouldn't be in a battle with the coven right now. I scan the room, taking a deep breath to calm the adrenaline as I look for a blonde with a black dress. Nothing. She probably fled. Which was either good because we could pass, or she was an evil bitch for letting her coven die off as a distraction for the main event.

"Mollock, the leader!" I yell, as I run to help Alana. She's stabbed this witch three times and everytime white flowers pop up in place of where the blood should pour out and she's still going strong.

He nods and runs up the stairs and a second later Deven follows for backup. Last witch. We took out a whole coven. After we work together and sever the head from the body, I look around,trying to count roughly how many. The floor is littered with bodies, but it seemed too easy.

"That's all of them besides the few that escaped with the coven leader." Alana gasps, trying to catch her breath from where she is bent down with her hands on her knees. "We were at this for what felt like an hour while you were still passed out."

"Yeah, I had one of those fun dreams within a dream thing." I look at her and frown.

She laughs. "I'm real, bitch. Let's go."

I laugh also. I feel shaky from the lack of rest and sustenance. That probably accounted for some of my paranoid behavior. Well, that and my stomach is hurting like a mother trucker. Great time to start your period in the middle of trying to save the human race. Mother red waits for no one. We catch up to the guys right as they are about to finish off the witch.

"Tell your Neek that this won't be the last he sees of Ashley's coven!" She snarls at me as we approach, and then flinches when Deven tightens his grip on her scalp and Mollock presses the tip of his blade further into her throat.

I wave a hand in the air. "Yeah, no thanks. You could have just let us pass. Even tried to help us with the last challenges and get your freedom. Instead you chose to be stuck up cunts and paid the consequences. So, no. Hard pass, *Ashley*." I say back to her, holding in a laugh at her name.

Alana doesn't bother, though, and laughs obnoxiously. "It's just like an Ashley to be a-"

"Cunt?" I supply.

She laughs. "Witch, but yeah, same thing." We laugh at the memory of a hunter in our village who used to tease and bully Alana when we were younger, named Ashley. We always hated her growing up. She's dead now, so that's something.

I snap out of the memory right as the guys kill her and Neek appears out of nowhere, striding over to me with purpose, not breaking his stare. There's something carnal and terrifying in his gaze that immediately sets my nerves on fire, but I didn't make an attempt to back up because the same look deliciously clenched my stomach, shooting pleasure straight where he made me feel good. He didn't stop until he was right in front of me, only to grip my face hard in both hands and pull my mouth to his.

I gasp from the sudden pleasure but immediately push him away, realizing I was in front of the others. Neek seems to ignore it though and turns around as well, facing them. "Which one of you sorry fuckers touched her without permission."

Oh shit, no, not this.

Mollock and Alana looked confused, as they would be, but Deven clenched his fists and lifted his chin. "Are you mad because you know who she really belongs to?" He paused, an evil smile on his face. Excuse the fuck out of me who the hell did he think he was? "Or that she enjoyed me touching her?"

I didn't even get the words out before Neek's air born

in his smoke form, ramming straight into Deven.

And then they're gone.

CHAPTER ELEVEN
THE LOLLIPOP ENEMY

FELLEN

"So what Fellen, you're still defending the fact that he could have gotten killed by the King and you don't give a shit!" Mollock shoots off as we walk through the rest of the *hopefully empty*, witch house. I should have just kept my mouth shut after he was taken, but that's not me and I couldn't help but fire off a smartass comment.

"First of all, I don't think he killed him." I pause and think, metally cringing because I really had no idea if he would or not. "Second, I think saying whatever's coming to him he deserves, after he pretty much held me down and dry humped me, is fair!"

He looks back at me with a glare and shakes his head like he's disappointed. I really don't give a shit. "He's still part of this team! We've all gone through some fucked up shit since we've been here. Him coming onto you doesn't mean you lose all faith in him or wish him harm from our enemy!"

It's not lost on me how Alana has been quiet through all of this, and if I had to guess, it's because she's mad at me. Other than Deven's looks, I honestly don't know what her or Mollock saw in him to open their damn marriage, turn it poly, and let him in their relationship.. but it must have been something great because she's looked hurt and scared ever since he disappeared. Which made me an ass friend for my comment but also for not telling her that he'd been sleazing on me for a while now.

I swallow my pride, a tiny bit anyways, as I reach out for Alana's arm, lowering my voice. "Listen, I'm sorry for not telling you that he'd been flirting or hitting on me." She just looks at me but doesn't respond other than to raise one eyebrow at me, so I continue on. "But we both know it's harmless because I don't want anything to do with him anymore. I brush it off and reject him, put him in his place or ignore him every time. If I was flirting back, then that would be shit on my end. I've turned him down one too many times and that's probably why he escalated to doing what he did. I planned on telling you guys as soon as I could because I realized his obsession with me had gotten out of hand and needed to be reined in."

Right when we find the exit out of this nightmare house and walk through the door leading outside and back into the swampy night air, she finally responds. "Opening your relationship to another person takes a lot of trust on everyone's part. I guess I'm just more pissed that he didn't come to Mollock or I sooner and let us know that he still had feelings for you. I know you're done with him, that's not the issue. And your comment," She pauses to let out a brief laugh. "Well, that's just you, Fellen. I'm not mad. Just irritated that he's been taken and then all this comes to light. It's the least of our worries right now. We just need him back and to continue on." She throws up a white flag with a small smile and the pressure releases on my chest a fraction. Not all the way because I know that Mollock is still being pissy, but it helps.

"You're right. Let's just get him back so I can kick his ass and settle this." I smile back and she rolls her eyes.

We all quiet down and stand on the edge of the trail that leads to the next territory. We don't have to guess what it is, because Neek's super tall ghost friend is standing there to greet us. Behind him the territory reminds me of the candy cane fields, but instead of candy canes for trees or obstacles, rainbow lollipop suckers of all shapes and sizes surround the area. Some mimic trees and have tiny lollipops growing out of the stick part. Some mimic bushes that have all sizes of lollipops in clusters. In between all of that chaos is unmarked graves everywhere. It doesn't matter how many baddies I've killed, graveyards have always creeped me out. Now we are facing one that looks like a candy factory exploded over the top of it. *Fan-freaking-tastic.*

Ghost guy smiles. "I'm letting you pass, so chill with the challenge stuff or I may have to kill you." He says it so nonchalantly that I can't help the laugh that slips out after looking at Mollock's frustrated face as he grips a salt bag at his side.

"I'm Zeek, by the way."

I raise an eyebrow. "Wow. Did you and Neek come up with those cute little names while you braided friendship bracelets."

Zeek throws back his head and laughs. "Something like that." He starts to turn but when we don't make an effort to follow, waiting on Mollock to lead, as this is also his territory, he turns back and looks at us confused. "Are you coming or waiting for something?" He looks around in mockery.

"Where is Deven?" Mollock asks.

Before Zeek can say anything I interrupt. "We will get him back, but the mission is first. We need to move." I start to go past him to continue, but Mollock reaches out and grabs my arm, stopping me before I can get too far. A growl that I have no idea where it came from slips out and he lets go of my arm before stumbling back looking terrified.

"What the..." He starts to say, looking intently in my eyes.

My heart kicks up at the way he's looking at me and I look at Alana who gasps. "What?"

I look at Zeek and his mouth opens a fraction but he closes it quickly before he swallows hard. "Okay, what the hell are you guys looking at?" I hate being left out, and more than that, I can't stand having people look at me like that.

"Your eyes. They changed when I touched you, they looked like..." Mollock trailed off and Alana comes over, stepping closer to me while staring intently at my eyes. "Blue fire." She says for him. I fidget under their stares and once again look at Zeek for help.

"You're the supernatural here, what does that mean? Did you do something to me? Did Neek?" It had to be a soulmate thing if that was the case. I mean, I could see the damn tether thing, and I've also seen Neek produce blue fire up his arms. That had to be it, right?

Zeek sighs before running a hand through his messy orange afro. "I don't think I'm the right person to ask on all of that, but listen. I may be the leader of this territory and willing to let you pass, but that doesn't mean every ghost here agrees with that. You're going to have to trust me to make it through, and we need to get going now to avoid trouble."

"Pfft. Figures," Mollocks quips back. "We have a team member missing, one turning into the land only knows what, and a supernatural leader asking for our trust. I feel like this is one big joke."

"What choice do we have?" I fire back, irritated at the implication that I'm turning into anything.

"Fellen is right. We need to move." Alana glides by me, unaffected by Mollock's stance on not wanting to move. Zeek continues on down the path and I follow them both, giving Mollock a look over my shoulder.

Since we entered this place, it's felt like the once inseparable bond between our team has been shattered. I hate it. I also hate the fact that no matter what happens at the end of this mission, whether we make it through or not, nothing would be the same between us from here on out. Especially me.

"Alana," Mollock calls out and she holds back to walk with him. I continue to follow Zeek, starting to feel uneasy about all of this. Maybe they were right. Maybe this was one big trick that we were falling into, because when were we ever so trusting with supernaturals? My trust came bowling me over when I saw the soulmate tether Neek kept telling me about, but what if it wasn't a tether at all? What if he just said that and in reality was turning me into a supernatural like him. A jinn? From what I read you have to be born like that, and even though the blue fire thing reminded me of Neek, no human could be turned into that. Vampire, werewolf, siren, ghost, hell, even a zombie, but not a jinn. Maybe the books were wrong though?

My internal debate breaks when I all but run into the back of Zeek, who's stopped and holds out a hand. "Something isn't–."

He doesn't get the words out before Alana's scream pierces the air. I whip around as terror flashes through me. She's gone.

"ALANA!" Mollock screams, looking around frantically.

"What happened?" I ask. Mollock is screaming her name over and over and right before he goes to run off in a direction she might be, I reach out and stop him turning to Zeek. "What happened?"

"It's Aaron."

"I don't give a fuck who it is. Get her back now or I will challenge you and you will die." Mollock threatens, and for once I'm on his side. This has gotten out of hand. We let our guard down. This could have been what they wanted this whole time.

"I told you not every ghost was okay with you coming on through!" He yells back and the blue glow around his body glows brighter. "We just need to go." He groans and grabs at his hair, pulling on it.

"NO!" Both Mollock and I say at the same time. I look at him and he tosses me a salt bag, which I catch and already know what needs to be done.

"Aaron could be using my wife as a skin suit. Trap her, and call for me. I'll do the same thing if I find her. We need to split up," Mollock says, before turning and this time I let him run off the trail and away from us.

My mind is going a thousand miles per minute and I needed to steady myself. Emotions didn't help. I needed to concentrate. I whirl around facing Zeek who still just stands there having the audacity to look guilty. "What kind?"

He knows what I'm talking about and sighs. "Poltergeist."

"Fucking hell!" That meant he could do a lot in the way of mental damage before we could find her. While ghosts like to get their power through possession, poltergeists got their nourishment from fear. "Where would he have taken her?"

"There is a set of deep caves that way." He points to our right, the opposite way Mollock ran. "That's where he usually is. And I don't know if you guys have any more items in your backpack, but you know that little bit of salt isn't going to work on him, right?"

I roll my eyes. "Obviously, but you're coming too." When he looks like he's about to argue, I hold up a hand. "You need to show me into these caves, help me find and take him down. If you're Neek's friend like you claim, and want to get out of Sweet Land so badly, you're going to need to make your buddy stand down. Because I'm not going any further without Alana."

"Right then, come on." He shakes his head in defeat,

even though he didn't even try to put up an argument and heads off in the direction he pointed to. The further back into his territory we walk, the thicker the lollipop woods get and the swirling colors start to hurt my eyes and almost give me a dizzy sensation. "Oh, right. Don't stare too long at the lollipops, they'll make you pass out."

"Wow." I scoff as I step around a headstone. "You didn't think to tell us that when we first entered." I glance back behind me when a phantom wind or probably a ghost, rushes behind me moving my hair. I hold my weapon tighter and glance around, pausing before taking off again. It felt like we were being stalked. Or maybe that was just the feel of this territory since ghosts were here. Hopefully Mollock was doing okay. If they meant to separate us, they got their wish.

"So does Neek know about the eye trick?" He asks, and as we top a hill, the sight of a huge wall of rock and the entrance to a cave comes into view.

"I thought you said you couldn't comment about what it is? But now you want to talk about it?" I catch up to him and we both pause, looking at the cave.

"It's not my place to guess why there's fire in your eyes, but I think it's something Neek would be better off knowing about."

"And why's that?"

He laughs as he throws his hands up in defeat as he starts walking again. "Hey, I'm just saying if I was having a supernatural reaction, I would think asking my supernatural soulmate would only make sense."

"And I would think that if I was the one human you all claim to save you, you wouldn't be hiding things from her." After that he just stops responding. That's fine by me. The closer we get to the cave, the spookier it gets. The wind has died and a cloud has blocked over the moons, making it darker than normal and I'm almost glad for Zeek's blue glow to help me see.

"I'll take care of Aaron, you just save your friend and get out of here." Zeek turns to stop me from entering.

"She's not some damsel in distress. She's one of the most skilled hunters we humans have," I snap in irritation. I can see the light of a fire bouncing off the cave walls, further inward but I can't hear anything.

He crosses his arms in front of him before stepping out of my way and planting his feet, with a raised eyebrow. "Oh okay, right. I didn't just think that we were going in there to save your friend." He smirks, along with his smart ass comment and I had to give it to him. That was stupid to snap at him like that.

"Fine." I take a breath. "You take care of Aaron, and I'll get her."

He huffs triumphantly before proceeding inside. I walk beside him, constantly checking my back and surroundings while he just looks unfazed. I guess he had a right to be. It wasn't like the residents of his own territory were going to attack him. The further in we walked the cooler the air felt, and the larger the fire light, along with shadows, grew on the walls around us. My team and I had only ever dealt with one poltergeist before on a hunt and it was one of the longest and most challenging hunts we had to date.

It had somehow gotten into the inner houses in our crafting village in the Bad Lands. There were seven hunters that had gone into the house of a small family before us, that never made it out. When we finally took our turn at entering the house to kill it, it was a shit show. Every one of the hunters that had gone in before us was strung up by their entrails and hanging from different parts of this house. We were separated and psychologically tortured for days before Mollock broke through, killed it and got us out. The walls would bleed, or close in on you. The floor would drop out with nothing but flames underneath. Loud music would blare, or there would be none at times, all the while this poltergeist would use images and tactics to scare the holy living shit out of you.

We never did end up rescuing the family of four. A mom, dad, 3 month baby boy and ten year old girl. The father was forced into madness after chopping up his family and eating them. By the time Mollock found them, or rather just him, he was on the end of smashing his head in with a hammer before he could save him. That whole thing still gave me the creeps to this day. The supernaturals here didn't seem like the monsters in the Bad Lands. Neek was right, but that doesn't mean all the supernaturals here were okay. Obviously this *Aaron* one, was a baddie to go against the leader of his own territory.

I just hoped Zeek could rein his resident in so I could find Alana sooner rather than later. I won't have my best friend suffering the same fate as that poor father did. She was almost there herself in that house when we got to her. She was just about to plunge a dagger through her heart. After doing some recollection of what went down with the team and hearing what all we went through, Mollock let us know that Alana's weakness was ghosts. It was fine. We all sought out our weaknesses and made them known to our group for the reason of training to overcome them.

"What's that?" I stop when I hear a moan, and look to where the shadows show…

"WHAT THE FUCK?" Mollock barrels through us, barging straight ahead. I didn't even know he was behind us, and I bite down my yelp as my heart flies into my throat.

"Fuck that scared me!" I breathe out trying to catch my breath.

Zeek laughs and goes to pat my back but I give him a death glare and he lowers his hand. "Is someone scared of ghosts?" He taunts and I scoff and go to follow Mollock right when I hear shouting.

It didn't sound good.

"Alana, what the fuck?"

I round the corner and my jaw drops.

She's on top of a guy, obviously a ghost, err, poltergeist. I'm guessing Aaron, and she is naked and having sex with him. *Holy. Shit.* I'm stunned speechless. Like, no words. Yeah, Alana, Mollock, and Deven were in a relationship, but not an open one to strangers. Also, the blue glow of her eyes says she's possessed. So not only are they mind fucking her, they're fucking her literally. She is conscious and seeing all this go down, unable to control her actions. This was beyond bad. I go to touch Mollock because he's not moving, locked in shock just like I am while his wife continues to moan, and go to town on another guy all while licking her lips and looking right at us.

"Okay, she's possessed. Just calm-"

He snatches his arm from me like I have the plague. "I fucking know that!" He breaks from his shock and finally bolts forward to go and get her but right as he gets close, she opens her mouth and fire floods out in a path through the air. Mollock ducks just in time while I'm now in more shock, I turn to Zeek.

He's in fucking shock. Yeah. He was a ghost, and even he was like what the fuck.

I snap my fingers in his face. "Hey! Fix this now!"

He clears his throat. "Yeah, she has a nice body."

"Dude, what the fuck? Now!" I use my anger and push him forward.

But he stops. "Aaron is using his poltergeist powers through her, while she is also possessed. Now-" He points to Mollock and I see he's now possessed too. "He's possessed." What. Is. Going. On. I grab my salt bag and hurry to untie it.

"Fuck this." Right when I go to make a half circle so I can catch them and unpossess their asses, Zeek stops me.

"It won't work. Go pull some of those lollipops from the ground. They have psychedelic powers. Just like they can put you in a trance and make you pass out, they can also wake you up!" He shoves me toward the exit and I temper my rage. Why the hell didn't he say that or get them before coming here? "I'll work on breaking them apart and getting Aaron reined in."

My only response is a growl of frustration as I sprint toward the exit. It's hard when I feel so weak and shaky with no food, but the adrenaline helps me to push on and now it's only me who can save them. I can't let my friends get taken down by some weird ass sex orgy.

Right as I breach the cave exit and spot a cluster of lollipops, Deven steps calmly around the corner right in my path, almost like he was waiting for one of us. I skid to a halt. "Deven! You're okay!" I grab his arm and pull him to the cluster, but he doesn't move. "Come on! We need to save Mollock and Alana. Poltergeist!" I urge him to move, half out of breath, and when he doesn't, I let him go. "I don't know what's wrong with you, but I can't stand here."

I start past him, thinking maybe he's possessed when he grabs my arm and pulls me back to him with a smile on his face. "I am okay, but you won't be."

"What are-"

I don't get the words all the way out before the butt of his gun slams into my temple and the world goes black.

CHAPTER TWELVE
ONLY A WARNING

I wake up a couple times, but not all the way. More like breached somewhat of a consciousness and then let my mind drift back to the peaceful blackness that did so well at hiding the pain racing through my body. My body shifts again, not on my own accord, and then I'm being lifted in the air. I can feel a pair of strong arms lifting me. My head rolls to the side and the pain of his bite shoots down my neck again as the person adjusts me to their chest.

I whimper uncontrollably as the scent of pine and bourbon assaults my senses.

"Shh, little omega. I got you." It's Rowen. He's walking me somewhere.

The man that did this to me.

That man that made me love him. So much so that I dedicated my life to finding a cure to help him. Made me chase him through the hell of this apocalypse, all over Russia, just for him to trap me and subject me to the same fate.

I thought he loved me.

"I have an escape for us. Just make it through the change and we'll be off this realm and onto somewhere better once you face your fate." I feel his hot breath and chin stubble against my forehead but don't react. He probably knows I'm awake. Probably some supernatural thing. I don't care. It's been so long since I was in his arms. I never imagined it would be like this, though.

Maybe if I keep my eyes closed long enough, when I finally open them, I'll realize all of this was just some insane nightmare instead of reality. Maybe he'll be human again? Maybe he'll love me again?

"You killed a lot of my pack to get to me, baby girl." There's a pause and then I feel like I'm being laid down. I fight to keep my eyes shut. Just a little longer. Just a bit more and I won't have to face him, or what he did to me. "Keep your eyes closed if you want to for now, but as soon as you survive the change, you will answer for your crimes."

And just like that, reality comes bleeding in whether I want it to or not. I guess I should have known this was never going to end any other way. A bolt of pain flashes through me so suddenly that my eyes pop open and a scream breaks out right as my heart stops and an instant cold sweat comes over me. The pain is intense, striking my head, fingernails, toenails and every tooth in my mouth all at once. Right when I think the pain might kill me, and the fleeting thought that I could be the percent that doesn't make the change, a pair of bright orange eyes grace my vision.

"Time to face the music, babygirl."

That voice and those words echo around and through me before I shift trying to fix my aching muscles.

What the?

My eyes spring open and at first it's hard to adjust from the double vision as I can see the two moons shining down on me, and a flow of nausea hits me. Reality slowly comes back to me as I try to shift my arms, only to realize they are tied above my head by the wrists from where I lay on my back on the ground. The double vision finally ebbs and I realize my legs are tied down, spread apart, and worse…I'm naked.

Deven.

The last thing I remember is that son of a bitch knocked me out.

I go to scream, but I know it's useless around whatever he shoved in my mouth and gagged me with. What. The. Fuck. I scream regardless as rage hits me like the force of a thousand fires. My stomach clenches again, reminding me right at that moment about my period, because cramps hit me so hard I falter in my scream and instead groan in pain. That's right about the time he decides to show his face as a cold sweat hits me.

"Time to face the music, babe," he says, with a humorless smirk. I'm reminded of weird deja vu that I can't place, but it feels like I've been in this position before.

"You, stupid, ass!" I try to shout, but it just comes out, "Hmm, mhhmmmm, HMM!" And he laughs.

"I can't believe you would fuck a supernatural enemy over me. Over someone you love, and I know you love me, Fellen!" He looks and sounds insane. His black hair is a mess, sticking out in different directions—complete opposite from his normal groomed look—and his dark brown eyes are bloodshot. I also notice the purple bruising around the skin of his left eye, along with the busted lip and a limp he walks with as he paces back and forth in front of me.

If he expects me to say something back to him, he should have ungagged me. I continue to listen to his bullshit while I maneuver the gag in my mouth with my tongue and try to push it out while wiggling my lips. Not that getting the gag out will free me, but it will give me a good opportunity to cuss the stupid asshole out. He's completely lost it, and not that I need a savior, but it would have been nice for Neek to make sure this type of shit wouldn't happen to me if he was going to measure dicks and mark his territory. He may have thought he taught Deven a lesson by the beating he clearly gave him, but it obviously only served to piss him off more. The one thing I could never stand about Deven is that he couldn't let old dogs lie. He had to keep arguing a point until he got his win or got revenge on someone, no matter how many times people told him to drop it.

"Don't look at me like that," he says in response to my death glare. I'm not sure what else he would expect from someone tied up. Then again, he did seem like he was completely insane right now.

"LLLL, EEEE, GGGGG!" Let me go, I shout, not giving a shit that I can't get the proper words out. I wiggle and thrash the best I can, my back and ass screaming in protest from the hard ground scraping my skin. This is insane. Our friends need our help. What the fuck was he thinking?

The whole time I thrash about, he stands there watching me with hooded eyes, and it's not lost that he's looking at my breasts. I'm going to kill him. This is insane. What's he planning on doing? Leaving me here to die by the fate of the ghost territory? Or is he planning on raping me? How did someone I grew up around and considered a valuable team member, turn around and be on this level of crazy?

"Keep doing that, babe. It's getting me hard and ready to show that fucking bastard what's mine," he says, before licking his lips.

I temporarily stop my thrashing and look at him. Is he serious? His plan is to tie me up and rape me? My heart starts pounding, and the thought of him doing that to me puts my situation in a whole other perspective. I'm pissed, hurt, and disgusted as I watch him take his dick out of his pants and start to stroke it. My eyes look up to his. He wouldn't really do this to me? He had to be trying to scare me?

I try to clench my thighs together as he starts walking towards me, and I give it my all to free myself. I pull on my arms so hard that the rope he tied me up with burns my skin, but I don't give a shit. I'm not going to lay here and be still for this motherfucker to have his way. This is beyond obsession. He's sick. Something must have gotten in his head from this land. He wasn't like this before.

I shake my head from side to side, begging him to stop as I scream through my gag. There was no telling how long I was passed out or what happened to Alana and Mollock. If I had to guess, they were still battling their way with the poltergeist, meaning I was alone with no help on the way. Regardless, as I move my head side to side, screaming and thrashing the best I can to break my restraints, I try to catch any signs of someone coming to stop this, but there's no one. And I doubt the ghosts of this territory would give two shits about what's going down and come to my rescue.

He lowers himself down to the ground, breathing in deep as he slowly trails his disgusting hands up my legs. The feeling of pure helplessness washes over me and pushes through the other strong emotions I'm struggling with right now also. Hate. Fear. Anger. Disgust. And before I know it, tears are flowing from my eyes.

I'm strong and I've always been strong.

Now, I feel nothing but weak.

"Shh, Fell. Stop these fake tears." He makes his way up to lean over me, licking one of my breasts on his way towards my mouth and his dick presses against my center. I whimper out, trying to move away, wanting this sick bastard to stop touching me. He's a fucking coward to do this to me tied up, because he knows it's the only way to have me. He's a weak piece of shit. "I remember how you used to love me pounding into you. You'll love it again, I'll show you."

I thrash again and whip my head to the side when he tries to kiss me on the cheek. I try to bring my leg up to slam my knee into his balls, but he has me tied down so tight that all I can do is wiggle side to side at best. Before I can bring my head back and hopefully headbutt the fucker, he slams a hand down hard on my cheek, pushing and holding my head down to the side against the rough dirt, so I can't move. When he kisses my neck, as he starts to push into me, vomit starts to form in my throat and I know I'm going to throw up and choke.

"Oh fuck, Fellen." He sucks air in between his teeth as he fully pushes into me and now I can't fucking stop it.

I cry. I fucking bawl my eyes out and if I could, I would never stop. I sob through the gag covering my mouth, but he ignores it as he continues his assault.

"You're so wet for me. See." He grunts out as he pulls back then slams into me again. The shame of him acknowledging my traitorous body has my chest hurting. "You're." Another thrust and I whimper. *I want to die.* "Fucking." Another thrust. *How could I be so weak?* "Perfect."

I zone out the best I can and concentrate on a cluster of colorful lollipops in front of me. If I never see these fucking things or him again in my life I would be a hundred percent okay with that. I fucking hate him. He better run far and fast because as soon as I'm free, he's dead.

I've never wished someone so dead before in my life as I do him. In this moment, I wish Neek would show up and obliterate him so this will just stop. Deven shoves in harder now while picking up the pace, using his other hand to grip any piece of me he can, as he sucks and licks on my neck and chest. I can feel the skin on my temple and cheek, still pressed against the ground, start to bleed, but I welcome the pain and try to hold onto it as he continues to defile me. I do all that I can to concentrate on the pain on the outside, instead of the pain he's causing inside me, but the slapping of skin and his disgusting moans along with heavy breathing break through all the same and I can't forget what's happening to me.

"I love you so much, Fellen," he says in my ear, as his sweaty forehead presses against the temple not shoved against the ground, and I slam my eyes shut with a whimper.

The nausea and vomit that has been building finally releases and I heave as it makes its way up my throat only to have nowhere to go but spray around the gag, out my nose, and choke me as my throat tries to work it back down making me hold back another heave wanting to come up. It burns my eyes and I can't get proper air in, leaving me to blow out my nose before breathing deep and whimpering from the pain. "Oh yeah. I'm cuming. You like it. I can hear how much you like it," he says, hearing my suffered breathing and twisting it in his sick head.

He finally stills and grunts out as he finishes inside me before kissing me all over my face. The feel of his nasty, hot cum shooting up in me will forever haunt my nightmares and I doubt even Neek will be able to save me from them. "You were perfect. I knew you would finally give in to me."

I lay still, or try to, but my body decides to start shaking all over. I can't even control it. He finally lets my head up, before crawling off my body and another round of vomit is threatening to come up when he pulls out of me. I shut my eyes again tight to keep from seeing him as I try again to slam my thighs together but I still can't and the shock that has me shaking has left my muscles weak. I'm so ashamed.

Why couldn't I have stopped this?

"You won't say anything to the piece of shit King or

the others, because if you do…" The pause makes me open my eyes, hoping to anyone out there that someone has shown up and killed his ass, but he's still there, eyeing my body. "I'll kill Alana and Mollock before we do this little tie up exercise again."

He says it so easy that between that and the look in his eyes I believe him, but did he really think they wouldn't find out? Right as he turns to walk away, he seems to think better of it and turns back around. "Here's a little piece of advice your *King* gave me, that I'll give you... Don't disobey me, this is your only warning."

Then he turns and walks away.

I wish I could feel something other than the memories of his assault, but it's like my body has a cruel sense of humor and I can still feel him touching me. I lift my head with a muffled scream and slam it back against the ground to make the muscle memories go away and fight off the nausea. I wish I could hide. Run. Curl up in a ball. I'm a coward. I sob, hating the fact I still can't cover my body or wipe the sticky mess of him away. His scent washes over me and I throw my head back again. I just don't want to be conscious anymore. I do it again, and again, feeling my throat raw from screaming each time, and finally my vision crosses, blurs and I welcome the sweet blackness that blankets my vision as I finally pass out.

NEEK

Another blow lands on me. This time a right hook and I grunt through it, feeling the skin around my eye bust open.

"You can stop this anytime, Neek," Thelia taunts. When the servant that was beating the shit out of me got too tired, the King decided to get his own hands dirty for once and took over. He kicks and cracks a rib, and this time I do make more of a noise. It hurt, but I wasn't going to let them break me.

"Just tell us what is so special about that human girl and we let you go." Another punch, this time to the mouth, and I spit out the blood and tooth along with it. Stupid fucker. I glare at the King's smug face, remembering it to memory for when I was finally free and could tear him apart.

I finally find my voice. "I told you, she's no one." They must have been watching us at the right moment, at the right time, because all it took was for them to hear Fellen could save us all and I've been here in the throne room, getting the beating of my life ever since. Neither of them look convinced and right when Ace goes to land another punch, Thelia calls out for him to wait.

She stands up from her throne, straightening her long, fitted black dress before heading over to us. "I think it's time we finally used one of our wishes." My heart stops in my chest as she makes her way, and a buzzing starts in my ears. Fuck. Anything but that. She sees the panic in my face, there was no way to mask it when she said it, and it makes a cruel smile take over her face. "Don't you think, my dear?"

He smiles back to her before looking at me. "Yes, I believe that will be more entertaining than this."

She gives an obnoxious laugh before stopping right in front of me. "Hmm, what should we wish for?" She puts her finger on her mouth and taps it while looking up to the ceiling. Being this close, I can see the faint wrinkles around her eyes. Fae are immortal, only because we age slowly. So in contrast to humans, it takes a Fae one thousand years to age one human year. Thelia and Ace were not only the most powerful Fae alive, but they were the oldest. Making them a lot more cunning, evil and bored then most, which was a cruel combination.

"Just spit it out," I growl, ready to figure out how to fight whatever fate they were going to bestow on me. I couldn't fight a wish but I would try with all my might, and if it had to do with Fellen, I just hope our soulmate bond was enough to keep me from betraying her.

This produces a squeal of giggles and claps from the

Queen, who is clearly entertained by my anger. "Ooo! I love when he gets feisty!" She walks over and wraps both arms around Ace's one while she continues to look at me with a giant smile. She was fucking insane, but it didn't take a genius to figure that out from the whole Bad Lands, Sweet Land shit she'd created.

"So, since you can't choose between your precious friends, and obviously losing all your ghoul friends did nothing to shake you..." She pauses as the memory of me screaming for them to leave and being too late to save them takes over. I was too late. Territory one was obliterated and with it, all the supernaturals that lived there. I pull hard at my restraints. I wanted to break them and then break her fucking neck as I roar out in pain for my friends lost. I was so ready for this punishment to be over. "After all this time, you still haven't learnt your lesson about why choosing humans over your own kind is bad."

I scream out, shaking the chains that hold me down again. She could wish for Fellen and her team's death and the Jinn would complete it in a nanosecond. This would all be for nothing and be over with, but from the Queen's love of sick torture I just hoped it was anything but that.

"I wish..." She pauses and the magic takes over me in an outward display. My limbs lock, as a heat assaults my body. My demon powers take over as it burns my angel side away. I grunt out in pain as a blue light starts to shine around me and in that moment I'm suddenly, irrevocably and ultimately hers. Thelia's voice floats around my head and the trance of the Jinn takes over, making me see, know and hear only her.

"Yes, my Queen." I say, automatically.

She claps in delight again, before schooling her expression and continuing. "For you to finally act like the human-hating King of Sweet Land that you are. I want you to despise them. Work with the land to kill them, instead of save them. Starting now."

I hear Ace laugh deeply as they start to walk back to their thrones and the curse of her wish takes over my body fully. My golden wrist cuffs heat to a dangerous temperature, even for me and I cry out in pain as the wish transforms my mind. I feel the soulmate tether in defense as my mind fights the magic and vice versa.

Humans are bad. Rage fills me with this, and I think of the death those humans have caused to my land, but at the same time a weird hurt comes over me.

Your soulmate needs you. Protect her. Protect the humans. Sadness overtakes the rage and I scream out, my body and mind in a battle of wills but I know what I must do. I know who my master is and who I must obey.

As fast as the onslaught of magic starts, it stops and I'm left breathing heavily, looking at the reflection of my bloodied face in the gray-colored, marble title below me. She snaps her fingers and the chains that held me down are gone.

"Let's test this, shall we?" Thelia asks and my head snaps to look at her. My master. I obey only her. She claps her hands and I can see Sweet Land in a cloud of magic off to the side of the throne room. I see three of Fellen's team members, but not her, walking with Zeek. I growl, watching Deven closely and something in my soul feels off. Wrong. But before I can figure it out, my master talks again.

"Who do you hate?" She asks, and I know this without an ounce of doubt in my whole being as pure hatred flows through my blood.

"The humans," I answer. I watch them walk through my land not phased at all, from the death they've caused.

"Who do you want to kill?" She continues, as we watch them approach a familiar body.

My heart stops and a flow of coolness that I associate with the lesser power of my angel side, flashes through me. I'm aware and have broken through the trance of the wish, as my soulmate tether shines and rage fills me. I open my mouth against my own accord to answer my master, but my soul mate is tied up, bloody and naked. I scream as blue fire licks up my arms. Something happened to her. Something...*who*...someone touched my mate. My mind can't process it, but I know with out a doubt in my being that someone fucking raped her and I can't see straight.

I lose it. My jinn takes over and transforms into my full smoke form. Not just a small wisp of blue smoke, but me. The real me, and the King and Queen gasp from the thrones as guards rush in.

"LISTEN TO ME, YOUR MASTER!" she commands.

Dark storm clouds surround me, with thunder rumbling and lightning striking the ground next to me as someone screams. I roar out, embracing the wind that has taken over the inside of the castle. I will kill them. All of them. Any one who touched her. Right as I feel the precedence of my power reach its breaking point—and I don't know how much more I can take of the two halves of my body fighting one another—the Queen says something that has my powers immobilized and I'm crashing to the floor as the cuffs around my wrists work to bind me to her once again.

She guessed it as she gasped out the words. "I know who she is."

It was over. I pant against the ground, feeling hopeless and afraid.

"I change my wish, Neekilahaud!" she says, using my true name to enStavee my mind once more, and this time I won't have a choice but to obey as that is the true name of both halves.

"Kill your soulmate."

CHAPTER THIRTEEN
THE TRUTH

ALANA

My time under the influence of the poltergiest is foggy at best, but I remember and *feel* enough to know I fucked him. In front of my team, and my husband *and* lover. He'd taken over and used my body as a conduit for supernatural things I should have never been able to do. I grab my throat as the memory of me breathing fire comes back and I shudder. It was like an extreme messed up nightmare. Really, since we've stepped into this land it's felt like one big dream.

It's only when my stomach growls that I'm snapped back to reality.

This isn't a dream and these messed up things really do keep happening to us.

I glance over at Mollock as we make our way out of the cave. He was possessed as well and taken over to join in on the fucked up shit that poltergiest made us do. I know he can feel me looking at him, but he doesn't glance my way or acknowledge me at all, other than to clench his jaw. So, I look away. He knows none of this was my fault, but he's been acting differently ever since we've been here. Angrier. Or maybe it's the land bringing out the worst in all of us? I'm not sure, but I need to concentrate on the next task at hand and that's my best friend.

Zeek informed us he sent her to get some lollipops to break the possession and she never came back. So while he worked to command them from our bodies, something must have happened to her and it scares me shitless. I can't in my whole heart see Fellen get taken down by a ghost, but you never know what can happen on a hunt or how one instant of letting your guard down has the possibility of changing your life. I could almost feel my heart squeezing in my chest before I blow out the anxiety. I need her to be okay.

The only other thing that was nagging at my mind was Deven.

He hasn't said two words to us since he showed up, other than to swear he didn't know where she was. Which was odd. We all heard him stand up to Neek and challenge him over Fellen, and then watch him disappear. Yet he had nothing to say on that matter. Neither Mollock or I were bringing it up either, but he acted like it never happened. He didn't act pissy or mad about the busted lip and black eye he had.Neek obviously beat the shit out of him. That isn't like Deven, something is weird.

All of this is weird.

I grunt out loud, unable to quiet my frantic thoughts anymore. "Okay, someone needs to talk now!" I demand and we all stop, including Zeek that I notice is giving Deven extreme death glares.

Both guys look at me, but it's Mollock who breaks the silence first by blowing out a breath and grabbing the back of his neck. It's his tell for when he is about to apologize and my anger dies down a bit. "Baby girl, it's nothing, okay? I know you weren't yourself and neither was I. I don't blame you for what you did. We're all tired, hungry and stressed. It's nothing." He knows exactly what I'm referring to because he keeps assuring me all this quiet, angry and out of character behavior for all of us is nothing. Bullshit.

"It's nothing?" I ask, my hands finding my hips on their own accord as my attitude flares. "We were just possessed and fucking one another. Deven," I thrust a hand out in his direction, "has been trying to hook up with Fellen and didn't even try to deny it, which made Neek beat the shit out of him and he comes back like nothing happened." I pause and take a deep, much needed breath. "Right at the same time Fellen just disappears!"

I grab my head in frustration. "Ugh!" All of them look at me. "We need to be coming up with a plan to find Fellen!"

Mollock grabs my elbow and I release the grip on my hair as I let him pull me into his chest. Before he can talk, I break the silence once again. "And everyone is acting weird," I mutter and his deep laugh rumbles through his chest, making me smile. Just a little, because they really were acting weird. I look at Deven in Mollock's arms, usually he comes over and helps to sooth me when I'm upset, but he hangs back and for a second I think I catch guilt in his stare, but I'm not sure. I don't need two men comforting me, I'm a grown ass woman and a badass vamp killer, but in our shared relationship that's just how things were. All three of us were close. Usually. Now it seemed like Deven was willingly pulling away and I wonder if it's because of Fellen.

Mollock pulls me away from his hug and kisses my forehead before lifting my chin and placing a gentle kiss on my lips. His touch always comforts me, and usually I'm not one to show affections on hunts or when were were in danger, but we'd been through so much fucked up shit already. It was nice to have five seconds of him holding me. It made me think that maybe everything was going to be okay. That maybe we might make it out. "I'm sorry. Just stressed, okay? Let's get Fellen and get through this." He reaches out a hand to Deven, who clasps it as before, pulling him into a quick hug, with back pats. "Three territories down and shit load to go, right?" He asks, and we all laugh but it's more forced than genuine.

Zeek walks ahead of us, not bothering to wait. "We don't need a plan to find her, we just need to keep looking."

I give the guys a look, because out of the short time we've known this ghost leader, he's been nothing but laid back and fun. Ever since Deven's been in the picture he's been agitated and pissy. We shrug it off and follow him as I call out Fellen's name.

"FELLEN!" I cup my hands around my mouth as I frantically look.

"There's no way she would have just pushed on out of here without us, right?" Mollock asks in disbelief, and before I can punch him in the face for that thought alone I hear him answer himself. "No. She wouldn't."

"Fellen has never left any of us behind. She's the most loyal of us!" I hiss in agitation. He knows that, too. Both him and Deven, so I don't even know why the question came up.

"We will find her, I'm sure," Deven adds, before picking up the pace, passing me on the trail to catch up to Zeek that we can see a good way away now.

I start to open my mouth to ask the question that's been burning in the back of my throat, but close it before I can. What if something bad happened to her? I don't voice it though. I'm too afraid of the consequences of hearing it out loud.

Mollock pulls me back to walk next to him.When I look up, I know what he's about to ask, so I cut him off.

"Not here."

"Then when? You need to eat, and just sipping water isn't going to cut it. We both know that."

I sigh in defeat and it's like my stomach heard his concern, because it chose that moment to growl. I put my hand over my stomach, which does nothing to quell the hunger growing inside me. "We knew this was going to be a challenge when we came here with this–." I pause again and hate the concern I see flaring in his eyes. "Condition," I continue, before looking away and back to scouring the land for Fellen. "But we can't let the others know, so unless you have a plan that I don't know about to get me nourishment, we are just going to have to push on like the rest of them."

He nods before kissing the top of my head. "Just say the word and I'll do anything to take care of you."

I give him a small smile, not fully able to give him thanks for his concern because of my starved and worried state. "I know."

"MOLLOCK! ALANA! GET OVER HERE NOW! IT'S FELLEN!" We hear Zeek yell, and then I take off running as fast as I can, my heart pounding in my chest from the unknown. I jump over a cluster of stupid lollipop bushes and come to a fast, skidded, halt as I see what Zeek is looking down on.

"Oh my gods, Fell." I hear the others arrive behind me and I turn into momma bear mode in a second. "TURN

AROUND AND GIVE US SPACE!" I yell at them in anger and appreciate that they listen, along with Zeek backing up and turning around as well.

Fellen lies completely still. Too still.Hands and feet tied up with rope and bound to giant lollipop sticks, while gagged with a balled up shirt that didn't look like Fellen's. The rope is from our bags.. I kneel down and feel her pulse. She's alive, barely. It's slow and her skin is ashen, slick with a cold sweat. I grab my knife and start cutting away at the rope on her wrists when I notice the knot. It's a hunter's knot. My mind races as I stay completely still and try to rein in my thoughts.

It couldn't be.

He wouldn't do this. It had to be a trick. A ghost did this, planted this here to look like…

"Alana, talk to us, baby girl," Mollock says, using my nickname and I know he's doing it to comfort me because usually it makes me want to melt into a puddle. But my head is fuzzy, and I'm struggling to reign in my hormones from the change I'm going through.

I go to undo the knot instead of cutting it. It's one we use to stay tight and unbreakable from being strained. Since her body is being pulled apart and her ankles tied down in the same fashion, there would have been no way for her to get out of it. It's like a chinese finger trap at this point.

It's Deven.

It had to have been.

I stand before I do anything else and slowly turn around, the pure anger, fear and disbelief coursing through me fuels something I've never felt before. "Zeek," I say in a low voice, as my heart thumps hard trying to explode in my chest and my whole body shakes from fear. He turns with anxiety written all over him, but he knows something happened and that it had to do with Deven, so I'm left with two choices, and since I know one will conflict with my husband, I choose the path of least resistance. "Restrain Deven."

"WHAT?" Deven yells, turning around right as Zeek turns into his ghost form, heading right at him.

"WHAT'S GOING ON?" Mollock shouts at me, coming over and glaring in my eyes. He thinks I'm possessed. I'm not.

I step to the side, and I hate that my best friend's body is exposed like this, but he needs to see what I'm seeing; to know this isn't some crazy guess. I look over to see Zeek has taken over Deven's body and has him kneeling on the ground with his face down. Good. Make it easier for me to kill the son of a bitch. I look at Mollock to see him shaking his head in disbelief before he goes to the ankle knots and checks those.

"He…" He's at a loss of words. So am I, but this is too much and he won't get away with it.

"Tortured and raped her is what he did!" I spit out

and he visibly flinches. "And he was just going to act innocent! Like we wouldn't find out!" I take a deep breath and clench my hands, trying to calm my nerves. "Get her untied and dressed. I'll take care of him."

Mollock opens his mouth and then closes it before nodding.

"You will need someone for a sacrifice," Deven says, looking up as Zeek talks through him. Even though I know it's Zeek in charge, I still struggle to look Deven in the eye for what he did.

"Why?" I ask, taking another step closer as I put my hand on my knife.

Zeek makes Deven stand up. "After the siren's territory, which is your next obstacle, you have to go through the molasses swamp and to pass you must sacrifice someone to get across."

"Fuck!" I swear this fucked up mission just keeps getting worse the further we go. Zeek is right though. If we need to sacrifice someone it should be that piece of shit. But just because a ghost possesses your body and takes over your movements and ability to talk, doesn't mean you're not conscious through it all, because you are. You can hear and feel everything going on around your body, you just have no control over it until the possession is complete.

I hear Fellen whimper and I look back to see Mollock undoing the last restraint on her left ankle, and she's starting to wake up.

"I won't be able to possess him outside of my own territory," Zeek adds and I cuss again, because that was the only thing I could think of to get him to be the sacrifice.

"But you were in ghoul territory when we first arrived," I counter. "So was the vampire and the King."

He nods. "Yes, but that was after you had defeated the territory and for the record, the King can go anywhere in the land at any time. Us? The residents, leaders or not, can not break from our territory onto another while humans are on ours or an undefeated territory."

I scratch my head trying to think. "So you're saying until we defeat the sirens, you can't enter it while we're there."

"Exactly."

I hear another whimper and look to see Mollock trying and failing to dress her as she's still not fully conscious. "I got it," I say and walk over, holding back fresh tears at my friend's physical state. Mollock nods, looking relieved, and stands to go talk to Zeek. I gently move her hair out of her face and hurry to dress her. I just want to hold her and keep her safe, to tell her I wasn't ever going to let anything happen to her again, but we need to get this over with now more than ever and I need to focus on getting her back to a fighting state.

"So what if we defeat the sirens and come back and get him with you still possessing him?" Mollock asks, and that's a good point.

"You can't go back in the game and besides—." He pauses and runs a hand down Deven's face. "There's been a bit of a rule change and let's just say even if you could go backward in the game, now there may not be a territory to go back to."

I finish getting Fellen dressed right when her eyes start to open, and I shift her head away from the guys, not wanting her to look at Deven. "Ouch." She grabs at the back of her head and I'm guessing she must have put up one hell of a fight for him to get her down like that, but other than the blood between her legs and at the back of her head, I don't see any other injuries but bruising and his nasty bite marks. I'm going to kill him.

"Shhh." I position her in my lap and hold her close, but that's not Fellen and she wiggles.

"I'm fine," she says, and it's not lost on me how hoarse her voice sounds. I let her go from my death hug as she sits up, but before she can turn toward the guys, I turn her face back to me, making sure to look her dead in the eye.

"We know it was Deven and we are handling it. Zeek has him possessed now." I watch as her cheeks redden and she looks away. She's ashamed and I hate that. There's nothing to be ashamed about.

"Hey," I say to her and she looks back up, and where I know I saw embarrassment before, she's already replaced it with the Fellen attitude I know and love. "Fuck him."

She takes a deep breath in and nods. "I plan to," she says in a deadly voice and my inner monster loves it. I hope she makes him suffer.

FELLEN

They catch me up on the plan and even though I know for a fact it's Zeek in there running that asshole's body by the way his eyes glow blue, I still can't look at him and it pisses me off even more.

I feel so fucking embarrased they found me like that.

So ashamed that I made myself black out so I wouldn't have to think or feel what he did to me, instead of trying to break free myself.

I shake away the emotions as I take a big drink of water and zone back into the conversation. They're still trying to figure out a plan for Deven and I hate that I couldn't kill him now.

"We will get some rest here for a while, eat some food and then move on once we all have more energy," Mollock says, and Alana nods before giving me a side eye. I know that her maternal instincts must be activating or something, because she's like my best friend slash mom at this point. She keeps asking if I'm okay and trying to comfort me, along with looking at me every five seconds like I'm going to burst into tears.

I already did that, and not that I don't feel like I could cry again at any moment, because I did feel like that, but I'm not going to. I'm not going to give that fucker the satisfaction of watching me break down as he sits cozy and way too alive across the fire from me.

"Here's the deal," I say, and everyone quiets down. I try to clear my throat of the scratchy sound, but I can feel that it's going to be there for a while. "I know you can hear me, Deven, and the fact that you were caught means you're not going to get away with what you did to me either way." I pause again and push down my rising emotions. "So you have one of two choices when Zeek leaves your body. You can let me kill you now." I pause and look around to my other teammates and they don't have any problem with what I just said, so I continue. "Or you sacrifice yourself for us when the time comes."

None of us expect an answer from him since Zeek is taking over his body, but Zeek answers with what his internal thoughts are to us. "He's fighting it. Fighting me being in his body. He's pissed and in denial."

"But you can see, right?" I ask in embarrassment.

Zeek nods Deven's head. It's one of their supernatural abilities to help them scare humans. They can view memories and hear thoughts. So, it's safe to say Zeek was able to see what he did to me. "I can confirm to your friends that he did in fact do what he's accused of."

Mollock gets up and walks away without another word and I can tell Alana wants to follow him, but she looks at Deven as she starts to stand, then looks at me and sits back down on the logs we drug over by the fire. I want to tell her it's fine, that she can go to Mollock, but I can't. I'm not ready to be alone with him, because Zeek being in his body or not…It would be too tempting to just kill the fucker.

"Just let him go," I say, after the silence is too much, and Alana stands automatically protesting but I stand also and quiet her. "We are going to have to let him go eventually."

"NO! We are not going to let that asshole just walk around here!" Alana shouts, and I flinch back by her outburst.

Before I can respond or even process, she marches over and mutters sorry to Zeek before she loses her shit on Deven's body, and I can't say that it doesn't satisfy the hell out of me to see her punch Deven hard enough to knock him down before kicking him in the ribs. Mollock chooses that time to come back, as his wife is beating the shit out of a lifeless body thanks to Zeek holding him down from the inside.

Alana is out of breath and spits on him before Mollock tells her that's enough and picks her up by her middle, moving her away. "ENOUGH!"

We let her have a breather, and the silence takes over to where that's all we can hear, and for some reason a laugh bubbles up and out of my throat before I can help it and they are all looking at me like I'm insane.

That's okay. I feel insane. "He threatened to kill you both if I told on him." I quieted down my laugh that was threatening to turn into tears, strong with sadness instead of humor.

They gape at me and then Deven, and suddenly Mollock is holding Alana back again as she tries to go after Deven with a knife. "YOU THOUGHT YOU COULD KILL ME?" she shouts, incredulously.

"STOP! JUST STOP! HE'S FUCKING DEAD EITHER WAY!" Mollock shakes her again, and I can see the tears in her eyes.

"Fine." She takes a deep breath. "Fine."

This is tearing all of us apart more than before. Not this, me. I'm the cause. All because I couldn't stop him from doing this, or I didn't bring it up sooner, or shut it down sooner.

"We need to rest and none of us are going to get that with him free." Mollock throws down a rope. The same rope Deven used on me. I can tell by the blood on it, and I stop myself from grabbing my sore wrists. That must have been what he walked off for. "We will have him tied up and gagged before pulling him along with us, like the animal he is."

Zeek nods in agreement, and we all sit there a while longer in silence before a phantom wind blows through our makeshift camp, strong enough to almost blow the fire out. I think it's Neek. I almost hope it is, but then the reality of my situation hits me and I curl into myself. I don't want him to see me.

I don't want him to know what happened.

I thought I did when I was going through it but now I just want to hide from it like the coward I am.

"The land isn't going to let you sit for long, so if you're going to get rest or whatever else, you need to do so now."

Before I can stop myself my mouth blurts out my thoughts. "Where's Neek?"

Deven spits blood from his mouth before moving his jaw around. "I wish I knew."

CHAPTER FOURTEEN
THE WISH

DAGGER

As soon as the ghoul territory fell, Neek's castle took a hit with incoming residents. This place was big, but not that fucking big.

I head over to Aspen, making my rounds for what feels like the hundredth time, asking everyone if Neek was back yet. I don't need to guess where he is. I know those Fae fuckers took him because one minute we are in the fallen ghoul territory and the next he just poofed and was gone. If I have to guess why they are suddenly so interested in him after all these decades, it would have to be because they either figured out the girl is something important or they were getting ready to just off us all like Neek thought.

"Any sign of him yet?"

Aspen shakes his head before running a hand through

his white hair. “No, and I’m guessing my territory is still intact since Zeek and his territory aren’t here yet.”

“No, but Ashley and her coven showed up a little while ago, disappearing off into their own wing without saying anything.” No one told them to come. They just showed up. Which sucks because we thought they would all be finished off by the humans.

“Fellen.” He looks around before lowering his voice into a whisper and leaning closer. Intrigued, I lean in also. “Does she look familiar to you?”

“Familiar how?” I frown at the question, because no she doesn’t and also why would she.

He shakes his head and mutters to forget it. Before I walk off he tilts his head, motioning to my right. “How is she?” He asks, referring to Savannah, who sits off to the side of Neek’s throne, looking a little worse for wear.

“She’s fine,” I scoff. “For now.” I know she can hear me, but I don’t care. It’s true. We practically had to kill her to get her to this state of somewhat normalcy and now she just looks like a corpse, but at least her eyes aren’t red anymore. We drained almost three pounds of blood from her before the compulsion would work to calm her down. I fucking hated doing that to my mate, but I wasn’t sure what else to do. She was practically gone from us because her mental side had deteriorated so badly.

The rest of my blood mates sit or stand around her, touching her somehow to get comfort after all the years we'd been apart. I would be right alongside them, but I had to concentrate on the bigger picture. I will never get her fully back to health unless we can get out of this land, and for that we need her and Neek locked away before the humans get any closer.

He claps my shoulder, breaking me out of my inner turmoil. "If we are going to do this, we are going to do it right and get the hell out of here. She'll get better." He nods, more to himself than me it seems, before turning to Rune and walking off.

Before I could get any further throughout the crowded space, Neek's blue smoke form appears and lands on his throne before he materializes into his Fae form. I hear some in the room gasp as I approach. "What the fuck happened?" I ask right away.

He looks at me with a sneer, and I lift an eyebrow. "That shit isn't going to work on me." I point to Savannah. "I got her in line, now talk." The room is quiet. Too quiet, because no doubt everyone in this room wants to hear what he has to say. He looks like shit, and I wonder why he hasn't used his magic to heal himself, but the expression on his face tells me bad news is coming. I'm guessing he wants the pain. It worries me.

"It's them or us," he says in a strong voice that echoes through the silent room. I'm tempted to interrupt him by knocking the shit out of him, because they obviously brainwashed him, but I keep quiet, trying to figure out his play. He said they were watching us. It could be an act, because he's been spouting save the fucking humans for months now. I don't believe for a second he's now saying kill them.

Neek stands from his throne as he looks around the room. "That's it. We've lived too long, we should have never sided with them in the first place! So I give you my full permission to kill them."

"But Fellen!" Rune interjects, in annoyance. "We would have killed them but you said-"

"I KNOW WHAT I SAID!" A rush of magic pours out of him, knocking everyone back a step from the force. He looks calm immediately after his outburst, and that's what worries me. Something isn't right. It's more than him putting on a show, he really feels this way. Or he's…

"Fuck," I mutter and look away. They made a wish. They had to. They must have wished for him to kill the humans. Or ask us to. Or allow us to? I wasn't sure. My mind is racing and I look over to Aspen and he can tell something is off too. I know because he has Rune behind him now and giving me a confused stare.

"Something to add, Dagger?" he asks, as he snaps and a Fae servant appears out of nowhere, which confuses me because we ate them all…again...but whatever. She hands him a gold goblet and he takes a drink before lifting his eyebrows at me, expecting me to continue.

"Yeah," I say, balling my hands into fists at my side

to hold down my anger. I see Aspen step beside me in a silent show of force, but I ignore it. "That won't work for us now." I pause and see a lot of silent agreement going on, from the nods in the room. I make sure I'm careful with my words because those assholes were most likely watching us now. "We continue on like we planned."

Neek lifts an eyebrow, while sitting up straighter and holds out a hand, blue flames now dance around his fingers. "Is that so?"

He was acting like an evil bastard from a cheesy movie, and the thought makes me laugh. "Yeah man, it's so."

"And what do you all plan to do about it when it only takes me a flick of my wrist to knock every single one of you out? Same goes for the humans." He raises both hands now, the goblet disappearing, and the fire jumps to the other hand. "I could cover them in these amazing blue flames and watch as their bodies writhe in pain. Watch as they scream for help and appreciate the fact that there is no help coming and they are suffering like Adrian and his clan did." He points over to the side where the witches stand. "Like the witches did."

Aspen steps closer. "You say that, but you don't mean it. She is–."

"My soulmate?" Neek says and I think the whole room holds its breath and now I see life spring into Savannah's eyes for the first time since draining her, and I don't know if it's a good thing or a bad thing. She knows what's going on so hopefully she remembers the plan before she goes crazy again. There's too much tension in this room and one slip up, one fight, where we find out we can tear each other apart and it won't matter if the humans make it through or not, we'll finish each other off before the Queen and King have to worry about us getting freed.

"It doesn't matter what she is to me. It matters what she is in general, and that's someone who's kind caused our suffering," he growls out, stepping away from his throne and moving towards us. "Someone who *killed* your daughter. *Tortured and raped* your daughter," he goads to Aspen's face, who lets out a warning growl. It doesn't take much to get the wolves angry and now he has half the room growling and pissed. I'm pissed myself and in shock at his fucking words.

"This is fucked up man, and you know it!" I warn and step closer, trying to block Aspen from him. "They got you under a spell, or used a wish! It doesn't fucking matter! The point is, we know what we want and–." I look at Savannah as she approaches Neek, who is so taken aback to see her normal he rears back to look at her. "We were going to have to lock you down anyway," I finish, feeling like a piece of shit.

The backup plan was for emergencies only. This was definitely one.

"Sleep," she whispers and the compulsion hits him before he can even blink and he hits the ground.

"Now what?" Aspen asks, and I growl in frustration.

"Grab his upper. I got his legs."

NEEK

You can't just change a wish.

You get three.

Thelia used two. Kill the humans. Kill your soulmate.

They work like extreme compulsion but a wish used after saying the jinn's full name is like living and breathing that command, aching and wishing it true yourself until you make it true.

The humans will die. My soulmate will die.

I feel the need for her wishes to be fulfilled bone deep, like an itch you can't scratch. What she wants, I want. I want them dead. I want them to pay for what they did to us. For what their kind caused us to do, and to suffer all these years.

The wish twists and turns in my soul, enslaving my thoughts, but I can feel a cool liquid pour through my veins as my angel side flares. For a second, I'm aware that I'm telling everyone to kill the humans and I'm trying to get the words to stop, but then the wish takes back over and I feel enraged with the need to have it fulfilled.

Every time someone says her name, my angel side flares again, if only for a second, and I feel something off with her. My soulmate. The one I need to kill.

Fellen.

It's gone as fast as it came, in a swirl of lust, hate and confusion, as everything goes black.

CHAPTER FIFTEEN
ICE CREAM FLOAT LAKE

FELLEN

It was pure tension the moment Zeek separated from Deven's body, but it didn't last long before Mollock tugged the rope tied to him that binds his hands together and walked ahead of Alana and I.

The siren territory was one big lake with colored blobs of brown, white and pink floating on top of it and between the eerie fog. I guess that was the ice cream? Which made sense since Zeek called it Ice Cream Float Lake. This situation would be laughable if it wasn't so tragic. There was only a small beach that water surrounded in front of us and wrapped into ghost territory behind us. There was no way around it. To make it across we would either be going in siren infested water or try to jump from one ice cream blob to another, that floated on top of the water. I'd never eaten ice cream. None of us had, but we'd learned about it from our limited schooling growing up, or in magazines or books. Apparently the taste was really good, cold and sweet.

I didn't care for sweets, and now that I'm going to hop on the shit and fight off sirens while I'm at it, it's fair to say that if this life ever changed for us not to be in complete and utter hell all the time, I still wouldn't try the shit.

"Neek will kill him if he finds out what happened before you get to the swamp." I hear Zeek warn as we start to cross out of his territory. I guess that was his way of saying goodbye.

I look back and nod. "Thank you for holding him down." Zeek nods before walking away.

We've all endured a lot so far, but I'm sure having to chill inside the body and mind of a fucked up rapist wasn't how he wanted to spend his time. Although he is a ghost and he could be loving it, there's no telling. We are just lucky that Zeek didn't end up an enemy instead of a friend.

"Fell!" Alana calls, and I realize I've just been standing in one spot looking at Zeek's back. Oops.

I snap out of it and turn around. "What's the plan?" I ask, as I see a head pop out of the water, too far away to see if it's male or female. Doesn't matter. If those assholes started singing, we were in for it.

"I'll grab the fabric," Alana says, and starts digging in her bag. Mine was gone so I hoped she had something I could stuff my ears with. I keep an eye out as I see more heads pop out of the water and my nerves start to rise with each siren that pops up.

"Here's how it's going to go," Mollock says as Alana hands me fabric and I start to work to tear it up to fit in my ears. "We are going to release you and you're going to challenge the leader," he says to Deven, before pulling off the gag from his mouth.

"And if I don't?" Deven counters.

"Then I push you in like this and we find another way around the swamp, but I know you and I know you have too much pride not to fight your way across here."

Mollock has a good point. I stuff one ear. "We don't have a lot of time," I warn and point to the water. There were too many of them now to count, and we needed to challenge the leader. We wouldn't be able to try and hop our way across when all it would take is one slip up and you're in the water, or one tune of their song and you would go in willingly.

"Just do it!" Mollock says, untying Deven before pushing him forward, toward the water.

"He doesn't have to," says a handsome voice and we all turn to see a sexy, butt naked man step out from around a glob of ice cream that breaches the shore. He is hung. That's the first thing I see, and quickly look away from his privates. Just having the experience I had, I'm not even remotely thinking about sex, but it didn't mean I wasn't wired not to look. Either way I feel ashamed and move my eyes up his pale white skin, washboard abs and onto his pitch black eyes. They sit above his sharp cheekbones, and reddish, brown stubble that covers his structured jaw. He combs a hand through his shoulder length hair.

It's not lost on me that we are all ogling the poor man. Err, siren, but then a wave of reality hits me when Deven talks. "Turn off the lust, asshole."

Mollock shakes his head from side to side, trying to dispel the power. "You mean to let us pass, then?" Mollock asks.

"My name is Stave. I'm the territory leader and yes, I will allow you to pass."

You could feel the but in the air. "But, what?" I ask, carefully.

His dark eyes slam toward me and I stand straighter as it looks like he's assessing me. "The one to save us all" he whispers in wonder and starts to come closer, but Alana steps in front of me. I don't need her to do that, and she never has before. It cements more shame in me and I step around her.

"We are the ones to save you, unless you have more information why you just implied me alone." I ask, and he tilts his head rubbing his chin before his eyes swing to Alana.

"You have a secret," he says, and I look over and she's completely still not breaking eye contact. That usually means she's hiding something. It doesn't matter; we didn't have time to make small talk. We'd just finished off any food rations we had in the last territory. We need to push through as fast as possible. For all we knew, they were just stalling us.

"It doesn't matter," I say, interrupting his creepy assessment of us. For a supernatural being that is extremely hot, he is at least one hundred of the creepy scale. "How do we cross, and are all the sirens on board with that plan, or just you?"

"They will attack anyone that goes in the water." He pauses and looks out to his clan members. At least I think that's what sirens call their members. Too bad the expert was also a psychopath, or I would ask him. Instead I'd much rather bite off my tongue. "And kill and eat you," Stave finishes and before I can help it, I laugh.

"It's really not funny, but the way he said it was funny." I say to the group when they look at me like I'm insane. "Okay, whatever." I wave my hand in the air to make them quit looking at me. I was still out of it from hitting my head to unconsciousness. "So we have to hop our way across?" I ask, clearing my scratchy throat.

He shrugs. "You could try, but the ice cream is really gooey and you'll probably just sink through."

"Right." I click my tongue, looking around for something we could use to cross with. We didn't think of that when we knew we were going to have to pass through Siren territory and good ol' Zeek didn't warn us.

"Then how?"

Mollock steps closer to him, bringing Deven along by his upper arm. "If you're going to pull some shit, start with this asshole. Otherwise just tell us what we need to do."

Stave laughs, throwing up his hands. "Okay, okay. I was just fucking with you," he says and we all sigh out in relief.

"So we can swim across?" Alana asks, and I have no idea why she asked that because none of us can swim. There is a small pond in Village R that can teach children to swim, but we were never taught. Now I'm regretting that. The plan was for us to build something to cross with, but we didn't know we would be stuck on a beach with sand and no supplies to build anything. I think with all the chaos we'd gone through we didn't think before crossing.

He laughs again. "Oh, no. You'll have to hop on the ice cream floats, or my tribe really will eat you," he says and I give him the exasperated look I'm feeling.

"Enough of this." I walk over and start to put my hand on the blob of ice cream that gives off a magic coolness, even though the rest of the air is humid. I think better of it and pause at the last second. "This won't be like a poison thing to touch, right?"

Stave walks over and dips a finger into the pink colored cream that suddenly smells like strawberries and puts it in his mouth, before pulling out his finger with a loud smack. "Nope."

"That doesn't prove anything. The wolves pulled that shit with the tree bark," I say in anger.

"Okay then, test it on the one who raped you," Stave says with a shrug and I'm bowled over by the fact he knew that. I don't comment on it though and move away as Mollock forces Deven onto the glob. He fights it, but only for a second before Mollock overpowers him and shoves his hand right into the cream. Stave may have been joking but the ice cream was gooey, and I wasn't sure it would be easy to jump on, let alone walk and get across.

We hold our breath and after nothing happens, Mollock pulls out Deven's hand, which Deven shakes out in anger. "Happy?"

"Thrilled," Mollock deadpans back.

I swing around and point to the siren. "Just stop bullshitting us if you're really trying to help and tell us how to get across."

"I was being serious. The first one you will need a boost to get on, but then you just hop across and don't lose your balance. That's all the help I can give. If you want to cross, I'll let you as much as I can."

"So your way of help is really like, no way of help?" That didn't make any sense.

He scoffs. "You don't hear them singing do you?" He takes a step toward me and I take a step back. "I'm letting you cross instead of eating you or feeding you to my hungry tribe out there. So go," he raises an eyebrow as he points to the ice cream blob, "before I change my mind."

I sigh as he turns and walks away, bare ass and all. "Okay, let's do this. Asshole first."

"Agreed," Alana says, as we watch Mollock boost him up.

Deven half crawls, half wiggles his way up as the ice cream starts to melt at his touch, but he gets on top. We all watch as he struggles to take a few steps, and the sirens float closer. I wish he would die with every fiber in my being, but he was the most agile one among our group. If he didn't make it across to the next float, I wasn't sure any of us would.

A chill cut through the air, causing goosebumps to ripple across my skin as a siren let out an eerie wail. "They are getting antsy, just go!" Alana walks forward, prepared to go after Deven as soon as he jumps.

"Fuck it." He steps back in the goo before pumping his arms up and down preparing himself to jump.

"JUST DO IT!" Mollock yells and we watch with bated breath as he jumps, barely making it to the next white ice cream float, landing in a crouch.

"He made it." I breathe, in both relief and frustration. Mollock and Alana nod and he bends down and starts to boost her up, none of us wanting to wait long but we are all scared shitless.

Give us a knife, gun or any makeshift weapon and

we'd make it work, but obstacles like this were too unpredictable and I hated to admit it but this is the most scared I'd been in this land yet. It didn't help that the atmosphere seemed to play up our fear, and a group of clouds partly shifted in front of the moon's light, making it harder to see.

Deven makes it to the next one, barely again, and this time lands in a belly flop that bobs the float around and the sirens hiss below him in anticipation.

"I love you, Mollock." Alana looks down and back at her husband. She must be scared, because I never hear those words from her.

"You got this, Lana. Don't let the fear creep in. Just jump, girl, you got it!" I cheer her on and clap my hands. I couldn't let her doubt herself, because that's when mistakes were made.

"Love you too, baby, but Fellen's right. You got this!"

She nods her head, takes a deep breath in and lets it out before she takes a running leap and lands perfectly on the next one crouching down to ride out the bobbing that happens from her weight. "Told yah, bitch!" I holler and hear her laugh.

A siren pops up right next to Mollock and I,hissing.

I hiss back, because fuck them. Mollock laughs. "You going or am I standing here all day?" He asks.

I shake my head. "Nope. We both need to go up at the same time or one of us will be stuck with no way to get up."

He assesses the situation and agrees. "Damn it. You're right. Let's just hope it holds our weight."

I nod, because I'm not sure, but there isn't much else we can do. I can't pull him up, and I can't scale the damn thing alone, he'll have to pull me up once he's up there. And that's what we do.

The texture of the cold goo wraps around my boots and I start to second guess why I thought this was a good thing when I realize there isn't much room with two people on these things to jump, but there's no going back now. "Go," I tell him, as we watch Alana and Deven make it to the next one.

"You sure?"

I nod. "Yup. They can't kill me anyway, remember?" I shrug and he laughs.

"Yeah, I forgot you're the almighty one that is the soulmate of a King." He laughs again, before getting in position and warning me to watch out.

He jumps and makes it and my anxiety relaxes. It seems Deven and Alana have got the hang of it and are doing fine as well.

Right when I go to jump, a rumble shakes the ground and the floats underneath us.

"WHAT'S THAT?" I hear Alana call, but can barely see her.

"I don't know, but Fellen, you better hurry!" I hear

Mollock answer and look right as he jumps and barely lands the next float with an oomph, and holds on tight until it calms down.

"He's right." I hold in the squeak of surprise and look down at Stave. "The King and Queen know what you are now and they won't make this easy."

I open my mouth to talk but he continues on. "Just hurry before it's too late."

I look on and realize how far behind I am and make a running leap and jump with Stave's words ringing in my head.

What did he mean by, before it's too late?

Fifteen giant, pain in the ass ice cream floats later and I finally land on the shore covered in cold goo. My arms and legs feel limp and I can barely move as I crash to the sandy shore, not giving two shits that now I'm covered in sand also. I move my head to see Deven tied back up. Mollock and Alana are way too friendly. She's in his lap kissing his neck and it confuses me how they think this would be the time, but whatever. I close my eyes for a second and wait for my racing heart to calm down.

I must have fallen asleep for a second because when I open my eyes, Alana is shaking me telling me to get up and the ground is shaking again.

I sit up as a wave of dizziness hits me from hunger and a cramp hits my stomach. I grit my teeth and look up at Alana, who gasps. I put a hand on my cheek to wipe the sand, but she still gives me a weird look. "What?" I ask.

She points to her right eye. "Your eyes are doing the thing again."

"Ugh." I complain and close them. Why do they keep doing this? And what the hell is going on with the stomach cramps? I thought I was starting my period, but maybe it's the weird soulmate tether thing I saw from Neek? Maybe he's doing something to me through the bond?

I wait for the ground to stop shaking and I stand up. "Stave said we needed to move fast when the ground did this back there." I point to where we jumped across the lake and I see sirens watching us from the water and sigh.

"I think it's kind of weird that the King, Neek or whatever shows up, says he needs to make it across and wants to help us, and then up and leaves." Mollock says, and the thought has crossed my mind.

"Yeah, but-" I start to say, it doesn't matter when I see blood on him. "Hey, are you okay?" I point to his neck and he covers it with his hand and steps back.

"Yeah, just landed rough." He turns around and stops the conversation and I turn towards Alana.

"Who lands on their neck?" I ask her, but she just laughs before giving me a shrug and walks to join him.

That's kind of weird.

"Ready to make your sacrifice?" Mollock asks Deven and I forget it and catch up to them.

We haven't left the siren territory, but I was guessing by the group, or tribe, of the sirens getting closer and closer to the shore, we wouldn't be able to stay much longer. I look forward to where the path that follows through the land comes out of the sand and straight through a dark green grass, with a bubbling dark liquid around it. A pile of black, gummy looking rope sits next to the path before it completely submerges in the bubbling liquid.

"Molasses Swamp."

We turn around to see Stave once more, and he's not alone. It seems his tribe is done waiting and although there are a bunch of sexy bodies among the group, they also look terrifying with their serrated teeth showing and pitch black eyes, all the while, hissing and growling.

"Time to go," I say and we start to move forward together as a unit.

"I'D USE THE LICORICE TO MAKE A BOAT!" Stave calls out to us right before we cross into the new territory.

"What's licorice?" Alana asks me and I shrug. I had no idea.

"I'm guessing it's what's piled right there," Deven says, jutting his chin towards the pile of black rope stuff.

The ground rumbles harder this time shaking us around and Deven loses his step falling before Mollock can help him. He catches himself from face planting into the bubbling liquid of the swamp at the last second, before screaming out in pain. Mollock rights him and the shaking stops.

I gasp as he pulls back his shaky hands that are bloody with skin sliding off them.

"What. The. Fuck." I don't have any other thoughts.

A pop sounds from the bubbling liquid and I look closer to what I thought was fog, is steam. It's hot. Super hot. I look at the licorice and it's half laying in the stuff and not melting. That was it. Make a boat and cross but–.

"Someone has to push us." I realize that at the same time Alana puts it together outloud, and we all look at Deven, who looks pale and close to losing consciousness after having his palms melted off.

I can't say I feel sorry. I think having to melt to death is a pretty fitting way to die after what he did to me, but I don't know how we are going to get in the boat and convince him to willingly walk into molten liquid and push us across either.

"I think it's rising and it's going to take a while to figure this out," Mollock says.

"And if I don't push you guys?" Deven asks, in anger.

"Then I slit your throat and you die all the same," I snap back, but he doesn't even flinch.

"We'll see," he says as he sits down, not bothering to help us, and that was fine by me. Let him sit and sulk.

"I guess we will." I don't even look back as I grab the

long, thick strand of licorice and help the others get to work.

NEEK

I wake up and it only takes me a minute to realize they tied me up in the same spot, and in the same way Savannah had been tied up.

It's laughable.

"I can get out of here at any time," I say, and Zeek appears in his kitten form, but it's Dagger that steps out of the shadows and answers.

"Territory two is gone." I figured as much when I saw Zeek. It just pisses me off more.

"And you're still not convinced that they need to die for destroying our home?"

"Our home?" Zeek asks incredulously as he takes his Fae form. "This is our prison and you need to tell us how to get you to snap out of this!"

"There isn't any snapping out of it!" I growl.

I watch as they look at each other, a silent conversation going on, which ghosts have the ability to do. Dagger looks shocked for a second then sighs before nodding.

"And you don't give a shit about Fellen?"

"No," I growl again, trying to bat the confusing

feelings of hot and cold away as my two sides battle for dominance of my powers.

"I'm willing to test that theory," he says in confidence and raises an eyebrow in challenge; I scoff in response and he shakes his head. "I wish I really didn't have to show you this, Neek."

I struggle against my bond, as he lifts a hand to place on the top of my head and I know he's about to project a memory on me. "Show me what?" I ask in anger as I try to get him away.

"This."

The binds are off and I'm walking up a hill, on a path through Zeek's territory. I hear Alana calling her name behind me and that's when I see something off. A brown thing wrapped around the stick of a lollipop. What the?

I walk closer and shock floods my system as Fellen's state comes to view.

The rest of his memories play out of the team finding Deven the culprit, and I scream out as I break from the memory and transform into my smoke form. The wish captures my mind. Telling me to kill her over and over. My soulmate tether flares and my angel powers clear my mind enough to think just for a second. I could kill her later, but for now…

The fucker is dead.

CHAPTER SIXTEEN
TORTURED HEAT

FELLEN

There was no way to fully make a boat out of the supplies we were given.

Instead, it's really just a raft, with lipped edges. Hopefully it's strong enough to hold all of our weight.

We test it with the front half in the water and throw Mollock on there first, because let's face it, if it can't hold him alone, it isn't going to be able to hold all of us. Once we get to the middle of the swamp, there was nowhere to go if it started to sink. We would have to just boil to death.

Fantastic.

Not.

Another problem is the rapist asshole to our backs, watching us finish up the raft as he continually assures us that we can rot in Hell before he'll push us across and kill himself.

The whole thing is weird.

He went crazy and did what he did because of his

psychotic feelings. Fine. But for him to not feel an ounce of remorse for what he did to me, even try to pretend to apologize or even explain himself to us, is just the shit topping to this mess. It's like he didn't care about any of us and sure we are literally telling him to die, but it would have happened before now if we didn't need to draw this out. He should have expected that.

Did he really think he was just going to get away with what he did and believe that his little threat was assurance enough for me "not to tell"? Fuck him. He should have known I didn't need to tell anyone, he was dead by my hands the moment he crossed me.

"Ready?" Mollock asks, as the ground rumbles beneath us again for close to the twentieth time. It has been getting worse, along with a heavy wind that I just hoped might help us to cross.

We nod and look back at Deven, who we had to gag again, along with hog-tie to keep him quiet and still. He already tried to run, but that only helped in us learning that we can't go back into another territory, just like Zeek had said. Only, we got to witness it when Deven took off in a hard run. Mollock gave chase, only for Deven to run into an invisible force field face first before landing on his ass, as blood squirted everywhere from his nose busting open.

It would have been comical, but the land was getting progressively worse trying to push us through, and all of our nerves were fried. We just wanted to get this over with.

Looking across the swamp, it wasn't wide at all. Really one hard push, hopefully, and we might make it right past the middle. We are assuming a good push, but we realize that the player you sacrifice to get across would have to get in the molten molasses and push the others across. But since we had a non-willing sacrifice, we are guessing Deven may push us at the least, even at that. From there we just planned to use counter balance techniques, along with some left over licorice rope to get the rest of the way across. If none of that worked then it was left open that we would have to sacrifice another player.

This could go wrong in so many ways.

Maybe if he felt sorry for what he did, he'd feel like making it up by sacrificing himself. As it stood, I didn't feel a damn thing from the death glares we were all on the receiving end of.

"Mmm!" Deven grumbles as Mollock pulls him to a stand, supporting his weight as Alana unties him. I want to spit in his face. Instead I look away and grip my weapon tight.

If all else fails, I have a plan. It was a bit morbid, but still a plan.

I turn back to the others as I decide maybe telling them the plan would help give the asshole some motivation to do right by us the first time and get us across. "If he won't get us across, let's kill him and use his body like a row."

Alana's eyes bug. "Umm." She stands and packs the rope in her backpack. "I mean, that would assure we actually get across." I see the panic in Deven's eyes and I don't care. It was a brilliant plan.

"Maybe, depending on weight," Mollock agreed, taking off the rest of Deven's bonds. That was true. We were still unsure about weight as it was and lifting a dead person and attempting to use their body like a paddle would be a lot harder than it sounded. He finishes freeing Deven before taking off his gag. "What's it going to be?" he asks him, and I already see the disagreement of our decision building in his stare, and stance. He wasn't going to go down, either way, without a fight.

We've taken all his weapons and supplies, so really we could just shoot him right in between the eyes and go forward with the plan, but that isn't the way and his death is owed to me.

I sigh before anyone else can speak and step toward him. "What you did to me was cowardly." It's hard to look him in the eye without flashbacks invading my head, but I use those to fuel my anger. "Pathetic," I spit and sneer, taking a step closer and he doesn't step back, just stands taller with a frown. "You aren't a man, and definitely not worthy to call yourself a hunter." Emotions start to pick up in my voice for some reason and I pause, clearing my throat to keep it from breaking. "If you want to fight fairly because you're not man enough to own your shit and take your punishment, then so be it." I step back and throw my staff to the ground opposite of the swamp, and the others step back, but I can tell they don't like this.

Beating him to death will be my pleasure, if I don't just decide to push his ass in the swamp before we can utilize his body. Deven gives a small laugh, confidence splayed on his face as he steps back as well and shakes out his arms. "You think you can fight me after I so easily subdued you before, then fine. I hate that I'm going to have to kill you all to live just because I took what I wanted like a man, but if this is how it has to be–." He pauses and shakes his head with a sigh, like this is an inconvenience for him. "Then so be it."

My nerves build as he steps to the right and I step left to keep him in my full vision, and then we circle each other. We'd trained half our lives together. He knew my tells, and I knew his, but to say we'd be evenly matched would be a lie. Where I excelled more at weapons training, he excelled at hand to hand combat. He did have an advantage, but that didn't mean I wasn't well trained, and with the hate I had for him, I wasn't going to let that asshole get me on my back a second time.

My eyes quickly bounce from his face to his left hand, waiting for him to take the first move, and he would. He was too confident. All I had to do was wait for his giveaway and I could evade and wear him down enough to get the advantage. I look up a half second too late as he lunges and I side step away, turning fast to kick out, but my boot doesn't make contact with his back like it should have.

"WAIT! WE NEED HIM!" Mollock yells, and my eyes slam to the source.

Neek.

My breath stalls as I watch him hold Deven to his front with a knife pressed into his neck. Deven's head rears back so far that his Adam's apple pops out right above the blade as he looks straight at me. "Cheater," he rasps at me in anger.

Does Neek even know what happened or did he just show up to see what was going on? I looked down and tried to calm my shaky breathing. I don't want him to know what happened to me. "I'm owed this coward's death," I whisper, finally looking Neek in the eyes. I open my mouth to say more, but shame slams into me at the way he's looking at me like he already knows what happened. He looks irate at the same time he looks concerned for me.

My soulmate tether pulls and I know it wants me to go closer to him, but I firmly stay in place, ignoring how bad I wish he would drop that piece of shit and walk toward me instead. This isn't the time for that and even if it was, that isn't me. I'd never needed that kind of comfort before.

Finally he speaks. "You are." My eyes slam to his again, and this time I gasp as I know now what the others are seeing in my eyes, because I see the same thing in his. Blue flames, hidden behind a malicious stare. "But so am I," he finishes, and smoke starts to whisper off his skin, as the flames in his eyes grow brighter and the ground starts to tremble again.

"Get on the boat," he commands Mollock and Alana, before looking at me. "You will get this coward's death in the way of his sacrifice across the swamp, but before he can fully succumb to his injuries…" he growls, pushing the blade further into Deven's neck, drawing a thin line of blood to trail down his skin. "He will answer to me for his crimes."

He knows what he did to me. I don't know how, but my cheeks redden all the same from the shame and I can't stand it. What does he think of me? How does he feel about me now? My flame has died down and I'm almost relieved he's shown up, even though that's not me. I should be arguing to allow me the kill. To let him blood coat my hands, but instead reduced to just the awkward shame I now carry. I suck in a shaky breath, "Neek–."

I start to say something, anything, because I'm not even sure what can make this more bearable. Knowing that he must think I'm a weak girl that can't handle myself? Or him thinking I need him to play savior when all my life I was the only savior I needed.

"Get on the raft, Fellen," he growls and I try not to flinch at the use of my name instead of Emerald. I take a step toward the raft as Mollock and Alana get it in position and Alana is climbing on before crouching at the front of it to steady herself. "Push them." Mollock helps me to steady myself as I climb on, the molasses popping angry, hot bubbles around the makeshift raft, that bobs gently from the majority of it being in the liquid. There is a sickly sweet smell coming from the swamp, like the rest of this place, although this has a burnt smell wafting off it.

Looking forward, you can already see the start of the next land, and it looks like a winter wonderland. Or what I can tell those used to look like on Earth. I'd never experienced snow, if that's what the white, soft looking land ahead of us was, but I guess we were about to find out. It did have a certain trick to it, as the ground gleamed happily like a thousand diamonds from the substance reflecting the moon's light. I just hoped we could make it through the vampires as fast as we have all the rest so far.

I look back right as Neek is shoving Deven toward the raft and if he didn't look scared before, he does now. The reality of the situation finally hitting him.

Us too.

Mollock crouches down and so do I, as Alana puts her arms around us.

We all look down.

He deserves it. I should look on proudly and watch him in agony as he pushes us through the molten liquid, but I can't.

Somehow I feel like this is still all my fault. I don't know how or what I could have done differently to avoid us all ending up here.

It feels like the silence might break us and we are all holding our breaths.

"NOW!" Neek booms and I see Deven's shaky hands land on the raft, and I close my eyes.

Before he starts to push, Deven finally speaks. "For what it's worth, I won't ever be sorry for loving you."

A chill breaks through me at his words. He's insane. Alana, Mollock and I all squeeze each other tighter as we begin to move.

And he begins to scream.

NEEK

Kill.

Kill.

Kill.

The wish's demands pound through my mind just as strong as the blood pumps in and out of my enraged heart.

She did this. She ruined my land. Destroyed it. Her and these humans.

I fight with every morsel in my being not to slit her beautiful throat and bathe in her blood, and while I fight that desire, I hold on to the fact that at least one of the wishes demands will be fulfilled. I almost forget why I'm fighting against the wish to kill her and then a pull happens within me, images of her green eyes flash throughout my mind and I gain reason, if only for a second.

I don't know what pissed me off more.

Showing up and seeing that piece of shit try to fight her, or see the injuries from him evident on her beautiful skin. A calmness fell over me and I ignored the tug of bond that demanded I wrap her in my arms, and grabbed up that piece of shit, fighting the urge to end him quickly.

I could work around the wish and the land's demand of no helping humans, by instating my own rule. The rule that I can exact vengeance on any human I wanted and that included torturing them. If the first part of that just happened to get them across and further into winning this game while the demon inside me demanded to stop this and kill them all, so be it. I was at war with myself, and what the wishes of my master and land demanded of me.

Bone deep, I knew this wasn't going to end well.

There had never been a jinn able to fight off a wish. It didn't matter how long you put it off for. The better half of me kept pushing to break through and fight the powers of my master, but the only chance of me ever getting free and Fellen not laying dead in my arms is if she takes control of me and claims me back from the King and Queen.

Seeing how the wishes strain on my reality continues

to poison me with murderous rage, I wasn't sure how long it was until I lost my mind completely and killed the only hope we had left.

I barely kept a hold of my restraint as that piece of shit pushed the raft as far as he could before his bones were melting as he screamed and cried in pain. It was music to my ears and right before he passed out, I snapped him out of there and back in the dungeon where I'd escaped from earlier. He's barely conscious and I'm guessing it's from the pain.

That wouldn't fly. Yeah, he only only had stubs for legs and I'm sure he was close to his heart exploding in his chest from the extreme temperatures his body was subjected to, but I needed him alive and awake for his torture.

A deep cough comes from behind me and I watch as Dagger comes down the stairs, waving a hand in front of his face. "Fucking shit, that reeks." I ignore him and get to work forming torture weapons with my powers, using ice. The witches had all sorts of torture weapons, but I didn't want any help with my plans for him.

The wish starts up with it's insistent demand for a kill and I block it out by instead replaying the memory of Fellen getting found after his assault. A growl slips out before I can stop it and I swing around, punching the asshole in the face so hard I hear a crack. It only barely rouses him, so I turn to Dagger. "I need him awake for this."

He sighs and bites into his wrist as I grab Deven's hair in a tight grip and throw his head back for Dagger's blood to pour down his throat. Drinking vampire blood to a human was the equivalent of getting stabbed with adrenaline. It would do fine to wake him and keep him conscious, whether he wanted to be or not. He squeezes out a good amount before drinking his blood up and licking his wounds shut. "I take it they made it acros-"

He stops talking and is gone.

That's all I needed to know. They were now in Savannah's territory.

Deven's eyes slam open and he sucks in a shocked breath. I don't gag him as he starts to scream, but instead relish in them. "Lesson number one." I turn after grabbing one of the ice tools I made and grab his shaking hand, not giving him a second to comprehend what I'm about to do before I pull hard and rip his nail from his thumb. "If you can't take the screaming, you aren't man enough to cause someone pain." I look him straight in the eye, my face as close as I can bear to get it to him and I pull another nail.

He cries out like the little bitch he is as his nubbed legs move from his sitting position. I should have hung him from the ceiling by his skin. I take a step back and look up wondering if I still had time to accomplish that before his whined plea breaks my thoughts. "Haven't I suffered enough? Kill me," he begs, ending in a screamed cry as I go back to pulling nails.

"I wonder if you would have stopped, if she would have asked you the same question?" I inquire and he hangs his head, sobs wracking his body, complimenting the shaking. His nervous system is in battle with itself, trying to keep up with the pain and vampire blood at the same time. No doubt still in agony from losing half his legs, but now this. It's almost as if the universe knew I needed the most amount of pain to accomplish this torture.

I finish one hand and decide that isn't enough.

I look back at the tools. "Please." Deven whines.

"Lesson number two." I grab the knife and turn back to him. "It compliments lesson one and I think it's a good one for you to remember when you're burning in Hell looking for your next victim." I reach out and grab his jaw tight enough that when he cries out I put the forceps in fast and pull out his tongue.

He's frantic now, tears trailing down his face and he tries to shake his head but I keep it still, squeezing the tool hard enough it pierces his tongue to hold it in place. "If you can't get the answers you seek, they don't need to speak." Hmm. I smile insanely at that one. "Fucking rymthes. It will be perfect for you to remember." As soon as I let go of his jaw, keeping his head from moving, I grab the knife and slice across his tongue, effectively pulling it off in one go.

Blood sprays across my face and I spit what little of

it got in my mouth back in his face as he starts to choke on his own blood from it pooling in his mouth. His eyes start to roll back in his head and I slap his face a couple times before shoving his head forward so the blood runs out and not down his throat. "Can't have you choking to death before we get to the good parts," I tell him and make a slow, deep cut down his arm.

"Almost makes you wonder what she would have said if you would have let her talk?" I wonder.

He throws up and I laugh before turning away to grab a bucket to collect the blood pouring down his arm. No use in wasting it. When that one is tapped, I'll move to the other. Fellen and her team must have been keeping the vampires busy enough for them not to smell the blood down here, which was both impressive and curious at the same time.

"Lesson number three." I chain his bound arms to the manacles hanging above him before kicking out the chair and letting him hang. He mumbles out a cry and the sound elates me, but it isn't enough for me to fully exact revenge on the coward that raped my mate. I rip down his pants and it seems to wake him up as his head elevates from its former position and his eyes widen in fear. I step forward as I show him my next useful item. A metal rod, with thorned vines wrapped around it.

"Don't give what you can't take," I growl out, thinking of him pounding into Fellen as red coats my vision and my powers beg me to turn, but I ignore them and slowly start to walk behind him.

He's begging me. Or trying to. Hard to hear him without a tongue. She probably sounded much the same when he gagged her. I imagine her crying out, tears running down her bruised face as she tried begging him to stop. I position the makeshift dildo to his asshole and he's screaming now and trying to wiggle his body away from me. Good. I imagine she did the same thing. "Seem familiar?"

Another outburst of tears and I laugh. "Oh, you're right. You probably whispered sick shit in her ear like the little pervert you are, just to help yourself get harder. How about this?" I look down and slowly push the tip I fashioned like a butt plug, into him as he starts to scream again. I lean forward, letting my chest brush against his back and whisper in his ear. "You'll like this, baby. It will feel so good."

I shove the pipe in as hard as I can with one hand as I hold his shoulder to keep his body still with the other and he screams so hard that there's no sound now but a rasp. Blood pours out of him, over the pipe and I pull it out just as hard and shove it back in. My rage wishing with every pull and push I could erase the thrusts he put into her, but I know it won't. I might not even fully ebb the hurt I feel for her soul deep, but it will ease the justification for revenge I'll feel later.

If only I can keep him alive forever so I can come down here and let out my rage when I think of how he touched her.

I want to continue to rape the piece of shit with this magnificent torture device, but if I do, he'll be dead in no time. I was sure he was close anyways, so instead I shove it inside him one more time and leave it there as I step back to study my work. It wasn't enough, but he was quickly burning through the vampire blood and almost ready to succumb to his injuries.

I wasn't going to let him until I finished though.

I walk around and eye his hardened dick and laugh. Perfect.

His head hangs but I know he can hear me from the whimpers he's giving me to let me know he's alive. I lift his head for him all the same as his eyes open and close on repeat. "I warned you." I pause and collect myself to finish the job, refraining from stabbing him in the heart. "I fucking warned you that she was going to be the death of you if you ever looked her way wrong."

"YOU TOUCHED WHAT WAS MINE!" I roar out and grip his jaw until I hear the break. I step back and roar out so loud the dungeon around us shakes, and concrete cracks, crumbling down on top of me. I'm enraged at him and myself for letting it happen. For not being there to stop it. For provoking the piece of shit. No matter how the wish corrupts my very core, the center will always live and breathe her until her last breath, or mine. I close my eyes as I remember feeling fear and pain while I was being beaten in the throne room and I knew it was hers but didn't know from what. He punched me on a cellular level, that affected my very being not being able to protect my mate.

I get to work fileting the skin from the arm I did cut, as I torture myself with images of her beaten and assaulted body. I don't talk. Not for a while and when I finally pull down, ripping to separate skin from muscle, the rest of his arm skin and let it hang over his hand, I know how this was going to end.

I make Dagger wake him up one more time and the screams start again as I slowly cut his balls off and then start on his still hard dick. Which confused the fuck out of me, but good. It would make this easier. When I'm finished his eyes are closed but he's still alive barely, not for long though. I lift up his head by his hair and his broken jaw hangs. I wait and his eyes crack open.

"You should have never gotten your dick anywhere close to what's mine." I lift it up so he can see it. "Now, choke on it." I shove it as far down his throat as I can, and he does exactly as I demand.

I step back and watch with a simmered rage, until he finally takes his last breath.

Somehow I still feel like he got off easy.

CHAPTER SEVENTEEN

YOUR ANSWER LIES WITH FROST

FELLEN

We stand at the border line before crossing from swamp territory, into vampire territory and watch the line of mixed supernaturals staring back at us.

"Are they there to help the vampires or to keep them back from us?" Alana asks, and it's a good question, because I had no idea, but I had a bad feeling about it.

Something about crossing the invisible line in front of us seemed so final, and I hated to even think the word, but it felt like fate or destiny was right there among the supernaturals staring back at us, like this was it. We were either going to get through this territory or we died. I clench both hands tighter around the staff as irritation floods my veins. "I feel like this is it, you know?" I say, hating to even voice that out loud, but when you know your time is up, you just know. It pissed me off. Neek was nowhere in sight and I felt foolish for thinking he'd be able to get us through the land. Maybe it was one big joke after all. Give the humans hope and then slam reality into their stupid, hopeful faces when they get to the finish line.

I look over to Mollock and almost rear back in surprise to see the tears built in his eyes. He scoffs before giving a small smile and shaking his head. "We've had one hell of a run through, right?"

Alana laughs outright as she rolls a vampire stake between her two hands. "It's not over yet. This is my time to shine, so I plan to go out swinging hard."

"Bring it in," Mollock says and we huddle into a circle, hugging each other tight.

The Bad Lands train you to be confident and never give up, but they also train to know when to recognize your final moment so you can go out worthy and not a coward. We were most likely staring at our deaths. So as we held each other, we said the hunter's prayer one last time. We acknowledged our lost team members, and prayed for our loved ones back home, taking extra time on Mollock and Alana's sweet babies. I hoped to everything that there would be one last miracle thrown our way and we would walk through this territory and onto the last just for them to make it back to their children.

"Who's ready to kick some ass one last time?" Alana asks, sniffling as we all pull back.

I pull the sad stick out of my ass and grin like a fool, feeling anything other than happiness but refusing to let a single tear drip down my face. "Let's do it!"

As soon as we step over the line, coldness like I've never experienced hits us with the force of a wind storm. It's a bitter cold that feels like it's freezing every part of my body at once. Even my lungs feel chilled with each breath. I shiver and bring an arm up, wrapping it around me to try and fight off the cold as we step further into the fluffy, cold snow at our feet. If that's what it was. This territory smells the strongest so far when it comes to the sweet smell, and every brush of wind sends the substance dancing up and around us. I swear I could taste sugar.

"This sucks." I don't need to state the obvious, but I couldn't help it. If we were going to fight all these assholes at once, why couldn't we at least fight in a decent climate? I hear Mollock chuckle as we continue on, the snow getting thicker at our feet and coming up to our ankles as we trudged through it and the once blurry line of supernaturals started to come into focus more. In the very middle of this line I recognized Dagger, Zeek, and Stave. I wasn't sure who the rest of them were, but the red eyes told me vamps, the orange told me wolves and the purple told me sirens. It seemed like we were getting a welcome party. I didn't understand how they were all here now, when we were told that they couldn't cross into another territory before we defeated it but it wasn't like I could say that. Maybe I could? But then did I really expect them to throw up their hands in defeat and say, "Ope, you're right we'll leave here".

"They tried to lock me down." A voice cuts through, coming from our right and not the line in front of us.

I train my attention towards the source to see a beautiful, blonde haired woman in a long light blue dress approaching us. This must be Frost. I couldn't help but wiggle from nerves. Apparently she was what they were all worried about us getting past, and I knew that had to be true from the color of her eyes. Vampires dawned bright red eyes, however, the older and stronger of them were identified by how dark the red was. Her eyes almost look black from how dark they were. I looked at Alana and she was ready, but I wasn't sure I was okay with her fighting Frost. I knew for a fact we'd never faced any vampire as strong as her. Apparently Mollock felt the same, because as Alana got into a fighting stance he did the one thing I've never seen him do…He steps in front of her. Just like I figure she would, Alana steps back to his side. I appreciate him making his fear known and wanting to protect her, but he had to know she couldn't be side lined.

"You could let us pass and no one would have to stop anyone," Mollock says to her as she continues her slow approach.

She is absolutely beautiful in a haunting way, that I almost feel mesmerized.

"I haven't lived this long and suffered the fate I had, not to appreciate the long con." She pauses when she gets within arms length, as she continues to study us, and we her. I was guessing she was talking about letting us through as the long con, but I felt her speech didn't end in her being on board with that idea. "However, I'm not one to blindly believe something without seeing it with my own eyes."

Her dark eyes train to me as she tilts her head and I try to hold back the shiver and stand straighter. "There's a rumor that you hold a Jinn's fire within you," she says, talking to me.

I finally find my voice. "I am his soulmate." I pause, licking my cold lips, trying to warm the numbness. "I have no idea why my eyes do what they do." Not that it's any of her business, but if she needs proof of this to allow us to pass, I would put away my urge to drive my staff into her neck, and be civil. "You guys will never know if you can be freed or not, if you don't try."

She throws back her head and laughs, flashing her long fangs. Fear trickles in. Maybe I said the wrong thing? "You want to test your theory?" She asks, and I glance at the others not sure what that means but I take it she means to bite me.

"SAVANNAH, NO!" I hear Neek yell and my head turns to him transforming into his Fae form, but before I can even blink I hear the others yell and then a sharp, deep pain is radiating down my neck, spine and seizing every part of me. The pain is so blinding that I temporarily lose my sight as my heart clenches in my chest and then it's over and she's ripped off me with a roar while I fall on the cold, wet ground, gasping for breath.

She fucking bit me!

My hand flies to my neck as I feel the blood flowing over my fingers and my vision waivers from the pain and reality of the blood flowing out of me.

I would either turn, or die.

A warrior scream sounds and I blink to see Mollock charging approaching vampires and I need to get up, but my muscles aren't cooperating with me, and I slip back down to the ground. Neek is leaning over me and I want to laugh. This is such a fast and shitty death. But I can't even do that. I didn't even get to fight. I messed up and my distraction was my end.

Right as my eyes start to close and welcome the blackness my slowing heart is placing over me, I hear Frost screaming something, but I'm not sure I'm hearing it right. It doesn't matter anyways, but the words float softly around my mind regardless as I take my last breath.

She's a jinn…

NEEK

I can't stop the thrill that rushes through me seeing Savannah bite deep into Fellen's neck. I'm both hopeful and terrified of her death. The confusing feelings battle within me, until Fellen's screams break my debate and I fly forward, tearing Savannah off of her.

She gasps and backs away, pointing a shaky finger at Fellen and I'm at a loss of whether to break her neck, congratulate her, or run to Fellen. I turn away and ignore the commands hammering in my head and go to grab Fellen when Savannah's words stop me.

"She's a jinn."

I straighten up and turn in time to see her blood mates racing towards the others in her team and them charging back. Within the confusing rush of things, Savannah loses her compulsion on the others and they are fighting back the vampires from the humans. It's a shit show and fray of chaos. I don't waste another second taking Fellen away. As far as I can, anyway. I can't take her to my castle. Not yet. Not until the vampire territory is defeated and either Savannah will yield or they will all kill each other in the fray. Either way I could hold Fellen here until it was over.

I just hoped I could hold off the wish's demands long

enough to heal her and keep her safe. I gently lay her down on the floor, away from where any blood was spilt and work to cover the mess left from killing Deven. Savannah would know more than anyone who Fellen would be, so I didn't doubt her words, but it didn't make any sense. Jinn weren't just born into existence. Not anymore anyway, and they couldn't be born from two humans, so if Fellen was born and grew up in the Bad Lands, how could she be jinn?

But Savannah worked as an identifier in Fae. She was one of the best around. She worked in Fae orphanages to identify a baby or child's lineage and help find their parents within their rightful communities. It did involve her taking a small amount of blood to achieve this. Nothing like what she took from Fellen, but that could be blamed on the savage soul she'd turned into while here. Either way I believed what she said, I just didn't understand it.

A few things lined up, though. The fire everyone has been claiming to see in her eyes was a jinn trait. One that is recognized right before a jinn claims their power. Which is only allowed once they are reborn from the flames, almost like a phoenix. Their bodies need to be rematerialized to allow them to have a smoke form. If what she said was true. How long would it be before I'd have to watch Fellen burn up and claim her powers?

And if she was a jinn, who were her parents?

Did that mean there were jinn Fae in the Bad Lands

that had been thrown there and forgotten?

I shake my head from the thought. That wouldn't be right. During our dream visits before she got to the land, she'd told me she was parentless; they died during a hunt. I doubt two jinn parents would be easy to take down. Red slithers in my peripheral as I push the bucket of blood over to the wall and toss the knife on the rusted work bench in the corner. She was having a nightmare, but how was I able to feed from her if she wasn't human. I frown as a headache takes over my head right when the incessant wish starts up.

Kill her while you can.

Kill her for your master.

Kill her.

Kill her.

"UGGGH!" I yell out, grabbing my head. I want it to stop, and I wish it was just as simple as ignoring the words but it wasn't. My feet were moving on their own accord back to the knife I tossed down.

To fight it, I transform and go into her nightmare.

My eyes adjust to a dark bedroom as I look around and spot her on a single cot, her body drenched in sweat and white sheets wrapped around her naked body. Immediately I'm seething, assuming she was dreaming about getting fucked by someone else but then she whimpers before a scream tears from her throat. I walk closer and see the bite on her neck and then remember the first nightmare I visited with her. It was almost like a continuation, but why does she keep–?

I pause mid thought and realize if Savannah is right and Fellen is a jinn, these weren't nightmares. They were memories of her ancestors. But that still didn't make sense. Jinn are able to view their ancestors' lives, lived before them to gain precious memories to help the knowledge of our race survive. But she wasn't viewing, she was living them herself. A man comes into view, shirtless and sits next to her by the bed and pats a wet cloth on her head, shushing her.

"It's okay, almost there. Your eyes have already turned. Once you survive this first shift, it will be easy." His voice is so familiar. I move around to the side of them and get a closer look at him. It's the guy she called Rowen from the first dream, but that wasn't right. He looked familiar in a way that my brain was screaming something I couldn't interpret and I hated that I couldn't place him.

He turns his head, training his eyes straight at me. I know he can't see me, because these are memories or a dream. But a memory runs to the forefront of my mind. A younger alpha wolf coming to Fae from Earth and announcing his plans to take over control of the Fae wolf packs.

I gasp, finally putting it together.

Aspen.

But how?

Fellen screams again before blood starts pouring from her ears, eyes, mouth and nose. I look away, still confused. She wasn't making the change to werewolf, or her ancestor wasn't. This wasn't making sense, and I couldn't take the confusion anymore.

I exit the dream and pace as I watch her sleep.

None of this made sense.

A gasped breath breaks my inner turmoil and I watch her wake, keeping my distance to make sure I don't follow the wish's demands.

She coughs and goes to grab her neck, but it's healed. I didn't even touch it, which confirms she is some type of supernatural. *Jinn?* I still wasn't sure. If she was, we maybe more fucked now then we were before hand. If I put her in front of the King and Queen to claim me, and they realize what she is, they will bind her and have two jinn at their disposal. Unless I claim her first, which would make sense for soulmates to claim each other as their true masters to protect each other. I needed to know how this was possible and her true name, if she even knew it.

"I need to know who you really are," I state as she sits up, confusion bright in her eyes. I would give her a minute, but there was something she wasn't telling me. There had to be. Jinn aren't just shit out randomly.

"Oh my gods, is that–?" I look at where her eyes are trained at the remains of Deven that are crumpled in the corner on the floor. I don't have time to toss him out to be eaten. I sigh.

"He got what he deserved." She can't see the full extent of what I put him through and I'm glad I had partially covered him before she awoke. "Answer the question, Fellen." My eyes fly back to the knife as soon as her name passes my lips, and this time my angel side can't counteract the wish. I grip the counter it lays on to keep myself from grabbing it like the wish wants. I growl from the effort of holding back and swing back around to look at her.

Why did I think having her here alone with me would be better than around people who could stop me from myself?

"I don't know what you mean?" She stands, and bites her lower lip with a frown. "I told you everything!" Her voice rises with frustration. "Whatever you guys are seeing is just this fucked up bond, or you," she juts a finger at me as angry tears build in her eyes, "did something to me!"

My frustration builds, causing an ache in my chest. "I didn't do shit to you! You aren't telling me the truth! Why are you dreaming of people from Earth, when it's been gone for thousands of years? How would you know what it looked like to even have those dreams if you weren't immortal?" I open my mouth to say something about Aspen, but stop while I'm ahead. One thing at a time and the way she was looking at me like I spit in her face told me getting anything from her was going to be a challenge.

"What do my dreams have to do with anything?" She counters, putting her hands on her hips and it makes me bark out a humorless laugh at her attitude.

"They have to do with everything!" I shout and she doesn't even bat an eye, but I'm too worked up to stop. "Tell me the truth about your parents!" I demand and now she does flinch back, almost like I slapped her.

"They don't have anything to do with this," she warns in a low voice.

"They have to!"

"They don't!" She screams, a tear breaking loose.

I stalk forward in anger. "How do you know?" I stop before I can reach her, because with the rage swirling within me, I'm not sure what I'll do with the wish's influence.

"BECAUSE THOSE AREN'T DREAMS THEY ARE MEMORIES OF MY PAST LIVES!" She screams and pushes at my chest, I let myself stumble back while I try to process that.

"You must be confused. Jinn can view their ancestors' lives, but they can't live them." I state, shaking my head.

"They are mine. In each one they call me Fellen or another name that sounds familiar."

This snares my attention and my heart slams in my chest. Her true name. "What name?" I ask.

She looks warily at me now as her temper dies down. "Why?"

"Fellen," I warn and this time I do step into her space and reach out, gripping her shoulders. "Tell me."

I take another step and push her against the wall and when I press into her we both gasp, unable to fight the pull we feel towards one another. I move her chin up to look at me with a shaky hand, because I'm holding back from wrapping myself around her like I truly desire. "I need to know to figure this out, to fight this-." I stop myself before I can say wish, and almost like it knows I'm trying to fight it, I start to squeeze her tight, unable to stop until I pull myself completely away from her with an enraged growl. "FUCK!"

I look back to her and she has her head tilted in confusion. It's fucking adorable and I hate it at the same time. She would never be mine while I fought this impulse to want her dead, and she wouldn't be mine anyways unless she makes it through this. I needed to know what was the truth with her.

"Just-." I start to demand for her to tell me, but she interrupts me before I get the words out.

"Fellenna." My head swirls with desire, power and feared recognition.

That name.

There was only one person with that name.

I knew that because it was outlawed for a Fae to be named it.

But it couldn't be. There was no way.

I shake my head and back away from her as my mind races.

"Neek, what's going on?" She asks in anger.

I look up to her and this time, I really look at her features and know what I'm seeing is true but I don't know how.

"That name is outlawed in Fae."

She continues to look at me like I'd lost my mind. Maybe I had, but I couldn't bring myself to repeat it just yet because if what I was thinking was true my soulmate was both my savior and a ticking time bomb. "Okay? So?" She's confused and pissed. I don't blame her.

"It was outlawed after the King and Queen's daughter was stolen," I continue, recognizing her mothers eyes.

"And?" She continues with an attitude, still not understanding. "Someone obviously didn't listen to the rules." She laughs. "We didn't get the memo in the Bad Lands. Either way that is just what I'm called in my past lives, and not even all of them. My name is Fellen."

I walk to her and now I see it.

Blue fire flares in her eyes. It would if she felt threatened. I'm guessing she would feel that way if her whole world was about to change. I gently trail the back of my hand down her cheek, wiping away another tear as I watch her bottom lip tremble.

"You are their lost daughter, Emerald." She sucks in a shocked breath and shakes her head in denial, but

I already know it's true the moment I say it. I still don't know how, if she claims to have previous lives, and remembers growing up as a child in the Bad Lands but it was true. I felt it through our bond.

The funny thing is, her parents just sealed her death.

Unless we could fight the wish, and them.

CHAPTER EIGHTEEN
IDENTITY CRISIS

ALANA

Fellen and Deven had been called on a special assignment to Village V. Rumors of a wraith getting in had everyone on high alert. I wanted to go with them, in fact Mollock and I both wanted to go seeing how Railen and Nebula were there, but unfortunately we were headed for an assignment to clear a vampire nest found twenty five clicks north.

Mollock set up the shift leaders for the villages as I made sure the team we were taking was ready to go.

A damn training team. I hated those. Inexperienced, gung-ho, and stupid at best. Deven and Mollock were the best at training the new hunters. Fellen and I, not so great. We didn't have the patience and honestly, they made our job ten times harder half the time, trying to save them.

The two moons were blood colored. It fit the atmosphere for hunting vampires and set my mood to badass. I loved it. I loved the feeling of adrenaline right before we busted into a nest. The nerves that played throughout you and never knowing if you would walk out of there. Adrenaline junky, is what Fellen called me. Either way, whatever I was, was appropriate to get the job done.

"If they know we're here, why aren't they coming?" Jessen asks, and I refuse the scoff because…training. Sigh.

"Just like you said. They know we're here, so there's no need to whisper." I look back at her before eyeing the rest of the team. Mollock places a hand on my lower back. That's his way of telling me to be nice. "Remember your training. Vampires nest, or hibernate, when they are low on food. It's like they are in a stasis until they smell blood."

I pause and strain my hearing as I hear something coming from behind us. Looking back and around, there is nothing but a tiny group of trees that surround the cliff face and cave we are about to enter. "Right now they are starting to stir awake, and will be groggy. It's the perfect time to attack. Hit them fast while they are weak."

Mollock starts to instruct them on positions, and I hear the noise again. This time I can tell it's rustling. Like leaves. I look up but even with the two moons' light, I can't see anything and it puts me on alert. My normal adrenaline high is starting to turn sour with fear and I can't shake the feeling of being watched. One inconvenient noise, fine, whatever. Two…well, it's better not to leave that to chance when you live in a land full of monsters.

They wait for my signal as I usually lead and Mollock gets the rear when on training missions, but I can't chance the noise. "Go ahead with them and I'll take the rear. I want to check this noise."

Mollock looks unsure, but we are training them on a mission and rule number one. Never argue or second guess your team lead. He nods and then uses hand signals for them to proceed. I turn and keep my back to my advancing team and look at the group of trees we'd been standing under. Vampires weren't known for their patience. If this was one, which would be highly unlikely since the nest in the cave was silent, then it would have already pounced from it's starved state.

I walk forward, gripping a stake at my side as I scan the area slowly, trying to remember what other supernaturals we'd faced lately that could be hiding. Werewolves were killed not too far from here last night, but that didn't make sense. They wouldn't be playing hide and seek, either. My nerves start to swelter and my heart beating hard was starting to get uncomfortable, but I pushed back the fear and proceeded on before stopping.

Why wasn't I hearing any noise?

I spin around and look at the cave. They should be taking down the nest right now. Something wasn't right. I growl in frustration and decided fuck the noise. But right when I start to race forward, a figure falls down from a tree ahead of me and I skid to a stop, raising my stake.

Vampire.

What the?

"Thank you for this meal, little one." He chuckles but

makes no move, right as the rustling starts again and I turn right as a female vamp lunges. I stab out and land my target but it's too late. She bit me and her venom has my knees giving out as she turns to dust and she hits some type of vocal cord because I can't even scream.

I look up now to see at least five more starting to approach me and I know we fucked up. It was a trap. How?

It didn't matter, it was too late. The feel of fangs sinking into any open space that showed flesh struck me with blinding pain. They weren't trying to kill me.

They were turning me.

Right as I give into the blood loss, Mollock's angry roar sounds above me.

"STOP!"

I wheel around to watch the approaching hoard of vampires stop in their tracks like magic and face Frost. I'm guessing their blood mate.

Mollock killed one of them and a werewolf was about to finish off Dagger when she stopped the mass fighting. I'm not going to drop my guard, but I do take a minute to lean forward and take a deep breath in before moving over to Mollock, who looks a little worse for wear. The sight pisses me off and a growl slips from my lips before

I can stop it.

"The only human here is him." Frost points to Mollock and my cheeks redden before she continues as shocked faces look back at us. "And he can't be killed by vampire code unless we kill her first," she states and I'm rooted to my spot.

I wasn't sure how much longer we were going to be able to hide the fact that I turned one month prior to coming into the land, but I hadn't expected anyone to just look at me and figure it out either. The urge to use my new supernatural abilities has been hard to push back and resist, but I have, other than drinking blood. Which Mollock gives me willingly and since I don't take too much, and learned how to heal the bite wound, he's fine.

"Is this true?" Dagger asks, stepping away from the werewolf, which transforms and stands naked next to him. I recognize the wolf as standing next to the alpha back in their territory and I wonder if that's his mate, or one of them.

I don't know why, but for some reason I look at Frost before looking at my husband. No point of lying if it might save us. "It is." I confirm as Frost gives me a smile and starts to approach.

She puts her hands up gently. "I'm not going to hurt you." This makes me think she's safe, for only a second, but then I remember that there is a human that they might want and to get to him she stated they have to kill me first.

Mollock's hands land on my shoulders as another growl rumbles through me and I want to just push on and find Fellen. Make sure she's okay and get back to this mission.

Get home to our children.

"I'm amazed that you've been able to resist your natural urges on your own, while pretending to be human and actually getting away with it," she says with awe in her voice.

I don't answer about that though. It's not why we're here. "Will you let us pass?" I ask, and she raises both eyebrows before sputtering out a laugh.

"I guess I will, seeing how the only human here is blood mated to a vampire." She laughs again.

I look to Mollock as a question slams to the forefront of my mind. "If you're the only human here, does that mean you're the only one that can free the humans?"

He just looks at me with fear and I don't blame him. What if by the end of this none of us are human?

Who will save them, then?

FELLEN

Something drastically good or bad must have happened between the time I was bitten and Neek stepping away from me with fear in his eyes after claiming I'm some lost

Fae princess, because he announced we could pass and then disappeared, leaving me to find a way out of the torture dungeon.

I don't stick around long, eyeing Deven's dead body and not wanting to wait and see if he'll come back from the dead and exact his vengeance on me for a second time. Although this time I'm pretty confident Neek made sure he was down for good. I follow the concrete steps up to a house filled with dusted sugar, and creaking wood floor boards, and the cold I must have forgotten about creeps back in.

I still couldn't process what he claimed me to be.

Jinn. I scoff out loud at the thought.

Long lost Fae princess. A laugh bubbles out this time.

Right. He was just jacking with me.

I pass a room with a lit fireplace that hosts coffins. I shiver, and not from the cold, but from the uncomfortableness about my situation of being in a nest for vampires. I spot a door leading to the outside from it being wide open and frosted snow flurries down in a storm-like fashion with harsh winds. I don't hesitate to step outside, because it's better than finding out if anyone's home. Plus I needed to find Alana and Mollock and hoped they were okay. Why couldn't he elaborate before taking off? Or was he wanting me to freeze to death searching for my team members that may or may not be dead?

A lump rises in my throat at the thought and memory

of the blurred fight happening around me right before I passed out. They would have been way out numbered. I take a deep breath and steel myself for the reality that they probably didn't make it.

One minute I'm walking through knee-deep snow. Next, Frost and Dagger are in front of me.

"For fuck's sake," I cuss, and she smiles. Not in an evil way like before, and it sets me on edge. "If you bite me again I will use this bullshit jinn stuff on you." I'm not even joking.

She and Dagger laugh, but he's the one to talk. "You can pass through, seeing how we can't eat you anyway," he says and I want to punch him in his face, because I can't even see the way out of this bullshit to leave even if I wanted to and I don't, seeing how I need to find Alana and Mollock.

"Your teammates are fine and waiting for you at the territory's edge," she says, pointing the opposite way of where I was going. I give them both a hard look before turning around and heading that way. I had no weapons. My staff was probably lying in the same spot where I got my neck half torn out, unless they grabbed it so honestly, if they planned to take me down, there wasn't anything I could do about it anyway.

"You will need us if you plan to hold back Neek."

I hear her speak before glancing to my right and seeing her beside me. Vampire speed annoyed me almost as much as sirens and their singing. "And you need me to get you out of here, although no one has still explained how that's to happen." I pause and look at Dagger, who's walking to my other side. "Unless someone cares to explain now."

Honestly, it was straight bullshit at this point all the things Neek fed me. All of them are extremely unbelievable, but the fact that I still haven't been told how us, or me, making it through the land will save them all is the most irritating of all.

Silence followed and I laughed. "Oh what, so I'm some lost princess and now a jinn, but I can't know why you all are so sure I can free you."

They both gasp and I take it I wasn't supposed to say that, but I didn't believe it was true anyway. It couldn't be. I wasn't born in a Fae castle. I was born to Ruby and Travis. They were skilled and incredible hunters who died way too young when a run happened in a village and they underestimated the power of ghosts. Past lives or not. It wasn't true and the fact that I had fire in my eyes didn't prove I was supernatural. I hadn't poofed into a bunch of smoke or had bangles on my wrists like Neek so, no, I wasn't that either.

"What?" I ask in annoyance, no longer scared at the threats to either side of me but annoyed by one and pissed at the other.

Frost's hand jutted out, grabbing my upper arm in a tight grip and my breath stalled in my throat as I took in her serious expression. "Don't utter that to anyone else. Ever," she warned in a serious voice and her eyes flash silver. Compulsion. I recognized it, but I didn't feel it blanket over me like it should have. I'd only been compelled once on a hunt and that was enough to recognize the incredible power of these supernaturals and fear that from them alone. But I didn't feel compelled.

I repeated it again, testing it and even though my tongue felt heavy repeating it, it wasn't impossible.

"She's a jinn now. That won't work," Dagger says with concern on his face.

I roll my eyes. "I'm not jinn."

"You are," Frost says with a nod. "And whether or not you believe it, I'm telling you not to repeat that for your own safety."

"So you believe it?"

She looks at me with skepticism, before looking at Dagger and then back to me. "Neek told you this."

I nod. "After I told him a name that I'm called in my past lives." It didn't really matter to me who knew about this or not.

"Well. For us and you, you better hope that's not the case." A haunted look falls over her face. "And like I said, I wouldn't repeat it."

We crest a hill and I see Alana and Mollock now, relief flooding my system so fast my knees almost give out. I stop talking to them because they aren't giving me anything useful and they walk beside me, not having much to say either, until we get to the border.

"I thought supernaturals couldn't cross over into territories until we defeated the land or something like that?" Alana asks, after I plow her and Mollock over with a huge hug and Frost explains she intends to help.

"The last territory will be different and plus, there's some things you need to know," Dagger says, cracking his knuckles. It's not lost on me how he keeps giving nervous glances to the gothic style castle that sits in Neek's territory. It's surrounded by fog and the only description I can come up with in my head is: haunted.

"Like?" I ask, as I tuck weapons into the belt Mollock is supplying me with.

"You wanted to know how you can save us all," Frost starts, "You, Fellen, are the key. Being his soulmate allows you to claim yourself as his true master to his current ones." I nod slowly, not really understanding, but listening to try to make sense of it all. "King Ace and Queen Thalia claimed him as their jinn when they entrapped us here. It's how he's burdened with being the King of Sweet Land, and bound by the rules of the land."

"Magically," Mollock added, piecing it together.

"Yes, but there's more. Jinn can grant three wishes to their owners." I hate hearing her say owners, but I bite my tongue and let her continue. "And they've used up some type of wish or wishes on Neek."

"How do you know that?" Alana asks.

"His behavior," Dagger supplies. "He was the one that pulled us all together to get you to cross once he realized you were his soulmate. He knew that if you could make it through Sweet Land and get an audience with the Ace and Thelia, you'd be able to take possession of him, freeing him and in turn," he turns around with his arms wide before coming back to face us, "freeing us who are trapped in this land."

"So I just go up to the Queen and King and tell them I'm his soulmate and bam, you guys are free?" I ask. It seems too easy and what about my, err, the human race that I'm trying to save. Would doing that negate the audience and the request to set them free? Because if I had to choose, soulmate or not, I would finish my mission and free the humans in the Bad Lands. The supernaturals have lived immortal lives, trapped or not. I needed to assure the survival of the human race.

I watch as they both look at one another and then back to me. "You need to say a certain phrase, along with knowing his true name," Dagger answers.

"His name isn't Neek?" Alana asks, stealing the words from my mouth.

"A jinn's true name is sacred. It's the only way you can claim them and become their master. You bind them magically and are in control of them physically, emotionally and magically until you use the three wishes they grant you," Frost explains. "And seeing how you are jinn, or…becoming jinn, you will have the same worry. It would be better for you to claim each other to keep someone else from capturing you."

The word capture swims around my head, and I swallow hard. "But I can't be a jinn right now." I bring a hand up and wipe the flurries from my forehead. "I can't transform into smoke, I can't fly. I can't–." I pause, trying to figure out what a jinn could even do and try to rake up the memory of that book Deven gave me before coming here. It feels like years ago, and other than the picture I can't remember much from what I learned.

"You will," Dagger assures. "There's a lot to it, but the main point is. Whether the Queen and King show up here in Neek's realm, or you make it past Neek and gain an audience with them, you need to find out Neek's real name and claim him so you are his true master, in order to free him."

Frustration pours through me. "So why hasn't he told me this or given his true name yet?"

Frost steps forward looking at the Sweet Castle. "I don't know that reason, but I can tell you that's your next step."

"You need to be careful though, like I was saying, Neek was all for getting you through the land before they made a wish with him," Dagger scoffs. "Then he came back saying all humans needed to die and was completely changed. Something is off with him, so–." He sighs as he shakes his head. "Just be careful. Making it past him will be hard enough."

"Yet, we've been told that about every territory and especially this one and we breezed right through," Mollock counters.

"He's right," I agree and Alana nods.

"That may be so, but this will be different," Frost says and shivers like she's cold or scared. It's weird seeing her do that, when she looks like a fierce ice queen. "A wish will corrupt a jinn's very being, right down to his or her soul until the wish is fulfilled. There have even been some who've died from not performing their master's wish."

I nod. "And if they wished for him to not let us pass, or kill us?"

"Then he may be able to fight it and that's probably what he's been doing so far, but he won't be able to forever. Unless you claim him or the Queen and King take back their wish by using another, it will happen," Dagger says before stepping over the line. "The sooner we get this over with the better. And Fellen."

He looks back at me with a grim expression. "Do not let anyone know what you told us." He looks to Alana and Mollock now. "Not even them."

CHAPTER NINETEEN
THE SWEET CASTLE

NEEK

As the King of Sweet Land, I feel the chains tighter than any other captive here at this moment. The land and wish work together, causing the very worst version of myself to take control. And all I can do at this point…is bend to their will, and let it take away any responsibilities of my soon-to-be actions.

In the blink of an eye, I could end her, and watch the very life bleed from her eyes with no remorse. Just as easily as I could lose myself in the irresistible taste of her kiss while trying to fight the curse put upon us. No one, not even myself, could know how this would turn out.

The jinn were said to be some of the most powerful beings to ever exist, but when it comes to defeating Fellen, I feel powerless.

I sit on my throne and grip the arm rests tight when they step into my territory. I know the exact moment, because the land whispers the threat of them in a phantom wind that teases me to destroy. I don't move. Instead I close my eyes and concentrate, using my powers to zone into their location. Fellen and her team, what's left of it, aren't alone. The distinct smell of blood, wolf and fish hit me and another scent that surprises me…incense.

I figure they wouldn't be alone in this with how hard the others want their freedom, but even with help…

I drop my head and stare at my frayed jeans as I grit my teeth together in anger. I stop the thought before it's finished.

If I didn't fight this, the chances of everyone in this room dying together were just one of the many possible outcomes. If I could snap my finger and put a pack of wolves down, this was child's play.

I shake my head as my soulmate tether flares to life and the feeling of euphoric pleasure drifts through me as her scent hits me. I'm both turned on and outraged by it.

"Fuck off," I growl at the Fae bitch in the corner. The one that I swore I've killed more than a dozen times, but yet keeps appearing despite her well-being. It could be a different servant, but either way, the constant hovering of them was annoying enough to make me slam my own head into a concrete wall out of frustration.

I glare at her in warning, because she still hasn't moved and I swear her body shimmers for a second, but I must have seen wrong. "Why aren't you leaving?" I ask in warning. She was about two seconds away from getting her throat snapped after I siphon her fear out until she is nothing left but a husk.

She finally looks my way. A smug expression on her face. "I'm here to make sure his majesty does his job."

"And if I don't?" I growl out, rolling my shoulders to keep myself from attacking her.

She smiles. "I'm just here to observe."

I go to head her way when the castle doors slam open. I sit back down and think of a way to meld myself to this chair. If only it was that simple.

Fellen rounds the corner, walking confidently into my throne room, followed by her team and the leaders of the territories…all of them, but Adrian, follow behind her. Even Ashley does and I'm taken aback, wondering how Fellen managed to get her on their side. Before I can speak, Zeek's voice is in my ear.

"Sorry about this, buddy."

Then, nothing.

FELLEN

"It worked?" I ask incredulously, because holy shit! If he was knocked out that meant we could pass through the land and we won! I turn around but I'm alone. What the?

"Not quite." I hear a new voice. One I've never heard

before and suddenly I realize I'm not even in the same place. I'm in a giant throne room like before, but this one is colored in different shades of red and blacks. I continue my appraisal of the area, coming to see a man and woman sitting upon thrones on a raised dias in front of me.

She looks terrifying. Her hair is a bright silver with streaks of dark red, and she looks both young and old at the same time, which confuses me. Her eyes shine so bright green, it almost looks like they glow and I look away from her to the man who sits on her right. He looks the same, age wise but where she is plumper in size, he has an athletically toned build, and pitch black hair. They were obviously a Queen and King of some type.

Almost like they were waiting for me to catch up with who they are, they sit patiently as they occasionally drink from golden goblets. "You're King Ace and Queen Thelia," I conclude out loud and I should be pissed, or terrified to be standing here after all they did to human kind, but something is so surreal about it, instead I almost feel in awe. How many times had I read that sign and almost didn't believe they were real? Now here I was, staring straight at them.

"Indeed," Queen Thelia says with boredom.

I open my mouth as my brain catches up to the fact that the first thing they said upon my arrival was…not quite. So did that mean we didn't make it through the land, but then why was I here? And *how* did I get here?

"What do you mean, not quite?"

Before she can answer, I get my shit together. "I request for all the humans to be moved from the Bad Lands into the regular Fae lands where they won't be hunted for sport ever again!" I panic because they just continue to look at me in boredom and then I remember Neek and freeing the supernaturals, but I never learned his name so how could I do that? The warning Frost and Dagger gave me floats to the forefront of my mind and I decide to not get ahead of myself. If anyone should be here to diplomatically ask for our freedom, it should be Mollock and not the headstrong, arrogant team member, but here we are.

"No," The Queen says, tossing her hand up nonchalantly.

"No?" My eyebrows raise to my hairline and I'm shocked silent. No? Just like that? She was just going to say no? My breathing stalls. Did I already mess up?

"No, I quite like the entertainment of watching them run around like scared rats." She snaps her hand and high above us a vision of the Bad Lands appear from her magic. The village we left are currently fighting off a hoard of zombies, ghosts and vampires. It's madness and they are extremely outnumbered.

I barely keep myself up right as sadness fills my chest and pierces my heart. "No," I whisper and then look away right as a house is broken into and a child is torn out in a zombie's clutch. I wasn't sure what a child was doing in the hunting village, but it didn't matter. It was awful to look at all the same. Anger rises in me and I'm suddenly hit with an extreme stomach pain but I ignore it, however, they don't.

I watch as both her and the King stand and then we are back in the throne room with Neek still passed out.

The Queen looks around in anger, before spotting the territory leaders. "What is she?" She squeals in anger as I grunt through the pains.

No one talks and I'm shocked they are willing to hold my identity a secret, but the faint color of blue smoke catches my eye. I look over to see it coming from Neek but then looking back, no one else seems to notice it.

What the hell was that?

NEEK

I'm dreaming.

Something I haven't done in a long time and probably thanks to Zeek and Ashley, I'm stuck in this state. It's clear she is keeping me locked mentally while he's keeping me trapped physically. I can't say I'm entirely mad.

Fellen kisses me back just as hard as I kiss her and tears trail down her face.

I go with it, because fuck it. For the first time I'm not wanting her dead. I'm just wanting her. If this is the only way I'll get her, so be it.

"I don't care if this was all a trick, or some game. I don't care if you hate me. I'm begging you to make me forget it. Make me forget him!" She cries, and I look down and now she's in nothing but black, lace underwear with bruises, blood and bite marks covering her skin.

My sick mind plays with the image of her when they found her after her attack. I try to pull away and she holds me tighter as more tears fall. "Just take away the pain, Neek. Please." She pulls me into a kiss and I moan, feeling the weight of desire taking over me. I want her, no matter what. Whether in a dream, reality, or even well after I'm gone. I will always want her, and to have her begging for something I know will make us both feel better. I can't deny her, even if I wanted to.

I grip her hips, her skin warm and soft under my touch and kiss her deeply, as she moans into my mouth.

Fuck I needed her.

I grab the knife I used to torture and kill that little prick still crumpled in the corner and move my fingers slowly inside her underwear, groaning when I feel her slick folds, before pulling them away from her and adjusting the knife to cut them off of her. She sucks in a shocked breath and the back of the cold, dirty knife is against her.

"Scared?"

She wiggles before closing her eyes and throwing back her head, arching her back, and I make sure to keep the knife steady and away from her sweet pussy. I lean over and take one of her pebbled nipples in my mouth, sucking and twirling my tongue around it before biting it. A moan flies from her and as much as I like to hold up and let the anticipation build, I can't hold back anymore.

"Scream, Emerald," I whisper, before cutting through the bottom of her underwear, leaving them crotchless, before turning the knife around and shoving the handle up her soaked cunt.

I can tell I scared her as her scream of Neek sounded more surprised than pleasurable. I shush her and rotate it up inside her, feeling her juices collect around the handle and on my hand. Blue is so thick in the air, I'm surprised I'm not choking on it and my cock is dribbling in anticipation of getting to feel her warmth. "I would never hurt you," I assure her, before kissing down her neck as I continue to fuck her with the knife.

She pulls back now. "Why do you have to kill me, Neek?" The lust is off her face now and concern fills it, causing me to halt my actions.

"*Emerald-*" I'm fucking shocked, because how did she know that?

"WHHYYYYYYYYYY!" Her piercing scream is so loud I can feel my eardrums burst before I can stumble back, drop the knife and cover my ears. The scream is so loud it would rival a siren's scream. My head feels funny and I close my eyes from the pain.

When I open them, I'm out of the dream and back to consciousness. Stave smiles at me and I realize between him, Ashley and Zeek that was a siren scream to bring me back. I'm surprised my ears aren't bleeding.

King Ace and Queen Thelia stand off to the side, anger splayed in their expression. "I SAID WHO IS SHE?" Thelia screams, and I start to stand, but see the Fae servant from before trying to sneak away and my attention on her makes the rest of the room follow where my eyes are trained.

"STOP!" Ace shouts and the servant stops. "Who are you?"

The servant girl looks nervously around before trying to dart from the room, but Ace throws out a hand and she hits an invisible barrier. I look over and hold in a gasp at Fellen, who is leaning on Alana for support and holding her stomach and she breathes deeply. Her skin is coated in sweat and has a bluish tint. Fuck. She's turning. The King and Queen approach the girl who is now trying to scoot back on her rear to get away from them and I take that moment to glance at Zeek who I can feel next to me.

I tilt my head towards Fellen and lean over, giving him the one thing I thought I wouldn't tell anyone, my name. His eyes widen, but he knows what to do and makes his way over to Fellen. She needed to claim me before she turned and they found out.

"I SAID WHO ARE YOU?" The servant is lifted in the air with Thelia's magic by an invisible choke hold as she grunts and grabs at the force, her face reddening.

Zeek is telling Fellen, but I'm not sure it will be enough and then the servant is laughing insanely, like someone just told the funniest joke.

Thelia grips her hand together and the girl is further choked to silence, but then her body is rippling with some type of magic before a blinding light flashes and the girl isn't there anymore. Instead a handsome man appears in her place, with dark brown hair, and dressed in long black and gold robes, like royalty would wear.

The Queen gasps as the King growls…and fuck.

"Kupua!" Thelia hisses.

He laughs. "Not quite. While my children are the kupua, most refer to me as Loki, God of Mischief. At your service." He bows and I hear Fellen getting worse and decide to make my way over to her during the distraction. I wasn't shocked by noises coming from everyone, because holy shit. A god hasn't been in this realm, in…forever. It's safe to say the Queen and King met their match with him.

Loki was the father of the kupua fae, or said to be. It's safe to say now actually looking at him that it's probably true and if that's the case, the Queen and King have a lot to answer for from their years of outlawing, torturing and killing the kupua. They were known for shapeshifting and their trickery, often used as spies, which is why their kind got outlawed and ordered to be eradicated in Fae. While it was pretty peaceful in Fae, the Dark Fae kingdom still ruled and tried all it could to take Thelia and Ace down, and the kupua were used so much by the Dark Fae that it eventually led to their end.

I see the other leaders giving each other looks and I know what they're thinking. If there's a time to take down the King and Queen, it's now. We either go out fighting or not at all, but I needed to be free first. Fellen needed to say the words. Now, while they were distracted and before she arose as her true self.

"I'm glad I made it for the family reunion, although I have to say I was hoping the jinn would hurry and kill her a lot faster than he did. We've been playing this song and dance for too long now and the joke's run its course."

Right before I reach Fellen, Aspen reaches out and grabs my arm with a look of fear on his face. Ace is saying something to Loki, but I ignore it. "Since he's shown up," he pauses and looks over to his mate and then back to me, "I remember her." He looks me dead in the eye and I know he's talking about Fellen, which means it's real and she does have past lives that apparently Loki had something to do with it.

"Because!" Loki yells out and changes his once humorous attitude for one of irritation. "For thousands of years you hunted and killed my offspring because you are nothing but fearful and ridiculous creators! So I did the one thing I could to get back at you and teach you a lesson, while I grew my offspring in the Dark Kingdom." I hold my breath and realize how this was coming to Fellen.

The King and Queen do nothing to answer him but threatenly hold magic in their hands as they glare at Loki in fear. "I stole your precious Fellenna and cursed her to live over and over again."

Thelia cries out, dropping her magic and covering her mouth with her hands. I almost feel sorry for her, but not quite.

"Where is she?" Ace threatens, and livid energy pours out of him. As the most powerful Fae *arguably* in existence, he's not one to rival with. Although, I've never seen a Fae face a God and live either.

Loki laughs and looks straight at me and I growl in response. "She lived over and over again. *Horrible lives. Horrible deaths.* And I cursed her to be reborn every time, never activating her Fae traits and never remembering her past until now. Which is fine, I needed time to rebuild my army in support of the Dark Fae, but now we will be at war and playtime is over. It's time for her to die, and what better way than at the command of her parents, and by the hands of her soulmate."

"Never." The King and Queen whirl around and look at Fellen in shock as I promise Loki in a low voice that it will never happen. I look to where Fellen is doing worse.

Her skin was now completely darkened. She would transform soon.

Thelia gasps, putting it together and the room stills. "For every kupua you took from me, she suffered each and every lifetime. And this little show couldn't play out better if I'd planned it myself." He pauses and laughs again. "Because I did plan it!"

He snaps his fingers and suddenly he's an overweight man, shirtless, dressed in tacky lu'au. I hear Alana and Mollock swear and Fellen is looking up from her crouched position.

"Why?" She grunts and a blue fire alights her fingers.

"Chief Oak was probably my greatest identity. Don't you agree, my girl?" He asks her and suddenly she's screaming in blinding pain.

Ace and Thelia falter, not sure whether to run to her or face the threat.

"Release me." I demand and now it looks like they've finally come to their senses. "YOU NEED ME, NOW!" I yell and Loki is back to his regular self and making his way toward Fellen, but the closer I move the more I want to kill her and it's too late, they know, everyone including the god knows what she is.

"WITH OUR LAST AND FINAL WISH WE FREE YOU NEEKILAHAUD!" Ace yells. He turns with a black magic balled in his hands and launches at Loki, who disappears.

My body ignites in a blue fire, as the magic hold they had on me burns away and my gold wrist cuffs melt off and face the ground with a clang. A weight is lifted that I couldn't remember being there, but I suddenly feel lighter, and my head clearer.

"NO!" I hear Thelia scream as she runs to Ace, who is holding his stomach and bleeding on the ground.

It was the only second he needed for me to be distracted before Loki snapped his fingers right as Fellen made her final transformation to a jinn, and they disappeared.

Just like that the world stalls and before the supernatural leaders could reach the King and Queen from their charged attack, they are gone as well.

I drop to my knees and right as the castle starts to shake, I scream letting my rage, fear and confusion take over.

We were there.

We were right there, and she slipped through my fingers in an instant.

I ignore the castle splitting apart and showing the stone path continuing now right into Fae. Apparently, we were free, but I ignored it all.

The rush of the supernaturals racing out and back to our home…I ignore it.

The cried screams of Alana and Mollock…I ignore it.

By the time I realize there is light shining on me and a sun is gracing Sweet Land, I finally get up and realize that

I can't let her go.

I won't.

"Where are you going?" I reel around, shocked at the heated words of Alana, shocked to see her and Mollock still here when it's clearly been a while since I've stayed in that state. The fucking sun was over Sweet Land, no more eternal night and everyone was long gone. Safe to say, days is how long I've knelt there in shocked devastation, and yet they remained. Determination is set in her glare and, for the first time since meeting her, I know she isn't human. She's a vampire. It's weird how foggy I'd been. How much of myself I'd lost to this land. No more.

"I don't care if I have to go to the realm of gods. I'm getting her back."

"We are coming with you," Mollock says and I shake my head.

I wasn't going by foot, it would take too long. "I'm not going by foot." I needed to get to my home village and get to a seer. I needed to figure out where she was first.

"We don't care. You aren't leaving us. It's not what she would have wanted!" She argues and I know she's right. I cuss and grab my head. Fellen was with Loki and now a jinn, which gave me no doubt he wouldn't kill her but instead claim master over her and use her, probably in this coming war. She could be in the realm of gods or in Dark Fae territory. Either one would be dangerous to enter.

I do have a few tricks up my sleeve and I may be able to use her friends to help get her. "Fall behind and die," I say, before walking out of the castle and stepping onto the stone path. I will transport us to where I need to go, but first there's something we need to do and it includes going into the forbidden worlds, which just so happened to be right in front of us.

You don't live this long and not know a few things.

So fuck the more powerful, threats of war, or even the god of mischief himself. I will move Heaven or Hell to find Fellen, and that's what I plan to do.

And I won't stop until my last breath.

THE END FOR NOW

Realm of Horrors Coming Soon

Pre-Order Here:

https://www.amazon.com/dp/B09Q7DF77P/

Thank you for Reading! I would love ot hear your thoughts on Amazon, Goodreads Reviews or in my Facebook Group! Please check out the first chapter of If You oNly Knew to read some of my other work.

IF YOU ONLY KNEW

If You Only Knew

Trigger Warning

This story contains subjects of abusive relationships, mental illness, suicidal tendencies, and loss of a child. It's intended for an adult audience of eighteen years or older, only.

CHAPTER ONE

GABRIELLA

"I don't understand why you just can't make it stop or go to a fucking doctor, Gabby! I mean, shit, you go to your regular monthly ones. Just tell him what's up, so you can get on something. This shit is affecting my sleep!"

I don't have the strength, mentally or physically, to say anything back to him. My lack of reaction causes him to huff before the slamming of the door vibrates the pictures on the wall. He's late for work, again. *My fault. Like always.* I had another one of my episodes last night.

At least since I've started to show, he's stepped back from hitting me. Not all the way, but enough to ensure he has a viable incubator. I'm sure I would have been smacked down hard for how mad he was this morning. I saw his hand ball up into a fist on more than one occasion since the start of the day. It was his tell for when he was about to *punish me*. He said I tore out all the bath towels and blankets from the hall closet, and no matter how many times he stopped me and put me to bed, I just went right back to it. Of course, I only remember glimpses of it. Grab. Pull. Grab. Pull. *Repeat*. I don't remember him stopping me or getting in or out of bed. I just know that

I woke up from what felt like a ten-second nap with my heart thundering so hard I could feel it in my throat. I felt disoriented for a couple seconds, but his screaming and clothes being thrown around brought me back to reality fast enough and I immediately knew what the problem was.

This is normal for me now. No sleep, and when I can sleep, I sleepwalk. So really I feel like I've gotten no sleep because whatever I end up doing is enough to make me feel exhausted the next day. It's better for me when I stay up for days at a time instead of sleeping. Then I *don't* sleepwalk, and then he *doesn't* get mad.

A large thud over a carpeted area sounds from behind me, followed by a scream and I'm snapped from my zombie-like stance. I look away from the door he slammed and shake my head to help my tired eyes focus, before grabbing my coffee on the way through the kitchen to Sam's room.

My sweet little boy sits on the floor, holding his head in a silent cry in front of his dresser, where it's clear he was trying to climb it by the drawers half open. He went from walking to trying to climb up on everything in his path.

"*Shhh. Shhh.* Oh baby, come here." I coddle as I set down my cup on the offending dresser and pick him up just as he finds his cry. I guide his head to my shoulder and rock him for a bit. When the screams die down, I lift his head up to inspect the damage. Yup, he'd have a goose egg. There was already an angry purple bruise forming. My nerves and adrenaline finally wake up from the hellish night I had, if just for a second, as I head to the kitchen.

"Owey. Owe. Ouchy," Sam whines as I get a frog-shaped baby ice pack from the freezer.

"I know, baby. I know."

I glance at the oven clock on the way out of the kitchen. *Ten minutes past eight a.m.* I let out a miserable sigh. It's still four hours until nap time for him *and* me. I need it. I'm bone tired. So much so that I, too, am on the verge of crying right alongside him, my chest hurts and the coffee only serves to churn my stomach. Of course my doctor would shit if he knew about the caffeine, but really, he'd probably shit if he knew I wasn't sleeping either.

It was just another day in Hell.

But also another day with my sweet baby. Well, *babies*. So despite how much I hate my life, I love them and they are really the only thing that keeps me going.

I get Sam settled on a program with his blanket and sippy of juice and look down to my belly. Another boy. Much to my husband's delight. The gender reveal appointment was the only one with this pregnancy he's bothered to come to, and the only time I've seen him genuinely smile since he started hating me. Of course I would be happy with either gender but I would have loved to have a little girl around. A tiny flutter graces my lower belly and I sigh as I rub the spot. Normally, I love the feeling of my baby boy wiggling around but now it just exhausts me further. My lower lip trembles as I head to the rocking chair near the corner of the room to look out the window. Sam's all-day baby shows occupy the TV and we have little internet service on my phone so there isn't much to do. I've taken up bird watching and reading. My former friends would have snorted and laughed about how lame I've gotten in these years.

When did this become my life?

I think back to the fairy-tale start of all this.

Isaac and I were high school sweethearts and have been together since we've been freshmen. He was the quarterback and I was the captain on the cheerleading team. *So cliche. So unoriginal.* But when you grow up in a small town, there isn't much else to anyone's story really. Most of our classmates hooked up with each other and got married as well. On our graduation day, he proposed at my party, much to my parents' disdain. They hated him. They still do. Maybe I should have taken the hint?

I, on the other hand, was ecstatic by the proposal. I thought I was in love. We had a fairy-tale wedding with pretty much the whole town in attendance. We got married under the dripping willow trees as the sun set, and then he whisked me off to a week-long honeymoon in a little beach cabin. Living in Alabama had its benefits. It was the week we returned from the honeymoon that we learned I was pregnant. Everything was perfect. He was the love of my life. And for the first little bit of our marriage, he was an attending father to all my baby appointments and super supportive when we found out I had a rare condition that required bedrest. He loved me. He did everything and anything for me. Surprise birthday parties. Presents and more, even outside of a holiday or birthday. It was all I could have ever dreamt of.

But isn't that what they all say?

Now I just play the part of a lonely, depressed, and abused housewife. No friends. Family fucked off after the wedding in silent disagreement with our marriage. No neighbors. Just me and Sam, and our goldfish, Elmo, all day…every day. Until my husband comes home drunk or almost drunk and starts his shit. Which is usually, the house isn't clean enough or I didn't cook the chicken quite right. Beratements and sneers are his usual go-to about how much of a shitty wife I am and if he could find someone better in this town, he would have already left me.

I pray every day he will. Find someone. Leave me. Or just not come home. Maybe a car crash? Maybe a work accident. Sometimes I daydream he will just leave without a word and only send a pile of cash each month to support us. I don't dare wish for a knight in shining armor to come save me. I had one of those and look how that turned out.

I can't even remember when it turned into this.

Was it when I started asking him permission to go out with my friends or go out in general? I had done that out of courtesy. *Honey, can I go out with Ashley?* It was always yes but then it turned into *why?* Or *no*. Then it turned into, *I don't like you hanging out with her*, and then after that, *I don't like you hanging out with them*. I slowly lost my friends one by one, because I was so in love with him I would have done anything he asked.

Or was it when he said I started to slack in my house chores due to being on bed rest and eight months pregnant? When he pointed it out, I slapped him. And that was the first time he raised his hand back. I got slapped in return. *Hard*. He knocked me unconscious when my head slammed into the oven. Was that it? Was that the gateway to him hitting me? Because since then, it has only increased and never fully stopped.

Sam was born, and bills increased. I still couldn't work because of a heart condition I developed with my pregnancy, and Isaac started drinking excessively because of money problems. We fought more and more and our sex life died. I could tell he resented me for not working. It got to the point that I just wanted a job and to get out of the house just to be away from him. I applied but when the condition was disclosed, I was almost immediately fired or not even considered. It pissed him off. It pissed me off. It even pissed me off when he tried to touch me or show affection. I hated his touch. His face. And then it turned into me wanting a break, so I called my mother and told her the truth. She didn't feel sorry for me and after a lot of, *I told you so's*, she asked me to come home.. Sitting in the car before leaving, I decided to send him a goodbye text. And that's when he pulled in. Was that when I gave up and accepted my fate?

The sound of tires squealing into the driveway moved my eyes to the rear-view mirror where I watched him pull in, fast. He had damn near put his truck on two wheels. Rain pattered the rooftop and windows of my Jeep Wrangler as I watched him slam his truck into park and the headlights go out. Before he even got out, I knew he was drunk and I was shaking, trying to grip the steering wheel. Why hadn't I hurried more? Why hadn't I just left when I had the chance and sent the text later?

I looked back at my sweet three-month-old baby boy bundled up in his car seat, fast asleep and ready to go. Maybe I could just have taken off? It would have been our only chance. My heart sped up as I put a shaky hand on the gear shift. He hadn't gotten out yet. I had time to put it in reverse and leave. But what if he followed in his truck? I couldn't put Sam at risk. Maybe I should have called the cops?

The truck door slammed me out of my debate.

He was out.

"Fuck. Fuck. Fuck," I whispered. My only chance was to lie. I dried my tears and acted like I was fine.

Two fast raps on the window and then the door popped open. "Gabby, where you going?" The smell of whiskey flowed into the car and I held my breath. It smelled like he drank the whole bar. His black hair was disheveled and sticking up in random places, and his eyes were half shut as he swayed in his spot. The smell of a woman's perfume, his open zipper, and the makeup smudge on the shoulder of his white shirt...wasn't lost on me either.*There was a time this would have destroyed me but it only cemented the fact that I needed to leave.*

"I, uh..." I swallowed down my clogged throat and tears, and smiled the best I could before clearing my throat. "I'm off to the store for a bit. I wanted to make some cookies and cakes for church Sunday. Bit of a random time but thought it would also do Sam good with the drive. He's gassy." The lie had come easy.

He squinted not believing me. I tried to talk but he interrupted me. "No. Come on. I need dinner warmed up and he shouldn't be out this late."

I clenched my jaw. "It's 6pm, Isaac. It's hardly late. Dinner is in the microwave." I reached for the door but he immediately stopped it.

"Gabby." He warned, before reaching in to grab my wrist but I pulled it back.

"No." That simple word was so hard to say because I never said no to him, but I had to stand up for myself.

"What did you say?" He snarled, sobering a bit. He looked to the backseat as my heart hammered out of control. Shit, the bags.

There was no turning back at that point. "No. We are

going out, we'll be back."

"The fuck you are Gabby! Now get out or I'll make you."

Fuck him. I thought. My fear turned to rage. I had to stop this even if he did get a few swings in. I'd had enough. He goes to reach for the back door handle where Sam is and I quickly lock the door before turning and kicking out to get him away from the car, but he's fast for being drunk and catches my ankle.

"Gabby fucking stop this and get your ass out now!" He squeezed my ankle tight and I screamed as he started to pull me from the car. The sound was loud enough that Sam awoke and started to cry. I held onto the steering wheel and tried to fight him but it only managed to piss him off more and before I knew it I was halfway out the car. My sweaty hands quickly losing hold on the steering wheel was my only lifeline.

"LET ME GO!" I cried out. We had no neighbors within miles or I would have screamed. Tears came and spilled down my cheeks as I screamed over and over while kicking out but it was no use and with one final pull he retched me from the car. On the way out, the back of my head slammed down hard, first on the foot rail and then the cement.

It caused the world to sway for a second, only to have come into focus with him over me as he screamed in my face. "YOU WERE FUCKING LEAVING ME! WITH MY

CHILD?" He sat down on top of me before I could get up and shoved my lit phone screen into my face. I couldn't hold in my tears now at my own stupidity. I had left the text message up on the screen that I had been writing when he pulled up.

"Isaac, I'm so sorry it has to be this way." He started to read my text out loud. I tried to buck him off with my hips. But he was too heavy and it only made him growl before putting more weight on me causing my already pounding head to feel fuzzy. I looked at the tire on the car and tried to keep focus on it, instead of his stupid face as the rain dropped down ontop of us. "Look at me." When I refused he grabbed my chin hard and forced me to look at him while he read. "I think it's better for us to have a break. Maybe things can go back to the way they were before things turned bad. I loved you at one point but now, I'm not so sure. Please give us some time. I'll be in contact."

I only saw the flash of lightning behind him for a split second before the force of his fist knocked my eyes closed. It hurt. Bad.

"You thought you could just take my son away from me and I would be okay with it."

Another hit, which was a slap instead and I could feel my left eye starting to swell. It wasn't enough for him so he kept hitting me repeatedly, and at some point he placed his other hand on my throat leaving me barely conscious. "Fuck you." I barely got the insult out when he finally stood before stumbling back from me breathing like a bull.

"Fuck me? I'll show you fuck me!" The rain had long died and if he had been drunk before, at this point he was cold stoned sober as he unbuttoned his pants. I snapped out of my beaten state and started to sit up.

"Isaac don't." I whimpered and then leaned to the side to spit the building blood out of my mouth. It felt like he knocked a tooth loose.

"Don't what Gabby? It's a little too fucking late. You won't ever leave me and I'll fucking make sure of it."

I scooted back as he took his hard cock from his pants. Everything in me ached and was in pain. Sam had stopped screaming but I still was worried without having eyes on him. I needed to go. I got on my knees and tried to climb into the car but suddenly he grabbed me by my hair and white-hot pain raced against my scalp. I screamed as he pulled me to stand. Slamming me up against Sam's door I got a quick glimpse of him awake, sucking his thumb from where my face is pressed up against the window. I closed my eyes as Isaac ripped down my pants and underwear. "This will hurt. A lot."

It was the only warning I got before he raped me over and over again. That night when he was finally finished, I collapsed and passed out on the concrete. He left me there for the night, and I awoke the next morning to Sam screaming in the car. I never tried to leave again. That night resulted in me being pregnant along with having to go to the ER the next day for anal bleeding and vaginal tearing. He tore me in both spots, it was the first time I'd ever had anal sex, so maybe that was normal, but the vaginal tearing was worse than when I had Sam.

Now, I don't fight anymore. Instead I put a numb smile on my face and go through the motions. Another pregnancy. Another bedrest diagnosis. Another day comes and goes where I'm trapped seeing his face.

Maybe it was all of it combined, the abuse, depression, loneliness. Or maybe it was brought on from the pregnancy? But I couldn't sleep with him. He forced me to physically lay in his bed but I couldn't allow myself to sleep safely around him. So I didn't. I would go days at a time with no sleep and then hit such a deep sleep at times, not meaning to. I would wake up in the kitchen pouring milk all over the floor, or with Isaac beating the shit out of me until I would come to my senses. *Sleepwalking*. It was my new thing he thought he could punish out of me.

I had a feeling it was brought on by my bouts of insomnia but I was too far gone to sleep now, even if I wanted to and it was no longer because I feared him. I was only numb to him. To everything. It was like my emotions just left me and I didn't have any more left. Sam would do something that before would elate me but now only produced a smile on my face. Big events didn't excite me or pull anything from me, emotions-wise. Weddings or funerals. And I used to cry at both. I was just here living in Hell and acting fine on the outside.

I don't know why I can't sleep now, or why I won't stop sleepwalking when I do.

The doorbell ringing snaps me out of my thoughts and I leave Sam on the couch to answer it. The peephole reveals a handsome guy, who's either a murderer or an alien, because there was nobody in this shit hole town that looked as good as him. It was almost enough to make my heart stutter, like it had long ago. Almost.

Murderer or not, I answer the door, my common sense gone along with my emotions. The man, who looks in his mid-twenties and is insanely tall, looks shocked for a second but recovers fast.

"Excuse me, Miss or Mrs.?" He corrects in a British accent when he glances at the ring on my finger. His accent does boost my heart for a second. "I was looking for an Alaric Miller." He lifts an eyebrow and looks me up and down. I'm so shocked by how sexy he is, I can only stare.

"*Miss*?"

"Oh, umm. Nope. Just me. Well, me and my husband's family. I mean our family." *Aaand* I was bumbling like an idiot. How long had it been since someone had gotten me this flustered?

A real concern draws his eyebrows together and he tilts his head in a way that highlights his strong jawline. "Are you okay?" His voice is genuine. Great. I'm about to go from a bumbling idiot to an almost crying idiot.

I clear my throat and put on a small smile. "I'm fine. Sorry, but there isn't an Alaric here and the last homeowners have passed away. About five miles down the road to the south is the Weston household. They might be able to help?" My heart slams at the thought of sending this handsome stranger away but I know even in my sleep deprived mind that this isn't a fantasy or a fairytale. He isn't here to sweep me off my feet, no matter how much I want to kiss him and see how it feels to be swept up in romance again. Where the heck were these thoughts coming from?

He gives a polite smile. "Well then, I will head that way. Thank you...Mrs.?"

I gulp and smile back. "Just Gabriella is fine."

He tests the name on his foreign tongue, making my heart palpitate and butterflies come out of hiding from within my stomach. "Gabriella." he repeats again before lifting a corner of his mouth in a sexy smile. He winks and then turns away. That's when I notice the Cadillac Escalade with blacked out windows. It looks brand new and his clothes look fancier than anything anyone wears here. I look down at my own three-day wardrobe of leggings and an oversize shirt. Sigh. My hair probably looks like a bird's nest as well.

He gives me one last look before getting into his SUV and backing out of the driveway. I sigh again in defeat of what could have been if I hadn't been so blinded by love at the age of sixteen. My headstone would say: Here lies Gabby, that didn't end up with a prince but a villain as her soul slowly decayed into an never ending darkness. I shut and lock the door and head back to my rocking chair. The life of Gabby was a mess for sure.

Continue Reading If You Only Knew, available on Amazon! Thank you for reading!

Connect with Me

https://www.facebook.com/chelsiiKlen

https://www.facebook.com/groups/2635684956688972

https://www.instagram.com/authorchelsiiklein/

https://twitter.com/chelsi_fountain